HELEN
THE WINE DARK SEA

Phoebe Conn

New York Times Bestselling Author

and

E. Gary Stickel, Ph.D.

FIC014000 FICTION / Historical

Cover and Book design by eBook Prep
www.ebookprep.com

April, 2016
ISBN: 978-1-61417-845-3

ePublishing Works!
www.epublishingworks.com

PART I

CHAPTER 1

Sparta
The Bronze Age, 1200 BC

In a playful mood, Zeus strode along the banks of the Eurotas River kicking up sprays of sparkling rainbows. He ducked under the falling drops to let a tickling stream roll down his back. He often came to the river on an idle afternoon, and today, he heard a woman singing with a voice as pretty as the songbirds. Her lilting melody drew him around the curve in the riverbank, and he slipped into the reeds to watch the lovely young woman bathe at the river's edge.

Swimming nearby, a regal white swan dipped his head in a silent greeting to the king of gods and Zeus nodded in return. The magnificent bird swam near enough to catch, tempting Zeus with a deliciously provocative idea. In an instant, he became the graceful swan and swam slowly toward the singing bather.

* * *

Leda had escaped her husband's palace and her fawning maids for a few precious moments alone. She had played along the riverbank as a child and sought to recapture the effortless joy before she was missed. The day held a glowing warmth, and she welcomed the water's chill on her bare skin. She turned as she squeezed the moisture from the ends of her long blonde hair and looking up, found a magnificent swan drawing close. A beauty of his kind, he fascinated her, and she remained still so as not to frighten him away.

The magnificent bird spread his wings wide and reached out to stroke her cheek with the tips of his gleaming white feathers before gently brushing the smooth swell of her pale breast as he drew away. He cocked his head to cast a sly look, as though expecting something in return. Tickled by his feathers, Leda laughed and took a backwards step, but he swam closer.

"Clearly you're someone's pretty pet, but I've nothing to feed you," she exclaimed. She slid her fingertips along the bird's gracefully curved neck.

The swan again spread his powerful wings to easily capture her against his breast. Surrounded by his feathery softness, Leda's breath caught in her throat, and the world began to spin. Drawn up into the swan, she felt as though she were flying, floating among the clouds. Lost in the exquisite sensation, she closed her eyes, but what she saw in her mind was not the handsome swan, but radiant Zeus, in all his physical splendor.

It was the god's mouth upon hers, his arms that held her in a fierce hold. She dared not open her eyes and lose such an incredible dream, but when he entered her with a forceful thrust, he felt fiercely real. He flooded her with pleasure so intense it skirted pain and yet she clung to him, wanting still more even if the cost were her life. He kept her cradled in his arms, his feathered wings caressing her very soul until she was too lost in him to remember she belonged to a mortal king.

Her maids found her seated by the river, stroking her knee with a gorgeous white feather from the swan's wingtip. She stood and endured their fluttering hands as they helped her into her long skirt and bolero, but she gave no excuse for eluding them earlier. As they walked back toward the palace, she turned to gaze at the river, but the swan had vanished, and she doubted she would ever see him again. When she gave birth to a daughter of rare beauty, she knew her as a god's child and named her Helen.

CHAPTER 2

Sparta
The Palace of King Tyndareus
Six years later

Leda pulled an ivory comb through the tangled ends of Helen's long curly hair. "Be still child. You cannot ride with your brothers looking like a wild creature from the woods."

Helen giggled. "I am a wild creature!"

"No, you are a lovely princess who must learn to behave as one. Today, you may ride with Castor and Pollux, but afterwards you must bathe and dress in finer clothes. You must be a fine lady tonight when we dine together."

Helen skipped away the instant Leda laid her comb aside. "Yes, Mother."

Leda went to the window and waited for her youngest daughter to ride by with her brothers. Helen sat a horse better than either of the boys, and when she was old enough to race, she was sure to beat them. Leda hated to put any limits on her high-spirited daughter and waved as Helen and her brothers rode by heading toward the open fields surrounding the palace. They were such handsome boys, but Helen possessed an awe-inspiring beauty. When she became of an age to wed, suitors would come from near and far to vie for her, but not today while she was still a carefree child.

Clytemnestra entered her mother's room carrying a bolt of linen. "Is this fine enough for us, or should I send the weavers back to their looms?"

Leda's eldest daughter favored her, with silken blonde hair and blue eyes. She was nearly old enough to draw interest from noblemen seeking a bride, and Leda was grateful she would be married and living in her husband's home long before men came calling for Helen. A rivalry simmered between the girls, but Leda kept a close eye on Clytemnestra, whose jealousy sparked most arguments. All thought her a lovely girl, but she went unnoticed whenever Helen stood nearby.

Leda ran her fingers over the cloth. "This is already perfection. Let's see to the dyes."

"Is there enough of the saffron to color this a bright yellow?"

"If that's what you wish, we'll find it." Leda hugged her daughter and turned her thoughts to creating fine garments for her family.

Helen's roan pony trotted along behind her brothers' showy white mounts, but she soon tired of their dust and took a trail angling toward the almond groves. The trees were filled with fragrant pink blossoms and offered welcoming shade. The boys were supposed to look after her, but they never did, and she did not care a whit. She loved making up adventures as she rode along, pretending to be a goddess riding to her shrine, or the queen she would one day be returning home to palace splendor.

When she saw someone ahead, she pulled back on the reins, but her pony trotted on toward him. He was quite the most beautiful man she had ever seen. He was tall and well muscled with thick, deep auburn hair and eyes of the same unusual bright green as her own. His fine clothing and refined bearing made it impossible for her to mistake him for a field hand.

"Who are you and what are you doing in my father's grove?" she called to him.

Zeus caught her pony's bridle. "I came to see you." He handed her a red, ripe pomegranate. "Do you use the seeds for dye?"

He was friendly and his tone too reassuring to cause Helen any fear, and she accepted the fruit and weighed it between her hands. "Thank you. I would rather eat them, but I do love their deep red for cloth. Now why have you come to see me?"

He smiled and scratched her pony's neck. "I'm a dear friend of your mother's, but you mustn't tell her we've met, or she'll be insulted I didn't tarry to see her. Are you good at keeping secrets?"

A bright twinkle lit his gaze and made her laugh. "Maybe, maybe not. How did you come here, have you no horse or chariot?"

"I have them, but today felt like a walk. You're a very smart little girl, are you not?"

"My father fears I'm too smart. Do you know him too?"

"Tyndareus? I know who he is, and he knows me. You must not tell him you have seen me either."

"How can I tell him? You've not given me your name?" She turned in her saddle. "I hear my brothers calling. They seldom notice when I've gone astray. Do you wish to speak to them too?"

Zeus moved close and brushed her cheek with a tender kiss. "I came to see you, dear child. Now go before they reach us and remember not to tell."

She lifted her hand to shade her eyes and raised up to gauge how far away the boys were. When she turned back, the fine-looking stranger had vanished. She pressed the pomegranate to her breast and vowed never to ever tell a single soul they'd met.

CHAPTER 3

Mount Olympus
Home of the Gods

Zeus's golden chariot was drawn by winged white stallions, and when they soared to cloud-crowned Mount Olympus, he found Hera anxiously awaiting him at his palace. "Beloved," he greeted his wife with a lingering kiss.

"Where have you been?" she asked peevishly. "Does it take an endless number of mortal maids to satisfy you?"

"They don't compare to you," he teased and drew her close.

She placed her hands on his chest, and his warmth tingled her fingertips. "That's true, but it's never enough for you, is it?"

"You are more than enough, and I haven't been out seducing pretty maidens. You doubt me too often, Hera, and it isn't becoming."

"Would you mind if I walked the Earth seducing princes and kings?"

Zeus stepped back, scowled and rested his fists on his hips. "Of course I would, and I'd kill them before they drew a breath to brag of it."

Her lush body curved in a graceful sway. "And you expect me to be less harsh?"

"I'll admit to a weakness for women, but none is as lovely as you, so you've no reason to be jealous. Today, I was merely walking through Sparta and enjoying the beauty of an almond grove in flower."

Hera's striking blue eyes narrowed. "More likely the female kind of blossom."

Zeus laughed. "I'm innocent of any crime, my dearest, don't make me guilty in your mind."

She swept him with a skeptical gaze. "Innocent for today, perhaps."

He again pulled her close and nuzzled her creamy smooth throat. "Isn't today enough?"

CHAPTER 4

Sparta
The Palace of King Tyndareus

Leda led the curly-haired, dark-skinned little girl into Helen's room. "Look what I've brought you. Omalu is a present from your father, and while she's young, she'll soon grow to be your favorite maidservant. You must treat her kindly while she learns how to please you."

Helen had been knotting scraps of fabric to form little people she could line up and toss about. "I'd rather have another pony."

"I said you will be kind," Leda emphasized. "You need Omalu to look after your pretty clothes. She'll see your room is in proper order rather than scattered with twigs and bark and whatever else you carry home from your rides. What is it you're doing now?"

Helen waved a fabric doll in the air. "I'm a goddess and these are my people. If they fail to obey me, I rip them to shreds."

Appalled, Leda raised her hand to her breast. "Please choose a goddess who is not so fierce. Artemis loves to hunt. Why not fashion some fabric deer and have Artemis catch them. Let Omalu help you."

The little girl took a small step forward.

"Can you tie a knot?" Helen asked, and separated some scraps for her.

Omalu nodded and climbed up on the end of Helen's bed. She was smaller than the pretty princess, but older by a year, and had big, brown eyes. She twisted a piece of yellow linen before tying knots and left a portion at the end for hair. She held it up, and Helen took it from her.

"Look," Helen cooed. "She knows how to make hair!"

"A piece of rope with a frayed end will look even better," Omalu offered shyly.

"Rope?" Helen's face lit with excitement. "Come, let's find some."

Leda stood back and Helen sprinted from the room with Omalu hurrying along behind. Clytemnestra had been such a sweet, calm little girl and so much easier to raise, while Helen provoked her so often she provided a continual challenge. She'd not imagined how quickly her headstrong little daughter would draw Omalu into her endless mischief.

Late that night when Leda was alone with her husband, she coiled her arm through his. "We must begin thinking of suitable husbands for our daughters. Clytemnestra will be a lovely wife for any nobleman, but Helen will need someone extraordinary."

Highly amused, Tyndareus laughed and patted her hand. "It's too soon to have contests for the girls, but I'll think on whom to urge to enter. There are sure to be many who'll want Clytemnestra, but Helen is so beautiful, men may compete for her for years."

Leda rested her head on his shoulder. "Clytemnestra must be wed first."

"Of course, she's the eldest and nearly as beautiful as her mother. Now come to my bed and remind me why I fought so hard to win you."

She licked her lips and smiled. "We were both fortunate." He trusted her so completely he had never doubted Helen was his, but she would never forget how Zeus, clothed in glorious white feathers, had blessed her.

The following afternoon, Castor and Pollux found Helen and Omalu playing in the dirt at the edge of the vineyard. All they saw were short lengths of rope tied with rags, scattered sticks and smooth stones from the river. "What are you playing?" Castor asked.

Helen looked up at her brothers. "We've made people of rope, horses with sticks, and the stones are ships. Omalu and I are fighting a battle, and my side is winning."

Castor squatted down beside her. He lifted a frayed chunk of rope. "Is this a mighty warrior?"

"Yes, he is, see the horsehair crest on his bronze helmet?"

Pollux laughed. "All I see is a mess that should be swept away."

Castor regarded the scene more thoughtfully. "No, this is definitely the site of a battle, and we ought to make our own rope warriors and practice planning strategy. Sparta has many enemies, and we'll have need of such skills when we're grown."

"You want to play in the dirt?" Pollux scoffed.

Helen used a bit of fabric to tie stick legs on another little twig horse. "If you see only dirt rather than a battlefield, go away and leave us be."

Castor sat and reached into the pile of rope for a piece. "I'll stay."

Pollux walked away muttering unflattering things about his brother under his breath.

Helen laughed. "You are my favorite brother, Castor. You must have always known it."

He touched her cheek lightly. "You must keep it a secret or Pollux will be jealous and give me no peace."

She placed the new little horse with the others. "I'm very good at keeping secrets."

"I doubt you have any worth telling."

She smiled to herself. "You'll never know. Now we must begin again once you've made your soldiers."

He reached for a few of hers. "What if I just capture these fine warriors here?"

She swatted his hand. "You may not capture my men until you have some of your own. It's not fair."

"Do you think war is fair?" he asked.

"There must be rules," she argued. "Besides, you have joined my game and must do as I say."

Amused, he glanced to the vast expanse of vivid blue sky overhead. "Mother has raised you to be a queen, but that day hasn't yet arrived." He worked on fraying and knotting his bits of rope as he talked, and they began the game anew as soon as he was ready.

By the next afternoon, Pollux became sufficiently intrigued to join in. He shoved dirt into bumpy hills, dug a hole and filled it with water for a sea. "This should look like a real battlefield," he announced. "We should have a pyre for the dead."

"Rope warriors can't die," Helen countered. "They get up to fight again and again, like the gods."

"Burning any would be a waste of good rope," Castor added.

The game had grown to the point Tyndareus came out to observe accompanied by a red-haired young man who viewed them with good-natured amusement. "You need to make tents for the warlords," Tyndareus got down on one knee to gesture with a grand sweep of his hand.

He looked up. "This is Menelaus, Agamemnon's brother. He's come to look at our horses. What do you think, do they need more than tents to make this site true?"

Menelaus knelt beside Helen. "Do you often play in the dirt with your brothers?"

Helen swept her hair out of her eyes with a small part of her arm that still remained clean. "They are playing with me. I began the game with Omalu and Castor wanted to play. Now Pollux has deigned to join us."

Menelaus laughed as the boys shrugged to admit they were indeed playing her game. "How old are you, sweet child?"

"Helen is six," Tyndareus answered. He noticed how closely Menelaus regarded her, and growing uneasy, he rose and stretched to his full height. "We meant to look at horses rather than play with my children." He took a step in the direction of the stables and Menelaus got to his feet and followed.

Castor waited until the men could not overhear. "He wants you, Sister."

She moved a rope warrior onto his stick horse. "He wants me for what?"

Pollux laughed at the innocence of her question. "At last we know something Helen doesn't."

Helen eyed him coolly. "Maybe it's not worth knowing."

"We'll have to wait and see," Pollux replied, and he went for another pot of water to refill his newly created sea.

Leda shook her head as her maidservants scrubbed Helen clean for the second night in a row. "You're dirty to the ends of your hair. How did making little rope dolls inspire you to play at war?"

Helen held out her arms, and the soapy water dripped off her fingertips into the large terracotta tub. "They were rope warriors, what else would they do?"

"And your brothers encouraged you. I'm angry with them too."

"Who's scrubbing them?" Helen asked.

"They can wash themselves," Leda argued, "so everyone will be clean for tonight's meal. Menelaus could not make up his mind on a horse, so he's staying the night."

"Castor said he wants me. What does that mean?"

Leda bit her lip. "It means only that he thinks beneath the dust, you are a very pretty little girl. Do not speak to him alone, Helen. You must never be alone with any man. Do you understand me?"

Helen thought of the handsome man who had given her the pomegranate. It had to have been all right to be with him. She gazed up at her mother with a charming, innocent gaze. "I understand." But she really did not.

Tyndareus, Menelaus, Castor and Pollux ate in the andron where they would talk about horses half the night, while Helen, her mother, and Clytemnestra, ate on the second floor of the palace where Leda had her rooms. Helen was hungry and chewed the last savory morsel from a rib. Her mother and sister were talking about the quality of a new weaver's work, and she soon grew bored with their conversation and asked to be excused. The instant her mother gave a slight nod, she bolted from the table and went to her room.

Omalu had eaten with the other servants and was seated on the end of Helen's bed creating a doll with a many-colored skirt. "I'm making a queen for you."

Helen watched her twist and tie scraps to form a doll larger than any of the others they had made. "I like her, but we must leave her here in my room rather than take her outside to our battlefield where she'd soon become dirty."

"The queen belongs on her throne, not on the battlefield," Omalu offered.

Helen climbed up on the bed. "I know, but if I were a queen, I'd don gleaming bronze armor and lead the warriors into battle myself."

Omalu laughed. "You wouldn't be strong enough to hold a sword."

"I will be when the time comes," Helen promised. "You'll see." She stretched her legs over the side of the bed and wiggled her toes. "Maybe I'll urge them on from the back of my horse."

"A good plan," the little maidservant agreed, and Helen giggled with her.

CHAPTER 5

Sparta
Palace of King Tyndareus
Five years later

Helen held her twined basket close as she moved through the field of saffron crocuses. The pretty lavender flowers were cultivated not for their beauty, but for their three bright red stigmas. Dried for spice, the stigmas also made a vivid yellow dye. Clytemnestra loved to wear flounced skirts dyed in every shade of yellow from pale to bright as the sun. Helen wore purple, or pomegranate red. She loved dark, deep colors, while her sister craved only the light.

Omalu followed closely behind, watching for the stigmas Helen missed or dropped. She used far more care and could remove the stigmas from a blossom without leaving a shattered bloom. Helen used the same brisk yank she would use to pluck feathers from a goose.

"We must be gentle," the dark-eyed girl

admonished, "or your mother won't let us come."

Helen glanced over her shoulder. She'd waited impatiently for the chance to walk in these fields, but now that she was eleven years old and the day had finally arrived, she felt only hot and sweaty rather than proud. "I'm not certain it would be a punishment."

Omalu shook her head. "You complain if you are left out and now aren't happy to be included."

Clytemnestra and her friends were moving far ahead on an adjacent path. They were singing as they pranced along, clearly enjoying themselves. "I'm beginning to believe this drudgery is called fun to fool us into doing it." Helen stretched to ease the ache in her back.

Omalu had to wait for her mistress to move forward. "I'm grateful to have something new to do."

Helen pushed herself on down the row and plucked the stigmas from the next bloom with exaggerated care. "Is this better, Omalu?"

"Oh yes, a tender touch works best. Ease the stigmas from the flowers so they won't be crushed between your fingers."

Helen waved her hand above the next crocus. "Is this too gentle?"

"Yes! Hurry, we must work more quickly or the amount in our baskets won't compare to what Clytemnestra and her friends gather."

"I really don't care," Helen replied. She had always preferred her brothers' company to her sister's, and after suffering through a day of gathering saffron, she would much rather be on horseback than strolling these fragrant fields.

* * *

Helen clenched her fists at her sides as her mother fit a colorful tiered skirt around her waist. "Clytemnestra is the one dancing in Artemis' temple, why must I go along?"

"So you'll know what to expect when it's your turn to dance. Your sister is old enough to wed, and we wish to dance and celebrate. Your turn will come in its own time."

Her mother had begun teaching her to dance as soon as she could walk. Clytemnestra had laughed at her lack of grace, but she was now old enough to perform the rhythmic steps and slow turns with a winsome charm, but she never lost herself in the softly strummed lyre music the way other girls so easily did. It was no longer enough simply to raise her arms and twirl in a lazy circle as she had as a child. Silent praise and prayers for a goddess were supposed to come with every step, and her mind tended to wander.

They would soon leave for the sanctuary devoted to Artemis overlooking the river Eurotas. Artemis was the Virgin Huntress, protector of mothers and their children. Once there, the women and girls would dance nude, but they would make their way to the temple wearing finely fashioned skirts befitting their status. Helen reached for Omalu's hand and skipped along behind Leda and Clytemnestra, delighted to think her sister would soon be wed and gone away for good.

The afternoon was pleasantly warm, the music of the flutes and lyres wafted across the sylvan landscape enticing Helen and the other little girls to dance on the grass. Stately cedar trees flanked the temple, and the temple's tapered columns were cedar as well surrounding the dancers with the wood's pungent aroma. Helen wove in and out of the other girls and then hopped in a circle around them. She made up steps of her own and as long as she did not bump into anyone, she heard no complaints. There were more giggles from the girls outside than prayers. Pretending to be Artemis in pursuit of prey, she pulled back the string of an imaginary bow and let an invisible arrow fly. It was much less effort than praying, and as close as she could come to reverence.

When they stopped dancing to drink from the river, Helen filled her mouth with the cool water and leaned back to gargle tickling bubbles in her throat. The other little girls stared at her wide-eyed, a couple laughed, but Omalu frowned and shook her head.

"You could at least pretend to be good," the maidservant urged. "Or I fear when it comes time for you to marry, no suitable man will want you."

Unconcerned, Helen tossed her curly hair and ran back to the temple to join in the next lilting melody. Her brothers played the lyre, and Castor had given her a few lessons, but given up when she showed minimal talent. She could play a few notes on the diaolos, the double flute, and beat a drum if no one were particular about having a rhythm. Thank goodness, girls were not expected to be fine musicians. For the afternoon, she was content to dance with her own playful steps, and let her mind move freely in her own inner world.

When they all grew dizzy and tired, Helen lay down on her discarded skirt alongside Omalu. She closed her eyes and breathed deeply. The mothers and their older daughters were still dancing inside the glowing temple, and the music floated outside around them in soft waves. Helen slept deeply, and her dreams were strange and sweet. When Leda woke her, she sat up and rubbed her eyes.

"I had the most wonderful dream about flying horses. They were white as milk and had enormous wings that lifted them into the clouds. Does Artemis own such a splendid mount?"

Leda wrapped the skirt around Helen's narrow hips and combed the fringed hem with her fingertips. "No, it is Zeus who owns a pair of beautiful flying horses, they're called Pegasai. They pull his golden chariot across the sky."

The heavens had dimmed in the gathering dusk, but Helen swept the sky overhead in a quick search. "Have you seen him coursing by?"

Leda would never reveal just how close she had come to Zeus, but she had not seen his chariot that wondrous day. "No, but his chariot flies above the clouds when he's on his way to Mt. Olympus, and no mortals are able to see him."

Helen frowned unhappily. "If I did by some chance, would he give me one of his fine winged horses?"

"I don't believe so, for how could he return home to Mt. Olympus?"

"He would still have one flying horse to ride." She followed her mother and Clytemnestra along the path to the palace. Their bare feet patted the dirt with a softer step than earlier in the day. Lost in the memory of the fantastic dream, she failed to notice how often Clytemnestra looked over her shoulder and frowned.

* * *

"I don't want you to be burned by the sun. Although you are nearly as tanned as our servants. I should keep you inside until you are as fair as a royal maiden should be." Leda pulled a long tunic over Helen's head. "You may watch the races from the roof terrace, but you may not run about among the horses. Do you hear me? You must not risk being trampled."

"This is Clytemnestra's day," Helen replied. "No one will look at me no matter where I stand."

Leda blessed her young daughter's innocence. "You must still be careful. Men wish to impress your sister with their strength and wealth. There will be contests, and many presents, and your father will choose the very best man to be her husband. In time a fine husband will also be found for you. A man who is a great rider, of course, you would never be content with a man who sat a horse poorly."

Helen nodded thoughtfully. "No, he must be a man who owns many fine mounts so I could ride a different one each day." She hugged her mother and ran up the narrow stairway to the roof. Omalu followed close behind.

"We are above the dust and have the best view," the maidservant observed.

"We do." Helen leaned against the stone railing circling the roof terrace. There were many young men gathered below ready to compete. They were handsome in their fine short tunics, but she gazed beyond them to their mounts. Some were raven-black, others bays and roans, all proud animals that pranced in place eager to run.

Omalu nudged Helen. "Look there, that fiery-haired man is staring at you. Do you see him?"

She followed her servant's gesture and recognized him. "He talked to us long ago when we made rope warriors. He comes to talk to father about horses, but I've forgotten his name."

"He's a handsome man."

Helen studied him a long moment, but saw no reason to compliment him. "He must want to marry Clytemnestra, or he wouldn't be here."

Omalu shrugged. "He appears to be more interested in you."

Helen doubted it. "He's just waiting his turn to race." She picked the winners by their horses, not the riders, and when the men turned to wrestling and boxing contests, she lost interest. The men had brought oxen and sheep to show their wealth and there would be feasts with fresh meat each night, but women never attended the raucous gatherings. With nothing to do the rest of the day, Helen took Omalu by the arm.

"Come, we can go to the river and fish. The air there won't be filled with dust and the stink of sweat."

Omalu carried their fishing lines. "I'll welcome the quiet. Why is it men prefer to shout rather than speak softly?"

Helen shrugged. "It must make them feel more manly. Will you remind me to look for a quiet man when it's my turn to take a husband?"

"A quiet man with a great number of horses?"

"Yes, he'll be perfect for me." She skipped along the trail and hummed as she fished, content to spend the afternoon with her maidservant away from all the noise and fierce competition for her sister.

CHAPTER 6

Sparta
Palace of King Tyndareus

Tyndareus made an excellent match for Clytemnestra with Agamemnon; the powerful Mycenaen high king possessed great wealth and was eager to wed the beautiful blonde. There were wedding clothes to sew, decorations to be made and feasts to plan. Uninterested in the preparations occupying the women in the palace, Helen avoided her sister's company whenever possible. She could ride again without having to weave her way through the abundance of suitors ready to race and felt free for the first time in weeks.

Omalu was afraid of horses, and Helen's brothers had little time for her, but she didn't stray far and often rode into the almond groves looking for the friendly stranger who had given her the pomegranate. She remembered him vividly, even if he failed to reappear. As she returned her roan pony to the royal stables, she found the red-haired young man she met years ago waiting for her.

"Are you still making warriors out of rope?" he asked.

"It was a child's game, and I'm eleven now." She jumped from her pony before he could grasp her waist to set her on her feet. She handed the reins to a stable boy who bowed and led the gentle pony away.

"What games do you like to play now?" the young man asked.

"I'm learning to use a bow," Helen announced proudly. Castor thought it fun to teach her, and she practiced whenever she could.

He appeared surprised and laughed. "Do you plan to be a huntress like the goddess Artemis?"

"Maybe. I've forgotten your name, if I ever knew it, and I'm often told to avoid strangers." He wore a fine linen tunic and a gold headband shone through his red curls. So even if he were a stranger, he was a fine looking and wealthy one.

"Very wise advice. I'm Menelaus, King Agamemnon's younger brother, so you shouldn't regard me as a stranger, but as a kindred nobleman."

She dragged her toe in the dirt in a wide arc. "Are you heartbroken Clytemnestra will marry him rather than you?"

He responded with a ready grin. "Not at all."

That surprised her. "But I saw you here with all the men who wanted her."

"Did you now? I came only for the races."

"Did Clytemnestra know that?"

"She probably didn't even notice me. I waited for you today, because I heard you loved horses as much as I do. You've grown since we first met, and your pony is rather small for you now. Are you ready to move up to a horse of your own?"

Growing cautious, she took a step back. His smile appeared genuine, but he had to want something in return. "Do you have horses to give away?"

"I own a few and would like to present you with one. When we are celebrating a marriage between our families, why should Clytemnestra receive all the gifts?"

It was a confusing answer, and she was uncertain whether or not she liked him. He was handsome she supposed, but she thought his generosity misplaced. "Will you give horses to Castor and Pollux as well?"

"No, they already own fine mounts, but you have outgrown your pretty pony."

That was certainly true, although no one had any time to notice her of late. "I'll have to ask my parents first."

His green eyes lit with a playful twinkle. "Yes, do ask them, and I'll give you a choice. There's a dapple-gray mare I believe you would like or would you prefer a bay?"

"How am I to choose if I have not seen the horses?" she asked.

He nodded. "You are a clever girl. I'll bring them both with me on my next visit."

"I must still ask if I may accept your present."

He nodded to agree. "I'll wait to hear from you then. Send a messenger to my palace so neither of us will be kept waiting."

She left him and ran inside. Her mother was overseeing the women weaving at the looms. "Menelaus wants to give me a horse. Is that too much?"

Leda turned slowly. "Clytemnestra is marrying his brother, so that's probably what has prompted him to offer such a generous gift. Your father will have to see the animal and decide whether or not you may accept and ride it."

Helen liked the idea of a horse even if she wasn't fond of Menelaus. She hurried away to find her father.

Tyndareus laughed at her confusion. "When you are a little older, many men will give you gifts, but you did the right thing in coming to me, and I must see the horse first. Menelaus is a wealthy lord, and if he wishes to give you such an extravagant present, you must accept it graciously. You dare not make an enemy of him."

"If the horse is swift I'll be grateful," Helen replied, "but how could I be glad if I can outrun him?"

Helen always amused him, and he hugged her close. She shared her brothers' love of adventure, and he was pleased Menelaus also valued her spirit. "I'll speak with Menelaus and insist the horse loves to run. Leave everything to me."

She kissed his cheek, and confident he knew horseflesh as well as any man, trusted him to help her choose the best steed Menelaus could offer.

Menelaus returned the day before the wedding. Leda was happy to have Helen occupied elsewhere, and her father walked with her to the stable. He passed his hand over the dapple-gray mare, winked at Helen, and then closely examined the bay gelding. "These are fine animals indeed. Do you have a preference, Helen?"

"Yes, I want the fastest. Let's race them."

Tyndareus turned to hide his smile. "What do you say to a race, Menelaus? I'll ride the gray if you'll take the bay."

"A course over flat land?" Menelaus asked.

"Yes, the same course you raced here a few weeks ago." Tyndareus called for bridles, and the horses were soon ready to mount. "Go up on the roof terrace where you'll have the best view, Helen. Maybe you'll see more than speed when we run."

She took Omalu up to the roof with her. "I'll accept the swiftest horse, but if I took them both, you could ride with me."

Terrified by the prospect, Omalu shook her head. "Oh no, I would slide right off the horse's back and break my neck. Don't ask it of me."

"I'm only teasing." Helen leaned against the stone railing circling the roof and waved. Her father and Menelaus trotted their mounts to the starting line and quickly broke away in a dust swirling gallop. The gray had the greater initial speed, but the bay passed the pretty mare to win. The choice was more difficult than she had expected, and she worried on her way down the steps and outside.

The gray was a beauty, and tossed her snowy mane as Helen came near. "This is a very fine horse, but I want the bay," she announced.

"Excellent choice," Menelaus exclaimed. "He'll carry you happily even if you ride all day."

Her father touched her shoulder. "You are still not to ride without an escort, your brothers, or a stable boy I choose."

"Yes, Father, I understand."

"What if I took her for a ride now?" Menelaus asked. "We won't go far."

Helen was already on the bay's back before her father had a chance to object. "Yes, you may go, but don't be away long."

"We'll come back soon," Helen promised. She took a firm grip on the reins and turned the bay toward her favorite trail. "Thank you. What's my horse's name?"

"He has none as yet. Call him whatever you wish." Menelaus swung himself up on the gray and rode beside her. He patted the mare's arched neck. "You ride very well. Did your father teach you?"

Helen thought a moment. "He gave me lessons, but I may have been born knowing." She tapped her heels against the bay's flanks and galloped away.

Menelaus sent a hurried glance over his shoulder, but Tyndareus had already entered the palace and had not seen how quickly Helen had outsmarted him. He clucked his tongue at the dapple-gray and sent her at a run after Helen, but he did not overtake her until she had pulled her new mount to a halt.

"You should not race ahead on your own," he scolded, his brows drawn in a hostile line. "There might be dangers you couldn't see."

She thought him too cautious and scanned the land she had ridden over all her life. The tilt of her chin made her intractable mood plain. "No terrible dangers have ever been encountered here, and my father's warriors could handle them if they did. We can return to the stable at a walk. Will that please you?"

"Yes, and we must race again another day when I'm riding my usual mount," he responded between clenched teeth. "Or would you prefer racing chariots?"

She was too young to control a chariot, but it would be like flying over the ground, and she looked forward to the day she would be strong enough to handle it. "I've never seen a woman drive a chariot. Have you?"

He ran his fingers through his windblown hair. "No, but I believe you could do it when you're grown, if any woman could."

"I hope so."

His mood lifting, his smile grew wide. "I'll await that day with eager anticipation."

Leda's eyes widened in horror. "You let Helen ride alone with Menelaus without a chaperon? His interest in her is decidedly premature, but she should not be alone with him. It's most improper."

Tyndareus rubbed his hands up and down her arms with a gentle reassuring touch. "He merely wants to ingratiate himself with our family, which will make him doubly careful she comes to no harm. Cease to worry. Helen will return home safely."

Leda waited outside to make certain. She waved as her daughter came into view and met her at the stable. "I came to see your new pet. He is a beauty, isn't he?"

This time Menelaus jumped down fast enough to swing Helen to the ground. "He's one of my finest, and Helen will find him an easy and comfortable mount."

Helen rubbed the gelding's soft nose. "It was time for me to have a horse. Maybe I'll teach Omalu to ride my pony."

Leda nodded to summon the stable boy standing nearby. She circled Helen's shoulders in a warm hug and urged her toward the palace. "Thank you, Menelaus. The horse is a beauty."

"Like Helen," he whispered softly to himself and nodded to her.

On the day of the wedding, Helen danced in the palace with the women and young girls. The music was loud, and their twists and turns often frenzied. When the brightly frescoed walls became a blur of red, blue and yellow, she fled the women's quarters with Omalu for the breezy air of the roof terrace. She was dressed in her finest clothes, a skirt with colorful horizontal bands and a pretty bolero, gold earrings and bracelets. Her long hair floated free, and she blew it out of her eyes.

"The women dance and the men drink and feast. Does it not seem a foolish way to conduct a wedding?" she asked her diminutive maidservant.

"It's not for me to say." Omalu had new clothing too, and ran her fingertips over her beautiful skirt. It was the prettiest one she'd ever owned.

Agamemnon's emblem, two royal standing lions embracing a sacred column had been beautifully wrought in gold and embellished on the front of his chariot. The remainder of the impressive conveyance had been decorated with flowers and ribbon streamers and stood out among the others lined up near the stable. Helen wished she could take one, ride away and not return home until dawn.

She'd caught a glimpse of Menelaus, or at least a flash of red hair, when Agamemnon had arrived. She knew none of his other kin, but no one expected her to be acquainted with another royal family.

"Are you hungry?" Omalu asked.

Helen shook her head. "No, the dancing made me too dizzy to eat, but there will be plenty of food later. If you're hungry, go find something for yourself."

Omalu leaned against the railing beside Helen. "I'm dizzy too. Are brides supposed to be lightheaded when their new husband carries them away? Maybe then they won't cry when they tell their family goodbye."

Helen's laugh bordered a rude snort. "Clytemnestra won't shed a single tear. She's heard Agamemnon's palace is even finer than our father's. It's told Mycenae is rich in gold, and she'll be the queen. She won't miss us, and I'll not long for her haughty company either."

They remained on the roof terrace until Leda found them. "I'm so glad you're here rather than in the stable in your new clothes." She drew in a deep breath, and released it slowly. "Time is passing too quickly. I remember being your age so clearly and watching my sisters marry, and then I became a bride, a mother, and I'll probably be a grandmother before you're wed."

Her mother was so young and beautiful; Helen could not even imagine her growing old. "Men don't mark time the same way as women, do they?"

"No indeed," Leda responded, "they count the years by the wars they have fought and love to recite their heroic battles endlessly. That's why women don't join them for a feast, where we would have to listen to their tiresome bragging the whole night. Now come with me. You must eat with your sister on the last evening this will be her home."

Helen went along without complaint, happy to celebrate her sister's departure in every way possible. Clytemnestra had burned her childhood playthings as a tribute to Artemis, goddess of life's transitions, but Helen had no collection of pretty toys to sacrifice, when hers were so easily lost and broken. When it came time for her to wed, she would have to gather some quickly, rather than disappoint Artemis by having none to offer.

Clytemnestra bathed in water scented with rose perfume, donned her beautiful new clothing, and Leda placed a crown of roses in her hair. The women lit torches to light her way in a lovely swaying line to where Agamemnon waited at the palace gates. He took her hand, and accompanied by the torchbearers, they made their way to his festively decorated chariot.

He was a tall man, with broad shoulders, thick dark curls and a rakish grin, but Helen didn't like him. He was a fierce warlord noted for his bravery, but he had never given her more than a distracted nod, and he struck her as being arrogant and cold. Clytemnestra walked beside him with her head demurely bowed, wearing a shy smile, while surely she relished becoming Agamemnon's queen. He was the high king, the most powerful ruler in all of Greece, which added to the young woman's innate pride.

Helen looked up at her parents and found her father wiping a tear from his eye. "You don't like him?" she whispered.

"Hush," he scolded. "I'm sorry to lose our dear Clytemnestra, but a young woman must go with her husband to his home. Her marriage to Agamemnon honors us all."

Leda held her husband's hand tightly. "Before you know it, we'll be lighting torches for you, Helen, and while we may shed a few tears, it will be a joyous day."

Helen wondered if Agamemnon would teach Clytemnestra how to use a bow, and quickly decided he wouldn't even think of it.

CHAPTER 7

Sparta
Palace of King Tyndareus

Time passed as quickly as Leda feared, and at twelve, Helen was considered at an age to marry. Leda worried about her daughter, however, for she showed none of Clytemnestra's eagerness to wed. Clytemnestra had already given birth to a son, Orestes, and as expected, exalted in being both a queen and a mother. Helen still preferred horses to men, and Leda thought they would be wise to wait until she showed some inclination toward marriage.

Tyndareus disagreed. "Helen is a great beauty and there will be a long and fierce competition for her hand. We could begin the contests now, and not see her wed for a year at least, perhaps two. By then, she should have grown more mature in her thinking."

"It's not her thinking that poses the problem," Leda argued. "She's smarter than most and doesn't hesitate to speak her mind. If she dislikes the men who come to woo her, she will say so. I refuse to allow her to marry a man who would abuse her for her independent ways."

He brought her fingertips to his lips. "Nevertheless, a clever man will know how to seduce his bride."

"Unfortunately, few men are as clever as you, beloved." She relaxed in his arms and escaped into the moment and left the decision unmade.

On a warm spring afternoon, Helen danced at the temple of Artemis alongside the Eurotas River with her mother, other noble women and their young daughters. The rhythms were as familiar as a heartbeat and growing overly warm, she slipped away to drink from the river. A boat came into view paddled by perhaps twenty men. The blue prow painted with owl's eyes gave the ship a regal presence, and she thought it must carry a king. When the boat neared shore and a gray-haired man leaped over the side, she realized too late she stood nude on the riverbank, and she hurried to hide among the reeds.

In his youth, Theseus had slain the bull-headed monster Minotaur on Crete, and lack of courage had never stopped him from taking whatever he desired. The King of Athens was now an aged widower with too many sad memories. He needed only a glimpse of an extraordinarily beautiful young maiden to know he had to make her his. When she ran from him, he overtook her and threw her to the ground.

Helen fought him fiercely but he was too strong to throw off, and he covered her mouth with his hand to stifle her piercing scream. She struggled as long as she could, but when he laid his arm over her throat and pressed down hard, she lost consciousness and lay limp beneath him.

Without a thought to her welfare, Theseus followed the wild song in his blood to ravage her with brutal thrusts. Desperate to keep her, he wrapped her in his cloak and carried her to his ship. He called to his crew to make haste, and they paddled the ship out into the swiftly flowing river.

Missing Helen, Omalu came down to the river in time to see the ship racing away. "Helen!" she called. She searched the reeds hoping to find her hiding, but found only the matted spot where Theseus had thrown her. She ran screaming toward the temple, fearing they would never see Helen again.

Theseus took Helen to his hill fortress of Aphidna, near Dekeleia. Her arms and legs were bruised from his firm hold on her. She'd been terrified the whole voyage that he'd give her to his men for sport. Worn out from worry and lack of sleep, she was so furiously angry she refused to look at him. In her mind, he did not exist, and she vowed to do whatever she must to survive and return home.

He had announced his name proudly, and caressed her curls, but she batted away his hand. "You're so lovely," he whispered. "I know you must be Tyndareus' daughter, Helen. No one ever speaks of your temper. In time, you'll grow fond of me."

"Never!" Her throat was bruised from his choking hold, making her voice low and hoarse. She kept a firm grip on his cloak to keep herself covered and turned her back on him.

"Never is a very long time," he replied with a deep

laugh. He had brought her to a mountain fortress near Athens rather than his palace, and the only women in residence worked in the kitchen. He summoned one to serve as her maid and to escort her to a room on the second floor. She was a tall thin girl with frizzy black hair tied back with a cloth braid. Her brown eyes appeared enormous while her nose and mouth were too small for her face. She looked thoroughly confused by Theseus' command, and when she took Helen's arm, the Spartan princess refused to budge.

Theseus waved the girl aside. "I'll carry you myself. You weigh so little you'll be no burden." Helen remained stiff in his arms, and he could barely manage the task.

They passed no beautiful frescos, nor finely painted rafters and columns. Helen saw only the cold ambition that had built the forbidding fortress of giant cyclopean boulders and cared not at all for Theseus' wealth and power. No king who raped young women would ever be admired, and she studied the chamber where he had taken her searching for a way out. The window was too narrow to climb through, and too far above the ground below to be of any use whatsoever. The wide corded bed was a grim reminder of how he had brutalized her by the river, and she moved as far away from it as she could.

"You'll want to bathe and new clothing will be found for you. Don't despair, Helen, you'll be well-treated here," he promised.

Her spine remained as stiff as a cedar tree's trunk. "If you'd ever wished to treat me well, I wouldn't be here."

He softened his voice, "How can you be unaware of your great allure? Forgive me, I'm a captive of your beauty."

Helen turned to spit at him, but he had already moved through the door, and the hinges squeaked as he swung it closed behind him. "Bastard," she fumed. She had been barely conscious for most of the journey to this miserable ugly fortress and was uncertain where they had beached the boat. She went to the window; hungry for the sight of anything resembling home, but the mountains surrounding the cursed fortress were unfamiliar.

Servants loved to talk, and gossip spread faster than a wildfire over dry fields, so her whereabouts would soon be discovered. Someone would come for her; one of the men her mother swore longed to marry her, or her father himself. All she had to do was wait. She scratched a mark in the stone beside the window with her thumbnail. She would count the days, and find ways to humiliate Theseus at every opportunity.

She had often been reminded she would one day be a queen, and she would act the part now. She paced the room, the oversized cloak swinging out behind her, her furious anger burning clear to her toes.

The girl from the kitchen brought in a wooden tub for her to bathe and followed with amphoras of hot water. More frightened than eager to serve, she quickly bolted out the door. She had dropped soap and a thin towel on the floor, and Helen debated whether or not to use them. Finally deciding she would rather scrub off Theseus' stench than hope to offend him by being unclean, she tossed aside his cloak and stepped into the tub.

There was a beautiful room with murals of diving dolphins in which to bathe at home, and tears stung her eyes as she thought of how far away she must be. She cursed Theseus with every breath and hurried to finish before he returned. The maid had not brought the promised clothing, and she ripped the wool blanket from the bed to wear rather than don the cloak stained with her virgin's blood.

Her mother had told her the bodies of men and women were created to fit together perfectly. Boys trained and wrestled naked so she knew how men were made, but she had never expected her virginity would be stolen rather than taken tenderly. Warlords kept women captives in their beds, but she was no prize of war.

She was forced to use the bed as the only comfortable place to sit. She huddled with her back against the wall, linked her arms around her knees, and waited for a chance to call Theseus a swine.

She was too disgusted by her dismal situation to be hungry, but when the girl brought her a bowl of mutton stew, some bread and wine in a stemmed clay kylix inscribed with an owl, she thought it would be wise to eat rather than risk becoming too weak to survive. She dunked bits of the thick-crusted bread in the stew and chewed slowly, but the flavorless meal compared very poorly to what their cooks prepared in her father's palace. A fortress would be home to warriors rather than a noble family, and perhaps they were satisfied with warm and plentiful food and cared little how it tasted. She tried, but could eat only a small portion of what she had been given and set the bowl by the door. She sipped the wine, and wished it were pure, sweet water.

At sunset, the light in the room grew dim. The girl returned to collect the tray, empty the tub and remove it, but she failed to light the fire on the brazier or to bring an oil lamp. Helen sat on the bed, closely wrapped in the blanket and wished Theseus dead. If he thought he could bore her into welcoming his wretched company, he had made a grave error. She had always spent much of her time alone, and preferred it now.

The frayed hem of blanket inspired her to rip off a strip and tie a few knots to create a doll warrior. She held it tightly in her hand and imaged herself adorned in shiny bronze armor holding a sharp short sword she'd swiftly thrust through Theseus's heart.

Theseus did not appear until late the next morning. He held several changes of women's clothing draped over his arm. Helen stood in the middle of the cold chamber, tightly wrapped in the blanket.

He shivered with the chill. "Was the fire not lit last night?" He laid the clothing on the foot of the bed. "I'll see to it now." He knelt at the brazier and used flint to strike a spark. He blew on the flame until the kindling caught fire.

Had anything been handy to use as a weapon, Helen would have bashed it against his skull rather than stand idly by, but there was nothing useful at all. He was dressed in a fine black tunic and wore a gold necklace and a large gold royal ring. Even if he had taken great pains to look his best, she despised him.

He brushed off his hands as he stood. "Such an oversight will not reoccur. I'll tell what servants can be found here to see to your every comfort, or I'll flog them all myself."

He had expected something in the way of gratitude, even if only a slight nod, but he had seen more cheer in the gaze of a venomous snake. Helen's curly hair floated about her head in wild disarray, and even wrapped in a blanket, she remained as slender as a reed. He studied her a long moment and began to wonder.

"I was entranced by your beauty at my first glimpse of you by the river. I thought you a lovely young woman, but today you appear to be no more than a wild child. What is your age?"

She gathered courage from the tiny woolen warrior hidden in her hand. She lifted her chin proudly. "I'm twelve, and you would be wise to send me home before my father's warriors reach your gates. They are a blood-thirsty lot and will rip you limb from limb for kidnapping and abusing me."

Clearly not frightened, he laughed and took a step closer. When she backed away, he took another step. "Your father may not find you for years, so I'll enjoy you without a worry. My Athenians can defeat any warriors who dare to attack us, as they have many times in the past."

His boast sickened her. "You'll not enjoy the slightest moment with me," she hissed.

"Fortunately, I'm a patient man, and will give you time to grow accustomed to your lot here. The clothing belonged to my late wife. If it doesn't fit, you'll eventually grow into it. If you are in a better mood tomorrow, we'll go for a walk in the sunshine. Wouldn't you enjoy time away from this tiny chamber?"

"Not with you."

"As I said, I'm a patient man, but do not abuse me for it."

She watched him go and a moment later the door again swung open. The kitchen girl entered with a bowl of porridge with numerous lumps, warm bread and another clay kylix of wine. Seeing the pretty clothing on the bed, she looked around for a place to set the tray.

"I could use a table," Helen offered. "Is there one no one is using?" She took the tray from the girl and set it atop the clothes. "You look like a clever girl, I bet you'll soon find one for me."

The girl shrugged, and left, but returned before Helen had finished eating the bread in tiny bites. There was a young man with her, an ungainly youth with the same frizzy hair and large-eyes, and Helen assumed they were brother and sister. He carried in a three-legged wooden table that was as crudely built as the bed.

"Thank you," Helen responded, and he blushed a bright red. "Do you suppose you could find a chair so that I might sit at the table while I eat?"

He sent a frantic glance toward the girl and the pair left in such a hurry they nearly collided at the doorway. They returned with the requested chair, he placed it by the table and stepped back.

Still clad in the blanket, Helen tried the chair and found it fit perfectly with the table. "Thank you again. The stone floor is very cold on my bare feet. Could you find something to serve as a rug?"

The boy lifted his brows, but the girl yanked on his sleeve to lead him out. They were gone a long while, but finally returned with a brown spotted cowhide they unrolled on the plank floor. They looked up, clearly hoping for a word of praise.

"How clever of you," Helen exclaimed. "This will do perfectly. Tell me your names so I can thank you properly."

"E-Emalia," the girl stuttered her name and took her brother's arm. "This is Oron."

Helen found a smile for them. "Thank you, Emalia and Oron. May your kindness be rewarded."

The pair bowed on their way out, and she had to raise her hands to cover a laugh. Her chamber now held a serviceable rug and a table and chair. Although far below her usual standards, it was a great improvement over what she had found upon her arrival, and she turned her attention to the clothing on the bed.

The skirts were of fine wool woven in colorful bands of red and blue, and the boleros were in matching hues. She wrapped a skirt around her waist and had to pull it up high before securing it with the braided cord to avoid tripping on the hem. The boleros were also too large, but offered a welcome covering after a rough blanket on her tender skin.

She moved the chair to the window and stood on it to improve her view, but no troops were gathering in the distance. They would be soon she was sure, and she would happily throw Theseus' severed limbs onto a funeral pyre herself!

She had been given fine clothes, and she began to wonder what more of Theseus' late wife's belongings could be found. That evening, when

Emalia carried in a thick slab of roast pork, conveniently sliced in thin strips so she would not require a knife, she thanked her warmly. "Did you serve the woman who owned these pretty clothes?"

Emalia shook her head. "Oh no, my lady, I've never left the kitchen before yesterday."

"I'd be grateful for a pair of sandals. Do you suppose you might find some in her room? She is dead, after all, and wouldn't miss them."

The girl appeared torn by the request. "I'm not allowed to wander the fortress."

Helen understood a table, chair and cowhide could be found without traversing the royal chambers. A pair of sandals could not. "I'm grateful for what you have brought me. A new fire has not yet been laid. Is it to be your duty?"

"Yes. I'll fetch more wood."

The girl dashed from the chamber, and Helen took the chair at the table and found the roast pork absolutely delicious. The cook could at least roast meat if not do anything more. Before she finished, Emalia returned with Oron carrying an armful of wood. He lit the fire in the brazier and they bowed as they left her. Although still a most unwilling captive, Theseus hadn't touched her, and she considered it a very fine day.

CHAPTER 8

Sparta
Palace of King Tyndareus

Leda had been hysterical from the moment Omalu had run screaming into the temple crying that Helen was gone. She had seen her daughter slip out of the temple and had expected her to swiftly return. Now she could not forgive herself for not following her. She cried herself to sleep in her husband's arms, but soon awoke even more distraught.

"How will we ever find her?" she sobbed.

Tyndareus smoothed her hair. "I've sent the palace guard down the river to question everyone who might have seen a boat. We'll know who has taken Helen soon, beloved, and no man would dare to do her permanent harm."

She burrowed against his chest. "You know precisely what any man will do with her, and it could destroy her soul."

He rubbed her back in a soothing circle. "She's a very strong girl."

The violent images in Leda's head gave her no peace. Her husband plied her with wine to lull her to sleep, but tears continued to roll down her cheeks in her dreams.

Many farmers and fishermen had seen the King of Athens' owl-eyed boat, but none knew his name. They recognized only someone of wealth, with gray hair and a muscular build. He had clutched something, or someone, to his breast, they were certain of it.

Castor paid each of them well. "Thank you for keeping a close eye on the river and our land." He didn't mention Helen's name to protect her, but he was soon convinced Theseus was the man being described.

"He wouldn't have taken her to Athens," Pollux offered, "but somewhere where she couldn't escape and find help to return home."

Tyndareus paced as they talked. "Take a few warriors with you. Remain hidden until you discover where Helen is being held. Then we'll plan an attack with a greater force."

"Tell Mother we'll find her," Castor responded. "We'll go now and not waste any time in the effort." Intent upon keeping his word, he strode out with his brother.

Theseus ushered an elegantly dressed woman into Helen's chamber. He appeared surprised to find it now furnished with a table, chair and a covering for the floor. "Helen, this is my mother, Aethra, and she'll look after you while I'm away." He waited for Helen to turn from the window. "You'll obey her, or she'll make you very sorry. Is that understood?"

"I couldn't be any sorrier than I already am," Helen replied. "If you'll not be here to torment me yourself, why not send me home before my father's warriors arrive? They'll make short work of you!"

Aethra was a petite woman and barely reached Theseus' shoulder. Her hair was snowy white and styled atop her head in a profusion of braids held with gold combs. Her unlined skin made it difficult to believe she could have given birth to a son of Theseus' age. Her smile held no warmth, and her eyes were an icy, forbidding blue.

"Don't worry, my son. I'll see to everything," her soft tone held a grating edge.

Helen straightened her shoulders. She could so easily overpower Aethra, but what would she gain this far from home? It didn't mean she would obey the little woman, however. "Whatever journey you plan may be your last. Your best course is to send me home before you go," she stressed.

He came close to caress her cheek, and she jumped as though she'd been bitten. "Then I wouldn't have you waiting for me when I return." His smile grew wide at the delicious thought.

Helen glared at him. "I'll wait only to be freed." She despised them both, and didn't see either one for the rest of the day. Her meals continued to be uninspired fare, but she ate as much as she could simply to pass the time. Accustomed to making her own entertainment, she stood at the window waiting for something, or someone to come into view, but the hills remained quiet without even an animal on the hunt to observe.

* * *

Soon after Theseus departed the next morning, Aethra came to Helen's chamber. "It's too fine a day to remain in your chamber. Come with me."

Clearly the diminutive queen expected to be followed, and Helen was too delighted to escape the dreary cell to argue. She wondered if Aethra would strive to simplify her own life by ordering her to do whatever she would eagerly do anyway.

Aethra led her out through the aule, the outer courtyard, and into the vegetable garden. She sat upon a stone bench and patted the place beside her. Grateful to be outside, Helen took a deep breath. The herbs growing nearby lent a hint of mint to the air.

"Does Theseus force you to live in this wretched cold fortress?" Helen asked.

"No, of course not, but he had need of me here. Fortunately, lust does not rule my actions, and we should get along well, if you'll choose to be civil."

No advantage would be gained from an angry outburst, and Helen moderated her tone, "Don't ask me to forget, or forgive, how I came to be here."

Aethra regarded her with a curious gaze. "You're as appealing as the goddess Aphrodite herself and should never be left unguarded. Don't blame my son for taking advantage as any virile man would."

Helen stood to walk the path circling the garden. She knew men thought her pretty, but it was no excuse for ill treatment. "If lust rules your son's temperament, then he's the one who requires a guard." To her complete amazement, Aethra raised a pale hand to stifle a light-hearted giggle.

"All men lust after a comely wench. Has your mother not taught you as much?" Aethra asked.

Leda had attempted to teach her a great many things, but unfortunately, that didn't mean she had learned them. "No, she did not, but from what I've seen, Spartan men are far superior to those of Athens."

Aethra rose to walk with her. "The same fiery blood flows in all men's veins. Now let's enjoy the day in a companionable silence."

Helen was delighted to walk and keep her own counsel while she clung to the hope someone would come for her soon. She imagined a whole army of bronze-clad warriors swinging their swords and shouting her name and storming the fortress.

Castor and Pollux followed their father's orders only in part. They took a fast ship rowed by twenty men, but those men were skilled warriors as well. With their sail raised for speed, they made their way down the Eurotus River and into the Gulf of Lakoia. From there, they followed the shoreline around the Cape of Malea and into the Gulf of Argolis. Always remaining within sight of land, when it grew dark, they steered the sleek ship into shore. They had brought rations for the voyage, but ate sparingly to make them last. At dawn, Castor and Pollux roamed inland to question everyone who frequented the shore and found Theseus had passed that way.

"The ship is a beauty," one fisherman swore. "I saw it once years ago, but it's still as fine a craft. Theseus was seated in the prow with a woman across his lap. A cloak shielded her face, but he would not have taken an ugly girl."

"At least she was not lashed to the mast," Pollux murmured under his breath. He paid the fellow, and they continued their journey, gathering information from every possible source. Athens lay on the other side of the Saronic Gulf, but a mention of a fortress at Dekelia intrigued them. When they finally brought their ship to shore above the village, Castor and Pollux entered alone.

Fishermen tending their nets saw few highborn men and recognized the brothers as people of importance from their fine garments, proud posture and confident stride. One made a low bow.

Castor greeted them with a ready grin. "We're seeking Theseus. Is it true he's in the fortress?"

The youngest of the fishermen stepped forward. "He was here, but he and his guard have sailed on another adventure."

Pollux swore angrily. "We'd wished to join him. Did you see a young woman with him when he left?"

The fishermen exchanged anxious glances before the youth continued. "He arrived with one, but allowed no one to see her. She wasn't with him when he sailed away."

Castor thanked them for being so helpful and after extracting a promise of secrecy, placed a few gold beads in their hands. "Come brother, let's be on our way."

Pollux followed and waited until they would not be overheard to speak. "It sounds as though Helen is a captive within the fortress, but Theseus would have taken his best men with him wherever he was bound, and there can be few left to guard her."

Castor nodded. "They'll be careless with him away and probably drunk every night. We can storm the fortress and free her in the morning while those fools will still be asleep on their beds."

"I want a closer look," Pollux replied. He led Castor onto a nearby rise where they could study the fortress. There was such little activity to observe, however, they soon ended their surveillance and returned to their ship.

That evening, Aethra invited Helen to dine in her chamber. The room was furnished for a woman of her status and lit by oil lamps. They sat upon royal chairs piled with thick cushions and the low tripod tables were spread with fare far finer than Helen had been given there earlier. The fish baked in bay leaves was quite good, but she had little appetite. She sampled a fig and stifled a yawn as the older woman bragged of Theseus's bravery.

"Where has be gone?" Helen asked, as though it were of little concern while she was counting the days until she could escape him for good.

Aethra smiled as though he had already returned. "He's gone to rescue the goddess Demeter's daughter, Persephone. She's been kidnapped by Hades and taken to his Underworld, the Kingdom of the Dead."

Helen sat up straight. "He's brazenly kidnapped me, and now gone to rescue a girl Hades took against her will? How can he oppose behavior that's as vile as his own? How can he possibly justify his actions?"

"More wine?" Aethra asked, ignoring Helen's outrage.

"More wine will not make me feel any the less abused. Theseus may rescue a hundred women, but as long as he holds me captive, I see no reason to praise his name."

"You're such a silly child. The King of Athens may do as he pleases, and while he's sure to grow bored with your tantrums, your beauty alone will keep you alive."

A servant stood in the shadows, ready to fetch whatever his mistress wished, but Helen considered the meal over. "I want to return to my chamber."

"You'll leave when I say you may." Aethra ate another bite of fish and took a long sip of her wine. "Your mother should have taught you silence is a woman's greatest asset. No man can bear a woman who refuses to acknowledge his presence. He'll exhaust himself to win her favor. On the other hand, he'll promptly flee a young woman with your vicious tongue."

"Which is exactly what I want!" Helen cried. "I've no use for the man, king or no king."

"Then you'll have a very unhappy life with my son. You cannot escape him, so you would be wise to learn how to enthrall him with your beauty."

"If he were my slave, I'd sell him to the dreaded mines." She suffered in silence as Aethra continued to offer advice on how to manipulate men to do her bidding. Apparently a woman's beauty was wasted if it wasn't used to control men. When the tedious meal was over at last, she nearly ran back to her chamber and welcomed the warmth from the fire glowing on the brazier.

She paced the small room and fought to recall her mother's half-heeded advice. A woman was to bathe daily, more often if she cared to, and her hair was always to be well groomed with a glorious healthy shine. Her clothing was to be beautifully woven and sewn and worn with pride. Pride was a favorite word of her mother's. A woman should draw herself up into a straight proud posture, while her steps and gestures must always be graceful. She should eat her meals slowly with dainty bites, rather than gulp down her food like a harried servant.

Throughout their days, Leda had provided a running commentary on deportment and a profusion of advice on how to run an efficient household. As for manipulating men, if her mother were even aware of such a skill, she hadn't discussed it. Or, perhaps she had thought it too soon to offer such intimate instruction. Whatever her mother's reason, Helen thought it wrong to practice silly wiles on a man when a straightforward request, or outright demand, would be so much simpler and much more to her liking.

Clytemnestra had mastered their mother's teachings on feminine perfection, undoubtedly making Agamemnon a deliriously happy man. The only king she'd accept would be an extraordinary horseman who was slow to speak. She fell into a restless sleep hoping this would be the last night she would have to spend under Theseus's distasteful *protection*. If the bastard had actually ventured into the Underworld, she hoped Hades would imprison him there forever.

CHAPTER 9

Castor, Pollux and their men waited unseen as fishermen brought their early morning catch to the fortress. Once the door in the tall gates had opened, they shoved the startled fishermen aside and stormed in ahead of them. Catching the few warriors there unprepared for battle, they unleashed their mission with flashing spear blades and with a brutal vengeance easily gained control of the stronghold.

Castor grabbed the arm of a serving girl cowering in a corner and yelled, "Where's Helen? Take me to her, and you'll come to no harm."

The sobbing girl dried her eyes on her sleeve and led him up the stone stairway to his sister's chamber and then darted away. Castor thrust open the door and after a momentary fright, Helen recognized him and leaped into his arms.

"I knew you'd come!" She hugged him tightly. "I heard yells and screams and knew it had to be you."

"We weren't the ones screaming." He laughed and smoothed her hair. She'd hurriedly dressed in her over-sized clothing, but she'd never been prettier. "Let's not waste any time in leaving. Have you anything to bring?"

She had no desire to keep the clothing other than what she wore and squeezed the tiny fabric warrior in her hand in grateful relief for her newfound freedom. It would be the only souvenir she'd need. An idea too good to ignore came to her, and she seized upon it. "I'd like to take Theseus's mother, Aethra, with us. She's a veritable fount of knowledge and mother will find a place for her."

His slow smile spread into a rakish grin. "Take his mother? What a splendid idea, Sister." He took her hand. "Let's find her."

"I know the way to her chamber." She skipped as she pulled him along. Shouts could still be heard coming from the floor below, but they were harsh instructions to the cowering servants rather than challenges to Theseus's vanquished warriors.

Aethra faced the door as they entered. She may have had to dress hurriedly, but she projected a queen's elegant dignity. Castor gave a mock bow. "My lady, you're coming with us. Gather your belongings; we mean to leave before the sun is high."

"I've no wish to accept your brash invitation."

He looked at her askance. "Did you wish to come here, Helen?"

"No, absolutely not, but I was kidnapped rather than invited. You're coming with us, Aethra. Now what do you wish to bring?"

"I refuse to go." She was too small to object, and when Castor swept her up into his arms, her tiny fists beat ineffectually on his chest.

"You mustn't be so reluctant to accept the hospitality of a princess of Sparta, my lady," he remarked with a low chuckle. "Pack whatever you believe she might need, Helen, and I'll have one of the men carry the chest to the ship."

"I'll hurry." Helen searched the carved chests to find Aethra's clothing. There was a small clay jar, a pyxis, used to hold perfumes and cosmetics. She wrapped it in one of Aethra's skirts and added it to the chest. Another small chest was filled with gold jewelry, and she carried that herself. She recognized the man who came to take Aethra's belongings, but he glanced away, and she wondered if he thought meeting her gaze would be disrespectful, or if no longer a virgin, she had lost her appeal. Aethra hadn't thought it a problem, but now she wondered.

Pollux waited at the foot of the staircase, and she hugged him tightly. "You are the best of brothers. I knew you'd rescue me."

He blushed deeply. "We should have arrived sooner."

"No, you arrived after Theseus had departed with his men, and that made your surprise attack so much easier."

Insulted, he stepped back. "Do you think we lack courage?"

"Certainly not, but we must thank the gods for the splendid timing of your arrival."

She stepped around the blood spilled upon the courtyard. Servants were dragging bodies into a heap for a funeral pyre. Emalia was among them, and when she paused to wipe her bloody hands on a rag, Helen caught Pollux's arm. "Is there room in your boat for a couple more?" she asked.

Pollux stopped beside her. "Whom do you mean?"

"The girl closest to us and her brother were kind to me. May I bring them?"

"If you can hurry them along."

Helen gestured for Emalia, and the disheveled serving maid looked over her shoulder at the other servants before running to her. Her worn sandals were splattered with blood, and she appeared terrified death might soon overtake her. "Yes, my lady?"

"I want you to come with us. Find Oron, bundle your belongings and hurry to our ship."

The girl's already large eyes grew huge. "Go with you to Sparta?"

"Why not? Do you enjoy the drudgery here in the hot kitchen? There will be a better life for you in my home. Aethra will need a maid, and you'll not scrub another grimy kettle."

The girl wrung her chapped hands. "I hate it here."

"Then fetch your brother and your things and come with us. I'll wait for you here for only a moment. Hurry or you'll be too late."

Emalia bit her lip, and her decision quickly made, she nodded and ran into the fortress. Helen looked up at the glorious blue sky and thought she'd never seen a finer morning for travel.

Emalia and Oron were painfully thin and possessed so few belongings they added little weight to the boat. They huddled near Helen in the prow and watched as the fortress faded in the distance. When only the mountains remained clear, they turned their attention to the bay and sat clutching each other's hands as the sleek boat sped through the water with swift strong strokes of the fine-muscled Spartan seamen.

Castor leaned close to whisper in Helen's ear. "They rushed to our boat, and Theseus's whole household might have sailed with us had there been room for them. How did you make pets of his people?"

"They're far from pets. I treated them respectfully, and they were so eager to please me, I hated to leave them behind."

Aethra sat stiff-backed in the ekrion, the canopy covered stern castle where Pollux made certain she had no opportunity to hurl herself into the sea. Helen nodded toward her. "Aethra will be our guest, and I doubt she'll beg to return home."

"When you subdue the enemy so easily, maybe we should fight with a legion of beautiful women rather than armed warriors."

Helen thought the idea daft. "Your swords set me free, rather than my own efforts. Besides, men are stronger and much better suited for a warrior's bloody trade."

The wind billowed their great sail, displaying the royal emblem of Sparta. Castor brushed her cheek with his fingertips. "You don't appear to have suffered too greatly."

She pulled away. "More than you can imagine."

"I can imagine more than enough, but you've survived as yourself. I told Mother you're a strong girl. You've proved it today."

Her hair blew free in the sea breeze. "We're all born strong, Castor. Theseus was a fool to believe otherwise." She doubted she looked the same, however, when she felt so different inside. It wasn't merely her innocence that had been stolen, but something deeper, and something far more precious had been lost forever.

* * *

Confident they'd not be pursued, the Spartans pulled their ship into shore that night, and built a fire to roast the tunny fish they'd caught in their nets. Aethra refused to eat, but Emalia and Oron didn't have to be coaxed to have their fill. The siblings weren't much older than Helen, and their simple joy over having ample fare amazed her.

"Why would anyone starve his servants?" she asked Castor. "They'll do far better work if they're well-fed."

"Perhaps Theseus is too mean to care." Castor passed her a kylix of wine. "I'd not thought you ever concerned yourself with the management of a household. Have Mother's lessons finally taken hold?"

Everything her mother had taught her had been of little value in the fortress. "Perhaps. She'll see I marry well, and what man would want a wife who couldn't manage their household?"

He leaned over to hug her. "Any man who vies for you will not care a whit if you can even recall the servants names, let alone assign them duties. You're too lovely to worry about anything when you'll please your man simply by existing."

"I might as well be a fresco if only my appearance matters."

"An artist could create wondrous frescos with your image, and probably will, but you're too lively a girl to be as silent as a woman painted on a wall."

She sighed to concede the point. "True, I've never been the retiring sort, but now, everything is different."

"It doesn't have to be."

Her brother was handsome with a lively sparkle in his blue eyes, but he saw only the surface, and she hoped it would be enough for other men.

Leda ran to welcome Helen home. She hugged her and smoothed the curls from her daughter's forehead to study her expression. "Did the beast beat you?"

"Only when he caught me at the river, but I'm home, and we needn't speak of my wretched captivity ever again."

Castor and Pollux kissed their mother's cheek, and she hugged them both tightly. "You've rescued your sister, and there's not a mark on either of you handsome heroes. Your father will want to hear every detail, but I'm happy knowing only that you're all home safely."

Hearing the commotion, Tyndareus strode into the courtyard, swept Helen off her feet and spun her around twice before setting her down gently. He turned to his sons. "I would swear I told you to find Helen and then summon more men, yet you dared to set her free yourselves? I don't know whether to be proud or angry that you disobeyed me."

"Proud," the brothers replied, their grins wide.

"It was an easier challenge than we'd expected," Castor added.

"Not all that easy," Pollux argued.

"I want to hear it all," Tyndareus answered. "You must be hungry, and we'll talk while we dine."

As the men entered the palace, Helen caught Aethra's hand and pulled her close. "This charming woman is Theseus's mother, Aethra. I want to show her how much warmer our hospitality is than her son's."

Taken aback, Leda stared a long moment at the petite woman. "Welcome, my lady. You'll be an honored guest, and your wisdom is sure to enrich our lives. "

Aethra looked past Leda to the beauty of Tyndareus's palace. "I'll not thank you until I'm certain you're sincere."

"Isn't she a joy?" Helen asked. "I've brought along a maid for her who'll need pretty clothing and sleeping quarters. Come, Emalia. My mother needs to see you."

The shy girl took only a single step away from her brother. "My lady, Oron will also need useful work."

"Have you cared for horses?" Helen inquired.

He shook his head. "No, but I can learn."

"Of course you can," Helen assured him. "Find the stables and tell the boys working there I said you're be made welcome. They know I come there often and will see how they behave towards you."

"I'm on my way," Oron replied, and he jogged away without looking back.

Leda had Aethra shown to a fine room and directed her serving maids to find Emalia clothing and to provide her with the necessary instructions. Grateful to be alone with Helen, she ushered her to the bathing room. "Whose clothes are you wearing?"

"A dead woman's. Burn them or give them away, I'll wear only my own clothing now." She tore away her borrowed attire and stepped into the tub. It was painted with charming fish that appeared to be swimming in the sea.

Serving maids filled the great terracotta tub with hot water. Leda dismissed them and pulled a stool close. "I'll never forgive myself for what's happened to you. Never."

The rose scented soap was soft against Helen's skin, and she spread the lather over her arms. Her bruises were too faint for her mother to notice, but she needed no reminders of how badly Theseus had treated her. "It wasn't your fault, Mother. I shouldn't have gone to the river alone, and Theseus shouldn't have leaped from his boat to catch me. His name should be forever cursed, but we shouldn't brood over what can't be changed."

Leda had to swallow hard. "You're not to blame for any of this, dismiss the thought immediately. Theseus abducted a young Spartan maiden dancing at a sacred temple, and the gods will punish him for such despicable sacrilege. I wish we could simply forget this outrage, but first we must be certain there are no unfortunate consequences."

Shocked by the thought, Helen shut her eyes tightly and began soaping her hair. "He only raped me once, not again and again."

"A woman needs to be with a man only a single time to conceive, but perhaps your youth will protect you. If not, there are herbs to…"

"Surely they don't grow with the herbs used to flavor our meals."

"No, but they can be found in our apothecary garden. Please don't fret you'll be forced to bear a child. I promise you it won't happen." She moved closer to help Helen shampoo her hair, and Omalu brought fresh towels.

Omalu wept as she knelt beside the tub. "Can you ever forgive me for not being with you? Together we could have fought him off, and you'd not have been taken so far from home."

Helen stood and wrapped herself in a lavender towel before stepping out of the tub. "He had a sharp dagger, Omalu, and he might have killed you. I'm grateful we both survived."

Omalu brushed her tears from her cheeks, and Leda dried hers before Helen noticed.

Helen rose early to go riding with her brothers. Still elated by their successful adventure, they teased and prodded each other, but after the initial joy of returning home, her spirits were noticeably dimmed. She'd hoped to lose herself in her former routine, but riding with Castor and Pollux no longer amused her. She looked toward the mountains, the clouds veiling the sky, and down at the well-worn path. Even with the brightness of the day, the familiar sights gave her no peace and her heart ached. Her ordeal at Theseus's hands would become widely known, and the story embellished by tales of her brothers' heroic rescue. People would stare at her, perhaps attempting to hide their curiosity, but they would regard her openly if they thought her unaware. She'd know though, and every glance would sting.

Castor pulled his mount to a halt. "It's not like you to be so quiet, Helen. Are you bored with our company?"

"No, merely sad. Continue your ride, I'll return home."

"Not alone," Pollux avowed. He and Castor turned their white mounts to remain with her. "Do you want to race?"

She shook her head. "No, I just want to be outdoors and feel the sun's warmth on my skin."

She looked over her shoulder, but they weren't being followed.

The brothers followed her glance. "We're alone. Tomorrow we'll bring food and stop along the way to rest and eat," Castor offered.

Helen nodded, but she doubted she'd want anything more than a berry or two. A wildness twisted inside her, a churning that made the thought of food obscene. She had eaten in the fortress to remain alive, but now, there seemed to be little point.

She recognized Menelaus's glowing red hair as he rode toward them. He was grinning as though he could barely contain himself, but she had to force a slight smile.

He flung back his cape as he greeted Castor and Pollux and then took up a place beside her and allowed them to lead. "I'm overjoyed to see you looking so well. I'd have gone with your brothers had I known you'd been taken. I wish I could have been the one to set you free."

Clearly he regretted missing an adventure, while she'd rather forget it all. "Could we talk of something else?"

"Whatever you wish. The wildflowers on the hillsides are especially lovely this year."

She couldn't help but smile at how quickly he'd granted her request. "Yes, they are, indeed. I wonder if we'll be able to create especially fragrant perfumes."

"You're far too beautiful to have any need for perfume, Helen."

She'd never thought him a fool, but his compliment rang false. Perhaps he wished to believe nothing about her had changed, but sadly she knew better.

* * *

Aethra walked with Leda through the herb garden, and paused frequently to suggest a better assortment or planting arrangement. "Herbs must be enticed from the ground," she directed, "not left to sprout wherever they wish."

Leda nodded thoughtfully. "I see what you mean. We've been rather careless it seems. Thank you for your suggestions."

Aethra stopped abruptly and regarded Leda with a narrowed gaze. "Is everyone here always so pleasant?"

She'd made it sound like a fault, and Leda couldn't help but smile. "Of course not. We have an occasional disagreement, but I prefer to keep our house as free of discord as possible."

"Hmm," the little queen dismissed the possibility and continued surveying the garden with a critical eye. "I suppose I should see the olive grove."

"If it's not too much for you today."

"Too much?" Aethra scoffed. "Do I appear to be too frail to stroll more than a few steps beyond my bed chamber?"

"Certainly not, but I don't want to tire you unnecessarily. We'll take this path to the grove. Perhaps you know something of creating dyes?"

"All there is to know. Do you plan to pull advice from my head the whole day through?"

Leda bit her lip rather than laugh at her amusing companion. "No, my lady, but I want to fully appreciate your wisdom."

Apparently placated, Aethra followed along the path. "Let's concentrate on cultivating olives for today."

"As you wish." Leda could not help but like the feisty little queen, and she understood why Helen had brought her home.

Tyndareus pulled Leda into his arms and tickled her ear with kisses. "Helen's beauty hasn't dimmed. How does she seem to you?"

Leda cuddled against his broad chest. "She's become even more fiercely independent, and yet she's quiet at times and daydreams of who knows what. Omalu stays with her, and they're as close as they've ever been. I'd wished for Helen to move beyond childish exuberance, but not in this horrible fashion."

"I'm being besieged by men who wish to take her for a wife. Whatever her mood, we should begin the courting competition. Even if she is unsettled now, and by the time the games are over and won, she should be content to have a husband."

Leda leaned back to study his expression. "We must wait, beloved, to be certain Theseus has not left her with child."

He nodded slightly. "It would be a king's babe."

"There will be no child," she stressed through clenched teeth. "Now let's find other thoughts for our evening together."

He slid his fingers through her hair to tilt her face for a kiss. "Like this?"

"Oh yes, like this." He understood nothing, but she loved him so dearly and wished an equally devoted husband for Helen. The real question remained whether Helen could become equally devoted to him.

CHAPTER 10

Helen rode with her brothers every morning and while her bay gelding wasn't nearly as swift, she raced them anyway. Every few days, Menelaus would appear, and she began to wonder if he weren't staying home several days in a row in a calculated attempt to make her miss him. He was as good-natured as her brothers and when her mood turned dark, he could still coax a smile from her. He had a rich rolling laugh and found her brothers' jokes endlessly amusing. Perhaps it was their company he craved rather than hers. She had thought a straightforward approach best with men, but now preferred not to inquire as to his motives.

Menelaus turned his mount to block hers, while her brothers continued on ahead.

He didn't frighten her, but she pulled back on her reins to gain space to ride around him.

"Wait," he asked. "You've been home two months. Some say your father will soon seek a husband for you. If there is to be a competition with games and races, I'll be the first to enter."

"Should I be flattered?" She whisked away an annoying fly and regarded him as openly as she always had.

The impertinent question won a small chuckle from him. "Yes, you should be enormously flattered, Helen. You should have a royal and wealthy husband, and I can provide for you very well."

She ran her hand down her mount's dark mane. "Shouldn't you be discussing this with my father rather than me?"

"He knows, and if I'm to be your choice before the games begin, you could save us all a great deal of expense and effort by declaring it now."

She dug her heels into her horse's flanks and cantered to reach her brothers. "You shouldn't have left me behind with him."

Castor wheeled his horse around. "Did he insult you?"

"Yes, but not enough to deserve punishment. Tell him I don't care who vies for me. I'm going home."

"I'll go with you," Pollux announced and followed.

Castor waited for Menelaus to reach him. "You've had your eye on Helen from the time she was a pretty child. Now you've insulted her, and she may be very slow to forgive."

"Was it wrong to say I intend to compete for her hand?"

"Yes, it's much too soon since we freed her from Theseus's fortress to bother her with thoughts of marriage. Now you'll have to begin again to impress her. Another horse, perhaps?"

Menelaus snorted. "I fear the gift of every horse I

own might not be enough to touch her heart."

"Then you'll have to win every contest. You ride well, can you run?"

"I'm a fast runner, throw a spear well and can easily wrestle a man to the ground. I can do it all."

"Ajax may come," Castor warned.

Menelaus yanked his horse to a halt. "Ajax? He's great-sized and strong, but not every contest requires his brute strength."

"True. Patroclus should enter too. He's a handsome lad. Odysseus, the king of Ithica, is sure to compete, and he's known for his cunning as well as his prowess in battle."

Menelaus gave a frustrated cry, "Am I known for anything at all?"

Castor had to laugh at his lack of insight. "Yes, your wealth, and it may be all you need. Our father will select Helen's husband, and while he might ask for her preference, it doesn't mean he'll grant it."

"Then I should have been riding with Tyndareus rather than Helen." Menelaus left Castor on the path and cut his own way toward home. There wasn't a man alive who wouldn't want Helen, but he didn't care how bruised and bloody he got, he was going to win her for his own.

Once reassured there would be no regrettable consequences from Theseus's assault on his daughter, Tyndareus called Helen into the megaron one afternoon. The painted griffins flanking his high-backed throne appeared to be smiling as they looked down on him. "Come, sit upon my lap as you always have."

They were alone in the ornately decorated room, and she slid upon his knee and looped her arms around his neck. "I already know what you wish to say."

He smoothed her curls away from her face. "Why don't you say it for me then?"

"You and Mother want a fine husband for me, and because men love to fight and race, there must be a competition like the one you held for Clytemnestra."

"Yes, and many of the same men may enter. They'll come from all over Greece, not only because they love to compete, but because they want you, Helen. You're a famed beauty and a rare prize."

Embarrassed, she shrugged off the effusive compliment. "I've never felt it, nor seen it."

He rested his forehead against hers and drew in a deep breath. "You must have heard rumors about your birth, perhaps a whisper or two about lord Zeus."

"If I heard his name linked with mine, I gave it no credence. You're my father."

He leaned back to study her expression. "I've raised you with love, child, and while your mother waited years to tell me, Zeus, the king of the gods, is your true father. He gave you a magical beauty others see even if it escapes you."

Dismayed she'd been shielded from such a significant fact; she gripped his tunic with a tight fist. "Then shouldn't my choice of husband be Zeus's concern rather than yours? Will he send a god from Mount Olympus to woo me?"

He sighed at the notion. "I've never seen Zeus walking among us and can't predict what he might do."

His comment prompted the vivid memory of a remarkable childhood encounter. "Years ago, I may have met him in the almond grove. He was tall, fair and very handsome with wavy hair and a beard that seemed to glow. His eyes were as green as mine. He gave me a pomegranate, and when I turned away to look for Castor and Pollux, he disappeared. He'd made me promise not to tell anyone we'd met, but didn't reveal his name. I kept the secret, but I doubt it matters now."

Amazement widened her father's eyes, and he squeezed her tight. "You saw him only once?"

"Yes, on one sunny morning, but never again. If I'd known he might be Zeus, I'd have asked to see his winged horses and to ride in his golden chariot."

"Let's keep this story to ourselves, Helen. If Zeus blessed you with a visit, he must be very pleased with you."

"Whoever he was, he was kind and friendly, but he should have given me his name. I would have paid closer attention."

He laughed and hugged her. "The gods love to play with our lives, that's why we pray to them and make sacrifices to keep them happy and unconcerned about us. Now I began this conversation meaning only to tell you it's time to marry. You needn't worry we'll force you to wed a man you can't admire. You've seen the men who've come here for feasts and festivals. Do you have any favorites?"

She waited a long moment to mention a name. "Menelaus has always been attentive, but I fear I've insulted him."

"How?"

"He said it would save everyone the expense and effort to vie for my hand if I chose now."

"Fool! He guards his wealth well and it increases each year, but he should not have approached the topic of the competition with you. I'll speak to him on his next visit."

"He may not return."

Her voice was soft, tinged with sorrow, and he set her on her feet and stood beside her. "He'll return until he has not a horse left to ride, and then he'll walk, but he'll be here again soon. I promise you."

She gazed up at him, her doubt clear in her troubled frown. "How can you be so sure?"

"Because I'd have done anything for a moment or two with your mother. Fortunately, she was inclined in my favor even before I won the competition for her hand. I'm grateful every day for her love."

"You forgave her for being with Zeus?"

He took her hand as they strolled into the courtyard. "There's nothing to forgive. The gods do with us what they wish. Zeus adores beautiful women, and your mother is one of the loveliest ever born."

They parted and wanting only to be alone to think, Helen ran from the courtyard into the almond grove and wandered among the pink flowered trees. The handsome man she'd met so long ago may have merely been quick on his feet rather than Zeus, who could appear and disappear as he pleased. She was troubled by the thought she might be a god's daughter. It was another worry atop many, and she promptly forgot Menelaus's bruised feelings.

Aethra dined with Leda and Helen in the portion of the palace reserved for women. She offered advice each time she swallowed. "You'd be wise to wed a poet, who'd remain home and entertain you with his poetry, lyre and songs. Warriors forever seek a new challenging enemy, and no woman looks forward to bidding her husband farewell without any real hope he'll return alive."

"Do poets enter contests of strength and endurance?" Helen asked.

"Some must at Delphi, Apollo's shrine, I suppose, and you'll know where such a man lays his head each night," Aethra assured her.

Helen glanced toward her mother, who was hiding a smile. "Would father welcome a poet to the family?" she asked.

Leda shook her head and paused to sip her wine before answering. "No, he wants someone strong enough to defend you should the need arise."

"Arise again," Helen emphasized. "Although I suppose I'd not be abducted from a renowned warrior's palace. Who would dare?"

"Certainly not," Aethra admitted, "but you must remember he'll seldom be home. Men are born wanderers, lured by their lust for gold and the scent of fresh blood to seek fame and glory wherever it exists, or wherever they might create it. Poets make the best husbands because they remain home and stay alive."

"You're speaking from experience?" Helen asked before Leda could hush her.

"No, Ageus was a warrior king just as Theseus is today, but they are a poor topic for conversation in this house."

"Indeed," Leda agreed. "These almond filled figs are especially fine this evening."

"A fig is a fig," Aethra announced, and Helen was inclined to agree.

Tyndareus sent heralds to announce a competition with Helen as the prize, and the word circulated quickly among unmarried noblemen throughout Greece. Some were daunted by descriptions of her beauty, while more were drawn to the palace of the Spartan king to gain a glimpse of her. The young men boasted of their talents in games and battles, but few other than Diomedes, the king of Argos, had any recent victories to celebrate. Odysseus was admired, and his fiery red hair made him a colorful contender.

Helen stood beside her father as he welcomed men to their palace, but one face soon blurred into another. They were a handsome lot, young, muscular and fit, but her cheeks ached with the tiresome effort to smile. When the last man had been introduced, and Menelaus had not appeared, she felt an unaccustomed pang of sorrow.

"What's wrong, child?" Tyndareus whispered.

"Menelaus isn't here. Not that I had any favorites, but he appeared to be so eager, and now he's stayed away."

"His brother Agamemnon is here," he remarked.

"He's Clytemnestra's husband, so he must be here only to observe the sport."

He pulled her hand to his lips. "Shall I send someone to inquire as to Menelaus's health? Perhaps he's fallen ill."

Helen shook her head. She hadn't seen him since the day they'd parted on the riding path, but she wouldn't beg for his company. "Let him be. Must I stay any longer?"

"No, go with your mother and remain inside the palace as long as you wish. I'll provide a frequent report of the men's progress."

She doubted she'd be able to summon the enthusiasm to care. The men filling the courtyard were laughing together and in a playful mood, but the hunger in their eyes reminded her of Theseus lascivious gaze and sickened, she rushed inside.

Omalu lured her onto the roof terrace where years earlier they had watched the competition for Clytemnestra's hand. However, the men were gathered farther from the palace for foot races and were difficult to identify at this distance. The maid raised a hand to shade her eyes. "I do see a red-haired man."

"It's probably Odysseus," Helen replied. She leaned against the railing and looked up at the sky. "He frightens me."

"Why? How is he different from any of the others?"

Helen closed her eyes a moment and carefully chose her words. "There was no desire in his gaze when he looked at me, but instead a keen relish for the challenge."

"I didn't realize you'd studied him so closely."

"It was impossible to miss." She turned her back to the railing. "I'd not expected so many men to compete, and I'm afraid whoever is chosen will brag for years of how he won me."

"But he'll love you!" Omalu exclaimed.

"Will he?" Helen studied her neatly trimmed nails. The constant use of her mother's creams gave her hands the appearance of a fine lady who did no more than direct the activity around her. She longed for so much more. "The chariot races should be more exciting to watch."

"I find this all exciting, my lady."

Helen laughed with her, but as the prize in the competition, she had so much more at stake.

Tyndareus rested his hands on his hips as he surveyed the rapidly growing mound of gifts suitors had brought for Helen. Leda thought they should accept them all. Helen refused to even offer an opinion and remained unimpressed. "I'll not accept any of them," he announced clearly. "That will settle the matter until your mate's chosen, Helen. Then we'll require a suitable bride price."

"We've already accepted the livestock," Leda reminded him, "otherwise, we'd be unable to feed such a large number of competitors."

Tyndareus nodded agreeably. "You're right. It was a wise decision and great benefit to our xenia hospitality."

He'd hoped to end the competition much sooner, but some men excelled at wrestling, others were swift runners, adept at throwing a spear, or possessed fine horses for the chariot races. An archery competition continued for days. Men who won their favorite competition believed they were far superior to the others who competed in several to show their prowess, but failed to win a single one.

Helen donned a purple cloak and veiled her head before leaving the palace to view the chariot races. She made Omalu also disguise herself and they made their way past the stables and hid behind a conveniently placed oak tree. Peering around the broad trunk, they watched as men paraded with their finest horses and bragged over who would be left choking on another's dust.

"Look, my lady," Omalu pointed toward a pair of jet back horses with a dazzling sheen and long flowing manes and tails. "Have you ever seen a finer pair?"

"No, and they are superb." They were being led to the row of chariots by a groom rather than their owner, and Helen held her breath as she waited to see who he might be. When Menelaus appeared behind her and tapped her shoulder, she nearly shrieked in surprise.

He was clad in a black leather kilt trimmed with gold and wore a proud grin. He held out a fine deerskin quiver filled with hawk-fletched arrows and a new back-bent bow. "I saw no reason to bring you gold trinkets rather than something you truly desire."

Her mother had taught her not to grab at offered presents, but it was difficult to politely hesitate now. She nodded to Omalu to take them. "Thank you. I didn't think you were here."

His grin grew even wider. "You've searched the crowd for me?"

Her cheeks filled with a bright blush. "It's only that you are among the few men I know."

"So you were looking for me," he teased. "Now I'm flattered. What do you think of my horses, the black pair?"

"Those are yours?" Omalu asked, her voice bubbling with admiration.

"Yes, and this is the first time I've shown them away from my own palace. They are not only remarkably handsome; they rival the wind for speed. You're standing near the end of the race, and you'll see."

Helen drew her cloak closer around her shoulders. "You mustn't tell anyone that you've seen me."

"And risk having men surround you and shout their name? Certainly not." He leaned close to kiss her cheek and strode off toward his chariot.

Omalu shifted the bow and quiver in her arms. "I've always liked him."

Helen looked over the other men milling about before the chariot race. Most were tall with glossy long hair and trim like Menelaus, while a few had burly builds. She'd looked forward to the chariot races, but she dreaded the thought of marriage. She hugged herself to stave off a sudden shudder.

"What's wrong?" Omalu asked.

Helen refused to give her fears additional weight by voicing them. She gazed up into the oak. "We might be seen standing here, and the branches will be easy to climb and provide a better view. Hang the quiver and bow on the lowest branch and follow me."

"I've never climbed as well as you do," the maid called, but she managed to stand upon the lowest branch and hang onto the tree trunk. Shielded by dark green leaves and clumps of acorns, they did have a far better vantage point. "This is high enough for me."

Men were gathered around Menelaus's team, and Helen wondered how he'd kept others from knowing he owned such a magnificent pair. The sleek horses tossed their manes, pranced in place and looked eager to run. Only a few men could race across the flat plains at a time, or collisions between chariots could cause horrible injuries, if not death, to both men and animals.

Menelaus steered his chariot to the starting line and waved in Helen's direction. Curious, other men turned to see who he might be saluting, but saw no one standing in the shade of the old tree. Helen held her breath until the men refocused their attention on the race.

If Menelaus were killed in a foolhardy attempt to impress her, she would never forgive herself. Many of the men already proudly sported scrapes and bruises from wrestling or falling while running, but a chariot race was a far more dangerous sport. Tears stung her eyes, but she couldn't look away. The course was a wide circle that would end close to where they hid near the royal fountain, but now feeling sick to her stomach, she'd only watch this one contest and return to the palace where she'd be shielded from calls of triumph or anguished pain.

Forgetting she was standing on a branch, Omalu jumped as the race began and then had to catch hold to keep from falling. "I can't see anything for the dust!" she cried.

Farther above the ground, Helen had an excellent view as the teams flew across the dusty plain. A man with a pair of grays burst ahead. Running a close second, Menelaus held back his team and let his rival lead for half the race. Then with a shout and a slap of the reins, he urged his horses into a wild gallop, and they flew as though they had sprouted divine wings and flashed across the finish line first. He turned his chariot away from the track and again sent Helen a jaunty wave.

She clung to the tree and drew in deep breaths rather than shout words of praise along with the cheering men. Menelaus had won such a clear victory, she doubted anyone would challenge him to another race, but she had seen more than enough for one day. She and Omalu reentered the palace with the same stealth they'd left, but Leda saw them discard their dusty cloaks and knew where they had been.

"Does the roof not provide a good enough view for you?" she asked.

Helen hid the bow and quiver behind her back. "No, I needed to be closer to watch the chariot races, but one was enough. I'll rest the remainder of the afternoon and see you when we dine tonight."

Omalu ran after her mistress, and Leda went up on the rooftop terrace to see what could be seen of the chariot races. It was a glorious day, and she recalled how excited she'd been when it had been her time for such a lively competition. Helen had been robbed of the innocent joy she'd experienced as a bride, but she prayed her daughter would still be happily wed to a man who understood her.

CHAPTER 11

Tyndareus grew weary of the competition. The noise of the games in the day blurred into drunken shouts at night, and he longed for a moment of blissful quiet. He'd had an ample chance to observe men he barely knew, and while some had impressed him as good men, others had revealed themselves to be unworthy fools.

They dined that evening in the megaron, seated around the estia, the great round fire hearth. Odysseus approached Tyndareus and put his fist to his forehead in a proper salute. "You appear preoccupied, my lord. Have you come to a decision?"

Sorry his expression had revealed so much, Tyndareus dipped his head. "There are many men here who'd make an excellent husband for Helen."

"I hope you count me among them."

"I do, but she's a strong-willed girl, and it could swiftly prove to be an unfortunate match. What I fear now is a riot among the others when I name the winner."

Odysseus rocked back on his heels. "The man will be much envied."

"Envy doesn't concern me. I'm more afraid of mayhem and murder."

Odysseus laughed then caught himself when he realized Tyndareus was sincere. "Why not ask every man to swear eternal allegiance to the victor? Then they cannot go back on their word and attack him."

Tyndareus regarded him with a slow smile. "It's an intriguing idea, my clever one, but it must be done before the winner is announced. It calls for a sacrifice so the men can swear in blood."

"You're very wise, my lord" Odysseus replied.

"It's always my hope." Tyndareus went directly to the women's quarters. He first thought of sending Aethra away, but he'd grown used to her pithy comments.

"The men are all in such high spirits," he began. "I've become concerned the winner of the competition might be abused by those who are rejected."

"Or murdered," Aethra interjected.

Leda gasped, but Helen quickly grasped the dire nature of the problem. "May I speak with you alone, Father?"

"Of course." Tyndareus took her hand and led her out into the columned balcony. "I will be forever grateful if you'll help me make the choice, Helen, or I fear the man might be in danger from you."

He was teasing, and yet his joke held a kernel of truth. She would be the worst of wives for the wrong man. "Menelaus won the first chariot race by an impressive margin. If you choose him, the men will believe his victory gives a true meaning to the games."

He studied her expression closely. "It would indeed. Is he your choice?"

Resigned rather than elated, she looked down at her toes. She wouldn't mention the gift of a quiver of arrows and a beautiful bow, but it showed how eager Menelaus was to please her rather than only himself. "Yes, I've never tired of his company, and I don't want any of the others."

"He's a fine man, one who could one day rule all of Sparta. You've made a wise choice." Relieved the matter was finally resolved, he kissed her cheek and returned to the megaron with a renewed appetite for the roasted wild boar.

When Helen entered her mother's room, Leda was quick to ask, "Is the matter settled?"

Helen sighed softly, and wished she could be as happy as she should be. "I believe Menelaus will make the best husband, and Father agreed."

"Agamemnon's brother?" Aethra asked.

"Yes," Leda responded. "Menelaus comes from a powerful family, and he'll do well by her. Now we must hurry with the wedding preparations."

Helen swallowed hard. Menelaus was a kind man, one she thought she could grow to love, but for now, she'd rather the games continued forever.

Tyndareus sent a servant to draw Menelaus away from the evening feast. The young man followed with a sure and steady step into the shadowed alcove. "I'm relieved you haven't taken more than your share of the evening's wine," Tyndareus greeted him.

Menelaus straightened his shoulders proudly. "I came to win Helen's hand, not to risk drowning in your fine wine. How many I serve you, my lord?"

"Come with me." Tyndareus led him to a storeroom where they wouldn't be observed or overheard. Spilled grain crunched beneath their sandals as they stepped through the doorway. "There are men who came here solely because they love the games, but Helen is a gift of the gods, and I won't give her to such a man. You've always struck me as sincere, and now is your chance to speak, my son."

Eager to do so, Menelaus broke into a wide grin. "Thank you for considering me as the serious suitor I am. I know Helen as none of the other men do, and it's not only her beauty that pleases me. I love the way she seizes a challenge, and the fearless way she lives her life. I want to lift away the sadness of her abduction and make her laugh everyday. I have a fine Spartan palace, and own more horses than she could ride in a year. I love her dearly and would never seek to crush her spirit as many men would."

Tyndareus raised his hand before Menelaus could add to what would surely become a lengthy accounting of his assets. "You are her choice as well, but don't let the others know the matter has been decided. I'll speak to everyone in assembly in the morning. Take care not to gloat or you'll surely provoke the worst of consequences."

"They would be worth it," Menelaus exclaimed, then caught himself. He lowered his voice to a whisper, "I understand and won't tell a soul tonight, and tomorrow I'll be proud but not overbearing. Temperance is admired by the gods."

Clearly reluctant, Tyndareus hesitated before speaking. "Helen has been badly mistreated, and you'd be wise to put her pleasure before your own. Always treat her gently, with the tenderness I'm sure you possess. Once she learns to trust you, she'll make an affectionate wife."

Embarrassed Tyndareus would think such a warning necessary; Menelaus was equally slow to respond. "I know how to please a woman, and I won't fail Helen."

Tyndareus gave his soon to be son-in-law an encouraging slap on the shoulder. "Thank you. I know you'll make us all proud, and what a grand union of our Royal Houses! Return to the feast, and do your best to remain sober so you'll have a clear head for tomorrow morning."

"I will, good king, although I do have a fine reason to celebrate tonight."

"Wait until the wedding," Tyndareus advised. He watched the young man walk away with new pride in his bearing. Menelaus was the man he would have chosen for Helen, and he was elated she had proposed his name before he'd had to. He hoped a happy marriage for them, but in marrying Helen, Menelaus would be taking on what could well prove to be the challenge of his life. Yet to join with the House of Atreus will be the envy of all of Greece.

Before the contests began anew the following morning, Tyndareus called an assembly in the great palace courtyard and announced he had come to a decision, but prior to giving the winner's name, he expected all the men to swear allegiance to the one who'd been chosen. "It's been a lively competition, and you've all shown your bravery and skill, but I must demand this last thing from you before we proceed."

Caught by surprise, some men scoffed rather than promise their allegiance to an unnamed man.

Someone shouted, "What if he's someone we despise?"

"You'll make the pledge anyway," Tyndareus replied. "Helen is a great treasure, and her husband shouldn't be at risk from a vengeful rival. Think of it as a way to protect yourselves. There are men who would kill for her, but I hope there are none among Greece's finest here today."

Odysseus stepped forward. "Lord Tyndareus, let me be the first to swear allegiance to the winner."

Impressed by his resolve, others agreed. A horse was sacrificed and men swore their allegiance with bloody hands. "We swear this vow by the gods of Olympus!" Slaves hastened to serve each one a kylix filled with the very best of their wine to celebrate.

Tyndareus waited until the wine had created a jovial mood. "Come stand with me, Menelaus." He waited for the young man to reach him. "I want you by my side when I proclaim you the victor." He raised his voice, "Helen will be Lord Menelaus's bride."

Agamemnon gave his brother a loud cheer, and while some men were deeply disappointed to learn they'd lost, more were generous of spirit and joined in the cheers. Menelaus took care to acknowledge his friends' good wishes without boasting of his good fortune, and as they'd all promised, no one raised a hand against him.

Helen's suitors departed en masse taking with them their guest gifts, boisterous noise and dust-swirling confusion. She remained in the palace

rather than appear in the courtyard to wave good-
bye, but her father bid each man a gracious
farewell. None was astonished by Menelaus's win,
but many were deeply saddened not to have been
the one chosen.

Now the matter of her husband was settled, Helen
searched her chamber for something to sacrifice to
Artemis, goddess of children. There was the frayed
wool warrior she'd brought home from Theseus's
fortress, but nothing more. The queen doll Omalu
had made for her had disintegrated long ago.

"I need something suitable to burn at the temple,"
she called to her maid. "I should have made dolls
and put them away to be ready, but as a child, the
thought of marriage held no meaning."

"We could make little stick horses. You're very
good at that."

Helen wished she could think of something more,
but reluctantly agreed. "Yes, they'll have to do.
Come let's gather sticks in the almond grove. Is
everyone gone so we won't be bothered?"

"Once your father announced Menelaus's name,
your other suitors had no reason to tarry. They're all
gone."

"Good, I shan't miss them." She grabbed her
maid's hand and hurried from the palace.

When Leda found them later playing with sticks,
as they had once loved to do, she tarried at Helen's
door. "I'd hoped you'd left your childhood pastimes
behind."

Helen finished tying a thread before looking up.
"Artemis expects a sacrifice from a maiden before
her wedding. I've no cherished toys to give her, so
we're making some."

Leda entered the chamber and sat on the end of the bed. "I'll miss you terribly."

Helen shrugged unhappily. "You've been so eager for me to wed, why are you suddenly filled with regret?"

"It isn't regret. Daughters naturally grow up and leave their parents; it's the natural course of life. I'll still be sad to see you go. I love your brothers, but daughters always remain closer to their mother's hearts."

"Menelaus comes here so often, his palace must be close. I'll ask him to ride here with me to visit you."

"Please do, but first you must become settled in your new home. Have you decided whom you wish to take with you? Omalu, of course, but are there others? What about the boy and girl you brought back from Theseus's fortress?"

Helen reached for another stick from the pile resting in the middle of her bed. "I'll think on it. I suppose I should ask Menelaus how many there can be."

Leda rose and kissed her daughter's cheek. "You're already thinking like a wife, and I didn't believe it was even possible. You do like him, don't you?"

"Yes, I do." She'd hidden the bow and quiver he'd given her under her bed. She'd not owned them as a child and wouldn't even consider sacrificing them to Artemis. "Better yet, I believe he really likes me."

"He's the most fortunate man in the world, and he adores you."

* * *

Menelaus returned the next morning with the dapple-gray mare. Flowers had been woven into the proud mount's mane and as before, Helen thought the animal a beauty. "Didn't we decide this once?" she asked.

The young man turned the beautiful mare to show her off from every angle. "Yes, we did, but I wanted to give her to you just to ride, you needn't race her. I promise you'll have no reason to run from me."

He had a wicked smile, and she understood his meaning. "Promise?"

"I swear it. May Zeus strike me dead with a lightning bolt if I don't." He laced his fingers together to provide her with a step. "Come, try her."

She looked for a chaperon and found Castor leaning against the stable watching them. "Will you come with us?" She had no virtue to protect she supposed, but she wouldn't shout it outdoors.

Castor disappeared only long enough to fetch his favorite mount. "I'll do my best to see Menelaus does not take advantage, dear sister."

Both men were teasing her, but the gray was such a pretty horse, she wasn't offended. She grabbed hold of Menelaus's shoulder, put her foot into his hands, and easily settled herself on the dapple-gray's back. "Does she have a name?"

"No, she's another one who comes when I cluck my tongue. Call her Shadow or Moonbeam, whatever you wish."

"What about Fog, Rain, or Mist?" she asked.

"Call her Jumping Frog if you like. My gifts come without any tedious conditions."

"Wonderful. Maybe I'll just call her Gift." She waited for Menelaus to mount his horse and rode toward the familiar path. The scenery had not changed overnight, and yet somehow today, the terrain glowed with an added sparkle. She glanced toward him. "Are you happy to have won?"

"Beyond happy, Helen. I'll have new frescoes painted in your chambers, but I want the artist to see you first. I've told him how beautiful you are, but my description, no matter how effusive, is woefully inadequate."

"Thank you, but your compliments embarrass me. Will I be able to watch him?"

"If you like. You must have a maid with you, of course, or I'll not allow another man in your chamber."

Now he sounded like her father. "I want to bring Omalu, she's been with me since we were both children. How many more servants may I bring to your home?"

He brushed away a gnat flitting around his eyes. "Bring your whole household if your mother will allow it."

She pulled a rose from Gift's mane and brought it to her nose. It had a deliciously sweet fragrance and made her smile. "She wouldn't, but will you always be this agreeable?"

He couldn't contain his smile. "It's my hope, but I'll warn you not to test me."

She frowned slightly. "Why would I want to?"

"Oh Helen, you're such a delight. Some women tease and make promises they've no intention of keeping, but you're as direct as a sunbeam."

"Are you sure it isn't the shine reflected from my blonde hair."

Castor laughed as loudly as Menelaus, and insulted, she tapped her heels against Gift's flanks and left them behind. They caught up to her, but she ignored them until her temper cooled. "You mustn't make fun of me. There's a great deal I don't know, or might misunderstand, but it's cruel to point it out so rudely with laughter."

"I didn't mean to be cruel," Menelaus insisted. "Please laugh at me whenever you wish, and I'll be happy to amuse you."

She eyed him askance. "I'll remind you of that vow often I'm sure."

"Yes, my lady, you probably will."

The stick horses burned with a bright flame in Artemis's temple, and while they were a small sacrifice compared to some young women's collection of childhood toys, Helen believed she'd completed her obligation. The others danced, to the metallic ringing of the sistrums but the drumbeat no longer echoed the wild thumping of her heart, and she circled the ring of whirling women and girls and moved into the shadows to watch.

Leda caught her hand. "Enough, we should leave before everyone notices how distracted you are." She guided her daughter outside, and they dressed quickly.

"Who wouldn't be distracted?" Helen responded. She tied the cord at her waist holding her skirt too tightly and had to ease it slightly. "I know what's coming, and a naïve virgin wouldn't."

Leda hugged her. "I wish there were a potion to ease your mind so you'd forget your time away from us."

"Then I'd lose a part of myself." She couldn't bear to glance toward the river and rushed along the path toward home.

Her mother caught up with her. "We'll have our feast in the women's megaron while the men have theirs. We'll have all your favorites. The cooks in Menelaus's palace should know how to prepare them too. You won't starve there."

Helen hoped she'd not want to, but she'd never longed to be a wife. She turned toward her mother. "Is it true that I'm Zeus's child?"

Leda halted as though she'd been struck and swayed before catching her balance. Her voice became a hoarse croak, "Your father told you?"

"Yes, and Tyndareus is my true father, not the king of Olympus who'd let me be ravaged without intervening."

"You mustn't blaspheme the gods!" Leda warned sternly. "Zeus cannot be everywhere at once, perhaps another of his pretty daughters needed saving."

"And he prefers her to me? That's not encouraging."

"No, he must delight in you, but I meant he cannot solve every wrong when men are so willful and brutal."

"And I'm about to marry one." Helen moved so quickly along the trail her feet barely touched the ground. She wondered if she'd be allowed to run, or ride, across the Spartan countryside as she always had at home. If Menelaus attempted to keep her closely confined, she might welcome starvation.

When they reached the palace, Leda directed Helen to the bathing chamber. "The water is already heated, and it can be reheated as often as you wish."

Helen waited for servants to fill the big terra cotta tub and then slid in. "There's too much perfume in the water," she exclaimed. "A light fragrance is good, but this water reeks."

With a twitch of her nose, Leda had to agree, and the tub was drained and refilled. "There, bathe with the rose soap, and you'll be as fragrant as a spring garden."

Helen sat quietly amid the soap bubbles as one of her mother's favorite servants shampooed her hair. "I suppose I really must think of whom to take with me. What about Aethra? She's not a servant, but her thoughts are amusing, and I'd hate to leave her behind."

Leda paced beside the tub. "You brought her here, so take her if you wish. After you've lived in Menelaus's palace for awhile, you'll be better able to judge whom you truly need."

Helen bent her head as the servant rinsed her curls with a fresh amphora jar of warm water. She'd leave home tonight with her new husband, and while she wanted to regard marriage as an adventure, she felt only numb. She recalled Clytemnestra's winsome smile as she'd ridden away with Agamemnon, but her own heart held not even a particle of the same proud, yet subdued enthusiasm.

Although the women's banquet prepared to celebrate her marriage held many delicious dishes with fish, olives and colorful pomegranates, Helen ate only a few bites of bread and goat cheese. She sipped watered wine and watched women she'd known all her life and their daughters sing and dance. It was as splendid a party as the one given for Clytemnestra, but the requisite joy still escaped her. As the night wore on, she began to fear

Menelaus wouldn't leave the men's banquet before dawn and then be too drunk to handle his chariot to take her home. She wished now she'd learned how to manage a team herself so neither of them would be in any danger of coming to harm.

Leda nearly skipped across the room. "Menelaus is at the gates, and it's time to light the torches." She offered her hand to help Helen rise. "He's a very handsome man and should be a fine husband for you."

"I certainly hope so," Helen responded and couldn't suppress a giggle. She hadn't meant to drink more wine than she could sedately handle, but the evening had been so very long and tiring. She wore a newly woven multi-colored skirt and fine bolero. With roses laced in her hair, a veil rested lightly on her long curls. Clinging to her mother's hand, she followed the torch-bearing women down the stairs and out into the courtyard.

That Menelaus had brought his magnificent black team to pull his royal chariot thrilled her more than the thought of becoming his wife. He offered his hand to help her into the flower decked chariot. She'd always liked his smile and found one for him. "Can we race to your palace?" she whispered.

He laughed and drew her between his arms before taking up the reins. "Stand here with me, and when we're out of sight, we'll let them run."

His tunic was sewn of fine linen, and his skin held the scent of myrrh. She took a firm grip on the front of the chariot rail and leaned back against his broad chest. He waved to her family and urged the dancing pair of blacks into a slow trot. "There's enough moon tonight to see well and let them run, but I should hold them back and appear to be a proper bridegroom rather than a reckless fool."

"I've never considered you a fool." She waved to her parents, who stood hugging each other tightly. Her brothers were waving with wild enthusiasm as though they were the ones being wed. Tears flooded her eyes as she realized how dearly she'd miss them all. Omalu, Emalia and her brother, Oron, would follow in a wagon at first light with her belongings, while Aethra would deserve a chariot for the trip. She took in a deep breath and turned to watch as the glowing torches faded into the distance.

She felt safe surrounded by Menelaus's strength, and the cool breeze lifted the lingering spell of the wine. She looked up at him. "It's a glorious night, isn't it?"

He bent his head to hear her and kissed her cheek. "It is." He slapped the reins to encourage the horses to hurry along the well-worn roadway, and they bolted to draw the chariot to near racing speed. Helen laughed as the wind tore away her veil. All too soon he drew the team to a placid trot, but she nearly jumped up and down from the thrill.

"Can we do this every day?" she asked.

"Ah, Helen, we'll do whatever we wish."

When they reached his palace, grooms came running to care for the high-spirited team. Menelaus laced his fingers in hers as they entered the columned porch to his palace. Had Tyndareus's palace been closer, she would have brought coals from her family's home to light a fire on his hearth. Any coals she might have carried tonight would have grown cold long before they entered the tall gates. His servants were waiting with brightly lit torches, all jostling to have the first glimpse of the famed Helen. She nodded her appreciation but failed to hide a yawn.

"I'll not have my bride fall asleep in the courtyard. Come, I want to show you your chamber." He escorted her up the main stairway and along the hallway.

She caught only a glimpse of columns painted in red and with gold ringed capitals and the first sight of his palace impressed her as being as fine as her father's. A fire burned in a brazier to warm her chamber, and vases filled with red lilies and wildflowers perfumed the air. Lanterns gave the room a soft golden glow, and she found his carefully planned welcome endearing.

The large chamber was decorated with a grape leaf border painted high along the walls. She turned to take it all in slowly, for this would be her home, perhaps for the remainder of her life. "You're right. The chamber could use some colorful frescoes, but we'll have to wait until after sunrise to judge the light."

"Let's amuse ourselves until then." He took her hand to seat her on the wide bed and knelt to untie her sandals. "You have such pretty little feet."

"Really?" Surprised by his compliment, she wiggled her toes. "I've never thought of them as being anything more than feet."

He stood, sat beside her and took her hand. "You don't appreciate how lovely you are, do you, my love?"

"It makes very little difference to me, but perhaps if I weren't so pretty, I'd have been safe near the river."

He hugged her. "I'd not meant to remind you of that awful day. Forgive me. Everyone will assume we've made love tonight, but we needn't if you're not ready. I'll wait until you want me."

His voice was low and as tender as his words. But if she chose to wait, it would only postpone the inevitable, and she saw no reason to push the challenge into another day. She knew enough not to admit she just wanted to get it over with. "You have very kind eyes."

A smile teased the corner of his mouth. "Thank you, and I mean to always be kind to you."

She looked down at their clasped hands. "I'd not have chosen you if I didn't believe so." She pulled her hand free to cup his face and kissed his lips lightly. "I mean to be your wife, Menelaus. You needn't treat me as though I were fragile tonight, when tomorrow I want you to teach me to drive a chariot and to use that handsome bow and arrows you gave me."

He leaned across her to ease her down on the bed. "No man has ever had a wife like you, Helen."

"I fear no other man would want one," she replied and welcomed his deep laughter. He moved slowly to undress her, his touch breeze light across her bare skin. He trailed kisses from her ears to the tender skin of her inner elbows before suckling at her breast. She ran her fingers through his curly hair and held him close.

She felt as though she were floating above the bed to watch his every move without any curiosity about what might happen next. He was so patiently adoring, she returned his kisses with an attempt at the enthusiasm he deserved. When he at last brought their bodies together, he waited, poised over her, and she smiled.

"I can truly call you husband now," she whispered.

He smothered her face with kisses, made love to her with a slow sweetness and fell asleep cradling her in his arms. She stroked his arm and wondered why her mother's description of the rapture of making love had escaped her. Maybe like love itself, the joy of being with her husband would come in time. For tonight, she felt safe in the warmth of his embrace, and it was enough.

PART II

PART II

CHAPTER 12

Troy
The Palace of King Priam

Cassandra huddled in the corner of the bedchamber and covered her ears to muffle her mother's agonized cries. Her own terror had increased with the growing size of her mother's belly, and now that she had gone into labor, Cassandra fought a near suffocating dread. Her gift of prophecy from Apollo foretold the worst of fates for the child, and he would decimate not merely their family, but all of Troy. When she at last heard the baby's first feeble cry, she rose on shaky legs and edged toward her mother's bed.

"It's a boy," Hecuba murmured. She kissed the infant's dark wet curls and passed him to a maidservant to wash and clothe. "Your father will be proud to have another son."

"Not this time," Cassandra vowed. "The child's birth is a curse on Troy, and you can't allow him to live. Smother him quickly and tell Father he was stillborn."

Horrified, Hecuba drew herself up in her bed. "How dare you speak of such vile things? He's a fine boy with bright eyes and sturdy limbs. I'll not hear another word spoken against him. Leave me, child."

Cassandra remained by her mother's bed. The three maids who'd attended the birth were staring her way, their expressions twisted with disgust. "Apollo blessed me with the gift of prophecy, and I see the future as you never will. I'll convince Father to put a quick end to the babe. What is one child compared to the fate of our beloved Troy?"

"Leave me!" Hecuba screamed.

Cassandra hurried from her mother's chamber to search for her father, King Priam. In the early afternoon, he often walked in the royal garden, and she rushed to his side. "Father, you know my prophecies ring true, and I'd never lie about a child, but Apollo tells me your newborn son will bring the destruction of Troy. His life must end before he's tasted a drop of his mother's milk."

Priam grabbed his daughter's shoulders to push her away. "Your mother has been safely delivered of a son?"

"Yes, but the god tells me the child will bring only evil down upon us, a disaster, and you must see he doesn't live out the day."

Priam brushed by her. "I must see the child for myself."

Cassandra ran after him. "There's nothing for you to see, Father. He has the innocence of any newborn, but his fate is a dark and dangerous one you mustn't allow to unfold. Troy's preservation is at stake."

Priam brushed her hand off his sleeve. "I'll decide for myself."

Cassandra halted at the bottom of the stairway. "You must trust me. Don't let the child live if you truly love Troy and your people as you swear you do."

Priam hesitated at the doorway of his wife's chamber, Cassandra's ghastly prediction echoing in his ears. Her prophecies had proven true in the past, and her harsh warning left him badly torn, for if he made the wrong choice, Troy could perish. The price would be too terrible to even imagine. He knocked lightly at the partially open door and was invited in.

"I hear we have a son."

Hecuba was more shaken by Cassandra's dire prophecy than by the rigors of childbirth. Sick clear through; she clutched the infant to her breast. "We talked about naming him Alexandros. He's as handsome a babe as Hector was. He favors you."

"Let me hold him." Priam picked up the small bundle and regarded his son with a thoughtful gaze. The little boy yawned widely and peered up at him, his dark eyes lit with curiosity. "He is a fine boy, indeed, but what will he be when he is grown?"

Frightened by his tone, Hecuba reached for the baby, but Priam stepped away. "You mustn't listen to Cassandra," she begged. "She's always harboring doom. Her prophecy is no more tangible than smoke in the wind, and it needn't come to pass."

"I want time to think and will keep the child with me." Priam turned away.

Fearing his decision had already been made, Hecuba sobbed and called after him, but abandoned, she wept alone.

* * *

Priam sent a servant for his son Helenus and carried the baby to the megaron, now empty after the morning's work was done. The fire in the round central hearth lit the colorful frescos of griffins, lions and stags arrayed upon the walls. Bold geometric patterns and medallions painted in bright reds, blues and yellows covered the ceiling. The capitals of the marble columns supporting the rafters held intricate designs wrought in gold. A multitude of swirling patterns had been lightly incised into the stone floor. Not a single space in the expansive room had been left unadorned.

The scalloped edge of the high-backed ivory throne was decorated with strips of gold, but unbearably uncomfortable for King Priam now. He held the baby on his lap, but no joy filled his heart at the birth. Apollo had given Casandra and her brother the gift of prophecy for a reason, but today he was loath to believe in it.

Helenus halted at the doorway. "You sent for me, Father?" he asked.

"Yes, come close and touch your new brother. I need to hear your prophecy."

The young man came to his father's side, but was reluctant to touch the infant. "Casandra has the stronger gift."

"This is no contest. Touch him and speak."

Helenus laid his fingers on the babe and quickly jumped back. "I see fire and blood, terror for us all. How can this be?"

Priam sighed deeply. "Cassandra foretold the same. The gods have sent a clear warning the child's future portends disaster, and I must not ignore it. I cannot bear to sacrifice him myself. Find someone who will take him away and see to it."

Helenus thought a long moment. "Agelaus brought cattle to the city and is still nearby. He's always eager to do your bidding. Shall I summon him?"

"Run." The babe had fallen asleep, and Priam folded the blanket up close to hide his face. Filled with a nearly unbearable sorrow, he thought of his beloved queen. Hecuba might never forgive him for what he was about to do, but he could not choose an infant over the fate of Troy. He had no choice, none at all.

As he followed Helenus, Agelaus looked around him mouth agape, obviously stunned by the magnificence of the megaron. He bowed deeply. "What is it you need of me, my lord?"

Priam remembered the man and nodded. "I have a task for you. My newborn son carries a curse that will doom Troy. You must take him to Mount Ida and sacrifice him to the gods. Go now, before anyone else learns of his birth. I beg you not to allow him to suffer. Kill him with a single swift stroke. Do you understand what must be done?"

Agelaus swallowed hard and reached for the child with shaking hands. "I have always been your faithful servant, my king." He took the child and placed him in the cloth bag hanging from his shoulder by a strap.

Priam stood, the weight of his horrid request plain in his slumped shoulders. "We will never speak of this again."

The herdsman bowed and passed by the stern-faced royal guards.

Helenus waited by his father's side. "Does mother know?"

"Yes, but a mother's heart is always open to her

babe, regardless of his fate. Do not mention the child to her. Let her rest undisturbed."

"As you wish." He raised his fist to his forehead in the royal salute and walked away through the megaron's wide double doors, his head bowed.

Grieved by the baby's tragic fate, Priam sat slumped upon his throne, warmed by the glowing central hearth, but forlorn clear to his bones. He lifted his gaze to the horses' heads carved above the wide doorway. How he missed the days when he could ride without worry toward the sun. Now the fate of Troy rested as a crushing weight on his shoulders, and he rose with no hope tomorrow would be any easier to bear.

Agelaus ran from the palace with the babe bouncing on his side. The infant cried with a soft, pitiful wail, and the sound tore the herder's heart in two. He and his wife loved children, and while he had promised King Priam to do what should be done, the longer he ran, the more awful the deed became. He raised the squirming bundle to his shoulder to comfort the tiny lad and ran on toward Mount Ida.

His legs soon grew as heavy as lead, and too tired to hasten on, he trudged to his own home. It was a humble cottage built from sun-dried bricks with a thatched roof, far from the palace's citadel, and the tiny infant was too weak to cry by the time he arrived. They lived within sight of Mount Ida, and this was as close as he would come to carrying out the king's dark command.

His wife, Sotiria, stared as Agelaus pulled the baby from his bag. "Where have you found this child? Is his mother not searching for him?"

"No, he is unwanted, and we would make fine parents for him. I want to name him Paris, after the bag in which I carried him."

His wife laughed at the thought, reached for the baby and smoothed his dark curls. "Well, little Paris, you cannot be more than a day or two old. He needs milk."

"We can make a cloth nipple and give him goat's milk."

She didn't know whether to laugh or weep. She watched the babe's face pucker up for a faint cry and nodded toward the door. "See to it now. I'll not have this fine babe starve to death in my arms."

Agelaus paused only long enough to give her a fleeting kiss and hurried outside. King Priam never traveled near his small home, and he had been forbidden to ever speak of the doomed child. If they never spoke of the babe, he would never have to admit that he could not bear to carry him to his death. A herder's son would never attract a king's notice, and the secret of Paris's birth would never have to be revealed. Comforted by the thought, he grew even more assured he had made the right decision.

Apollo, Deity of Light, Music and Prophecy, found mortals endlessly amusing. The depth of Cassandra's sorrow touched him, however, and when she came alone to weep at his temple in Troy's citadel, he appeared in a radiant shimmer. "You needn't pray before my shrine when I'm here close enough to touch."

Casandra drew away from the blinding light. "Have you heard my prayers? I've given no prophecies since the one condemning my infant brother, but my whole world has come to ruin because of it."

He reached out to touch the braid coiled in her tousled hair. His voice was low and tender, "How so, my pretty one?"

"My mother cannot bear to look at me. My father winces each time he does, and my poor brother Helenus, is treated no better. My family wants only good prophecies that foretell Troy's victories in battle or its enrichment with great wealth. They shun me because of my dire warning about my tiny brother, and yet how could I have kept quiet when so much could have been lost? You've given me a means to protect Troy, and I could not have remained silent, could I?"

"Of course, not." He lifted her from her knees and embraced her. "They should know not all prophecies could possibly be good."

"They may know it, but they still blame me. No, they hate me for revealing what I saw." Her eyes glistened with tears.

He lifted her chin with a fingertip. "What do you see now?"

The light around him had dimmed so she could appreciate him in all his beauty. He was taller than mortal men, with shinny curls and dark eyes alit with mischief. He had wrapped her in his strength, and she relaxed against him. "You are too handsome to describe."

"Thank you. I find you lovely as well." He bent his head to kiss her, lightly at first, and then with a lustful vigor.

She pounded her fists on his bare chest and struggled to break free. "No, you must not. I'm meant to be a mortal's bride."

He laughed and the sound echoed in the hollow temple. "In time. First let me show you what passion is meant to be."

The scent of frankincense floated on the air, the dark heady fragrance had seemed reverent until now. She had come seeking solace, not an ardent lover, and Apollo's power terrified her. "It's not passion I need," she begged.

He played kisses along the smooth swell of her breasts. "You came seeking me because I am precisely what you need."

She shook her head. "No. My life is in tatters because of a single dire prophecy. I have no wish to make everything worse."

He tightened his embrace. "You've no desire to lie with me?"

Huge tears rolled down her cheeks. "No, but I cannot compare to a goddess."

"Perfection becomes tiring," he assured her. He cupped her breast and ran his thumb over the crest. "You are a delightful creature, Cassandra. Bend to me."

Terrified she would be consumed by his heat, she shut her eyes tight and fought to make him understand. "I sought only a moment of peace."

Greatly annoyed, he released her with a quick shove. "You pray to me, but refuse to feel me deep inside you?"

Shocked by the bluntness of his question, she shook her head, and her curls flew in a dance of terror. Her voice caught in her throat, "I want only your comfort."

"Yet you've refused the way I generously wish to give it," he scoffed. "Gifts given can be taken back, and from this day forward, you'll escape all blame, for people will no longer believe in your prophecies. Your voice will become as a rattling wind."

He vanished in a soaring spray of light leaving her dizzy and sick clear to her soul. What had she done? She hadn't meant to anger her god Apollo so badly he would curse her, and she sank to the cold flagstone floor and wept until she had no more tears.

Aphrodite, goddess of Love, laughed at Apollo's downcast expression. "Whatever could be wrong? Have you finally found a woman who refused to melt beneath your magnificence and heated ardor?"

He snarled at her, "Be careful what you say."

"Or what?" She circled him slowly. "I don't see a mark on you, so you cannot have lost a battle and come home to mend. Is your poor heart broken? Who would reject the most handsome of the glorious gods?"

He drew back his arm, but she easily eluded him and sprinted away. Her insulting laughter rang in his ears, and he would have cursed her too had he been able. A hideous cackle drew his gaze upward to Eris, the goddess of Discord, who hovered in the rafters, her black wings fluttering. "You dare laugh at me?"

She angled her wings and flitted to the ground. "A mere chuckle of appreciation, dear Apollo, for there has been little to amuse me today."

He strode off rather than fight her fury. Eris loved nothing better than an argument and if given the chance, could hurl insults for all of eternity, but he had had his fill of contentious women for the day. He headed for Dionysos' palace to drink with the god of Wine until no insult mattered.

CHAPTER 13

Troy
The home of Agelaus, the herdsman
Ten years later

Paris sat on a stone outcrop playing a panpipe to serenade the cattle. His tunes were sweet, but the placid creatures continued to chew the grass without any show of appreciation. Prompted to give up the effort to entertain them, he gazed toward Mount Ida and wished for a human friend. His father was proud of him, and his mother so loving he dared not complain, but the days alone in the meadow were often far too long. Their brown and white spotted hound lay stretched out by his side.

Moved by boredom, he got to his feet and stretched his arms above his head. "Let's run!" He took off down the hillside facing away from his herd, and the dog eagerly raced beside him. They made a slow circle and returned to the hill to find the cattle unaware of their absence. He caught his breath, and continued to run in a loop until he was so tired he was grateful to sit and rest.

He scratched the hound's ears and hugged him. "Tomorrow, we'll run faster and farther, you'll see. The next time there are races in the village, I'll win." He propped his arms on his bent knees and hoped the fair weather would last.

Market day in the village brought farmers, herdsmen and artisans to trade produce, livestock and handmade wares. There was no celebration with races that day, but Paris still loved being in the village where cattle were not the only thing in view. When he saw a pretty little girl with thick, curly black hair, he tried not to stare, but she turned and caught him. A bright flush flooded his cheeks, and badly embarrassed, he dipped his head to hide it. When he looked up, she was standing close enough to touch.

"Who are you?" she asked. Her brown eyes held a hint of gold and shone brightly with curiosity.

"I'm Paris," he responded. "Why do you need to know?"

She clasped her hands and twisted herself this way and that. "I want to know everyone. Aren't you going to ask my name?"

She looked a couple years younger than him, but some girls were small, and it was difficult to accurately judge her age. "Go ahead and tell me."

"I'm Oenone, and I herd my father's sheep. We sell the finest wool in the valley."

He glanced behind her. "Where are these fine sheep?"

She silenced her giggles with both hands. "They don't come to market."

"So you expect me to believe these superior wool-producing sheep exist without seeing them?"

"Yes!" she exclaimed, and walked away with an arm-slinging strut.

Agelaus approached with a bag of flour, and Paris reached out to help him carry it. He turned to follow the little girl's path through the village, but soon lost her in the crowd.

"I've not seen you smile so wide. What do you find so amusing?" his father asked.

Paris shrugged. "Nothing. I just like coming to the village."

"Good, when you're old enough, I'll send you to get what we need, and I'll stay home."

Paris looked forward to that day, but it was Oenone who lingered in his mind rather than some far distant future.

Several days later, Oenone came riding up the hill on a shaggy brown pony with twigs and leaves tied into his mane. Paris leaped to his feet and surveyed his herd with an anxious glance. "Are you hoping to startle my cattle?"

"No, I meant only to startle you." She slid off her pony, sat down in the tall grass and leaned back on her elbows. "Did you know we lived so close to each other?"

He had not dared ask his father about her and risk being teased, or more likely, scolded for thinking of girls at his age. "No, but I'd not have gone to visit you even if I had."

She twisted a handful of her dark curls as she spoke. "Why not? Do you spend all of your days talking to cows that don't answer?"

"No, I play my panpipe rather than talk."

"My pony loves the panpipe. Please play something for him."

The instrument lay by his foot, and he bent down to scoop it up. "I don't feel like playing now."

"You'll play a tune for your herd, but not for my beautiful pony?"

He studied the pony with a thoughtful glance. It looked very old and tired rather than beautiful to him. The plants threaded into his mane made him look as though he'd traveled through the wilds alone, but he did not want to hurt her feelings by saying so. "How can you tell?"

"He pricks his ears forward to better hear a tune. Don't you know anything about horses?"

"We own a few to ride when tending cattle."

"I don't see any horses." She stood and brushed off the back of her baggy clothes.

"They are with the larger herd grazing on land on the opposite side of our cottage."

She took the reins and swung herself up on her pony's back. "I'm gathering herbs for my aunt Chrisoula. She's teaching me to use them to make cures for all manner of troubling illnesses."

"But it's the gods who send sickness. That's why we make sacrifices to keep them content."

She regarded him with a condescending stare. "There are people who fall ill who couldn't possibly have offended the gods. Some suffer accidents or are wounded in mishaps, and my aunt tends them. Now I must be on my way, and it's your turn to come and visit me."

He watched her go, and noted the direction, but uttered no promise of any kind. His job was to watch this herd, not run about the valley with little girls. He had wished for a friend, but Oenone wasn't what he'd imagined at all. He'd learned the patience to watch his family's stock, and she jumped around like a frightened hare. If her people really did own sheep, he doubted they would allow her tend them.

Agelaus heard the sound of a panpipe as he came to the meadow in the late afternoon. He also played, but he had never learned more than the songs his father had taught him. Paris had far more talent and made up his own tunes. His mother loved to hear him play, but this music was slow and melancholy, and Agelaus didn't want her to hear such sad music.

"Has it not been a good day?" he asked as he approached the son he loved so dearly. "The cattle look content."

"Everyday is the same," Paris replied, "which is good for the herd." Oenone's visit had made the day unlike any other, but more perplexed than happy, he wouldn't smile and give his father cause to wonder why.

"Perhaps it's time for you to tend the larger herd. I'll find a pony for you, and you can come with me. Cattle can run as fast as a horse when frightened. A herdsman must also protect them from predators and poachers, but you've had no such threats here."

Paris's eyes lit with joy. "May I go with you when you lead cattle to the citadel? I want to see the king."

Agelaus laughed, but he would never allow such a trip. "You are much too young, but King Priam doesn't concern himself with cattle, so you'll miss nothing by staying at home."

"But someday I may go?"

"We'll have to wait and see." He had moved his family closer to Mt. Ida where the pastures were rich and thick. Some thought the gods had blessed the land, especially the highest peak now crowned with a glowing golden cloud, but Agelaus didn't dwell upon them. Instead, he thanked only himself for having the courage to keep Paris alive. He believed no evil would come from having saved the life of such a handsome boy.

Paris fought to hide his disappointment when Agelaus returned from the village with a gray pony that had seen far too many winters to make him proud, but he knew his father could not afford a finer mount. He loved his parents too dearly to reveal his desire for more than they could give, which added a deep layer of guilt to his sorrow.

"You must learn to ride him before you attempt to herd more cattle," his father announced. "Today, ride around the meadow, and take great care not to frighten our stock. When you're comfortable on your horse's back, I'll give you a chance with the larger herd."

"Yes, Father. I'll do a good job." He'd been shown how to use the reins to turn the pony and how to stop him with a gentle tug. Thinking he knew all there was to know, he rode out to the meadow and circled the herd he thought of as his own in ever widening rings. His hound trotted along beside him, wagging his tail, perhaps equally glad to do something new. The day was warm, and stifling a yawn, Paris imagined himself to be a powerful king marshalling his armor-clad warriors for battle. With such placid charges, he could lose himself in dreams of heroic adventure without any fear there would be something he'd miss.

He patted his pony's neck and nudged him on each time he stopped to graze. He hoped keeping a careful watch on their herd might be far more exciting, but he really looked forward to the day they'd drive their cattle to Troy. He couldn't wait to see King Priam's palace even if he would never be invited inside the royal precinct. Knowing somewhere splendor existed, beautiful women and coffers of jewels and gold, filled his imagination to overflowing. He thought people everywhere must know of the great beauty and wealth of legendary Troy.

Ready to give the sturdy pony a rest, he dismounted to allow the docile animal to graze. He played his favorite melody on his panpipe to serenade the herd as though they deserved his abiding love, and let his imagination soar free. His hound looked up at him and wagged his tail, waiting for the next command.

That evening, Paris wiped his last bite of bread over his plate to savor the flavorful drippings. "How old must I be to become one of King Priam's warriors?" he asked nonchalantly, as though the question had not I burned his mouth all day.

Agelaus choked, and recovered after a deep cough. "You are a boy barely old enough to ride a pony. Warriors are full-grown men. They have mastered fighting with a sword, a lance and bow and arrows. They know how to protect themselves with a great-sized shield. You could not even lift one."

Not discouraged, Paris pressed on. "Must I wait until I am grown to train?"

His mother shook her head. "We are herdsmen not warriors. Troy is powerful and has been at peace for many years. Who would dare to assail us? You're not needed. Be grateful you have a home and animals to tend."

"I am grateful," he insisted. "I truly am, but I could be a warrior for a while and seek some glory then return home to raise cattle. Couldn't I?"

Agelaus rose from the table. "You'll not speak of becoming a warrior until I say you may. Is that clear? Do not upset your mother with thoughts of blood and death. Instead, thank the gods our enemies fear the power of Troy. That's why we live on this beautiful holy mountain in peace."

Paris searched their faces for even a faint sparkle of hope. "I don't plan to die."

His mother laughed. "No warrior does, but it doesn't protect him in the throes of battle. You should want a long and happy life, and you must stay here with us."

Paris went outside to gaze at the stars and wished his family knew a warrior he could ask, but none lived in their village. He brightened at the thought he might meet one when they drove their cattle to the city. He would pretend he had forgotten all about them until then, but he could hardly wait. A shooting star flashed above him, and he took it as a good omen for his hopes.

Oenone rode into the meadow, her pony's mane festooned with dangling bunches of sweet-scented rosemary. She called to him, "If you're now riding a horse, why haven't you come to see me?"

Paris's mind had wandered in many directions, but not in hers. "I'm too busy watching our herd to travel through the countryside searching for you."

"Then it's a good thing I've come to see you." She slid from her pony's back and sat upon a rocky outcropping. "I name all of our sheep. What do you call your cattle?"

"Name the cattle?" He laughed and shook his head. "I think of them only as a herd. I know which ones wander if not closely watched. That's enough for me."

"You spend your days here in the meadow, with only cattle for company, and you don't give them names?"

"My hound is company enough, and the pony fills the days too."

She regarded him with a sidelong glance. "What are their names?"

The hound looked up at him, as if waiting to hear. Paris had raised him from a pup, but no one had ever told him to give him a name. "He comes when I whistle, so he doesn't need a name, and if the pony came with one, I haven't heard it." He bent down on one knee to hug the dog and looked up at her.

"Do you remember my name?" she asked.

"Oenone. I have a fine memory and remember everything I must."

"Good. Now I've herbs to gather and must be on my way." She bent down to kiss his cheek, hopped upon her pony's back and rode away at a bouncing trot.

He'd never been kissed by a girl, even a little one like Oenone, and felt only embarrassed rather than pleased. What a peculiar child she was. He wondered who watched her sheep when she rode around the meadows shadowed by Mount Ida. Maybe she had a brother or two and they took turns. He really didn't care, and wouldn't waste another thought on her. He rubbed his cheek as though he could remove the light touch of her lips, but the tingling sensation remained, and it wasn't at all unpleasant.

* * *

Oenone would visit Paris every few days, and then not return until the next full moon. She liked to ask questions to which he had no answers and for a long while he regarded her as a nuisance. When he'd begun watching the large herd, he'd been afraid his father would discover them talking together and send her away. He had grown used to her, he supposed, but he didn't really like her all that well. But when he didn't see her, he missed her, and that confused him.

"Let's go hunting," she greeted him one day. She carried a small bow and arrows and looked out over the meadow. "We might find birds that would be delicious to eat."

"Does your father send you out to hunt for food?" Paris asked.

She slid off her pony and kept a firm hold on his reins. "No, but he wouldn't refuse a plump partridge if I brought one home."

"We might be able to trap a rabbit with a snare," he proposed instead.

She shuddered and crunched up her eyes. "Then we'd have to kill it and skin it."

"Well, you'd have to pluck the feathers from a bird."

"I know how to do it, do you?"

He'd seen his mother wring a chicken's neck and shove it into boiling water to loosen the feathers to ease in the plucking. "Yes, I do, but my job is to tend the cattle, not pluck chickens all day."

"Do you even know how to shoot arrows with a bow?"

"I could do it," he claimed without ever having held a bow.

"Get a bow and practice so the next time I come to see you, we can hunt."

She rode away before he could argue, but she always made him feel as though he ought to know something he didn't. That night, he asked his father about making a bow and arrows.

Agelaus gave his back a weary stretch. "I told you not to mention becoming a warrior until I said I was ready to listen."

"I'm thinking only of going hunting. I've seen partridges fly over the meadow and they're good to eat, aren't they?"

"They're delicious, but fly faster and higher than you could shoot an arrow."

"Then I should trap them with snares before they leave their nests. I could go out at first light and hunt before the cattle need to be watched."

"I suppose you could try. I know a bowyer who makes fine bows of yew wood and sharp arrows too. I'll find a way to trade him for them."

Everyone in the village bartered for goods, but his father was especially adept at making fine trades. "Maybe I could go with you and see how they're made," he asked.

"I need you here, Son, you won't be an apprentice for another man."

Paris nodded and went into the house for supper. At least his father hadn't refused to allow him to hunt, but otherwise, he felt trapped on their land despite how often his mother told him to be grateful they owned cattle. His grandfather had been a herdsman, and his father before him. Herding should be in his blood, but he knew deep down inside he was meant to live a far more exciting life than the one into which he'd been born.

He longed to know what lay beyond Mt. Ida and the village he knew so well. He took care at mealtimes not to eat more than was his share, but his dreams could be as grand as he dared imagine them.

CHAPTER 14

Troy
Home of Agelaus
Seven years later

Paris became so adept at hunting, his arrows hit their mark more often than not. He'd won challenges in town on market day, and while he never uttered the word warrior, he believed he was well on his way to becoming one of King Priam's best men. Oenone had hunted with him as they grew older, but over the years her interest in the sport had waned, while he'd become ever more enthusiastic. Her visits had dwindled to a very few, and he'd never admit how often he searched the horizon for a sight of her.

She'd been a pretty child, but now old enough to wed, she was a dark-eyed beauty with a lush figure that drew every man's eye on market day. She preferred mixing potions with her aunt to flirting with suitors, but she wasn't unaware of the admiring glances sent her way.

* * *

Paris left the cottage early one morning to hunt and caught sight of three men on horseback separating a dozen cattle from their herd. They were so pleased with themselves they failed to glance over their shoulders until an arrow pierced the trailing man's upper arm. The wounded thief screamed and clung to his horse's back to dodge Paris's fury of arrows. Terrified for their lives, the thieves abandoned the cattle they'd stolen and galloped away.

Paris rode after them until they parted into three separate directions at the border of his father's land. Positive they'd not return, he let them go rather than chase down one. He gathered the straying cattle, herded them home and picked up the arrows lying in the grass.

Agelaus met him seated upon his own mount. "I heard a scream. If there were cattle thieves out, you should have come for me."

"There was no time to summon you, and I managed on my own."

"With the bow in your hand?" he scoffed. "Did you wound them all?"

Paris swung down off his horse and stepped on the end of his bow to bend and unstring it. "Only one, but it was enough to send them fleeing, and they won't come back."

"Because they'll be afraid of you?"

"Yes, and they'll remain afraid. I've no time left to hunt. Is breakfast ready?"

"So you've chased away cattle-thieves and now you're hungry?"

Paris watched his father's grin widen. "If I'd eaten breakfast first, we'd have lost a dozen of our best cattle." He went on inside and entertained his mother with a colorful account of his adventure. His father told anyone who would listen about his brave and clever son.

Oenone greeted Paris as soon as she came close enough to be heard. Nowadays, she rode a black mare, a far finer horse than her first pony. She hadn't come to race, however, and held out a broken arrow and the loose bronze tip. "I believe these are yours."

Their cattle were grazing quietly, and he could afford a few moments of inattention. He slid from his horse's back and reached for the arrow. The bronze point could have been anyone's, but he recognized the fletching on the shaft as his own. "Where did you find these?"

"My aunt broke the arrow before pulling it from a man's arm. He claimed he and a friend had been hunting when the mishap occurred. She knew he was lying, but wrapped his arm in healing herbs and sent him on his way."

Paris made no effort to hide his disgust. "He's a thief who tried to steal our cattle and didn't deserve such tender sympathy."

"Perhaps not, but Chrisoula never asks if a person is good or bad when they come to her. She sees only their illness or wound." She dismounted and dropped the reins to allow her mare to graze.

"Do you intend to do the same?" he asked.

"No one comes to me as yet, but someday they will, and I'll decide then." He'd grown so tall she had to look up at him.

He turned the broken arrow in his hands. Blood had left a deep red stain. "Did your aunt know the man?"

"She described him as a foul-smelling stranger, and he must have ridden a long way from here by now."

"I hope so. I aimed for his back, but a man on horseback is as difficult to strike as a running deer."

She turned and brushed her curls from her eyes. "Did you intend to kill him?"

"I meant only to keep him from stealing our cattle. If he'd died, he would have deserved it."

Her brows dipped in a puzzled frown. "There was a time when you weren't so fierce."

He laughed as though it were a compliment. "You didn't use to be so pretty. Does your father know where you are?"

"He concerns himself with our sheep," she responded with a slow smile. "This morning, I'm gathering herbs as I often do, but I'm expected home soon."

The grazing herd shifted with lazy steps. "I wish I had some entertainment to offer. Some men in the village like to fight bulls. We keep ours separate, or they'd fight on their own. The next time you come, I'll set them on each other to amuse you."

She shook her head sadly. "You've never come to visit me with flowers, poetry, or songs. A fight between bulls isn't a proper way to impress me."

Bewildered, he watched her mount her horse and stepped forward to catch her mare's reins. "I'm seventeen and not ready for courting."

Her dark curls tumbled around her shoulders as she looked down on him, and her voice was soft and sweet, "And if I wait for you to grow older, I'll be too old to wed. Good day."

Until that moment, Paris had not thought of taking a wife. He intended to be a warrior, and they didn't wed until after they'd left the king's service. Oenone would be a grandmother by then. He thought of the men who came to market day. The ones who were of an age to marry had very little to recommend them. He'd never thought of Oenone as having a husband, but the prospect of her marrying one of those fools proved surprisingly painful.

Oenone's aunt Chrisoula, was a tall, slender, flame-haired woman who possessed a magical touch. She could simply wave a healing herb above an ailing friend and cure her. She listened closely to her niece's comments on Paris and responded with the wisest advice possible. "You must make the man come to you."

"And if he shows a maddening disinterest?"

"Ignore him and flirt with a man who'll adore you."

Oenone tied red ribbons around the rosemary sprigs, stepped upon a stool and reached up to hang them from the rafters to dry. "You've taught me to see too much."

"Impossible."

"No, I see what a young man will become, and how a thick middle will one day be a huge belly that will surely crush his wife beneath him."

"Truly a man to avoid," Chrisoula agreed. "But a thin man can fall ill and die too soon and leave you with children to raise alone."

"Any man could die, but some are too short and have such large feet I can't help but laugh when I see them waddling my way."

"Be kind," Chrisoula chided. She pulled the string tight on a bag of juniper berries and added it to the herbs hanging overhead. "Look for a man who makes you laugh."

"I enjoy laughing as much as any girl, but I'll never be drawn to an amusing ugly man."

"I've seen such men with beautiful wives, so not every girl shares your opinion."

Oenone sat down on the stool and brushed off her hands. "I'm sorry I never knew my uncle. You must have loved him dearly."

Chrisoula drew in a deep breath and sighed softly. "He was as handsome as a god and always thoughtful and kind. He had the most beautiful voice and could make everyone cry with a sad song or laugh with a happy tune. I will miss him until the day I die."

"You could not save him?"

"He was thrown from his horse and dead when I found him. I held him all night and kissed him good-bye in the morning. Another has never touched my heart, but you are of an age to have a husband, and we must widen our search to find you a good man."

Oenone loved the scent of rosemary and held a branch close to her cheek. "Now we are where we began. I want Paris, but he will take too many years to be grown."

"A cruel trick of fate. Perhaps he'll surprise you."

Oenone was far too practical a girl to cling to such an unlikely hope.

"When should a man begin building his house?" Paris asked his father. "If he waits until he finds a girl to wed, he'll have nothing to show her, but if he begins building early, he'll have no time for courting."

Agelaus nodded thoughtfully. "A perplexing

problem indeed. I've always hoped you'd build your house close to ours. Let's look at the land and decide where a good place would be."

Paris took a backwards step. "I didn't say I was ready to begin."

"You needn't start building today, Son, let's just look for an appealing site. You don't want to be too close, but you shouldn't be too far away either."

They walked over land they had traversed for years, this time with new eyes. "This rise provides a pleasant view of the valley," Paris offered.

"True, and wood you'll need for doors, windows and to frame the roof won't be too difficult to haul from the pine forest."

"Gathering rocks for the foundation will be a chore," Paris complained, "and it might take a year to make enough mud brick for the walls."

"You'll need thatch for the roof," his father added. "We'll trade for whatever you need."

Paris pulled in a deep breath. "Did you build our house?"

Agelaus chuckled at the memory. "You were too small to remember, but I did, with a great deal of help from men in the village. They'll help again for beef."

"I own no cattle," Paris reminded him.

"Our herd will all be yours when I'm gone," Agelaus offered. "You're welcome to all you'll need now."

"Thank you." Paris studied the land and wondered how one went about planning a home so nothing was forgotten. "I could learn to build furniture," he murmured.

Agelaus slapped him on the back. "You're very bright and can do whatever you set your mind to."

Paris bent down to pick up a stick and drew a rectangle in the dirt. "The front should face Mount Ida, so I'd have a view of the sunset, or would it be better to face the rising sun instead?"

"The rising sun," his father said. "It's a good way to greet the day."

Paris felt as though he had greeted too much that day. He rose and tossed the stick aside. "I need to think of everything first."

"It's always wise to have a plan," Agelaus agreed.

As they started for home, Paris turned to walk backwards and faced his father as he spoke. "What do you think of having our bulls fight? The bulls would do all the work, and I could gather all I'd need from the men's wagers."

"Ah, now there's an idea." Agelaus had a good laugh over it, and then grew serious. "Our red bull has never been the friendly sort. The black is too tame to do more than turn and run. We'll need to find a man with a bull he thinks can beat ours. I won't wager our bull though. A cow perhaps, but we won't bet the bull himself. If I brag a bit, there will be someone who believes his bull is stronger. Give me a chance to inspire some interest, and we'll see what happens."

Paris broke into a wide grin. "We could use the ring for animals in town. From what I've seen, bulls don't need a great deal of room."

"No, they like to butt heads and paw the ground, but they don't race around each other. Let's not tell your mother about this yet. She'll think us daft for sure."

"A secret it is," Paris agreed and went off whistling.

***

Unfailing good humor made Agelaus popular in the village. When he mentioned his family owned a particularly mean-tempered bull, speaking as though he were seeking only a sympathetic ear, two men immediately offered their bulls for a match.

"I don't know," Agelaus mused thoughtfully. "I wouldn't want either of you to lose a bull to injury and blame me."

Edremus was a short, portly man with close-set eyes who loved a bit of sport wherever he could find it. He rubbed his hands with jovial enthusiasm. "I've never seen a bull suffer more than a scratch he'd scarcely feel. Bring your bull to town on the next market day, and I'll bring mine. We'll see which bests the other."

"My bull will fight the winner," Manyon quickly offered.

"We could all use some entertainment," Agelaus admitted. "But there ought to be a prize for the winner. What do you say to three young cows? Will you wager that much?"

"Yes, of course," Edremus agreed. "I'll be happy to bet cattle I'll never lose."

"We'll have to wait and see," Agelaus answered. "I'll have Paris bring the bull to the next market day, but remember that I've warned you both about him."

His friends nodded, chuckling over the certainty of a win.

Paris feared he wouldn't be able to coax the red bull into walking to the village unless the beast grew accustomed to being led by a rope. The bull grew bored with the lessons early each day, but they made slow, steady progress.

"What a fine bull you are!" Paris praised him repeatedly. "Every cow will be in love with you." The red bull snorted and regarded him with a fierce black-eyed gaze, but undaunted, Paris persevered. On the day agreed upon, the red bull came willingly, as though he's learned several fine cows were to be his reward.

Agelaus whispered, "We're reluctant to do this, remember."

"Of course," Paris responded. "Red should be the first bull to enter the ring so he'll have a chance to grow used to it."

They arrived early and released Red into the ring. The wood-fenced enclosure was more often used for sheep than cattle, but it was large enough for the bull to circle at an easy lope. When Edremus led a brown and white spotted bull into the ring, Agelaus warned him again of how foolhardy this challenge might be.

"Talk to me after the bulls become acquainted," Edremus replied. He jostled another man aside for a better place to stand outside the ring and watch.

Paris had great confidence in Red, but the brown and white bull was of an immense size, and he feared the match might be closer than they'd anticipated. "Are we the ones being foolish here?" he whispered to his father.

Agelaus dipped his head. "Just watch."

Red turned when the brown and white bull was led into the ring. He lowered his head and snorted what had to be an insulting bovine taunt. The brown and white bull stood still with no more than a swish of his tail. Red pawed the earth scattering clods of dirt. When the spotted bull made no move to respond, Red charged and the beasts butted heads with a loud thump. Red was a powerful bull with shoulders thick with muscle. He kept his head down and shoved the brown and white bull back with a force that made the crowd cheer.

Paris had thought Red would know how to fight well, and yelled encouragement. His bull pawed the ground and forced his opponent into a slip-sliding retreat. The brown and white bull made a brief attempt to lunge back, but Red planted his hooves in the dirt, snorted and refused to move. Paris held his breath, hoping the fight would soon be over, and fearing something terrible might occur. When Oenone slipped through the crowd to reach his side, he whispered, "Do you ever use your herb cures on bulls?"

"What an interesting thought, but your bull is unlikely to need them."

Paris studied the length of her thick, dark eyelashes, and she caught him. "Why are you staring at me rather than the astonishing spectacle you've staged with your bull?"

He laughed and shook his head. "I see you so seldom, that's why."

"Whose fault is that?" she asked.

Before Paris could think of a coherent reply, the brown and white bull broke away and trotted to the far side of the ring, clearly surrendering the fight. The men surrounding the ring shouted and cheered, and those close enough slapped Agelaus on the back.

Agelaus raised his hands. "The bull belongs to Paris now. Congratulate him." He caught Edremus's eye and waved. "Bring the three cows to us tomorrow."

Several men eagerly offered a bull to fight, but Paris raised a hand to stop them. "Manyon has been promised the next challenge," he told them. "While we'll win again, I won't promise matches beyond that one."

Oenone handed him a wreath of wildflowers. "The winner deserves a crown."

"Thank you." Paris took it, letting his hand brush her palm. "I'll wait until Red's temper cools before I hang it from his horns and lead him home."

She nodded. "Undoubtedly a wise decision."

When she turned away, he reached for her arm. "I'm doing this for you."

"Why? Infuriated bulls don't impress me."

He leaned down to whisper, "Would a fine house and my own herd impress you?" he asked.

She responded with a slow smile and touched his cheek. "I'll wait until I see them."

He couldn't promise she wouldn't have a long wait, but the sweetness of her expression gave him hope it wouldn't matter.

Manyon's bull was as black as a moonless night and had an evil glint in his eye. "I don't like the look of him," Agelaus whispered.

"He may be all looks," Paris answered. They'd again arrived early so Red could enter the ring first and mark it as his territory. The black bull trotted right up to him, head lowered, and pawed the dirt.

Red dipped his head, butted the black bull with a powerful lunge and shoved so hard the black bull stumbled and went down on one knee. The men in the crowd gasped, but the dark bull quickly recovered to give a hearty push back of his own. Red snorted, pawed the ground, and hit the black bull again. They stomped, twisted their heads against each other and shoved with all their strength but neither bull gained any ground.

"We've a real fight this time," Manyon shouted.

Paris nodded, but he had every confidence Red would win. He imagined bulls viewed time differently, and could butt heads for days, but a short while later, the black bull turned away and trotted to the opposite side of the ring. The crowd stood silent for a moment, then those who'd backed Red began to laugh and shout. Paris hadn't seen Oenone that morning, and a little girl in her father's arms handed him a carefully woven flower crown. He thanked her, but again took the precaution of giving Red time to rest before they made the journey home.

Ares, the god of War, viewed the fight from a gold-lined cloud, highly amused by how easily Paris won with his red bull. Zeus thought the bouts only mildly diverting. "You simply don't find humans as entertaining as I do," Ares remarked, his dark eyes aglow with mischief. "I like the boy, but I wonder how he would react if his bull were to lose a match."

Zeus responded with a sly chuckle. "I'm sure you could arrange it."

"Of course, I could. What sort of a bull should I be? I'm thinking perhaps the shade of thick cream."

"The pale color would fool them into believing you would pose little threat."

"My thoughts exactly. I mustn't be too large, however, or Paris might refuse to allow his bull to battle me."

"Perhaps you should be on the small side."

"Yes! What a splendid idea. If I appear to be a bull of little consequence, my victory will be all the more surprising and sweet."

They spent the afternoon refining Ares's plan and looked forward to playing it out soon. Gods though they were, they had very little in the way of patience when it came to interfering in human affairs.

The red bull won every fight and men were now coming from distant villages to bring a bull for a contest. Paris remained modest as to his bull's prowess, and rather than brag, he issued challenges and welcomed all who responded. On an especially bright morning, the expected man did not appear, but a cream-colored bull stood waiting in the enclosure. Thinking it was the bull the missing herdsman had offered, Paris led Red into the ring.

Now used to the game, Red moved toward his opponent, sniffing the air, and pawing the earth. He lowered his head, but before he could charge, the cream-colored bull rammed him with a head-clash that shook the earth and brought an admiring crescendo of praise from the crowd.

Oenone stood at Paris's elbow. "Who owns the white bull?" she asked.

"I'm not certain, but it looks as though it will be a fierce fight." He leaned over the top railing for a better view. Men near him shouted encouragement to Red as well as the newcomer. Unmindful of the cheers, the bulls locked horns, shoved and shoved back, bellowed deep threats and kept at their battle far longer than the other bouts had lasted.

"There's something wrong here," Oenone cautioned Paris.

Agelaus agreed. "That's no bull I've ever seen, and I fear we'll lose today."

Paris wouldn't admit to being equally worried. Each of the cream-colored bull's head-butts were as damaging as the first, while Red's slowing responses showed he had begun to tire. Paris would have to let the match play out, but when Red finally broke away, he could not blame him.

"That's no ordinary bull," he murmured to his father.

Oenone handed Paris a flower crown. "You must still declare him the winner."

"I will." He waved the crown and let the noise of the onlookers ebb before he called for the owner. When no one stepped forward, he circled the outside of the enclosure to reach the cream-colored bull and dropped the crown over his horns. The crowd cheered and gradually dispersed, but still no one came forward to claim the winning bull.

"We'd not agreed on a bet, so I owe the owner nothing," Paris told his father.

"Take Red home. I expect someone will come for the white bull soon," Agelaus advised.

"Do you want to wait?" Oenone asked.

Paris shook his head. "I've had enough of the village for today." He entered the ring and led Red away on his rope. When he turned back, the cream-colored bull seemed to shimmer in the sunlight, and he rubbed his eyes rather than believe in magic.

Ares spun the flower crown on his finger. "I won as I'd expected, but the boy was very gracious about the loss."

"But he thought it a fair win," Zeus reminded him.

"It was fair," Ares argued. "I was a bull after all."

"An enchanted bull that could not have been beaten by any earthly beast."

"A minor complaint," Ares insisted. "I took care not to break the red bull's spirit and leave him too frightened to fight another day. He'll never face me as an opponent again, and I doubt there's another bull alive that can best him."

Zeus took a long sip of wine. "What's the boy's name?"

"Paris, and I'll remember him."

"We forget nothing and no one, you fool."

"Perhaps not, but Paris may prove useful someday, and I'll recall where to find him."

Zeus covered a wide yawn and left to find Hera for an enjoyable afternoon.

That Red had been beaten inspired several men to argue vehemently for a re-match with their own bull. Paris listened, and certain Red would not be beaten again, he agreed. No one had seen who'd come for the pale bull, but Paris wanted him quickly forgotten. The first re-match was with a brindle bull with a twisted horn. He was a sturdy beast, but slow and Red challenged him repeatedly with swift head-butts and deep bellows.

Oenone came close enough to rub against Paris's side. "Red looks very strong today."

Paris didn't take his eyes off the bulls. "He does."

She held a flower wreath she'd woven from the wildflowers she'd gathered along the way into the village. She scolded herself for approaching Paris when he preferred looking at bulls to her and draped the floral crown on a nearby post. She took a step away and then several more, but when Paris failed to notice, she followed her aunt Chrisoula's advice, made her way to her mare and rode away.

CHAPTER 15

Mount Olympus
Home of the gods

Wedding plans were underway for a water nymph, a dear favorite of Zeus. He wanted the day to be perfect and confided his fears in his lovely wife as she trimmed his hair. "Eris thrives as the goddess of Discord and will make a horrid mess of things. You know she will."

Hera brushed a shorn curl from his shoulder. "Let's not invite her, beloved. Then the wedding and feast will be over before she even hears of it."

"I doubt it will be so easy. We're only delaying the inevitable, and we'll surely choke on the foul stench of her blazing anger later."

"She'll have to pretend she doesn't care about the wedding, or she'll look pathetic. She's too proud to abide that shame," Hera posed.

He turned to look up at her. "Fine, we'll not invite Eris, and she'll not be missed. Weddings are yours

to perform. Will your peacocks be ready to pull
your chariot?"

She bent down to kiss his ear. "They're happy to
prance and fly across the sky whenever there's an
opportunity. It's endearing that they're so vain."

"Is vanity a fault in those of us who are perfect in
every way?" he asked.

The haircut complete, she came around him to sit
upon his lap. "We're gods, my darling, and radiate
perfection. We may have a few minor faults, but the
peacocks are merely birds, pretty though they may
be. They love to strut and show off their
magnificent feathers and bob their feather crowns
to gather praise. I love them, but even without their
proud strut, no one could possibly fail to see them."

"All I see is you," Zeus responded, and Hera
smothered her laughter against his newly shorn
hair.

Despite Zeus's plan, Eris learned of the nymph's
upcoming wedding and fumed at being overlooked
just as he'd feared she would. She cursed and
stomped until she grew hoarse and exhausted, but
by then, a delicious idea had occurred to her. She
needn't foment discord with shrieking fits when it
could be so easily aroused with trickery. She had a
golden apple made and inscribed, *To the Fairest*. It
was a gorgeous prize for the winning goddess, but
she laughed gleefully at how difficult it would be
for Zeus to choose the winner. No matter whom he
chose, the goddesses he passed over would scheme
to pay him back for the insult, and he'd never know
any peace.

At the wedding, she stood quietly on the edge of
the circled guests and waited for Hera to proclaim

the nymph and her mate wed. Once the celebration had begun, and nectar flowed into golden goblets, she tossed the beautiful apple into the guests' midst, and hid behind a column to observe unseen.

Hermes flew and caught the apple sailing through the air and read the inscription. "*To the Fairest*. For whom is this treasure meant?"

"Give it to me," Hera responded. "I'm the queen of the gods and rightfully deserve it."

"No!" Athena argued. "I'm the goddess of Wisdom, and I know the pretty apple is meant for me."

Aphrodite moved forward with a sultry dancing glide. "I'm the goddess of Love and the fairest among you all. The beautiful apple was intended for me."

Hermes shrugged unhappily and called to Zeus. "It's for you to decide, my lord, as chief among us, it's your right to choose."

Hera pressed close to her husband's side. "I must be your choice."

Aphrodite turned in a seductive swirl and reached out to caress Zeus's powerfully muscled arm. "You can easily see I'm the fairest. Your decision should be easy."

Athena refused to concede. "I'm far fairer than either of you. Your vanity clouds your mirrors as well as your thoughts, and you refuse to see the truth."

Zeus raised his hand rather than allow the goddesses' strife to continue. "This is not a choice I wish to make," he announced. "Ares, who was the handsome boy with the champion bull you challenged?"

Ares was often paired with Athena and hugged her to his side to make his own choice clear. "Paris, my lord. He lives on Mt. Ida near Troy. Shall we summon him?"

"No." Zeus turned to his messenger. "Hermes, you must find him and ask him to choose. All three of you lovely goddesses will accompany Hermes to Mount Ida, and you must promise to abide by Paris's decision."

"The boy herds cattle?" Hera asked, clearly astonished her husband would suggest such an absurd option. "How can his judgment possibly be better than yours, my love?"

"I'm sure it isn't, but I'll not allow the decision to haunt me forever. You three must go with Hermes and don't return until the matter is decided among you."

Paris drove his herd to the highest of Mount Ida's peaks, Mount Gargarus, where the deep green grass grew thick. He played a lively tune on his panpipe until his herd of cattle suddenly grew skittish. He stood and quickly searched the hillside for a predator, a lion perhaps, but the countryside stretched out in peaceful calm. A sudden jolting crack of thunder made him flinch, and he gazed overhead filled with both fear and wonder.

Hermes parted the billowing pink-tinged clouds, and the radiant messenger of the gods flew down on his winged sandals. He carried the glowing golden apple and his Caduceus, a golden wand with two writhing serpents entwined on its staff. Behind Hermes, Hera, Athena and Aphrodite floated down to the earth. Awestruck, Paris stared at the magnificent beings and fell to his knees.

Hermes took Paris's arm and raised him to his feet. "You're a strapping lad, handsome as well, and you needn't cower before us. We've come to have you decide a matter, and you must consider your answer carefully before you give it."

Paris nodded awkwardly, and stuttered, "I'll do so."

"What an agreeable lad," Hermes enthused. He gestured toward his lovely companions. "Zeus commands you to judge one of these goddesses as the fairest, the most beautiful, the most divine."

The goddesses glowed with the same sparkling shimmer as Hermes, and Paris shaded his eyes with his hand to see them more clearly. "I know cattle and little else, to me you are all very fair, all beautiful, all divine. May I split the apple into three equal parts? Then each will be fairly acknowledged."

Hermes shook his head regretfully. "You have no choice, mortal, and can't deny the will of the gods. You must select one goddess and give her the golden prize."

Paris glanced around him desperate for help, but only his cattle were near and they were unmindful of his dismay. "So be it, but I beg those I don't choose not to punish me."

Hera took a step forward. Her hair was the deep brown of rich earth and curled atop her head to accent her vivid blue eyes. She was the tallest of the goddesses, and bathed in the fresh scent of falling rain. "You needn't fear us. Zeus will accept your choice and so will we."

Athena's raven black hair was adorned with golden combs, and a haunting touch of lavender perfumed the air around her. Her luminous gray eyes were framed with thick black lashes. Her smile offered warm encouragement. "You needn't be afraid. Just give us your best, Paris."

A wreath of red roses crowned Aphrodite's golden blonde curls, and the flowers' lush perfume danced on the air around her. Her sparkling eyes were more gold than green. She dipped her head and gazed at him through long fluttering lashes. "You're so handsome, Paris. Let your heart guide your decision."

Dazzled by each one, their gorgeous gowns and sweet perfumes, Paris shrugged helplessly. "Perhaps I could see you more clearly if you were to disrobe."

Amused, Hermes slapped him on the back. "It's clear you're a deep thinker. Do any of you object, my lovelies?" he asked the goddesses.

Hera unfastened her golden belt, and her delicate ivory hued gown pooled around her feet. She turned slowly and glanced over her shoulder. "I'm Hera, queen of the gods. Examine me closely and you'll find no flaw. Choose me, and you'll rule Asia and be the richest man alive."

Paris swallowed hard. "You're offering me such a grand bribe?"

"Not a bribe," Hera laughed, "but a generous reward."

Athena whirled around him in a dizzying spin before discarding her colorful multi-hued gown. "I'm Athena, goddess of Wisdom and Defensive War. Choose me, and I'll make you the wisest man who ever lived, and you'll always be victorious in war."

Her figure was as perfect as Hera's with high, full breasts, a narrow waist and gently rounded hips.

Their legs were long and their feet tiny, and he feared he'd never be able to choose.

Aphrodite came so close her pale pink gown brushed his arm as she released the gold and silver braided belt, and the sheer fabric floated to the ground. She spoke in a tantalizing, honey-smooth whisper, "I'm Aphrodite, your goddess of Love, and who could be more beautiful? Look at me." She raised her arm to coil her golden hair above her head and let it cascade into a shimmering cape over her shoulders. Her lush figure was as exquisite as Hera and Athena's.

"Choose me," she invited in a seductive hush. "I'll reward you with the world's most beautiful woman as your very own."

An innocent rustic lad, Paris fell instantly in her thrall and spoke without hesitation, "You should have this!" He grabbed the golden apple from Hermes and placed it in Aphrodite's outstretched hands. "Now, goddess, where is my prize?"

Aphrodite responded with a deep throaty giggle. She scooped her gown from the grass and disappeared in a golden mist.

Hera and Athena donned their gowns before circling Paris with resentful gazes, and the depth of their jealousy thickened the air. Hera's voice was a deep snarl, "Your choice will bathe you..."

"And your city," Athena added.

"In blood and fire!" The two goddesses pointed at him, their gesture evil in its intent. "Trojan fool!" They turned away and dissolved in a sparkling mist plotting the destruction of Troy.

Paris couldn't believe his eyes. He turned to Hermes, confused and filled with dread. Hermes dropped an arm around Paris's shoulders and gave him a brotherly hug. "It's always dangerous to insult a goddess, although Hera and Athena were convincing in their insistence you'd not offend them. You have won a prize from Aphrodite, however, and should go to Troy to claim it."

"How?" Paris asked, so frightened he could barely form the question, but Hermes had already vanished as the goddesses had, and his lowing cattle were again his only companions. Stunned by the whole astonishing encounter, he sat with a thud and cradled his head in his hands. He'd met three goddesses, each more beautiful than the next, but who would believe him if he told such an outlandish tale?

His father would laugh and be certain he'd fallen asleep and dreamed the whole dazzling episode. His mother would smile and pat his shoulder as though she often had similar dreams. Oenone would believe him, he was certain she would, but how could he admit he'd chosen Aphrodite's offer of the world's most beautiful woman? It would only make her angry and sad. When she was so pretty, why had he asked for another woman? Should she learn of it she'd never forgive him, never.

He should have taken Hera's prize, ruled Asia and been blessed with untold wealth, or Athena's gift of wisdom and victory in battle which would have given him everlasting heroic fame. Both choices struck him now as far better than Aphrodite's, but they hadn't given him any time to think. They'd forced him to choose quickly, and Aphrodite was the very soul of love. No mortal man could have resisted her.

No one he knew had ever seen a god or goddess, and shaken to his soul, he stood on wobbly legs and vowed he'd never tell anyone what had transpired that afternoon. He hoped to someday reach Troy, and the woman Aphrodite had promised could be waiting for him there, but until that day, he would cherish the memory of the confounding afternoon in his heart and not share it. Then no one could damn him as a fool for his choice. But Hera and Athena's angry departure left him deeply uneasy about his future.

Waving excitedly, Agelaus rode out to where Paris watched over their grazing herd. "King Priam has sent men for a bull to be a prize at the funeral games honoring his dead son. They want Red, and I couldn't let them take him without telling you."

Unable to believe the chance to visit Troy had presented itself so quickly, Paris needed a moment to gather his thoughts. "Red sires strong calves and will make a fine prize," he agreed, barely able to contain his excitement. "This is my chance to see Troy, and I'm going with them. They probably don't know much about caring for cattle and Red will need me to lead him."

Agelaus tightened his grasp on his reins. "They must know enough or King Priam wouldn't have sent them. They can handle the bull. You're needed here."

Since the day the goddesses had visited him little more than a week ago, he'd thought of little other than making his way to Troy, and he'd not miss this unexpected chance. He straightened up to his full height. "Haven't I been a good son to you?"

"You have surpassed all my dreams, Paris, but you're still needed here."

"I want only to see Troy as you have," he argued. "I'll return home when I can."

Agelaus frowned unhappily. "So many come to see the games each year, all you'll see is the backs of a huge crowd."

"Then I'll see that. I'm old enough to go on my own."

"It's not a matter of age," Agelaus complained, but when Paris refused to listen to any of the reasons he posed, he reluctantly gave in. "I'll ask our cousins from the village to watch the herd and go with you. That way I'll know you'll be safe."

"Is Troy a dangerous place?" Paris asked, too excited to be apprehensive.

His father shook his head. "No, but there are thousands of people living there and not all are noble."

Paris leaped upon his horse's back, and they drove the herd closer to home. He was briefly tempted to tell his father he'd been told to go to Troy to find his gift from Aphrodite, but no matter how he rehearsed the story in his mind, he couldn't make it sound convincing. He'd take Red and let the world's most beautiful woman find him.

As they neared Troy, Paris gazed up at the grand city surrounded by its massive well-built walls, the walls, his father told him, had been built by the gods, Poseidon and Apollo. The Pergamon, the Citadel, rose above the city with King Priam's magnificent palace and temples of the gods at the crest. They glowed in the sunlight as he imagined Mount Olympus would.

As they entered through the Scaean Gate, he marveled at the enormous crowd gathered together.

He'd not even realized there were so many people in the whole world. In the village, he heard a low murmur of conversation, but here in Troy, he was surrounded by raucous noise. He kept looking up at the citadel with the gleaming royal precinct, but the milling crowd quickly jarred him back to reality.

The multitude shouted rather than speak in normal tones, often with shrill voices, and they created a constant din. There were bright pennants flying from merchants' stalls, and the sellers touted the worth of their wares at the top of their lungs. Paris had never seen such an array of exotic goods, but Troy was the hub of a vast trading network with gold from the Hittites' Empire, ivory from Egypt, and frankincense and myrrh from Babylon.

He and his father followed the king's men to the pen where the prize bull was to be shown. Red entered the enclosure and circled at a trot ready for a challenge but none appeared. "He expects to fight," Paris noted with forced calm.

"Several of his calves show the promise of being even finer bulls when grown, so we won't miss Red for long," Agelaus assured him.

A young woman walked by in a colorful tiered skirt and bright bolero and immediately caught Paris's eye. When she turned toward him, he nodded, but she wasn't nearly as pretty as Oenone, and he quickly looked away. Surrounded by noise and color, he caught the familiar smell of garlic in the air. Someone was cooking one of his favorites from home.

From horseback, he could see so many dazzling things he grew dizzy. "I wish I could have come sooner."

Agelaus shrugged. "A child would swiftly become lost, so you were better off to wait until today."

"I'm taller than most men now," Paris responded proudly. "Even on foot I can see over the crowd. Where do they have the games?"

"The sporting grounds are on the flat area on the sea side of the city. I don't want to tarry here. Look around, we'll find a present for your mother and leave for home."

Paris had waited too long to visit Troy to rush away, and Aphrodite had given him an especially good reason to stay. "I'll not miss a chance to watch the games before we go, Father. Our herd won't even notice we're gone."

Agelaus dared not disclose the true nature of his fears, and hoping they could observe the games and depart without notice, he gave in. "We should leave our mounts here where they'll be looked after. A walk will do us good after our travel."

Paris's grin grew wide. "Thank you." He dismounted and handed his reins to one of the king's men and nearly danced in place as he waited for his father to make ready to go.

King Priam loved hosting ceremonial games and paced along the walkway behind the battlements on the high wall enclosing the pergamon of the royal city of Troy. The sky was clear, and the air off the sea invigorating. His sons Hektor and Deiphobus stood at his side. "The others racing chariots will provide little competition for you two."

"Are you sorry or proud?" Hektor inquired with a sly smile. He was a handsome young man, tall and muscular with thick black curls and laughter brightening his dark eyes. Deiphobus had finer features and a slender more elegant frame. He was an equally fierce competitor, however.

"I won the last time we raced," Deiphobus reminded his father.

Priam nodded. "I've not forgotten, although Hektor may have the finer team today."

"If he can control them," Deiphobus countered.

Hektor took a playful swing at his brother and Deiphobus countered with his own. "Come, let's go on to the sporting grounds and be ready when our turn comes."

Priam watched his sons walk away toward the Scaean Gate, the main entrance to the city. He was proud of them, but still missed the baby son he'd lost so long ago.

At Paris's urging, Agelaus found a place to stand on a gentle rise above the oval-shaped grounds. "We'll have a fine view here," the older man said. "But we should go before the close of the games to avoid being caught in the rush of people leaving."

The noise of the gathering crowd rolled over Paris and the bright colors stung his eyes. He'd never thought his clothing shabby, but when so many others wore garments in a beautiful array of colors, tunics and skirts without a single stain, he hoped no one would notice his dusty country clothes. He saw many beautiful women with make-up and elaborate hairstyles and doubted any would even look his way.

"They always begin with chariot races." Agelaus pointed out the two horse teams being led into the broad clearing. Drivers gestured for the surrounding crowd to move back and a surge of movement rippled around them. "Next to King Priam's high field throne, there's an altar for Zeus. Gods love the games even more than we mortals do."

Paris had never seen a chariot race and unable to stand still, he jostled from foot to foot. He liked the black team better than the bays or grays. "What fine horses they have."

Agelaus nodded. "They are known as the horse taming Trojans. Those young men are King Priam's sons, Hektor and Deiphobus. They win most races, but here come men leading several more teams, so we'll have a good race with real competition."

"Have you ever ridden in a chariot?" Paris asked.

"A few times as a boy," his father replied. "It can be a wild ride if a man fails to control his team. Some here are undoubtedly hoping for a bloody accident where both men and horses will die. Unfortunately, spectators could also be killed."

"Why would anyone hope for that?" Paris asked with a puzzled frown.

"There's a meanness to a crowd that you don't see in a single man," Agelaus offered with a shrug. "I hope we see only a fast race rather than a tragic one."

Paris straightened his shoulders. "So do I."

The chariots were light in weight with small platforms for a charioteer to stand and a semi-circular front guard covered in leather to protect him from the horses flying hooves. Paris could see the inherent danger even as the men lined up their teams near King Priam's throne. He had expected the king to shine like a god, but he made his way to his throne, a mere white-bearded mortal in fine robes. If only there were some way for him to impress Priam, then his dream of becoming a warrior might come true. With no chariot to race, or any knowledge of how to drive one, he would have to wait for another chance to come his way.

The Royal Herald began the race with a shout and swung a red pennant. Just as Paris had expected, the chariots burst forth like sparks from a torch. The man with the black team drew ahead as they swung around the curved track. As his father had feared, a chariot swung wide and careened into another man's. The charioteers jumped clear as their chariots flew apart in a rain of splinters, and the horses ran on dragging what little remained of their once fine chariots. The race slowed long enough for the men to catch their loose teams, and then continued to a rising roar of the crowd.

The man with the handsome black team won, and the crowd roared in praise and applauded. The winner jumped from his chariot to salute King Priam with a fist to his forehead. "Which son is he?" Paris asked.

"Hektor, although Deiphobus's bay team ran a close second. Have you seen enough? Are you ready to go?"

"What will they do next?"

Anxious to leave, Agelaus sighed unhappily. "Boxing. The men wrap their hands with leather thongs and fight to the last man standing. It will be brutal and bloody."

"I could do that." Paris pushed his way through those standing in front of them, creating a narrow aisle as he made his way into the clearing.

"Wait!" Agelaus yelled, but his son was too fast to catch. The men who'd stood ready to fight laughed when Paris joined them, but one had extra leather and wrapped the young man's hands even as he called him a fool for entering the fray.

Paris waved to his father, and stayed on the outside when the men spread out into a wide circle. The man nearest him wore a fierce expression, but his punches were wild and weak, and he went down with Paris's first blow to his chin. Unsure of the rules, Paris found another man to box and then another. Life as a herdsman had made him tough and strong, and he fought with a keen relish none of the other combatants possessed. When he turned to search for another opponent, he was surprised to find he had beaten them all.

The surprised crowd cheered, and he saluted King Priam as he'd seen Hektor and Deiphobus do. He was awarded a beautiful red leather headband, which he handed to Agelaus. "Do you think I might meet the king?" he asked.

That was the very last thing Agelaus would ever want, and he shook his head. "No, we'd not be thought worthy. Come before someone challenges you to another fight you'll be too tired to win. I don't want to take you home all bloody and beaten."

Too excited to feel a single blow, Paris wiped the sweat from his brow on his arm and shook his head. When foot races were announced, he grabbed his father's arm. "I can run. I want to race too."

Agelaus closed his eyes and moaned softly. "Do what you must, if you'll not listen to me."

"This is only one day, Father," Paris chided. "Let me show what I can do."

Paris jogged to where the race would begin and took a place beside Hektor and Deiphobus. Despite their fine clothes, they looked like ordinary men to him, rather than royalty, and he smiled and nodded a greeting, which they ignored. He was quick, but it would be a long race, and he stayed back until the finish line came into view. He ran then as he did in the shadow of Mt. Ida, and sprinted past the early leader to win by a wide margin. He waved as the crowd cheered and won another fine headband.

* * *

Deiphobus bent over to rest his hands on his knees. "That boy is swift. Who is he?"

"No one," Hektor replied, "but he's fast. Let's catch our breath and challenge him to another race. He won't have the same speed a second time."

"Neither will we," Deiphobus warned.

"I will even if you won't," Hektor vowed.

Paris was surprised the king's sons wished to race him again. "Are you certain?" he asked them. He had run for the sheer joy of it at home, and they didn't look as though they spent much of their time outside the palace. He didn't wish to embarrass them, as surely that wouldn't be wise. A shorter distance was chosen this time, but Paris didn't intend to let them sprint by him. Meaning to impress King Priam, he ran as though propelled by the wind and again won easily and received a third headband.

Agelaus grabbed his son's arm. "Come quickly before they show their disappointment with their swords!"

Paris doubted there was any such danger until an armed guard appeared just ahead of them. He looked over his shoulder and found an approaching guard there as well. Turning again, he found Hektor and Deiphobus coming toward him carrying highly polished bronze swords. He pushed Agelaus behind him.

"It was only a foot race," Paris called to them. "How can you take up a sword against me?"

Neither of the king's sons responded. They tried to catch Paris between them, but he was too fast on his feet and sprung upon Zeus's altar where the god would protect him.

Frantic, Agelaus shouted to King Priam, "Paris is your son, your majesty. I couldn't sacrifice him as you asked. Punish me if you must, but save him, he's blameless, and he's your own!"

Astonished, Priam leaped to his feet. He'd seen Paris win three trophies, which was remarkable, but not noted a likeness to Hektor and Deiphobus until that moment. Paris had his sons' height, their thick black hair and lean muscular build. He was a handsome youth beneath the dust and sweat, but he'd believed the boy he'd given to Agelaus long dead.

"You disobeyed me?" he shouted.

Agelaus couldn't lie with Paris's life at stake. "Sire, he was too beautiful a babe to sacrifice. He's a fine young man, your highness, and deserves to live."

Astonished by their exchange, Paris looked between the two men, the father he loved, and the king who might have sired him. "How can what you say be true?" he yelled to Agelaus.

Agelaus hung his head rather than admit King Priam had wanted his newborn put to death. The crowd had grown hushed as everyone strained to hear the unsettling conversation.

Hektor and Deiphobus had been small when they'd been told a baby brother had died soon after birth. They recalled their mother mourning with near endless tears, but to have that lost child presented now as a brother, was more than they could calmly accept.

"Call Mother here," Hektor shouted. "She'll know her own child."

Priam sent a servant to fetch his wife. He sank down onto a stone bench and stared at Paris, searching for any sign Agelaus's claim might prove false. The young man was strong and swift, valuable assets his other sons possessed, if not in such abundance. Although he also thought Agelaus would lie to save his own son from Hektor and Deiphobus's anger.

Priam scolded them as they waited for Hecuba. "Put away your swords. The games celebrate the victor, and you've shamed us all by turning on him. If he is faster than you, congratulate him and wait to race another day. Troy needs such strong young men to defend and honor her."

Hektor and Deiphobus exchanged a resentful glance, sheathed their swords and handed them to an attendant. They could abide losing to one another, but not to a sweaty uncouth boy from the countryside. They were royalty after all, and he was nothing but a lowly commoner in their minds.

Hecuba came running, holding her colorful skirt to avoid tripping. "What is this?" she cried. "How can my tiny son live?"

Paris was as confused as the queen and waited to hear Agelaus retell the story. Prophecies meant little to him, and clearly he'd proved the dire one condemning him to death as false for Troy stood as beautiful and prosperous as it had ever been. Who would dare to challenge the mighty Troy?

Hecuba had grieved for her lost babe every day since his death and quickly discounted the prophecy at his birth. "I recognize him as one of ours. Bring him to the palace where he can bathe and dress properly in fine clothes befitting a prince. When he returns home such a fine young man, surely his fate will benefit us all."

Paris jumped from Zeus's altar to follow Hecuba's maidservant. He turned and called to Agelaus, "Come with me."

Agelaus had expected his head to be struck from his shoulders at any moment and hurried after Paris before King Priam thought to order it. The royal entourage re-entered the Scaean Gate, made their way through the lower city and through the gates of the citadel to the palace's main entrance. This was the second time he had been inside the palace, and it overwhelmed him as on the day of Paris's birth.

Paris was enthralled by the palace's lavish beauty. He'd grown up in a low-ceilinged thatched roofed cottage, like all the others in the village, and he'd only dreamed of how grand King Priam's palace must be. Glorious frescoes of lions chasing deer decorated the walls, stately columns supported the roof and the rafters and ceiling were painted in intricate patterns in red, blue and gold. The stone floors held incised designs he hated to step on with his badly worn sandals.

He waited for Agelaus to come even with him. "How can I be a prince rather than your son? Has nothing you've ever told me been true?"

"I saved your life," Agelaus whispered gruffly. "Be grateful."

Dazed by the madly improbable day, Paris shrugged helplessly. "What will Mother say when you come home without me?"

Agelaus stopped mid-step. "It will surely break her heart. Come home with me and tell her what we've found here yourself."

"Will King Priam allow me to go?" Paris asked.

"He must deeply regret ever giving you to me, and he'll do whatever you ask. At least I hope he will."

They'd reached the bathing room and servants quickly filled the terra cotta tub with hot water for Paris to bathe. A slave pulled off his tunic and tossed the worn garment into the glowing coals of the brazier used to heat water.

"That's all I have to wear!" Paris cried.

The slave bowed. "Our queen wishes to see you in new clothes, my lord."

Hoping they'd appear, Paris stepped into the tub. At home, they scrubbed themselves clean with a pot of hot water and a rag. He'd never seen a bathing tub and slowly settled in. He burst into a wide grin. "The warmth feels really good. You must find such a tub for Mother."

Agelaus nodded as though such a thing were possible. He sat upon a stool and waited while the slave shampooed his son's hair, but Paris insisted he could bathe himself and did. A second servant entered carrying a white tunic, kilt and several pairs of new leather sandals.

"One should be your size, my lord," the servant said as he laid the sandals beside the tub.

Paris raised himself from the tub and took the towel offered. If life in the palace held so many surprises every day, he would appear to know nothing of any use at all. He donned a more serious expression, wrapped the kilt around his hips and the first pair of sandals he tried were a perfect fit. He tied the laces rather than allow one of the servants to kneel and do so.

With his hair still dripping upon his shoulders, he

felt ready to go. "Does Queen Hecuba wish to see me now?"

"Yes, my lord, come with me," the first servant replied.

Befuddled by continually being addressed as such, Paris gestured for Agelaus to follow. Even the corridors in the palace were beautifully frescoed in reds, blues and gold, with exciting scenes of horses and wild boar hunts, but he doubted he would ever come to think of it as home.

King Priam sat with his wife on gold and ivory thrones in the grand megaron. Each studied Paris closely as he approached and while Hecuba was the first to smile, Priam soon joined her. "He is clearly one of ours," he proclaimed. "We must have a feast to celebrate his return."

Paris was awestruck by their magnificent thrones and the grand murals behind them with two great griffins and the famed stallions of Troy prancing on either side. "I've long hoped to become one of your warriors," he blurted, and embarrassed his boldness might offend them, he took a backwards step.

Priam nodded thoughtfully. "So we might one day have met."

"I'd hoped so," Paris responded. "It's why I entered into your games."

Hecuba leaned forward, "You'd no idea you were our son?"

Agelaus answered for Paris. "No, my queen. I raised him as my own and taught him to herd cattle. We came to Troy to bring the bull wanted for the grand prize for the games."

Priam laughed. "You've won your own bull Paris, have Agelaus return him to his home. You'll remain here with us."

Paris straightened his shoulders. "I should return home long enough to tell my mother what I've discovered here."

"How thoughtful you are," Hecuba exclaimed. "We named you Alexandros. Do you like the name?"

"I've always been known as Paris, and I'd rather keep the name. It suits me, I think," he replied. "If it won't offend you," he added.

Charmed by the innocence of his expression, Hecuba agreed. "I lost my Alexandros so long ago, I'll accept that you've returned as Paris."

"He's a prince," Priam reminded her. "He'll be Alexandros to us and our Trojans. I can't say I'm displeased with you, Agelaus, when you've taken such good care of our son. Stay and enjoy the banquet tonight, and you may leave with Alexandros tomorrow."

Agelaus bowed low. He hated to think how deep his wife's sorrow would be to lose her son, but with Paris there to tell the tale, she would have to accept the life of a prince of Troy far surpassed the life of a simple herdsman's son.

CHAPTER 16

The enticing aroma of roasting meat filled the megaron and Paris was so hungry he had to swallow hard rather than drool. "Do they eat like this every night?" he whispered to Agelaus.

"No, they eat a simpler fare, but this is a regal banquet celebrating your return to the family. You should enjoy it, but with what we've seen of your brothers' open resentment for you today, I'd advise against drinking more than a single kylix of wine."

Paris scanned the large room assessing the threat. "You fear they'll do me harm?"

Agelaus nodded. "Jealousy can be a bitter drug, and you must remain cautious. Here's another of your brothers."

Helenus approached them to introduce himself and called to another brother, Aesacus, to join them. "You'll find you've many brothers here," he explained. "But not all of them are Hecuba's sons and princes as we are."

Confused at how that could be, Paris frowned slightly. "I've not had a brother, and I hope none will wish to turn a sword against me ever again when I wish them no harm."

Helenus hadn't forgotten his dark prediction when Paris was born, and he took care not to come near enough to touch him. "You've won our father's protection, and our kin won't defy him."

Hektor and Deiphobus were seated on the opposite side of the megaron and deep in a conversation that Paris was grateful not to overhear. "I mean no one any harm. If I must reassure everyone daily, I will."

Aesacus was slightly shorter than Paris and looked up to regard him with a friendly grin. "You couldn't have walked among us and not been recognized. Come, sit with us and enjoy the feast."

Paris nodded for Agelaus to follow, but the humble herdsman sat well behind him and kept a careful watch on all those gathered nearby. He worried Paris would always be regarded as a lowborn herdsman rather than a prince, but his mother had taught him well, and his manners wouldn't call his behavior into question.

It had been a long and exciting day, and Paris had to cover his yawns rather than appear rude. Slave girls carried trays of the most delicious roast boar and venison he'd ever tasted, but he ate sparingly as he had at home. He looked over his shoulder to the man he'd always called Father and found him yawning too. He'd been shown a room they could share, but doubted they could find it without help now.

King Priam had just risen to speak of his joy at his son's return, when Laocoön, a priest from

Poseidon's temple, strode in. Dressed in a flowing robe, he was an imposing sight, but the fierceness of his expressions appalled the ruler.

"We're celebrating my son's return, and you're welcome to join us," the king announced. The crowded megaron had grown still, and his deep voice echoed against the beautifully decorated walls and the four blood-red columns flanking the great central fireplace.

"Where is this cur of a son?" Laocoön shouted.

No coward, Paris shoved himself to his feet. The priest wore a hostile sneer, but he'd done nothing to insult him or Poseidon. "I am here." Agelaus rose to stand behind him.

The priest's long white hair twined over his shoulders like roots. Bushy eyebrows veiled his dark eyes, but his threatening scowl remained unmistakable. "You were cursed the day you were born, and you should have been sacrificed before noon. Order his death tonight, King Priam, or Troy will perish. The gods have decreed it, and the gods must be obeyed."

Priam shook his head. "I obeyed when Alexandros was born, Laocoön, and it caused my beloved queen and me unspeakable grief. I'll not sacrifice my son a second time, and Troy's fate will rest with me as it has all the years of my reign. Troy has enjoyed peace and prosperity all of Alexandros's life. That disproves the existence of any damning curse. Go and pray for the gods' continued blessings and do not trouble us again with such dire evil talk of curses."

The king's spirited defense filled Paris with pride, but all around him men argued in hushed whispers, some siding with the smoldering Laocoön and others with Priam. Paris turned to look at his father, and then swiftly gauged how close they were to the wide doorway. Agelaus nodded. Paris was fleet of foot, and could escape, and he trusted his father to lag behind and cause a scuffle to delay anyone giving pursuit.

The king scanned his guests, his relatives, countrymen, and his own dear sons. "Challenge me now if you dare, but no one will touch my son, Alexandros, while I live to prevent it."

A tense moment passed before Hektor rose with Deiphobus. He saluted his father with a fist to his forehead. "We stand with our father and king."

Paris was amazed when the men filling the megaron rose to their feet, one here, another there, then in a rolling surge, all had stood. "To the king!" A man raised a two-handled kantharos, took a drink and passed the painted clay jug to the next man. It was refilled with wine many times before it reached Paris, but he took a deep swallow and handed it on to Agelaus who dared take only a sip.

King Priam sent guards to accompany them when they wished to retire, but even with armed men outside their door, neither slept well.

Two of King Priam's warriors, Orthris and Kastros, accompanied Paris and Agelaus home to their village. They left shortly after dawn with Paris riding his faithful horse for the last time and leading his champion bull. King Priam had given him a fine bay gelding with a thick black mane and tail, and Kastros led him as Paris's mount for the return trip to Troy.

Kastros was among the youngest of the warriors with a slim build, easy manner and quick smile.

Orthris was a husky man in his thirties, who appeared thoroughly bored with the chore of looking after Paris. He turned often to cast an eye on the trail behind them, but no one followed.

The trotting bull kept their pace slow and provided Paris with time to consider how greatly his longed for trip to Troy had changed his life. Agelaus looked equally lost in thought. "You'll always be my father," Paris reassured him softly. "King Priam and Queen Hecuba may have given me life, but I'd have perished within hours had it not been for your kindness."

Agelaus nodded. "I saw no evil in you and told your mother that I'd found an abandoned babe. That I hid the truth from her all these years will shock her as greatly as what you must reveal about who you are."

"Did you plan to tell me someday?"

Caught by the insightful question, Agelaus shrugged helplessly. "Not when I believed the price would have been your life. Have you been unhappy with us?"

Turning shy, his father looked away, and Paris reached out to grasp his arm. For as long as he could remember, he'd wanted more than a simple herdsman's existence, but he'd never complained to his parents when they loved him so. "You've given me a good life, and I'll miss you."

"You must promise to visit your mother whenever you're able," Agelaus insisted.

"I will," Paris promised, but when their cottage came into view, he knew after spending the night in King Priam's splendid palace, he'd never feel at home again there.

His mother ran into the yard to meet them, and then stopped suddenly when she saw the warriors. Their bronze helmets caught the sun in a flash of fire, and she feared something must be terribly wrong. "What's happened?" she cried.

Paris slid from his mount's back and Agelaus led their horses and Red around to the rear of the cottage. The warriors remained on their mounts until Paris waved to them to rest for a while. They'd left Troy without buying a present, and Paris wished he had something pretty to put in his mother's hands. He hugged her tight.

"Do you remember the night Father brought me home?"

Tears flooded her eyes. "You've always been ours as though I'd given birth to you. Who told you otherwise?" She admired his new clothes and ran her hand over his chest to feel the fabric. The pale blue wool was the finest she'd ever seen.

Paris told her about his adventures in Troy, his voice soft and caring as he described how he'd boxed and raced. He brushed away her tears. "I'll give you the three leather headbands to keep. Father has known all along that I'm a prince, but I'm as surprised as you are to learn I'm King Priam's son. I don't understand why I'd be cursed at birth, and in praise of all the gods, father didn't either."

"How could there have been a curse when we've had such a happy life together?" his mother asked.

"King Priam came to the same conclusion. I should have brought you something. I'll come with gifts on my next visit."

A sad smile trembled over his mother's lips. "We'll understand if you have little time for us.

You've always been as handsome as a prince, and now you are one."

He leaned down to whisper in her ear, "I don't feel any different, Mother, and I'll always love you."

Agelaus came to his wife's side. "Will you forgive me for lying about Paris all those years ago?"

"What lie? It's true his parents didn't want him, and we did. You've been a joy, Paris, and you'll always be our son." She wiped her eyes on her hand. "You should go and see Oenone before you return to Troy. She should hear your story too."

Paris sucked in a deep breath. "I'd thought I'd have a different life."

"One never knows what the gods have planned," Agelaus offered. "Now you must be on your way before King Priam forgets your name."

"He'll not forget him," his mother argued, "but you should be on your way."

"I'll come again as soon as I can," Paris promised. He kissed his mother's cheek, hugged his father and turned toward the warriors who stood waiting nearby. "There's someone else I need to see. Her home isn't far."

Kastros nodded. "We're here to do your bidding, my prince."

Orthis mounted his horse without comment. He waited while Paris swung himself up on the bay he'd been given and followed, still keeping a close watch for unexpected danger.

Oenone twisted the tunic to squeeze out the last drop of water before laying it on a bush to dry. She was helping her aunt with the laundry, and she stirred the kettle over the fire to make certain all their clothes were washed clean. She wiped her hair out of her eyes on her arm.

"Well, what is this?" Chrisoula asked in a hushed whisper. "Has Paris become a warrior?"

Oenone whipped around to see the three men approaching. Paris smiled and waved, but the warriors following him stared straight ahead. Embarrassed to be caught doing the wash, she dried her hands on her skirt and pretended it was a fine time to entertain callers.

"Come ride with me." Paris extended his hand and pulled Oenone up in front of him. "Be still a moment, and I'll tell you a tale you'll never forget."

Oenone looked back at her aunt who stood with her hands on her hips. She was a beautiful woman with long red curls and had captured the warriors' full attention.

"Where did you get such a fine horse?" Oenone asked.

"He's a gift from King Priam." Paris rushed through the astonishing change in his circumstance in as few words as possible. "I'm to live in Troy's palace with the rest of his sons, but I'll come back to see you often."

Oenone choked back her tears. "No, you won't." Green fields stretched out all around them, and she marveled at the earth's beauty. The simple life they'd shared would no longer appeal to him. He'd never build the house he'd promised, nor would he become her husband. His dreams for their future had meant so much to her, but she hid how deep her hurt ran.

"You'll forget me before the next moon rises."

"We've grown up together, Oenone, and I'd forget

myself before I forgot you. You're much prettier than the girls in the city, and I'll bring you a gift the next time I come."

All she'd longed for was his love, and he'd never spoken the words. "I don't need gifts."

"Then I'll bring something for your aunt."

"You mustn't make promises you won't keep."

He gave her an affectionate squeeze. "I mean what I say. I plan to come home often, and maybe you'll be happier to see me the next time." He turned the bay and let her down gently in front of her cottage. He nodded to her aunt. He'd seen her once in the village, but the woman didn't appear any happier to see him than Oenone had been.

"I wish you both a pleasant day," he said in farewell, and headed back to the city with Orthis and Kastros following close behind. The whole world had opened to him and he didn't look back.

Chrisoula listened as Oenone recounted Paris's astonishing story. "So he's been a prince all alone," she mused aloud. "When he returns, and he will, you must convince him that if he's ever wounded, you'll be the only one who can save him."

Frightened by the thought, Oenone's voice grew shrill, "Why would he ever have need of me? Wouldn't the palace have many talented healers?"

"Perhaps, but none will have remedies as effective as yours. Promise me you'll tell him."

Oenone looked down at her hands, they were chapped from doing the wash. Paris would meet beautiful young women in the palace, who never lifted a finger to do any sort of work. Their skin would be pale, their long hair glossy, and their perfumed bodies slim and graceful. They'd be dressed in gorgeous clothes and gold jewelry. She doubted any could hunt as well as she could, but most women couldn't and the thought made her smile.

"I'll tell him, but I'll not hold my breath until he returns."

"That's wise. Now let's finish the last of the laundry and be done with the work for today."

They heated more water and the steam rising from the kettle hid Oenone's tears. She preferred gathering herbs and mixing potions to the hard labors of housekeeping. She felt numb, as though someone dear had died, and what she'd lost were her own precious dreams.

Before they were in sight of the city, Paris pulled his mount off the trail. "I need to learn how to use a sword. Can one of you teach me?"

"Now?" Kastros asked, swinging down from his horse.

"Yes, why not? We can let our horses graze awhile and not be late returning to the palace."

Orthis also dismounted and led their horses toward a promising patch of grass. Left with Paris, Kastros understood he'd be the one giving the lesson. "We'll need to borrow your sword," he called to his fellow warrior.

"Take care with it," Orthis replied. He handed the bronze sword to Paris, who'd not expected it to be so heavy.

Kastros removed his helmet and set it aside. They'd not carried their shields, and one wouldn't be needed for this practice. "How much do you know?" he asked Paris.

"Know about what?" Paris replied. "I hunt with a bow and arrows, or a spear, and do well, but swords are meant for fighting men, and I've never held one."

"Hold it with both hands," Kastros instructed. "It must become part of your arms."

Paris swung the sword in a wide arc and liked the heft of it. Without considerable practice, however, he doubted he could fight long with it. He was strong, but wielding a heavy bronze sword was something new and his muscles soon began to ache. "Can you work with me everyday? I want to be able to handle a sword as well as Hektor and Deiphobus."

"They began with wooden swords as boys," Kastros replied.

"Then I'll have to work very hard to match them now."

Orthis shook his head and looked away.

Paris met often with Kastros, and while no one would describe him as being adept with a sword yet, he gained the strength to swing the heavy weapon in a flurry of blows on Katros' shield. He was determined to make his father Priam proud, but also to possess the skill to survive should Hektor come after him again. Hektor was the eldest prince and heir to the throne of Troy. While Paris knew he posed no threat to his brother's eventual rule, it appeared Hektor would need time to accept it.

He ate each night in the megaron with Priam and his brothers, but he took care to sit near Helenus or Aesacus, who were friendly, rather than Hektor and Deiphobus who had never shown him a bit of warmth. He made sure to always be the last to enter the large hall so he'd know where they would be before he sat down to eat.

"Do you like women?" Aesacus asked as he passed a kantharos shaped like a donkey's head.

Paris barely contained a derisive snort. "Of course I like women." He wished to pass unobserved until he knew everyone in his newfound family and how they behaved with each other. He'd not tell Aesacus he'd been visited by the three goddesses, whose beauty outstripped all women on earth. It was a delicious secret he cherished and nurtured to himself, and for a brief moment, he swore there was a heady hint of Aphrodite's roses in the air.

Aesacus laughed at Paris's look of dismay. "The palace has many pretty slaves, and they're eager to become a prince's favorite. Do you see the girl with the serving tray near Father?"

She was pretty, with long sable hair and a slim figure. "I do."

"She's one of father's favorites, so you must avoid her. Hektor is married to Andromache, who is a great beauty, and he's faithful to her, but the rest of our brothers enjoy the slaves' company."

"What about you?" Paris asked.

Aesacus took a bite of mackerel baked on a bed of bay leaves. "I have some favorite companions, and I don't mind sharing. Shall I come to your bed chamber later to introduce one?"

Paris searched for an answer that wouldn't insult his new brother, or Aphrodite, and finished chewing a bite of bread spread with goat cheese before he spoke. "I grew up with a very pretty girl, and when it comes time to take a wife, I may choose her. The palace is all so new to me, and I don't wish to insult anyone over a slave someone else may favor."

His brother shrugged. "Probably wise, but tell me when you grow lonely, and I'll find you some affectionate company."

Relieved to have successfully changed the subject, Paris nodded and helped himself to the fish.

* * *

Hecuba sent a maidservant for Paris, and he found her in the courtyard gathering a bouquet of roses. A young woman with a crown of fair braids had been talking with her, but bolted when she saw him and raced away. Hecuba welcomed him with a graceful wave. "Come walk with me, my son," she invited. "I'd hoped you could spend a few moments with Cassandra, but your sister recalls her original dark prophecy so vividly, she cannot bear to be with you. She becomes overly excited so easily, but I do hope you'll forgive her. She's been cursed by the gods."

"Yes, of course." Paris shortened his stride to hers. Silver tinged her dark hair at her temples, but she was still a lovely woman. He couldn't think of her as his mother, however, but only as a kind lady.

"How are you finding your new life with us?" she asked. Her voice was soft, as though they were exchanging secrets.

He had never had to think so hard before he spoke as he had to in the palace. "This is a fabulous place, and you and King Priam have been so kind to me, but it's still difficult to think of this as my home."

She nodded thoughtfully. "It must be very different from a herdsman's life. Do you miss spending your days in a meadow on Mt. Ida with your cattle?"

"My cattle never challenged me with clever words as the people do here." He hoped she was teasing and laughed, and was relieved when she laughed with him. "Yes, it's a very different life here, with so many people, and so much to learn, I'm kept very busy with all of it."

"Good. I've chosen some fabric for the woman who raised you, and I want you to take it to her tomorrow. You may have told her how grateful I am for all she's done for you, but she deserves to have something more than simple words."

"Thank you, my Queen. That's very kind of you, and I've wanted to take her a present." His eyes filled with tears at the thought of how eager he'd been to leave home and how lonely his parents must be without him.

Hecuba touched his arm. "Please call me Mother. Come and go whenever you wish, Paris. Is there anything else you'd like to take with you? I have more jewelry than I can ever wear, but I doubt your mother would be comfortable wearing anything I'd send."

"She is a wonderful seamstress, and fabric is a far better gift," Paris replied. He wondered if he should ask for something for Oenone too, but thought she'd rather have a new bow and arrows than a trinket from the palace. He'd learned where the cooks got their spices, and he'd take some of them home too.

"Come with me now, and I'll give you the cloth so you'll have it when you're ready to leave."

Paris followed the queen inside the palace and up the grand stairway to the women's quarters. He waited by her door, and it was Andromache who came out to hand him the neatly folded bundle. She was a rare beauty with abundant curls and dark eyes with impossibly long lashes. He recognized her although they had not been introduced, and he felt the heat of a bright blush fill his cheeks. He nodded when he couldn't gather his wits to speak.

"Hecuba has added needles and thread. You'll find them when you unroll the cloth."

"Thank you." He took the bundle and bolted down the stairs for his room. He sat on his bed and worked to slow his breathing from frightened gasps to a steady rhythm. He thought he was allowed to go wherever Queen Hecuba wished to lead him, but when Hektor had taken an instant dislike to him, he knew better than to smile at his remarkably pretty wife.

Andromache returned to her chair and adjusted the folds of her tiered skirt. Made of panels of bright-embroidered blue, it was one of her favorites. "Paris is a handsome lad, but he's too shy to even look at me. I've never thought of myself as being so frightening."

Beautifully drawn young dancers circled the clay vase Hecuba had chosen for the red roses she'd picked. "It's more likely Hektor who terrifies him, but he'll grow accustomed to us all in time."

"I doubt I should tell my husband that I've spoken to his new brother."

"That would be very wise, my dear," Hecuba agreed. She placed the vase on the small tripod table beside her chair and sat back to admire the fragrant bouquet.

"Is it wrong for a woman to keep secrets from her husband?" Andromache asked her mother-in-law.

Hecuba laced her fingers in her lap. "So much of our lives doesn't concern them, and why mention something they might misconstrue as overly important? I welcome your questions, and you may be assured whatever you confide in me goes no further."

"I've no real secrets to share," Andromache hastened to explain. "My life is so pleasant here, I'm perfectly content."

Hecuba paused as a serving girl brought them wine and a plate of figs. "You mustn't appear to be too content," she warned, "or Hektor might fear you don't need him. If you choose to appear to be preoccupied occasionally, he'll worry you're unhappy and be inspired to improve your mood in whatever way he can."

Andromache understood perfectly and smiled at the thought. "Thank you. You give such wonderful advice."

"I do my best," Hecuba replied and turned the conversation to the beauty of the season's roses.

Paris left the palace with the fabric gift for his mother, and a basket of spices, but he'd thought better of taking Oenone a new bow and quiver of arrows. It had been a long while since she'd hunted with him, and he didn't want her to think he still considered her a child. He'd found pretty ribbons she might tie in her hair and hoped she would like those.

As they rode along, Kastros and Orthis regaled him with the colorful stories of past battles warriors loved to tell. Paris's skill with a bow and arrows had impressed them. Orthis had become as friendly as Kastros, and had produced a sword for Paris to use for practice.

Paris was relieved to find everything in order at his parents' home. His mother had baked bread and gave them each a warm slice. The warriors thanked her and took theirs to eat near their mounts while Paris entered the cottage with her.

"I promised to come home with a present for you." He kissed her cheek and handed her the carefully folded fabric. "It's a gift for you from Queen Hecuba, and I've brought a basket of spices, too." He set it aside on the table where she kept her cooking things.

She sat down with the fabric on her lap and ran her hands over the exquisite cloth. "This is far too fine for us, Paris."

He knelt beside her. "You deserve such pretty things. You're a talented seamstress and can make skirts, boleros and tunics for you and father to wear."

Tears glistened in her eyes. "I'll save this until I become accustomed to owning something so fine, but I don't want to make our neighbors so envious they won't speak with us."

Paris hadn't thought of how easily that would happen when no one in the village had clothing made from such finely woven cloth. "Your son is a prince, so you should have beautiful clothes."

She touched his curls. "I'm so proud of you. Are you happy at the royal palace?"

"I miss you and Father," he answered truthfully. "I'll ride out to find him, but before I go, tell me the news of the village. Has anything remarkable happened?"

He listened as his mother mentioned several young girls who'd asked to be remembered to him. "And Oenone," he inquired. "Do you have news of her?"

"I've not seen her. I suppose I would have heard if she had anything to tell."

"Of course." He waited until they could find nothing more to say, and then kissed her good-bye.

Agelaus saw Paris riding toward him laughed and waved. "You've come all this way again?" he asked.

"I brought a present for Mother. How is Red doing, has he fought other bulls?"

Agelaus nodded. "I gave him a good rest after his trip to Troy and back, and he's won again as easily as before. There's been no further sign of the white bull that disappeared in the blink of an eye. Some think it was a trick of the gods."

Paris shook his head as though he couldn't accept it, but after his own breathtaking experience with three goddesses, he wondered about it too. "What can I bring you the next time I come?" he asked.

"Save the gifts for your mother," Agelaus insisted. "If you're going to stop and see Oenone before you return to Troy, you better be on your way."

Paris hated to tell his father farewell, and yet he itched to go. He promised to return whenever he could and led Kastros and Orthis to Oenone's home. She was working in the garden, and looked as startled to see him as she had been on his last visit. He noticed Orthis looking past her for Chrisoula, and understood why the man had been in such high spirits that day.

He dismounted and carried the ribbons to Oenone. "Your garden looks especially full this year."

"It will keep us well-fed," she responded.

He leaned close to whisper. "It appears one of my warriors was hoping to see your aunt. Is she here?"

Oenone rested her hoe against the cottage and went inside to fetch Chrisoula. The redhead soon appeared brushing flour from her hands. "How good to see you again, Paris," she called. She looked up at Orthis, who promptly dismounted and clumsily removed his helmet to talk.

"Come with me." Paris took Oenone's hand and led her away from the others. "I brought some ribbons for your hair. Is there something you'd like me to bring for you on my next visit?"

She took the pretty package, but left the ribbons tightly wound. "I'm surprised you've come back twice," she answered.

He turned to walk backwards and face her. "Why do you think so little of me now?"

She looked down at her bare feet. "You've become a prince of Troy, a different man, and I'm the same simple village girl."

"Don't you remember my saying that you're prettier than the girls in the city?"

"I might recall it," she hedged. "Aunt Chrisoula made me promise to tell you that if you're ever hurt, you must send for me to care for you. No one else will be able to heal your wounds. Promise me you'll remember her warning."

Taken aback, he stared at her a long moment. "Troy is enjoying a lengthy peace, so I'm unlikely to be gravely wounded, but I'll call for you if I am.

Now let's not be so serious. Have you heard a new song or tune?"

She laughed. "The entertainments in the village aren't nearly as exciting as they must be in the palace. If you'd heard a new song, please sing it."

"I've heard so many," he confessed before realizing how small it would make her world seem. "I'll learn the words to my favorites and sing them to you someday soon."

He meant what he said, and this time when he rode away he turned back to wave. Oenone was standing with her aunt, and the breeze ruffled her curls, but she didn't smile.

CHAPTER 17

Paris listened more than he spoke, but when there was so much to learn about the life of a prince, he continually felt at a disadvantage. He stayed on the outer edge of any gathering and did his best to melt into the shadows. He avoided controversy by refusing to take sides no matter what the issue, but still drew more darkly skeptical glances than smiles. Undiscouraged, he worked hard to master a warrior's skills and Kastor and Orthis proved to be patient instructors. The bronze sword grew no less heavy, but as his stamina increased, he could swing it more nimbly and use the deadly weapon for longer bursts of power.

Lonely, he lay upon his bed at night with his hands propped behind his head and ached for home where every sight was familiar. He'd noticed more than one pretty slave girl glancing his way, but thoughts of the beautiful woman Aphrodite had promised him kept him from inviting any to his chamber. Thoughts of his promised love filled him with an unending joy. She might be petite, or tall and slender. Her hair might be black or golden blonde, and her eyes could be blue or green.

He could imagine the light touch of her hand on his bare chest, or how her whisper would tickle his ear. He was certain her voice would be low and sweet, and every word that past her lips memorable. Hermes had urged him to go to Troy to find her, but he was growing very tired of the lengthy wait. Perhaps she wasn't even in Troy, but in another city where their paths would eventually cross. If she were the most beautiful woman in the world, she must already have many suitors. He hoped they were a dumb ugly lot, bald, or missing blotches of hair, with broken flattened noses, and chipped teeth. He laughed at his own talent for imagining the worst, and often fell asleep happier than when he'd gone to bed. He hated having to wait, but believed the lovely woman he'd been promised must arrive soon, and she'd be worth every day of the wait.

Menelaus arrived at Troy with a dozen ships. King Priam had not expected a royal visitor, but hastened to make him feel welcome. He sent members of the house guard to invite the Spartan to the palace, and Menelaus came with a train of men bearing armloads of gifts for the Trojan king.

A handsome man with red hair and a neatly trimmed beard, Menelaus accepted the Trojan king's hospitality, but he'd come on a pilgrimage to visit the tombs of Lycus and Chimaerus, sons of Prometheus. "A plague has swept Sparta, and the Oracle at Delphi has sent us to make sacrifices on their tombs to bring an end to the grievous sickness."

"I'll provide escorts," Priam volunteered. "You must dine with us tonight and set out for the tombs at dawn."

Paris had only dreamed of other lands such as Sparta, and the visitors fascinated him. They spoke the same language and wore similar dress, and yet there was something about them that set them apart. He sat closer to King Priam than he usually dared to overhear as much as possible. Apollo spoke through the Oracle, so the cure he'd offered would surely end the plague and health would be restored throughout Sparta.

He slept very little that night, and early the next morning, he was ready to accompany Menelaus to the tombs. He'd become known as a fine horseman, and his presence caused no curiosity or alarm. Menelaus rode the stallion he'd been loaned with an easy grace, and Paris admired him all the more.

"Tell me more about Sparta," Paris asked as they rode along.

Menelaus regarded him with an indulgent half-smile. "It's a gorgeous land with majestic mountains and valleys lush with grain. Our olives are delicious, our wine beyond compare, and the women the fairest ever born. The gods blessed me with a wife often called the most beautiful woman in the world."

Latching onto Aphrodite's phrase, Paris leaned forward. "What makes her such a beauty?"

Menelaus laughed at the innocence of his young companion's expression. "She's a daughter of Zeus, with curly blonde hair, eyes of a vivid green, and beautiful beyond description. She's angry with me for a dalliance with a slave girl, but I hope she'll have forgiven me by the time I return home."

"Why would you want a slave when your wife is such a beautiful woman?" Paris asked, clearly astonished.

"Her question exactly," Menelaus confided. "It happened after a feast. I'd had too much wine, and when the slave gave birth to a pair of red-haired boys, the secret was impossible to keep. I've sent the girl and the twins to live in my brother Agamemnon's palace, so Helen will not be reminded of their existence, but she's still been slow to forgive me."

Paris sucked in a deep breath. He'd not expected the woman Aphrodite had promised him to already be another man's wife, and it confused him completely. But if Menelaus had betrayed Helen's trust, and sired twins with a slave, then perhaps she'd be eager to leave him.

"Do you and Helen have children?"

"A daughter, Hermione, who is nearly as beautiful as her mother. I miss them dearly."

Paris kept his thoughts to himself as they continued on their way. He'd dreamed the woman who was meant to be his would instantly recognize him as well, but he'd not imagined she might be already wed to another and have a child. If Helen were the one, why would Aphrodite complicate his life so entirely? Yet even with this nagging worry, thoughts of Helen were impossible to suppress. He rolled her name silently on his tongue, and smiled as he drew her into his heart.

Paris had asked nothing of King Priam, and he hoped this one request would be granted. "I'm eager to learn all the world holds and want to visit the famed Achaean Palaces. If I had a ship, I could sail along with Menelaus and return home when I'm ready. I'll speak of your wisdom and generosity with everyone I meet and bring awe and respect to Troy. There might also be new trading opportunities to develop."

Impressed by his newfound son's sincerity, Priam was inclined to be generous. "Phereclus has built many fine ships, and I'll provision one for you and provide men to sail her. As a prince of Troy, you should have an escort of several royal ships on your journey. I wish I could travel with the ease of youth, but alas, the throne of Troy cannot be left empty."

Paris remained to listen to his father's advice to be circumspect in all he did while away, but in his mind, he was already gone. "It will always be my hope to make you proud," he insisted as he bid him a good day.

He watched his ship being readied, and with gentle suggestions had a figurehead carved of Aphrodite. He left frequent floral tributes at Aphrodite's temple and prayed she would bless his voyage.

Going home to tell his parents of his plans would only worry them, so he chose to wait until he returned, and impress them with the most beautiful woman in the world at his side. Then he would have a real story to tell. He gave Oenone only a brief thought. He couldn't tell her the real reason for the voyage, and he couldn't bear to lie to his once dear friend.

Cassandra heard of Paris's plan to sail abroad. She gazed out a lofty palace window and was overcome by a vision of roiling storm clouds colliding on the horizon. Terrified, she rushed to find Helenus. "Paris mustn't go!" she warned. She rent her black locks of hair and screamed, "How can we stop him?"

Hoping to calm her, Helenus rested his hands lightly on her shoulders. "Once Paris was allowed to live, all may have already been lost. Father has given his consent, and we can't stop him now no matter what we do."

"But we must try!" Cassandra begged. "You see it too, don't you, Helenus? Paris's foolishness will cause Troy's doom! Come with me to Father."

He took her hand. "I'll go, but don't expect to be believed."

King Priam dismissed his advisers as his children approached him on the terrace. As Helenus had predicted, he listened to Cassandra's fears, but promptly dismissed them. "The terror you foresee will never come to pass. Troy is too strong to be defeated by whomever Paris might unintentionally insult in Achaea. Let your worries go. I long to see you carefree and happy once again."

Cassandra bit her lip rather than cry out, but each time she caught a glimpse of Paris, a horrid sense of doom rolled through her, and she couldn't pretend not to be sick clear to her soul.

A feast was planned before Menelaus departed for Sparta, and while Paris was equally eager to go, he admitted only to a desire to see other lands. Men had volunteered for his crew, and they were a sturdy lot who would also serve as his guards. Kastros was among them, but Orthis had never loved the sea and preferred to remain in Troy. Experienced crews would sail the remainder of his small fleet, and each day he grew more eager to go.

Hecuba had gathered gifts for Paris to present to Menelaus and his queen. There was a finely made short sword with an engraving of a lion hunt along its blade for Menelaus. Exquisitely crafted gold bracelets were wrapped in soft, woven wool, and she'd also included a beautifully decorated pyxis holding perfume made from the roses in her own garden for his queen. The gifts were placed in an ivory inlaid wooden chest that was remarkable in itself. He thanked her for her generosity, taking care not to smile too widely.

"We must always be generous," she stressed. "It brings not only admiration, but a true respect for the wonders of Troy."

"I understand." He kissed her cheek and carried the chest to his bedchamber to await loading before dawn. His life had changed so radically in the last few months, and he dared not imagine how greatly it would continue to change if Helen preferred him to Menelaus. With Aphrodite's blessing, Helen might fall in love with him at first glance. From what he'd come to believe about Menelaus, however, he was too proud a man to let his wife go. For the moment, he rested all his concerns at Aphrodite's feet and concentrated only on impressing Helen.

King Priam produced a heavy box of gold for Paris to give Menelaus once he'd reached Sparta. "I've gathered clothing for you as well. You must present yourself as Prince Alexandros, and never mention ever herding cattle. The Spartans are proud aristocrats and with such knowledge, I doubt they'd show you the proper respect."

Paris draped the leopard skin cape over his shoulder and liked the weight of it. Agelaus had taught him to keep a close watch so lions didn't take any of their cattle, but he'd never seen a leopard. The skin was soft, smooth and beyond beauty. "Thank you. I'd like to hunt for a leopard someday. They must be magnificent animals."

"Indeed they are, but a menace to both our people and herds. My best advice for your trip is to listen more than you speak, and listen carefully. A bit of information you gather in Sparta may later come to have great meaning for us."

Paris rolled the hide between his arms and held it to his chest. "I understand a fool never stops talking, while the wise man speaks only when he has a good reason."

King Priam smiled. "Precisely. I trust the men going with you to remain loyal, but you must be firm with them. Don't allow them to waste their time or yours. They should run to do the bidding of a prince of Troy."

He'd had such little practice at overseeing another's work, he doubted he'd ever command as much respect as Priam's other sons, but he would remain sober and provide a good example. "A fierce glance should be enough to keep the men eager to do their share of the work."

"Yes, a stern expression is vital. Make them earn a smile."

Paris thanked his father for his sage advice and bid him, his mother, and the royal entourage farewell early the next morning. A fine breeze billowed their huge red sail emblazoned with the emblem of Troy, a rearing white stallion. He gazed up to thank Aphrodite for blessing the voyage.

A fanfare of horns blared and Priam led his assembly in a farewell anthem. The song stirred Paris's heart, and he wished he knew all the words. He'd never been on a sea faring ship, let alone a royal flagship and while he'd heard warnings he might become ill, he thrived in the salt-scented air. Certain he'd been born for adventure, he could barely contain his excitement as they crossed the wine-dark Aegean Sea. Yet nothing he had dared to dream or imagine had prepared him to meet Helen.

PART III

PART III

CHAPTER 18

Sparta
The palace of Menelaus

Oron, the stable boy who'd come from Theseus's fortress years ago, ran to meet Helen after her morning ride. "My Queen, Menelaus has returned home!" he yelled.

Her day now ruined, she wheeled her high-strung gray mare in a tight circle and rode away. There were a dozen different directions in which to go, and she chose the solitude of a trail she seldom rode. There had been no recent deaths from the plague, so his sacrifices in Troy must have won the god Apollo's sympathy. Unfortunately, he hadn't won hers.

She'd chosen Menelaus to be her husband, and their years together had been remarkably free of strife until…. She refused to even think the girl's name. He'd complained he'd been in a drunken stupor and scarcely remembered the night, but she refused to accept such a miserable excuse. He'd never gotten lost on the way to her room on any other occasion, so why would that one have been any different?

Perhaps it hadn't been, and he'd often prowled the palace and come to her from a slave's bed more times than he could recall. Had the twin boys not been so obviously his, he might never have admitted how deeply he'd betrayed her. That he'd carried the secret for so many months had left her feeling unclean and no amount of perfumed baths had eased her disgust. Other kings might have favorite slaves and spawn bastards by the number, but she'd never thought Menelaus could behave in such an unconscionable manner. He had not been gone nearly long enough for her to miss him, and now that he'd come home, the sorrow of the very sight of him would be renewed.

Menelaus carried their daughter Hermione into Helen's bedchamber. The little girl's arms were tightly wound around her father's neck. He stopped at a safe distance before speaking. "I missed you."

Helen turned away from the window overlooking the rolling golden plains. She couldn't find a smile. "Did it surprise you?"

"No, not at all, but I'd hoped you'd miss me as well."

She had been unable to feel anything more than the breeze brushing against her skin on her daily ride. She changed the topic rather than insult him in front of their daughter. "The plague hasn't spread, and many who were ill have recovered their health, so your trip to Troy assuaged Apollo's anger and provided as great a benefit to Sparta as you'd hoped."

"That's very good news." He kissed his daughter's cheek and set her down. She ran to her mother, and Helen scooped her up into her arms and hugged her. He remained where he stood. "A Trojan prince, Alexandros, has accompanied me home for a visit. He's a very earnest young man. He's brought presents for us." He extended his hand. "Come, I want you to meet him. He's a fine horseman, and you might even find the Trojan amusing."

Helen doubted it and shrugged. "Possibly." She placed Hermione on her feet and took her hand. "Let's meet our guest, Dewdrop, we're expected to be cordial. Smile so he'll see how pretty you are."

Menelaus brought Helen's hand to his lips before lacing his fingers in hers. "Hermione looks so much like you as a child."

"Does she?" Helen responded. "She's much sweeter, and you'll never find her playing in the dirt with warriors and horses made from rope and sticks."

"I'd be enchanted if she did, just as I was with you."

Helen recalled the day vividly. He'd interrupted their play, and she'd been annoyed rather than impressed by him. She'd known nothing about the world then, and now she knew far too much.

As Paris waited for the royal couple, he compared the throne room to King Priam's. It wasn't nearly as large and lavish. Instead of a gold and ivory throne, there was only a stone chair, although it was handsomely carved. Rather than the beautiful frescoes of prancing horses and the horse-taming men of Troy, here the walls were decorated with scenes of warriors following Ares, the god of war, into battle.

* * *

Menelaus and Helen made their way to the megaron where a handsome, dark-eyed young man with a charming smile awaited them. The fire from the central hearth made his face glow. The leopard skin thrown carelessly over his shoulder added a dashing wild touch to his demeanor she rather liked.

"Do you enjoy hunting?" she asked, her voice a soft melody.

"Yes, my queen. I brought my bow and spear hoping for just such an opportunity."

"We must arrange a hunt soon," Helen suggested to her husband.

"I'll see to it, my dear," he promised.

Paris didn't know how he'd found the breath to speak, for Helen possessed a luminous, spellbinding beauty, like the sun bursting through heavenly clouds. Her long curls shimmered as though they were laced with golden thread. Her eyes were a startling bright green, and her delicate features were lovelier than any of the goddesses from Mt. Olympus. She graciously accepted the gifts he'd brought her, exclaimed over the beauty of the bracelets, and added them to those already on her wrist. All too swiftly she excused herself and left them with her little daughter trailing. The pretty child would surely grow up to be as striking a beauty as her mother.

He had to draw in a deep breath to gather himself rather than appear to be a love-struck fool. Helen had been kind and welcoming, but there had been no joy reflected in her gaze. She'd followed tradition and extended the palace's hospitality as though she'd memorized the words years ago. She hadn't glanced toward her husband when she'd spoken to him. If she couldn't even bear to glance his way, then Menelaus's fears she'd not had time to forgive him appeared justified.

Alexandros was welcomed to the palace with a proper feast. Menelaus ate without tasting a bite, and talked of Sparta until they were both yawning and could no longer stay awake. He excused himself and went to his wife's chamber.

Moonlight lent the room a soft glow, and he cast off his sandals and tunic and lay down beside her. He pulled her into his arms and kissed her forehead. "I don't expect anything from you, but I want you to know where I've spent the night."

She smelled the wine on his breath, and wondered if he'd drunk it to enjoy the feast, or merely for courage to join her. She was used to his scent and embrace, the way his muscular body curved against hers, and how his hair fell across his face as he slept. He was a reasonable man, but she'd pushed him, and probably to his limit. Wisely, she didn't reply.

Paris had not expected Helen to ride with them on the hunt and was elated when she did. She wore a beige hooded cloak over her skirt and bolero to avoid the chill of the early morning air, and with curls flying loose near her face, she looked impossibly young. Her perfect skin held a peachy glow and made her appear no more than seventeen or eighteen and very near his age. Girls wed at thirteen or fourteen, so it was possible she was not yet twenty, or if that, no more than a few years past.

She rode a powerful bay gelding that she handled as easily as an obedient pet. Dawn broke over them with rose-hued streaks and promised a fine day for a hunt, but again, Paris saw no joy in Helen's gaze. Menelaus had told him that weather permitting, she rode everyday, and often spent afternoons giving Hermione riding lessons on her pony. There was always more to do than any woman could accomplish each day, but Paris couldn't bear how little joy Helen appeared to glean from what anyone would assume would be the perfect life in such a fine palace.

He hadn't noticed the quiver on her back until she rode ahead of him. Oenone had been an excellent archer, but she was a country girl, not a queen. Helen continually surprised him, and when they spotted a fine fallow deer with a regal rack of antlers leaping through the edge of the forest, Menelaus gestured for her to take the first shot. To Paris's utter amazement, Helen brought down the deer with a single arrow, and there would be tasty venison at tonight's feast. She rode home ahead of the men, and while they had not exchanged more than a nod of greeting, Paris was desperate for a chance to talk with her without Menelaus standing close enough to overhear. He'd have to find a way to let her know he saw her sorrow, and how deeply he wished to make her smile.

Hermione loved her white pony, but she was content to ride her in a slow circle outside the stable rather than venture any farther. Helen had been patient with her little girl, but couldn't continue repeating lessons Hermione had already mastered. When she saw the Trojan prince approaching, she welcomed him as a break in their routine.

"Good afternoon," he greeted them. "What a handsome pony. What's his name?"

Hermione cocked her head and observed him with a slyly critical glance. "*She* has a fancy name, Cloud Crest, but I call her Cloud Baby, or just Baby. Do you own many horses?"

"My father, King Priam, owns more than I have counted, and I may ride whichever one I choose. The countryside is so pretty here, when do you ride? I'd like to go with you."

"She prefers to ride here in a small ring where the palace is never out of sight," Helen answered with a weary shake of her head.

"Aren't you tired of the same view?" he asked.

Hermione shrugged. "I don't want Cloud Baby to get tired."

"No, of course not, but she might enjoy carrying you to the olive trees on the nearby hill."

Helen smiled at how easily Alexandros led her daughter into venturing the short ride. She walked alongside him as Hermione rode Baby. The gentle pony's mane hung down over her eyes, and she went wherever Hermione wished to go.

Alexandros was a handsome young man, but his sheer eagerness for life made Helen uncomfortable. "Tell us something of Troy," she asked before he could direct the conversation with questions she'd rather not answer.

"It's on the Aegean Sea and faces the sea channel, the Hellespont. The citadel and palace are at the top of a hill and possess a commanding view clear to the horizon. The city spreads around the hill and across the plain. It's said the walls were built by Poseidon and Apollo and will never fall. I wish you could come with me to see it."

She found his company unsettling on dry land and dismissed the thought of a voyage together. "I prefer to remain in my homeland where the ground is firm beneath my feet."

"Our land is equally solid," Paris assured her with a dry chuckle.

"I was referring to a trip across the sea," she explained. "Travel by boat doesn't appeal to me."

"I found it exhilarating. The whole world borders the sea and the wind carries us wherever we wish to go. I'm so glad I came here. Now that I have a chance, I must tell you how impressed I was with your skill with a bow."

His dark eyes danced with the admiration Helen so often saw, and she wouldn't encourage him. "I grew up with two brothers who taught me more than most girls are allowed to know."

"And clearly King Menelaus appreciates your skill."

They were at the foot of the hill, and she decided they'd gone far enough. "He understands me." She reached for the pony's bridle to turn her toward the stable. "Come, Cloud Baby, we've gone far enough for today."

Paris walked beside her. "Perhaps I could ride with you in the morning."

"I prefer to ride alone accompanied only by my own thoughts. Besides, Menelaus has another hunt planned for the morrow."

"Will you come with us?"

Clearly Alexandros was not easily discouraged, but she preferred evading his company rather than revealing how little it was appreciated. "No, he means to go after wild boar, and insists it's too dangerous for me to join in the hunt. Did you say you'd brought a spear with you?"

"Yes, I did, so I'll be ready."

"You still need to take care," she warned him as they parted at the stable. Hermione turned to wave at him as they entered the palace courtyard, but Helen didn't reward him with any lingering attention.

Omalu combed Helen's hair with gentle strokes. "Your husband is home from his voyage, but you seem no happier than when he left."

"Let's talk about perfume. The queen of Troy sent a rose scent that's completely overwhelming."

"Perhaps you should dab a drop on your ankle rather than your wrist."

"Yes, that's what I'll do and perfume my sandals rather than the air all around me."

Omalu bent slightly to observe her mistress's expression. "Your visitor is very handsome. Do you like him?"

"I don't dislike him," Helen answered.

"You don't like or dislike anything," Omalu chided. "You're walking in the lost land of in between."

"I know where I am," Helen assured her. She reached for the ivory comb to finish her grooming herself. She bent over to run her fingers through her curls and shook them into place as she sat up.

Omalu removed the lid from the pyxis Queen Hecuba had sent, sniffed the rose perfume, and wrinkled her nose. "This is far too intense." She folded a bolero Helen had discarded and retuned it to a carved chest of clothing. She continued to straighten the chamber until she could no longer be still.

"Menelaus has always been very kind to me. He's a good man. Why won't you forgive him?"

Helen drew in a deep breath and released it in a soft sigh. "Some things can't be forgiven."

"Of course they can. Has it not occurred to you that one day you might need his compassion and forgiveness?"

Helen turned to look up at her long-time companion. "My life is so peaceful and well-ordered, how could I ever do anything to offend him?"

Omalu shrugged. "I don't even want to imagine, my lady, but no marriage has only sweetness."

"Which reminds me, you should have had a husband long before now. Do any of the men here appeal to you?"

The dark-haired young woman covered her giggles with both hands. "There are so many handsome men here, I can't make up my mind."

"I've always liked Oron. He has a way with horses and would surely be equally gentle with a woman."

Omalu went to the window, rested her arms on the sill, and looked out. "Our paths seldom cross, and I don't know him well enough to have an opinion."

"Shall I send you to the stable each morning to see that my mount is ready for my ride?"

"He already knows when you'll come."

"Then we'll have to think of another reason for you to speak with him." Helen smiled at the fun of matchmaking, but she was eager to delve into anything other than her own problems with love.

* * *

"I speared an immense boar near here on our last hunt," Menelaus bragged to his guest. "We feasted on delicious pork for many days."

Paris heard appreciate murmurs from the palace guard. Apparently they fondly remembered either the excitement of the hunt, or the beast's succulent flavor. As the forest thickened, shadows grew long and deep over the leaf-strewn ground, but no boars appeared, immense or otherwise.

Wild hogs were known to be vicious and cuts from their tusks could gouge the bone. Not wishing to be caught unaware, Paris leaned forward to listen, but other than the birds chirping overhead, there was no sign of game. Menelaus signaled for his men to stretch out in a line as they moved through the woods, but he kept Paris close by his side.

When they at last came upon a boar, the bristly creature had been dozing in the sun near a fallen oak. He grunted when confronted, his tiny eyes bright gold specks in his dark gray hide. Taking them in, he rocked his head from side to side, and then turned and jogged away as fast as his short legs could carry him.

Menelaus raised his hand to keep his men in place while he and Paris pursued him. "How many boar have you taken?" he asked.

Paris had never even seen one this close and wouldn't claim any kills. "None, I've hunted only lion and deer."

"You take him then," Menelaus offered with a wave. "Aim for the shoulder to pierce his heart or lungs for the quickest kill. A wounded boar may turn and attack. Don't risk it."

Paris definitely hoped to avoid such a dangerous consequence. Mounted, he easily overtook the running boar and threw all his weight into spearing him. Mortally wounded, the boar's high-pitched shriek pierced the air, he fell to his knees, rolled to his side, and after a few feeble kicks, lay dead.

"Excellent!" Menelaus shouted. He rode close to slap Paris on the shoulder. "My men will dress the beast, and we'll feast on him tonight." He shouted at a retainer, "Take care cutting the tusks, and I'd add them to my war helmet."

Paris felt sick rather than proud. He yanked his spear from the dead boar and wiped the bloody bronze blade on the grass. He tried to shake off the memory of the boar's agonized scream, but it continued to echo in his ears.

"I believe I prefer taking deer with my bow and arrows." He watched as one of the palace guards produced a rope and with the aid of his companions, strung the boar up from a nearby tree. Dangling by its hind feet, it looked even larger than when it had first been sighted. He turned away as the man slit open the abdomen and began to dress the carcass.

"I also love the chase with deer," Menelaus agreed, "but the hunt for boar offers a brutal excitement and keeps everyone well-fed, and it's a fine manly sport."

Paris's mouth felt dry, and he swallowed hard before he spoke. "Of course it is. Thank you for letting me make the kill."

"I take pride in being a generous host."

Paris's smile wavered on his lips. He'd come to Sparta to meet Helen, and he refused to leave without her. Fortunately Menelaus didn't even suspect his motives, or he'd be as dead the boar.

When they returned their mounts to the stable, Paris was disappointed not to see Helen with her daughter. He'd enjoy talking with Menelaus for the rest of the morning about fine horses, but he saw no sign of a white pony. He supposed he might have inspired the little girl to venture away from the stable with the short ride she'd taken yesterday, but he was sorry he'd missed them.

He nodded as Menelaus pointed out a mare he expected to deliver fine foals. "She is a beauty. I like the depth of her color."

"She's as black as her sire. I always use blacks to pull my chariot. They appear to be fast even standing still, and I've never lost a race with them."

Paris was too embarrassed to admit he'd never ridden in a chariot, let alone driven one. When Menelaus began to wave, he was elated to see Helen and Hermione approaching. The little girl bounced upon her pony's back and called to her father.

Helen slipped off her gray mare's back and keeping the reins in her hand, approached Paris. "Hermione has at last decided she loves to ride. Thank you for taking an interest in her yesterday. You've given her the courage to venture away from the palace."

The pretty little girl was adorable, but when Paris was so enraptured with Helen, he was deeply gratified by her compliment. He looked down at his sandals in a vain attempt to find a witty response, and when he looked up, Helen was walking away with Menelaus, who held their daughter. Hermione waved, and he raised his hand to respond. He held his breath, and when Helen glanced over her shoulder and smiled, he nodded and thought he had made some progress after all.

He looked around and was relieved to find no one looking his way. He supposed all of Menelaus's men and kin were in love with Helen, but he'd seen something in the gentle curve of her smile that gave him hope.

The first light of dawn lit Helen's chamber when Menelaus rolled toward her on their wide corded bed. He propped his head on his hand. "I must go to Crete to arrange for my grandfather's funeral," he said. "It won't be a long trip, but it's expected I go."

She sat up slowly and pushed her hair out of her eyes. "I hope you'll have an uneventful journey."

"I do love the sea, but not nearly as much as being home with you and Hermione."

Helen hugged her knees. "Now that she's decided she loves to ride, we'll have adventures of our own while you're away."

He left her bed and stretched. "Perhaps by the time I return, you'll be in a mood to offer an affectionate welcome."

She watched as he wrapped a finely woven crimson kilt around his hips. He was trim and fit, with the same muscular build he'd had when they'd wed. She doubted he'd ever run to fat as less active men did, but his appearance had never posed a problem. She let him leave her chamber without offering any hope that she would regard him differently upon his return. The hurt simply ran too deep. Too awake to go back to sleep, she gazed out the window. It would be another glorious warm day, perfect for riding, or even making perfume.

She made a mental list of all that needed to be done, but didn't leave her bed until she had to.

The roast boar had tasted even better than Paris had expected. The feast had lasted long into the night, and the wine had flowed freely. Everyone there accepted him as a prince, and didn't observe him closely as though hoping he'd reveal himself to be a fool. He hadn't noticed when Menelaus had left the megaron, one moment he was there, and another he was not. Paris had stood and gone to bed, weaving a bit on the way down the corridor. He didn't awaken until mid-day, and couldn't believe Menelaus was gone.

He found Helen seated in the courtyard with her maid, Hermione and an older woman who was too elegantly dressed to be mistaken for a servant. "Good day, my queen. Is it true Menelaus has sailed for Crete?"

"He didn't tell you?" Helen asked.

She looked surprised, and while he doubted the subject had been mentioned last night, he wasn't completely certain. "No, I didn't know. Does he expect me to wait here for his return, or leave for Troy so soon after my arrival?"

Helen brushed a flying curl from her eyes. "You're our guest, Alexandros, please remain with us as long as you wish."

He didn't want to ever leave her. "Thank you." As far as he knew, men didn't sit with women during the day, and he left them with a determined stride as though he had somewhere to be. He went out through the gate and walked to the vineyard where he could sit on a bench and puzzle out what to do. He had such little experience with women, other than his own dear mother and Oenone, he had few resources upon which to draw. He possessed such a powerful secret, and he longed for the chance to share it with the woman he adored. Now that Menelaus had gone away, he hoped one would soon present itself.

Helen possessed too restless a nature to lie sleepless upon her bed, and she went up to the roof terrace to search for the peace that eluded her during the day. She drew her cloak over her shoulders and leaned against the railing near a large vase with a blooming rose tree. It's heady perfume filled the cool night air, and she was content to study the panoply of stars overhead. It was late, the household still, and when she heard someone on the stairs, she slipped into the shadows rather than greet them.

Unable to sleep, Paris had sought the stars as a reminder of home. Looking up, he saw fireflies flitting through the sky competing with the stars' brightness. There was a faint scent of Helen's perfume on the night air, and he hoped she was still there. "Helen?"

She recognized his voice and stepped into a ray of moonlight. "Did you not have enough to eat, or is your bed not comfortable?" she asked.

"The meals served here are splendid in every respect, and my bed is the most comfortable I've ever slept upon. I merely wanted to gaze at the stars and think of home."

She returned to the railing. "Is there someone you miss?"

He reached for her hand and brought it to his lips. "No, there's no one. I have a story you may not believe, but it's the truth and really happened."

His touch was pleasant, but she withdrew her hand rather than rest it in his. "I love a good story. Please begin."

He leaned against the rail so their shoulders would touch. "While I was born a prince, I was raised by a herdsman and spent many hours watching our cattle graze. One day a bolt of lightning pierced the sky, and as I looked up, the gods' messenger Hermes, and behind him, I was amazed to see Hera, Athena and Aphrodite floating down from Mt. Olympus. They'd come to ask me to choose the most beautiful goddess among them."

Helen turned toward him. "Are you sure this wasn't a dream?"

"I knew people would doubt me, so you're the first person I've told. I assure you it was real, not a fabulous daydream. With her golden hair, Aphrodite looks very much like you. Hera and Athena also offered bribes, but Aphrodite promised to give me the most beautiful woman in the world if I chose her."

Helen's voice was a soft whisper. "And did you?"

"Yes, and I've come to Sparta to find you."

She watched the sparkling fireflies and remained silent a long moment. "Wait, there has to be more to your story. Why would King Priam send a son to be raised by a herdsman?"

He'd hoped she'd be enchanted by his talk of goddesses, but now feared she needed to know so much more. He didn't want to say too much and spoil what might be his only chance to impress her. "Does is really matter?"

"Yes, I want to know why a prince wouldn't be raised by his royal parents."

"There was talk of a curse, which clearly isn't true." He told her about his fighting bull and how it had led him to Troy. He explained how he'd been reunited with his royal parents, but didn't reveal the depth of his brothers' hatred for him. "I'm a prince now as I was born to be, and I love you."

His heartfelt declaration sounded all too familiar, and yet still touched her. "I saw Zeus once as a child, and he didn't mention your name."

"Did he tell you whom he'd chosen to be your husband?"

"No, our conversation was very brief, but I've seen a god, so I believe you could have seen Hera, Athena and Aphrodite. Was she really the most beautiful goddess?"

"Each one is beyond compare, but Aphrodite offered you and with that promise, I couldn't have chosen either of the others, although I worried about offending them."

He was such a sincere young man, but clearly had forgotten how mischievous the gods could be. "The gods love to play tricks on us. Am I to have no say in this? I was kidnapped once, with a very terrible result, and would not recommend it."

He leaned close to brush her cheek with a tender kiss. "I thought Aphrodite would have cast a spell so you'd want to be mine."

His breath was warm against her cheek, and suppressing a shiver, she looked up at the night sky. "Apparently she neglected to weave one."

"Then I'll have to convince you on my own."

Stifling a laugh, she turned toward him and unwittingly stepped into his kiss. His lips were soft and the pressure sweet rather than insistent. She raised her hand to stroke his hair and relaxed into his embrace. Perhaps it was only the beauty of the night, or maybe truly Aphrodite's magic, but the feel of him, and his taste were so familiar, she felt as though she were coming home. When he at last brought their first kiss to an end, she pulled him close for another and made it her own.

Growing breathless, he spread tender kisses along her jaw. "I've seen how sad you are, how unhappy your life is. Come with me. Let's sail the wine-dark sea to Troy."

"Impossible. I cannot sail the wine-dark sea with you to Troy."

"Why? Bring Hermione and all the servants you wish. We can sail at dawn and you need never look back. I have a swift royal ship awaiting us."

She rested her head on his shoulder. "Hermione adores her father, and I would never take her from him."

"Bring whomever you wish, but come with me. I'll never betray you or give you any reason to be sad."

Moving back a step, she found they were engulfed in a golden sphere of swirling, spinning fireflies. She was struck by the magical moment, but gathering her wits, she broke free of his relaxed embrace. "You mean that, but sorrow often overwhelms me without a reason. Ride with me in the morning, and we need not speak of tonight."

She left him to run down the stairway, entered her bedchamber and threw the bolt. Alexandros was filled with a young man's dreams of love, and she'd been wrong to encourage him. That it had felt so right was merely a cruel twist of fate. Menelaus would never let her go no matter how pretty Alexandros's promises were. She sat on the edge of her bed, as lonely as she'd ever been and wished the handsome Trojan prince had never heard her name.

As Paris turned, the fireflies spun around him, their path gradually widening until they'd all flown away. Aphrodite might have sent them, and while they'd been pretty, he wished she'd turned Helen's heart toward him instead. Maybe Hermes and the goddesses had all been laughing at him, teasing him with a prize he could never have. But if he hadn't been inspired to go to Troy, he'd not have discovered who he really was. If Menelaus hadn't visited King Priam, he wouldn't have known Helen's name.

He believed he'd been guided to her from the moment Aphrodite had won the golden apple. They were fated to be together, if only he could convince her he was her true husband. It couldn't be impossible, or he wouldn't have found her so easily. Inspired, he planned for the morning rather than sink into despair.

CHAPTER 19

Aethra stopped Helen as she prepared to leave the palace for her morning ride. "I sleep so poorly, I heard you pass by my chamber very late last night."

Theseus's mother missed nothing, but Helen made no attempt to fool her. "I went to the roof terrace for the comfort of the stars. I find their constancy endlessly reassuring."

The white-haired little woman regarded Helen with a narrowed glance. "Menelaus was a fool to leave you here with a young man as handsome as that Trojan Alexandros. He's clearly enamored of you. Could your husband have done it deliberately?"

Helen hadn't mentioned Alexandros, and wouldn't admit she'd spent time alone with him. "Menelaus isn't given to plotting intrigues."

"Perhaps he's lacked a reason." Aethra walked with Helen into the courtyard with quick tiny steps.

Puzzled, Helen wondered aloud, "Are you saying he might have left hoping I'd behave horribly and have something to confess upon his return?"

Aethra raised her hands in a nonchalant wave. "It's merely a possibility. He'd be gracious and forgive you no matter what your indiscretion, but then you'd have to forgive his, wouldn't you?"

Helen looked down and smoothed her lavender-hued tiered skirt. "I'd rather not believe he'd even consider such a mean-spirited ploy."

"But what if he has? With forgiveness a certainty, why not behave any way you wish? When Alexandros is so eager to please you, why not allow him to do so?"

Helen laughed rather than reveal how appealing the prospect might be. "You're not usually so wicked, Aethra, and I'll not take what is purely conjecture as advice." She bid her a good day and walked out to the stable trying not to run.

She chose to ride the big bay gelding rather than the pretty gray mare. If she quickly tired of Alexandros's company, she'd be able to leave him on the path without having to worry he'd overtake her. She told herself it would make her safe, rather than reckless for riding with him in the first place.

Oron had known little about horses when she'd brought him there from Theseus's fortress, but over the years, he'd developed a real talent for handling their prized mounts with a warm word and cool hand. He helped her upon the bay's back.

"Thank you, Oron. Are you happy here?" she asked.

His face lit with a wide grin. "Yes, my queen. This is the best home I've ever had. I hope I've pleased you and your husband."

She glanced toward the palace, but there was no sign as yet of Alexandros. "You have. Are you lonely, have you considered taking a wife?"

"A wife?" His voice broke on the word, and a deep blush brightened his dark tan. "What woman would have me?"

"You're a handsome young man with an agreeable nature, have none of the pretty girls here told you so?"

Clearly deeply embarrassed, he shook his head. "Few come to the stable."

"Then I'll have to find a way to bring you into the palace so they can meet you." She turned her mount toward the path and left him to wonder what the future might have in store.

Rather than being deeply disappointed, she began her ride relieved Alexandros hadn't met her at the stable. Perhaps despite the foolish way she'd welcomed his kisses, she'd convinced him his attentions could lead nowhere. When she rode over the rise in the path and found him waiting for her beneath a wild pear tree, she was surprised, but couldn't hide her smile. Even if she hadn't wanted to see him, now that he was here, the day was doubly bright.

"Good morning," he called to her, and urged his mount onto the trail beside hers. "I'll pretend last night didn't happen if that's your wish."

He exuded the joy that escaped her, and it was all she could do not to reach out and touch him. "My whole life is pretense, so I'll not deny we exchanged a few kisses."

"It was more than a few," he chided.

He had the most beguiling grin, and she wondered if Aethra might have guessed the truth, and his presence was meant as a temptation. "Let's race." She tapped her heels against her mount's flanks and left him in a burst of musical laughter.

Paris had never heard her laugh, and he raced after her. He'd asked for one of Menelaus's finest horses, but her bay flew down the trail, and while he gained on her, he couldn't overtake her. When she stopped and spun her horse in a tight circle to face him, he was so dazzled by her smile he could have landed in the dirt and not felt a twinge. He leaped from his horse, reached up to catch her waist and pulled her down beside him.

"You have the most beautiful smile," he vowed between kisses. "This is the first time I've seen joy light your eyes."

She gripped his strong biceps. Happier in that moment than she could recall ever being, she reached up to kiss him. In an instant, he created the same magic they'd shared last night, but again, it seemed more fantasy than real. "Aphrodite must be toying with us."

"No, she means for us to be together." He wrapped her in his arms and lifted her off her feet. "This is the way our whole lives should be. Come with me to Troy and stay with me forever. The city is huge, and your world here is so small. You belong in wondrous Troy."

"A guest does not steal his host's wife," she cautioned. "Please consider the dreadful repercussions."

He laughed. "Menelaus can't battle Troy, it's far too powerful. The Troad, the kingdom it commands, is vast compared with little Sparta. Your husband's warriors would be outnumbered a hundred times over, and my brother Hektor has never been defeated in deadly combat. Come with me. It's where you belong. You'll be the brightest and loveliest of Troy's treasures."

She stepped out of his arms and moved away. "You're asking me to make the choice as though others wouldn't be hurt if I abandoned them."

"Bring whomever you'd miss. My royal ship is large." He pressed close behind her and looped his arms around her shoulders. "It's what the gods desire, Helen. We mustn't refuse their generous gift of love."

Resting against him, she closed her eyes and fought not to imagine the worst, but simply to feel his strength and affection. Tired clear to the marrow, she longed to go somewhere fabulous and new, to Troy where he'd promised love would never end. She looped her hands over his.

"I need time to think."

He turned her slowly to face him. "No, you need only this." He kissed her until she leaned into him, all luscious woman and sweet surrender. Still, it wasn't nearly enough. He drew in a ragged breath. "Let's ride to the sea to view my ship. Then maybe everything I promise will become more real to you."

She held his arms to remain steady on her feet. He was offering her time to think even if he didn't realize it. "Fine, I'll go with you, but we mustn't be away from the palace for too long, or I'll be missed."

He helped her mount her horse and nearly leaped upon his mount's back. "I've come with fine sailors who can chart a course for wherever you'd care to go. Egypt is filled with wonders. Would you like to go there?"

"Travelers have spoken of Egypt," she replied. "I hadn't thought I'd ever see it."

"You will if you want to." He reached for her hand as they rode along the trail. He could smell the scent of the sea in the distance, and wished he could convince her to leave with him now.

By nightfall, Helen still had not given Alexandros her answer one-way or the other. The love he offered was almost too much to accept. Almost. She paced her room as she weighed the cost of leaving against the lingering sorrow of remaining with Menelaus, where everyday she became a more hollow shell. When she heard a faint knock at her door, she didn't hesitate to open it.

Paris slipped into her room before she could change her mind. "I'll sleep with you here, or you may come to my bed, but tonight we should be together."

His voice was husky with desire, and she melted against him to welcome his kisses. "We should stay here," she whispered. She took his hand and led him to her bed. "For tonight, let's lose ourselves in love and not think at all."

He rolled her long gown over her head and traced her tempting curves with his fingertips. He held her close to press her breasts against his bare chest. "As you wish."

She peeled away his kilt and placed her hands on his chest. His height and handsome muscular build were so easy to appreciate even in the dim starlight slanted through the window. There was no going back now, and she eased him down beside her on the bed.

"There's no rush," she whispered. "We have until dawn."

He wound his fingers in her hair to hold her still for a flood of deep kisses. "Let's make tonight last forever."

She'd expected him to take her in a heated rush, but he spread teasing kisses over her cool skin as though forever had already begun. His adoring touch was light as he explored her body with a patient curiosity that made her tingle inside. He'd proved to be love itself, and she floated in his embrace craving still more. She tipped her hips in a silent invitation, and he responded with a slow deep thrust. It was an ageless dance, and he overwhelmed her with a stunning pleasure. She wrapped him in her arms and sighed into his ear the words of love she hadn't dare speak aloud.

When Paris could draw the breath to move, he sat up and rolled off her bed. "Gather whatever and whomever you want, and we'll leave now. We'll sail with the dawn, and you need never look back. I'll protect you with the royal guard, and we'll find endless joy in Troy."

He was insistent, as though the shared ecstasy of making love had sealed them as husband and wife. He kissed her once again, his taste luscious, and all her doubts fell away. She gave him her hand eager to go.

When Menelaus returned from Crete, he found the palace servants fleeing ahead of him rather than running to welcome him as joyously as they always had. Helen wasn't in the courtyard, and when he found Omalu in tears clutching Hermione's hand, he feared the very worst.

"What's happened? Where's my queen?"

Omalu bit her lip in a futile attempt to stem her copious tears, but failed. "She's left us, my lord, gone in the middle of the night with Alexandros. She took Aethra and Emalia, and they sailed for Troy."

"She did what!" he shouted, and when Omalu cowered away from him, he ushered her into the palace. He drew Hermione into his arms and gave her a fierce hug. "When did she go, how long has it been?" he asked.

"It was the second night you were away. None of us can believe what's happened, but...."

He nodded and softened his tone. "You needn't say it. I know Helen was deeply disappointed in me, but it's Alexandros who's to blame for this outrage, not her. At least she had the sense to leave my darling Hermione with me." He gave his little girl another loving squeeze.

"What are you going to do?" Omalu asked between tear-filled hiccups.

"I'll go to Troy and bring her home. What else would I do? No one heard her call for help?" he asked, the faint hope she'd been kidnapped lighting his expression.

"No, it was a calm night like any other, but when we awoke the next morning, she was gone. We've talked of nothing else. Had Alexandros tried to take her against her will, she would have fought him with a lioness's strength, and we would have run to her. Nothing in her bedchamber was overturned or out of place. She and Alexandros simply vanished into the night."

Too upset and angry to comment on how they'd snuck away like thieves, he called to a palace guard to send word to ready the army. Heartsick, he left his daughter with Omalu and went upstairs to Helen's bedchamber.

Her wooden clothing chest was empty, and her gold jewelry was missing from her delicately inlaid box. He sat down on her bed and rested his head in his hands. He'd not once thought of Alexandros as dangerous, and felt a fool for leaving him with Helen. Why hadn't he had the sense to take the Trojan to Crete, or send him away before he'd left? He'd hoped only to make Helen miss him enough to welcome him again to her bed. It had not crossed his mind how swiftly she'd welcome another.

Actor stood waiting for Menelaus at the bottom on the stairs. A respected elder, he felt he must offer an opinion. "Sire, as heroic as our Spartan troops are, we are only a few hundred men and not a match for Troy's host of thousands of seasoned warriors."

Menelaus quickly strode past him. "That may be true, but this is a matter of honor I can't ignore."

"Yes, my lord, you must act, but go to your brother, Agamemnon, first. As high king of Greece, he can muster a force to match Troy's. You'll save Sparta's brave men from a needless slaughter and regain your honor."

Menelaus stopped and turned back toward him. After a long moment, he nodded. "You're right, Actor, as you always are." He called to another guard. "Ready my chariot, and I'll ride to Mycenae. My army can ready for war until I return."

The guard banged his sword against his bronze breastplate and ran for the stable.

Entering the enceinte of Mycenae, Menelaus lashed his high-spirited team and looked up at his brother's hilltop palace fortress. It's massive cyclopean stone walls loomed ahead. Above the massive lintel at the lion's gate was a huge triangular stone with a sculpture of two huge powerfully muscled lions confronting a sacred column. Their golden heads were turned to face any visitor, their jagged-toothed jaws snarling with the might of their powerful king.

The tall gates swung open and twelve of the elite palace guards marched out, each covered from their fierce eyes to their shins in great plates of bronze armor. Their helmets were made of dazzling white rows of wild boar's tusks, an awe-inspiring sight, meant to frighten any visitor. They recognized Menelaus's crest on his chariot, lowered their spears and split into two lines to allow him to pass.

A trumpet blared the fanfare of Sparta in respect as Menelaus rushed his chariot through the gates and up the wide ramps to the gate of the royal courtyard. He threw the reins to a bowing attendant and strode through the blood-red columned portico into the megaron.

As high king of Mycenae, Agamemnon lived in a palace twice the size of Menelaus's. His dark, thick curly hair fell into his eyes, but no one mistook the fierceness of his gaze. Known as the Lion of Mycenae, there was a sharp cruelty to his features that Menelaus hadn't inherited.

He'd watched his brother's approach from out on the parapet, and startled by a clap of thunder, spilled wine from his kantharos. He hurried down to the megaron to discover what had sent Menelaus to him at such a frantic pace. He dismissed his advisors to be alone with his brother, but he wasn't moved by his tale of loss.

"Of course you want Helen back, and the Trojan prince's treachery insults us all. But we needn't raise an army to attack Troy just yet," Agamemnon posed. "To capture Troy would give us a great prize, expand our trade into the Black Sea, and bring enormous wealth, but such an assault must be thoughtfully considered. First, we should show we are honorable men. I'll send emissaries to King Priam to demand Helen be returned to us. Troy is known for their love of peace, and our request should be granted."

"And if it isn't?" Menelaus demanded. Weary from travel, his eyes were bloodshot, his posture sagged, and he appeared totally forlorn.

Agamemnon had never looked more regal and responded with a wicked grin. "Then I'll raise the greatest army the world has ever seen, and we'll go to war to claim Helen as our own. With the combined might of Greece, Troy will surely fall and shower us with its riches, and beautiful women for our beds."

"All I want is Helen," Menelaus stressed. "I refuse to lose her to a Trojan prince, or any man, who'd dare steal her from our Spartan home."

Agamemnon offered fine wine. "You have every right to your fury, but a cool head is needed now. A show of restraint will work to our advantage. Either Helen will be returned to you, or if not, we'll be ready for war with all the forces of Greece and seize her as well as Troy."

Menelaus shuddered. "You may love war, but I don't relish the bloodshed it will surely cause. I should go to Troy myself."

"No, you're the king of Sparta, and the matter of an errant wife shouldn't command your full attention. Don't let King Priam know how highly you value Helen, and he won't be prompted to demand an excessive ransom."

"I'll give him whatever he asks."

"You will not," Agamemnon nearly growled. "Don't let Alexandros's folly become your own. What did you make of Priam when you met him?"

"He was restrained at first, but became more cordial. My sacrifices to Lycus and Chimaerus did rid the plague from our land, but I'd have let thousands die had I known there was any danger I might lose Helen."

Passing by, Clytemnestra saw her husband and brother-in-law in close conversation and entered the megaron. "You're not looking well, Menelaus. I hope you've not fallen ill."

Menelaus stood and straightened his shoulders. "I'm only sick at heart. Helen has fled Sparta with a prince from Troy. I mean to get her back."

Astonished, her eyes widened in surprise. "Has she been kidnapped yet again?"

"No. She appears to have left willingly, but it doesn't matter. I'll bring her home soon, no matter how great an army we must raise."

Clytemnestra leaned against her husband and wrapped her arm around his. "You'd risk good men in such a venture? Why not let the whore go to her everlasting shame?"

"Helen is your sister!" Menelaus cried.

She kissed Agamemnon's cheek and turned away. "Helen has never thought of anyone but herself. She's disgraced us all, and I no longer have a sister. Forget her and take another pretty woman as you wife."

"Never," Menelaus vowed through clenched teeth. Clytemnestra had a beauty that hid her true selfish nature, but he'd already known she and Helen weren't close, and now he understood why.

* * *

Agamemnon's emissaries arrived in Troy bearing golden gifts for King Priam and were welcomed into the palace. "Have you also come to visit the tomb of Lycus and Chimaerus?" Priam asked. "I'd hoped no more of your people would succumb to the plague after the sacrifices Menelaus made."

The emissaries exchanged a startled glance. While tall, muscular men, they had been chosen for their wisdom and cool heads. The elder of the two responded, "Sire, Menelaus's pilgrimage was successful, and the illness has not spread. We've come to fetch the Spartan Queen Helen and return her to her husband and rightful home." His voice was pitched low, merely stating a fact, without making a strident demand.

Priam responded with a puzzled shrug. "We've not seen her. Why would you expect to find her here?"

The emissary spokesman continued, "She left Sparta with your son, Alexandros, while Menelaus made a brief voyage to Crete. He's willing to forgive her and sent us to escort her home."

Priam shifted as his ivory and gold throne became increasingly uncomfortable. "Are you certain she left Sparta with my son?"

"There is no doubt," the emissary assured him.

"None whatsoever, sire," his companion added.

After a stressful moment, Priam released a regretful sigh. "I can't say whether Helen is with Alexandros or not, because he has not returned here to our home. They may be together wherever they are, or they may not, but they are not here. You may return to your King Menelaus and assure him we have not seen either Alexandros or his queen."

Rather than turn belligerent, the emissaries bowed to the king and returned to their ship rather than insult King Priam with any further questions. Their mission had been a simple, if dangerous one, and they feared returning home with no answers.

Menelaus went to his brother's palace when summoned, but he understood from the messenger's expression the news wasn't good. He knew the men who had been sent to Troy and trusted their judgment. He paced Agamemnon's megaron as they spoke together. "You've no doubt as to King Priam's sincerity?" he asked.

"None, my lord. His surprise at our visit was genuine rather than pretense. He looked sincerely befuddled, as though he could not even imagine Helen being with Alexandros. The breach of honor was his obvious consideration."

Deeply discouraged, Menelaus dismissed them and looked toward his brother. "Where could he have taken Helen if not to Troy?"

"Phoenicia," Agamemnon replied with a shrug, "or Cyprus, perhaps he took her into Egypt. It doesn't matter where they went. That he took Helen is certainly grounds for war. My emissaries saw a great deal. They counted able-bodied men as well as the king's warriors, and the number of ships along the coast. The Trojans believe they are safe behind their mighty walls, but we can draw them out, and they'll be easily defeated, as they're no match for our superb warriors."

"I wouldn't count on it being easy," Menelaus warned. "War never is."

Agamemnon chuckled. "We'll have a righteous cause, and warriors who've never been cautioned against being brutal. Troy and her riches are already ours. Alexandros will return home before long. His passion for Helen will be the ruin of Troy, and you'll not only have Helen returned to your bed, but as many Trojan women as you'd ever desire."

"You understand nothing," Menelaus lamented. "Helen is the only woman I'll ever want, and there will be no others."

"You're love-struck by the gods, Brother." He laughed, shook his head and then paused before making a thoughtful suggestion. "Do you remember how Tyndareus forced all of Helen's suitors to swear their allegiance to you?"

"I do."

"Good, so will they when we call upon them to keep their vow. Alexandros may have thought you'd be unable to force him to return Helen on your own, but he couldn't have realized you'd come with the immense army of allies we'll raise. Think of it! All the kings of Greece will join us, and it will be the greatest army ever assembled. The bards will sing of this war for a thousand generations."

Menelaus sat slumped across his chair and swallowed the last of the wine in his cup. The bloody images flooding his mind were not anything he'd want bragged about or remembered. "I just want Helen, my Helen," he whispered to himself.

CHAPTER 20

Egypt
Land of Refuge and Adventure

Troy carried on an active trade with Egypt, and the men with Paris knew a welcoming bay where they could erect tents along the shore. He gathered thick carpets and soft pillows from nearby villages and built a miniature palace for Helen. He asked her to call him Paris, the name he'd always known, rather than Alexandros. His descriptions of his youthful adventures filled her days with laughter. At night, he enveloped her in the magical sweetness of his love, while hauntingly beautiful music from harpists and flutists floated on the perfumed air.

He awoke one dawn to find her peering through the opening of the pavilion. "It will be another golden day," he proclaimed and drew her into his arms. "What if I found horses to ride, would you like that?"

She turned to face him and stroked his cheek. "Very much. We should go early before it becomes too warm."

"I notice nothing but you when we're together."

"You must learn to see far more." She kissed his eyelids. "I love staying here and simply watching the sea and letting the days roll past without a thought save those of each other, but one day soon, shouldn't we return to your Troy?"

He hugged her tight. "One day," he promised with a teasing glance, and he smothered her lilting giggles with kisses.

Later, they rode along the edge of the surf, and the horses' hooves sent up drenching salty sprays. Helen had never spent such carefree days and loved how eager Paris was to amuse her. She refused to let her mind drift past the moment to the life she'd left behind, and gloried in the beauty they shared together.

In the afternoon, Paris and Helen often played knucklebones, which involved tossing anklebones of sheep and catching them on the back of the hand. It was a silly game she'd played as a child with Omalu, but Paris made any pastime fun.

One afternoon, an Egyptian servant brought them a beautiful new game to play. "It's called *Shebahu er sabu,* or in your language, Hounds and Jackals."

"I love games. How is it played?" Helen asked.

The servant responded with a respectful bow. He set down a rectangular wooden box, and pulled out the hidden drawer to remove the game pegs, which had beautifully fashioned animal heads. The top of the box formed the game board. A painted palm tree in the middle separated two lines of carefully drilled holes.

"The palm represents the sacred grove of our god Osiris, god of the dead," he explained, his voice low as though he were sharing a greatly prized secret. "The jackal pegs are carved of ebony and the hounds of ivory," he continued. "One player chooses the jackals, and the other takes the hound pegs. The point is to move your jackals or hounds through the holes in the game board on your side until you reach the last hole, marked with the hieroglyph, *shen*, for eternity, then you may take one of your opponent's pieces. As you move along the board, you may use these curved lines, or secret passageways, as short cuts to move closer to the eternity hole. You can also cross to the other player's side if you land on the line connecting them, or secret doorway. That way you can chase them. The first player to take all the other player's pegs is the winner.

"Roll these four wands to see how many holes to move your piece through. One side is black, the other white. If you have the jackals, you count the wands that land on black. If you have the hounds, you move on the number of white sides facing up."

Eager to play, Helen sat down facing Paris. She picked up one of the long black pegs. "I want the jackals. I love their sharp pointed ears. Do you mind being the hounds?"

"Not at all. Hounds are most welcome on a hunt."

He winked at her as though she were the game he was after, and she had no desire to escape. "This appears to be much more challenging game than knucklebones."

"Indeed it is," the servant responded. He stayed only a moment to answer their questions and then left them to play on their own.

Both quickly mastered the rules as they played, and they turned their games into a lengthy tournament. But the next day, neither could recall who had won. The following afternoon they played again, and after laughing until they nearly cried, they drifted into a loving game all their own.

Aethra was not nearly as content in Egypt as Helen and Paris were. She walked along the palm tree lined shore with Emalia in the early mornings, staying well away from the sailors and their wild games. She spoke to them only to criticize their sloth and when the provisions they provided fell beneath her standard, she went with them to supervise the buying of better quality fare from the nearby villages. First a small pony had to be found for her to ride, but the sailors assumed from her imperious manner that she must be Helen's mother and quickly followed every direction she gave.

Paris was amused by the clever little woman, and took care not to incite her wrath. They had been in Egypt more than two weeks when Helen revealed Aethra was Theseus's mother rather than a relative from her own household.

"He may be the King of Athens, but she's far happier with me than she ever was living in his shadow," she explained.

Helen had not confided the details of her kidnapping, but Paris was astounded she could not only have escaped Theseus, but taken his mother with her. "He didn't demand her immediate return?" he asked.

"He was unable to leave the Underworld for a good long while, and I've no idea what concerns him now." She stood and stretched. "I love living by the sea. It's salty like our blood."

"I love you." He wrapped his arms around her waist and rocked her gently. "Were life here not so perfect, I'd take you home to Troy, but I hate to bring this enchanted time to an end."

She rubbed against him. "We'll make our own enchantment in Troy."

"Yes, we'll do that, and it's so beautiful you'll never wish to leave." He whispered in her ear, describing the life they'd share, but each night, the stars overhead bid him to stay.

Hektor ran into the megaron. "Alexandros is home, and he has the Spartan Queen with him!"

Shocked by that odd announcement, King Priam rose slowly from his throne. "We'll withhold judgment until we meet her."

"You'll forgive him for bringing this strife to our shores? Had he wished to bring a terrible war down upon us, he could not have chosen a swifter way to do so."

Priam didn't respond. He straightened his shoulders to assume a proud pose and walked out onto the courtyard where he had a view of the sea. He recognized the royal ships at the shore, and waited not at all patiently as his son made his way up the hill to the palace. He ignored Hektor's sputtering and searched for the proper way to greet the young man he'd mourned for so long. That Alexandros was alive was enough for him today, and he'd make no damning accusations, at least not yet.

Paris held Helen's hand as they entered the palace courtyard. Several of his brothers stood beside their father, along with their wives. Some appeared merely curious, while others, like Hektor, were smoldering with barely suppressed rage. He pulled Helen close. "I'm home father, and this is Helen, my beloved wife."

"The Queen of Sparta," Hektor muttered under his breath.

Priam had never seen a more beautiful young woman and thought her golden radiance must rival Aphrodite's. The sparkling tips of her fair curls floated on the gentle breeze and bounced against her waist. Her delicate features were perfection, and her bright green eyes seemed to see clear to his soul. When she dipped her head slightly and smiled, his knees weakened.

She seemed to be of the gods, and enchanted by her, he drew in a deep breath to find his voice. "Welcome to Troy, dear lady. Please think of our fair city as your home."

Helen watched the others' stances shift, some bracing themselves and others relaxing slightly. They were a handsome family, regal in appearance and bearing. Priam must have been as handsome as Paris in his youth. Now his head was crowned with silver white hair, and his face framed with a grand beard. She wished she'd prepared a poetic way to respond to his greeting.

"Thank you for your kind welcome, my king."

Hektor took a step forward. "Your husband sent emissaries to escort you home. Did you believe you could leave Sparta and not be missed? You are Helen of Sparta."

Paris spoke before Helen could answer. "I'm now her husband, and her life is here with us. Henceforth, she'll be known as Helen of Troy."

Priam ended the discussion with a wave of his hand. "We sent the emissaries away, and we'll send away anyone else who might come for you, my dear. Let's give our thoughts to preparing your welcome. You'll find Troy honors Xenia, the custom of gracious hospitality, like nowhere else on earth. A fine chamber must be found for your comfort."

The king took notice of the two women who'd followed his son and Helen into the courtyard. The tiny one was as beautifully dressed as Helen in a colorful tiered skirt and elegant bolero, while the young girl was more simply clothed. "Quarters will be found for your servants as well."

"I'm Aethra, mother of the Theseus, King of Athens, and no servant," she proclaimed with a forceful stamp of her foot. "This young lady is my maid, not Helen's."

Priam smiled at her spirited announcement, while Hektor rolled his eyes. "Alexandros has made an enemy of Athens as well? He should never have been allowed to leave the palace."

Helen's voice was sweet, so soft others had to lean forward to hear. "My lord, Aethra has been with me for years. She is a dear companion and could not be left behind."

Having only just heard of her son's return, Hecuba rushed out to greet them. She swept Helen with as astonished glance and reached out to take her hands. "You do possess a goddess's loveliness, my dear. Welcome to the house of Troy."

Hektor gazed up at the endless sky, and nearly choked on a rude snort.

* * *

On Mount Olympus, Hera lay back on her couch and smoothed her long gown over her thighs. "This is almost too easy."

Athena had polished her helmet until her reflection shone in the bronze. "You mustn't become complacent," she warned. "Aphrodite will protect her beloved Paris and the Trojans, and Apollo will as well."

"Poseidon will join with us to take the Greek's side," Hera reminded her, "even if Zeus has stubbornly insisted he'll remain neutral."

"Helen is his daughter. Will he stay neutral if the war goes against Troy?"

Hera shrugged. "I've never seen him equivocate. He may protect Helen from harm, it's true, but that doesn't mean he'll safeguard all of Troy. Although he has said of all the cities on the Earth, he honors Troy the most."

"I've heard him say it," Athena sighed unhappily. She pulled her crested helmet down over her black curls, and her gray eyes sparkled with glee. "I love the courage mortals show in war and how gloriously red they bleed."

"I prefer to observe the mayhem from afar where the air isn't filled with the overwhelming scent of their death."

"It's my favorite aroma," Athena responded and strode away with a warrior goddess's long stride. The snakes depicted on the bronze Aegis covering her breast were the locks of the dreaded Medusa, whose look caused a swift and terrible death. As she moved, the serpents appeared to writhe with life, a sight that would leave any mortal spellbound.

* * *

The welcome feast lasted long into the night, and Helen had ample time to take in the magnificence of the megaron of Troy. Its columns were of polished stone, not the cypress wood of Sparta, and their smooth rounded capitals were coated with gold and reflected the flames in the torches lighting the huge room.

She did her best to return Hecuba's gracious, affectionate enthusiasm. Although her own clothing was very fine, her attire had never been of great interest to her. She smiled as Hecuba declared she must have the finest apparel Troy could provide, but she'd be happy with what she'd brought with her until new garments could be made.

Hektor's wife, Andromache, sat to her left and while she added little to the evening's conversation, Helen regarded her as pleasant enough. Hektor's black tunic was decorated with a wave-patterned trim and was as dark as his countenance. She hadn't missed the hatred lighting his gaze. She hoped to improve his mood by befriending Andromache. "Do you like playing games?" she asked her.

Andromache blushed. "I do, but I'm not very good at any of them."

Helen described the Egyptian Hounds and Jackals, and while several of the women seated with them had heard of the game, few had played. "I'll teach you all," Helen offered. "I've brought a gorgeous game set with pieces made of ebony and ivory with gold and silver collars. It's a pleasant way to pass the afternoon, and I hope you'll love it."

Aethra had left the celebration earlier in the evening, and when Helen could no longer remain awake, she also asked to be excused. Andromache walked with her to her bedchamber. "I do hope we can become friends, even if our husbands aren't fond of each other," Helen said, mindful of her great understatement.

"You know of the curse?" Andromache whispered. She sent an anxious glance over her shoulder and looked relieved they were alone in the corridor.

"Paris mentioned it in passing, but not the details, are they gruesome?"

"We've been told to call him Alexandros, his true birth name." Andromache followed Helen into her bedchamber. The spacious room had a balcony overlooking the sea and was as comfortably furnished as her own room. "I've just heard parts of the story. You must ask his sister, Cassandra. She and their brother, Helenus, gave dire prophesies the day he was born. I'd never even heard of Alexandros until he appeared at the games and was recognized as one of King Priam's sons. Anyone who knew of his birth thought him long dead."

"Fortunately, he is very much alive." Helen stepped out on the balcony. She loved being able to look out at the sea as they had in Egypt. Moonlight brightened the water, and the view seemed to stretch to the ends of the Earth. To the east, she saw the swan-like sail of a white ship as it entered the Hellaspont, the famed sea passageway to the Black Sea.

She turned to smile at Andromache. "It will take me awhile to meet everyone, but I'll look for Cassandra tomorrow."

Andromache took a step toward the door. "She keeps to herself, and you probably shouldn't tell Alexandros you want to speak with her. Some things are better left unsaid. Good-night."

Helen thought their conversation curious indeed, and she wasn't certain whether she'd just been warned against speaking to Cassandra, or to Paris. She had long kept her own counsel and wasn't even tempted to confide in Paris until she'd learned all she could about the curse hovering over him. He didn't seem concerned about it, but he was the daring sort rather than an introspective man who'd brood over his fate. He had been acknowledged as a prince of a fabulous city, and everything had been going his way. He'd taken her for a wife, and they'd been welcomed upon his return to Troy. Clearly if there had once been a curse, it hadn't touched him.

Paris hadn't kept count of the kantharos of wine passed his way, but he feared he'd taken too many long swallows. He found Helen's chamber, but stumbled through the doorway. "I beg your forgiveness," he murmured. "I shouldn't have celebrated my own homecoming with such enthusiasm."

"Come and lie down beside me," Helen invited, but he fell across the end of her beautiful ivory inlaid bed still clothed. She laughed and left him where he lay. Her first day in his home had been a full one. Troy was as magnificent a place as he'd promised, and she doubted she'd ever tire of living there, or being with him. She craved his tender touch, and she intended to make him happy all of his days. She brushed her fingers through his hair, whispered a good night, and left him to enjoy his wine-laced dreams.

* * *

Helen woke early the next morning. Paris hadn't moved during the night, and he slept so soundly, she dressed and left her chamber without waking him. She made a mental note of the frescoes decorating the corridor so she could return to her own chamber rather than wander aimlessly. Troy was known for its horsemen, and many a fresco featured a rearing stallion, or a magnificent herd running wild. She stopped the first maidservant coming her way.

"Would you please show me to Cassandra's bedchamber?" she asked.

The girl took a quick backwards step. "You wish to see her?"

"Yes, why not? Is she ill?"

"No, although some might say so," she stuttered, clearly unsure how to respond. "Come this way, my lady." She looked down the corridor the way Helen had come.

Helen reached for her arm. "Wait. First tell me what I might find."

The girl shook her head. "One never knows. Maybe you should wait for her to find you."

"She wasn't introduced at the celebration last night. Does she prefer her own company?"

"I've already said too much."

The girl looked too frightened to say more, and Helen had to be content to be shown to Cassandra's door without learning why. She knocked lightly, but there was no response. "Princess Cassandra, it's Helen. Do you have time to see me?"

After a long moment, the door opened only a crack, and Cassandra peered out with a dark, piercing gaze. Her black hair flew about her head in wild disarray, and her sleep gown fell off one shoulder to expose a thin, bony arm.

She looked older than Helen had expected Paris's sister to be. She smiled anyway. "I'm Helen, Alexandros's wife. Have I come too early?" she asked.

Cassandra slammed the door shut without speaking. Startled, Helen knocked again. "May I bring you something to eat or drink? It's going to be such a lovely day, and I thought you might show me around the palace."

Cassandra failed to respond and left Helen feeling uneasy. She started back to her own room, and met Hecuba on the way. "I fear I'm awake too early."

"I'm up with the dawn as well. Come into my chamber and join me for something to eat. My maid always brings more date cakes than I can possibly enjoy."

Helen followed her new mother-in-law into her bedchamber. It was easily twice the size of the room she'd been given, and decorated with gorgeous frescos of dolphins swimming in a rippling sea. They were so superbly painted, the playful creatures appeared real.

Out on the columned balcony, a maidservant set up folding chairs and a small tripod table for a tray of figs, pears and little cakes. Just as Paris had promised, she'd found Troy to be a dazzling place, and sacred Mt. Ida could be seen in the far distance exerting a silent blessing.

Once seated, Helen tasted one of the cakes. "These are so good. Thank you."

"Some should already have been sent to your room. I didn't expect you'd be roaming about yet, but since you are, we can talk together as we couldn't last night."

Helen brushed cake crumbs from her skirt and reached for a slice of pear. "I love your son. Is there anything more you need to know?"

Hecuba smiled and shook her head. "I suppose not, but I hope you'll be patient with those who are slow to offer their affections. Everyone is comfortably set in their place here, and I'm afraid my love for Alexandros has made some feel set aside."

"I understand." Hektor had looked ready to spit venom when she'd been introduced, and it appeared a great deal more than time would be required in his case. "I did learn some names yesterday, and hope I won't confuse them while I learn the rest. A gift of your patience will be greatly appreciated."

"You'll have it." Hecuba tilted her head to study her newest daughter-in-law more closely. "There's a highly polished bronze mirror in the bedchamber you were given. Haven't you looked in it?"

Surprised by the odd question, Helen shrugged. "Only to comb my hair and straighten my clothes. No one has ever accused me of being vain."

"You are remarkably unaffected by your exceptional beauty, but others, like my husband, are simply dazzled by you. You have an other-worldly glow, as a goddess would have walking among us."

Embarrassed, Helen discounted the compliment. "Perhaps it's only the sunlight reflected off your beautiful shining sea. Troy is such a magnificent place, and I'll love living here. How might I help you today?"

"Your company is all I ask. Alexandros should show you around the palace so you'll be able to find your way without becoming lost. It's a bit of a labyrinth I'm afraid. Tomorrow, or perhaps the next day, I'll have my seamstresses show you some of our fine fabrics. Please don't regard me as presumptuous, but my daughters and sons' wives love adding to their wardrobes. No woman ever has too many pretty clothes."

Helen would rather have discussed horses, but clearly Hecuba regarded new fashions as a must. "Thank you. I'd love to have something new."

The conversation flowed so easily between them, Helen dared ask the question that demanded an answer. "I've heard Cassandra's name, but she wasn't with the women last night. Is she ill?"

Hecuba pursed her mouth and looked away. "Apollo gave her and her brother, Helenus, the gift of prophecy. She offended the god somehow, and now drifts in her own world of imagined catastrophes. Some of our family has been unkind to her, but if you seek her out, you'll find her to be a fragile soul who doesn't deserve ridicule. I can already see you're too genteel a woman to stoop so low."

"Of course not." They spoke a while longer, and when excused, Helen returned to her room. She found a tray with date cakes and fresh pears on a small table by the door, so a servant had come in, but Paris hadn't wakened. She sat down beside him and leaned over to kiss his cheek. He opened one eye and quickly closed it.

"Is this what I can expect from you each morn?" she asked. "I'd hoped to go riding. Is it too late to visit the parents who raised you?"

He rolled over on his back and covered a wide yawn with both hands before looking up at her. "First, I need to find a fine horse for you, so tomorrow would be better, or the next day." He reached for her hand and laced her fingers in his.

She squeezed his hand. "If we stay here, will you show me around the palace so I don't become too easily lost? Can we do at least that much today?"

He kissed her fingertips and rolled off the end of the intricately inlaid bed. He stood and stretched his arms above his head. "I need to bathe, dress in clean clothes, and then we'll see every chamber of the palace if you'd like."

"Not everyone will invite us in," she replied.

"Most will," he assured her.

She took a slice of pear and went out on the balcony to wait for him. Troy fascinated her, and she studied the way the city spread out around the hill with trails leading down to the surrounding wall. More people than she'd ever met lived behind the massive walls, but the great main entrance, the Scaean Gate, stood open and men and women walked in and out freely.

In the distance, across the Trojan Plain, she could see fishermen with boats in the water, royal ships like the one that had brought them there, sturdy merchant ships, and what had to be warships aligned on the beach beyond. Clearly the Trojans loved to sail far and wide to trade. The view along the shore constantly shifted, but as entertaining as it was, she was anxious to ride and see the surrounding countryside.

When Paris returned still shaking drops of water from his hair, she relaxed against him and folded her hands over his. "Your mother warned me not everyone would be glad we're here."

"I can't deny it, but how did she expect you to respond?" He nibbled her ear to make her giggle.

"I don't know. Maybe she didn't want me to be hurt if some of your family are rude."

He turned her in his arms. "If anyone is rude to you, I'll make them very sorry."

His brows dipped in a stern line, and while she'd seldom seen him scowl, it made him look quite menacing. "I don't want to create conflict here. I'd rather find a comfortable place within your family. Being a guest in Troy is very different from being queen in my own land."

He kept her tightly wrapped in his arms. "I'm very new here too, but surely Troy will prove to be a fine home for us both. Now come with me, and I'll show you all I know about this wonderful palace."

This was the life she'd chosen, and she nearly danced along by his side as they made their way down the colorful corridor.

Hektor made his preferences clear. "You are to avoid the Spartan whore. Turn your back on her whenever possible. It's a disgrace to Troy to harbor her here."

Disappointed, Andromache frowned but reluctantly nodded. He'd been the first to mention Helen's name that morning, but she couldn't understand the fury of his anger. "Perhaps it's belief in the curse that will make it come true."

"No, it's the fact the curse was ignored that will take us to the brink of a terrible war. It makes me ill to look at Alexandros, and all I see of Helen, may all the gods damn her, is a misty golden blur."

She let him go without arguing, but he'd never know what took place in the women's quarters. She'd been drawn to Helen, whom she found kind and engaging, and wanted her for a friend. Even if Hektor couldn't see past the Spartan queen's radiant beauty, she'd found her to be warm and friendly and wouldn't respond by being haughty and aloof. Hecuba had welcomed her, and she'd follow her mother-in-law's example and let her husband believe whatever he chose. Surely no harm could come from that.

* * *

The citadel had its own surrounding defensive wall, and as Paris and Helen walked along behind it, she noticed something sparkling on the path. "Look at this." She picked up a red stone and turned it in her hand. "How pretty this is. It's both smooth and shiny. I wonder if someone's lost it from a piece of jewelry."

He took it and rolled it between his palms. "Ask my mother. She'll recognize it if it belongs to someone."

It slipped from his hand as he returned it to Helen and although she tried to catch it, it fell upon a rock. When she picked it up, it left a spot of blood on her finger. "How strange this is. Stones don't bleed." She wiped it off, gave it a small scrape upon the citadel wall, and another drop of blood appeared.

Paris was equally astonished. "That can't truly be blood, it must just appear so. There must be some magic within the stone, but I don't sense any danger in it, do you?"

She wrapped it tightly in her fist, and no feeling of dread overcame her. "No, it has only a pleasing warmth."

He leaned down to kiss her. "If no one claims it, I'll have it made into a necklace for you. We'll call it your blood-stone necklace. It's a good omen from the gods showing they favor our love affair, and with a blood offering too," he laughed.

"It would be striking, but perhaps the stone is too delicate to wear."

"A gold setting will protect it." He took her hand, and they continued their walk, but the way the breeze tossed her curls was so enchanting, there was only one place he wished to go. He leaned down to whisper a beguiling invitation, and her enticing smile was the perfect reply. Every day he thanked Aphrodite for giving him such a passionate wife and thought himself the most blessed of men.

Cassandra darted around a corner when she saw Paris and Helen coming her way. It made her shake with terror to look at the deadly pair. She saw the black wings of death flapping above them, but her father saw only Helen's astonishing beauty. His guilt over condemning Paris to death had to weigh heavily upon him as well, and he saw only the young man's charm. Every day the ill-fated pair walked through Troy brought their beloved kingdom closer to its ultimate doom. Would no one believe her until the streets ran red with torrents of her people's blood?

CHAPTER 21

Mycenae
Palace of King Agamemnon

Agamemnon drew powerful allies to his cause with an inspiring reminder of the allegiance the men had sworn to Menelaus when they had courted Helen, and a promise of the great wealth of Troy and the oncoming trade with the Black Sea cities would bring. There would be the precious metals, gold and silver, tin and copper to make bronze, Chinese jade, cinnabar, and timber to build ships among many other wonderful items to trade, such as the gemstones lapis lazuli and garnets. He slanted each appeal with whatever the particular man craved, and as expected, greed alone brought the loyalty and commitment of troops and ships he'd sought.

Menelaus heard it all, but demanded one last try at diplomacy. "I'll take Odysseus, who is a wise counselor with me and sail to Troy. It's possible Helen has grown to regret leaving me and will choose to come home. If we fail, you'll have an even stronger argument for war than mere rampant greed. If we assault Troy, thousands of our good men will surely die."

"Not a ship of our army has set sail as yet," Agamemnon replied, "so there's time for you to conduct what is surely a fool's errand. But do you truly wish to risk bringing another bout of laughter to your name? You've lost Helen once, and for her to refuse you anew would severely damage what's left of your reputation."

"Pride means nothing to me without Helen." Menelaus clenched his fists at his sides. "Let others call me a cuckold, my only concern is my wife, my queen, and I intend to bring her home. Fight Troy for insulting Sparta in the first place if you need an excuse for war, but I want Helen safely home and in my bed where she belongs!"

Growing tired of their tedious argument, Agamemnon stroked his graying beard. "You are a king in your own right, so do as you please, but use your time in Troy to gain every insight you can possibly gather for our cause. Each gate is a weakness in their thick walls. Find others, my brother, and make our war work easier."

Menelaus tossed the last of his wine down his throat and strode away to find Odysseus and be on their way.

Menelaus fixed his eyes on the eastern horizon and said little to Odysseus on the voyage, but he was grateful for his company. By the time Troy came into view, he'd gone over what he wished to say a thousand times in his mind, but he'd decided to show strength with a brief demand rather than attempt to shame Alexandros into returning his wife.

"If Priam again claims Alexandros and Helen haven't returned, we'll leave without calling him a liar," he told Odysseus, "but it will mean war with Troy."

"Agamemnon has made everyone eager for it," Odysseus replied. "Look at how the palace gleams on the hilltop. Priam must already see us approaching and know why we've come, but I doubt he'll meet us on the shore."

"No, he'll wait in his grand megaron on his ivory and gold throne. I don't mean to fail at this, but we'll not risk our lives in a foolish display with our swords either."

"Agreed. Helen may be tired of Alexandros and long to return home with us."

Menelaus looked at him askance. "That's doubtful, but Priam won't be anxious for war, and he has to know it's coming if she's not returned to me."

Odysseus nodded. "Indeed, he must, my friend."

Paris found Helen playing Hounds and Jackals in Hecuba's megaron in the women's quarters. "I must speak with you," he took her hand and urged her to her feet. "Forgive this intrusion, Mother, but Helen must come with me."

"Come back if there's time," Hecuba responded, and the young women with her were amused by what they mistook for a call to passion.

Paris hurried Helen to her bedchamber and closed the door behind them. "Menelaus has arrived with Odysseus demanding that you be returned to him. I kept out of sight to avoid inciting his rage, but I never thought he'd come after you when Sparta would be so badly outnumbered in an attack on Troy."

Helen rushed onto her balcony to scan the harbor and saw a dozen Spartan ships with Sparta's emblem on the sail. "He's brought a few warriors, but not his whole army, so apparently he hasn't planned an assault." She looked over her shoulder. "Your father promised to send away anyone who came for me, but will he actually do so now that Menelaus has arrived?"

"He will," Paris assured her. "He was steadfast in the decision, and you have his protection. Menelaus will return to Sparta, thoroughly humiliated he even made the effort to come here, and we'll not hear from him ever again. Trust me."

She turned back to the sea. "He was my husband, and I don't want him humiliated in any way."

He rested his hands on her shoulders. "You did it yourself, my love, when you left him. He'll sail home on the evening tide, and we'll be done with him."

A chill ran up her spine and made her shiver. "I wish I believed you."

"Are you afraid?" he asked.

She could see it all so clearly now and nothing was going to be as easy as Paris had assumed. Menelaus would not bear shame well, and he'd find a way to make her and all of Troy pay.

Priam had become devoted to Helen and while he sympathized with Menelaus's despair, he refused to allow him to see her. "She's made her choice," he offered with a sad smile. "She is loved here and has my protection. Return to Sparta, lord king, and forget her. Make another beautiful woman your queen."

Menelaus was so angry he could barely see. He knew the hellish war Agamemnon would soon unleash on Troy, and that gave him an advantage Priam didn't even suspect. He raised his voice, "Helen is rightfully mine, and if beautiful women are in such great supply, then it is Alexandros who should look for another wife. Is he not man enough to face me himself?" He stood with Odysseus beside him, as though anchored in place, and silently dared Priam to move him.

"Even knowing the reason for your visit, I've welcomed you," Priam began, with a weary shake of his head. "I've made the decision to protect Helen, and I'll be the only one you'll see. I assume you'd rather return to your ship than dine with us this evening." He gestured for the armed guards who had escorted the Spartans into the megaron and they came forward to show them the way out.

Odysseus laid his hand on Menelaus's back to steady him, and badly outnumbered, they left without drawing their swords for a fight. Menelaus looked over his shoulder and regarded them all with a deadly glance more threatening than his angry words.

Late that night, Helen lay awake in Paris's arms. She'd remained on her balcony and had watched Menelaus and Odysseus leave. What courage it must have taken him to stride into the palace when Priam could have so easily ordered his death. Odysseys's skill with a sword was well known, but he'd not have been able to protect himself or Menelaus while the palace guard surrounded them.

Until she'd seen Menelaus walk away, she'd not considered the danger he'd faced in coming for her. His posture had remained proud, but she knew his heart must be broken. His red hair glowed in the sun and for a moment she longed for him to turn so she could gaze upon his face a final time. He didn't glance back to look for her, however, and the chance was lost.

She'd left the sadness surrounding her at Sparta, but every time she saw a little child in the palace, memories of her daughter brought a painful ache to her heart. A tear rolled down her cheek. She'd chosen Paris and Troy after all, and this is where she'd live out her life.

Agamemnon was not surprised by Menelaus's failure to bring his wife home, and he quickly set about gathering his huge fleet at Aulis. Each king summoned commanded many ships, crewed by warriors eager to fight for gold and glory. Every day more ships sailed into view to rousing cheers, but when all those expected had arrived, the wind abruptly ceased and the fleet remained stranded where they were anchored. Tempers flared, arguments rose at the slightest provocation, and Agamemnon feared the attack on Troy might never take place. Each day he became more frustrated to the point he could bear no more.

Calchas, a priest and seer of great renown, came to Agamemnon with a slow, shuffling step. "My king, a Greek warrior has killed a deer in Artemis's sanctuary, and then dared to brag his hunting skills surpass those of the gods. The goddess of the hunt is so greatly offended she's holding back the wind to punish us all, and stalled the fleet here at Aulis."

"Then we must move swiftly to make a sacrifice to Artemis to ease her rage," Agamemnon responded. "Finally! Something that can be done."

Calchas's gray hair was thinning, and he looked up at Agamemnon with clouded blue eyes. "Only a pure blood sacrifice will appease Artemis," he warned. "You must sacrifice your daughter, Iphigenia, for nothing else will satisfy the goddess."

"But Iphigenia is blameless." Agamemnon staggered back, but caught himself before he fell. "She's a beautiful child who deserves to live a long and blissful life."

The seer shrugged. "The purity of her blood is what Artemis demands, none other will do. Without her sacrifice, there will be no voyage to Troy."

Agamemnon collapsed upon the ground and wept. Night had fallen before he had accepted the awful reality of what he had to do. He called for Odysseus. "Go to my palace and bring Iphigenia to me. Don't allow Clytemnestra to become suspicious. Tell her our daughter is to wed Achilles and to bring her finest clothes."

Puzzled, Odysseus asked for more. "Does Achilles know he's to be wed?"

"There's no need to trouble him. Calchas says I must sacrifice Iphigenia so that Artemis will release the winds, but I don't want her to dread her death. Let her come to Aulis for the happiest of occasions, and she'll die a quick, and I pray a painless death."

Odysseus stared at the troubled king, shocked and heartsick at his request. "Are you certain this is what must be done?"

Agamemnon nodded. "It makes me ill to even think of it, but it must be so."

"Perhaps the wind will be blowing a gale by the

time I return with her, and she'll live to reach old age."

"I pray to all the gods it will be so."

Iphigenia was a slender girl; her blonde hair was nearly white, her skin pale, and her eyes a lovely sky blue. When Odysseus looked at her, he saw only a reflection of Clytemnestra's fair prettiness and not a bit of Agamemnon's sly darkness in her. "Your father has arranged your wedding to Achilles, our greatest warrior, child, and we must hurry to Aulis for the celebration before the fleet sails for Troy."

Clytemnestra took her daughter's hand. "Are there to be no other suitors, or games to decide who'll win her hand?" she asked.

Odysseus responded with a disarming smile. "On the eve of war, we can't stop for games."

"Is Achilles handsome?" Iphigenia inquired, her gaze open and trusting.

"He's a fine looking young man," her mother replied, "but you're too young to wed, especially with a war coming that might soon leave you a widow."

"Achilles is too fine a warrior to be easily injured, but come with me now and discuss your concerns with your husband when we arrive. Bring your prettiest clothing, Iphigenia. You're a beautiful girl and will make a lovely bride."

Clytemnestra thought the whole matter strange. "I'll not waste my breath arguing with you when Agamemnon is the one who's decided this. I'm sure you can promise us a wild chariot ride."

"Indeed I can, my lady."

* * *

As soon as Iphigenia and her mother arrived, Agamemnon hugged his daughter to his chest and rubbed her back. "I love you so, Iphigenia." He took a step back, and her sweet smile made what had to be done all the more excruciating. "We must go to Artemis's temple, and we'll discuss the wedding later. Wait for us here, Clytemnestra." He nodded to Odysseus to enforce his request.

Clytemnestra meant to follow. "If you are in such a rush to make the match with Achilles, why should I wait here?"

"Do not argue, my dear." Agamemnon took Iphigenia's hand and started off at such a brisk pace she had to run along beside him.

"Something's wrong," Clytemnestra cried, but before she could follow her husband and daughter, Odysseus grabbed her from behind in a forceful hold and lifted her off the ground.

"Don't frighten the child," he whispered in her ear. "She must be sacrificed for Artemis to release the wind so that we may sail for Troy." When that horror hit Clytemnestra, her anguished howl came from the bottom of her soul, and he clapped his hand over her mouth to silence the awful sound.

"It will be quick, and she'll not suffer," he promised, but she fought and kicked and struggled to break free. Too strong to be overpowered, he understood the depth of her sorrow and tightened his hold to keep her pressed close to his heart.

As they reached the temple, Iphigenia saw several of her father's warriors gathered at the entrance, but no handsome young stranger. "Where is Achilles?" she whispered.

Agamemnon pulled her around to face him. "I love you with all my heart, but a sacrifice must be made. Do not hate me for this."

The pretty girl didn't understand her fate until three of the men came forward to catch her and laced her hands tightly behind her back. Horrified, she screamed for her father, prompting the men to tie a gag over her mouth. Shocked and betrayed, she pled with her eyes, for surely she was not meant to be the sacrifice. When carried into the temple and lifted upon the altar, she struggled to break free, but a man grasped her ankles to hold her down. The priest raised his sacred knife above her throat.

Before the blade stuck its mark, the temple blazed with an otherworldly light, and Iphigenia vanished in a cloud of golden smoke. The men were blinded by the bright flash and knocked off their feet by its power. They sat up slowly and rubbed their eyes, and tried to speak, but a dull roar rang in their ears and made it impossible to understand one another. The priest leaned against the bare altar for support. When he regained his sight and could hear, he waved the rope that had bound Iphigenia's wrists, and the cloth gag.

"Artemis took her!" he exclaimed. "I saw her golden bow slung across her back as she gathered Iphigenia into her arms. Surely the goddess has taken the girl to Mt. Olympus, and they were transported in that flash of light."

Agamemnon sat where he'd fallen. There was no blood on the altar, or the priest's knife, and no sign of his lovely daughter. He stared at his warriors, all of them shaken and dumbfounded. When one helped him to his feet, his legs barely held his weight. "What am I going to tell her mother?" he mumbled to himself.

The priest was ecstatic to have seen Artemis, but as he questioned the other men, he found he was the only one who'd glimpsed more than the glaring light. The temple had been rocked to its foundation, and dust filled the air. "I have seen the goddess," the priest kept repeating. "I've seen Artemis in all her glory."

Agamemnon rested until his strength returned, and he could walk without weaving like a drunken fool. As he approached his tent, he heard Odysseus speaking in a low soothing voice, doing what he could to calm Clytemnestra, but it was a chore better left to him. He ducked to enter his makeshift dwelling.

"Let her go," he ordered.

Odysseus raised a brow, but still astonished by what he'd seen, Agamemnon hurried to explain, "We entered the temple, and Artemis flew down from Mt. Olympus and swept away with Iphigenia. There was no sacrifice."

Enraged, Clytemnestra brushed off Odysseus's hands. "Liar! You've killed her! How can chasing a whore to Troy mean more to you than our own dear daughter's life? Helen should be damned and forgotten!" she screamed.

She wheeled to face Odysseus before he could slip away. Her voice was choked with tears. "You told us a monstrous lie to bring us here willingly. Does Achilles know how badly you've used his name?"

Agamemnon gestured for Odysseus to leave at once. "Don't blame him for my lie," he chided. "I wanted Iphigenia's last day to be a happy one. Now she'll dwell on Mt. Olympus with the gods. We could not have wished a better fate for her."

As soon as Odysseus had left them, Clytemnestra struck her husband with a fierce backhanded blow. "Another preposterous lie! You killed my baby, and I'll despise you forever, even after your death! May everyone you've gathered for this insane venture drown on the way to Troy!"

Agamemnon tried to catch her, but she ran from the tent, called to a warrior to bring her chariot and left the camp with her team at a full gallop. In an afternoon he'd lost both his daughter and wife, but he suddenly saw a leaf blowing in the air and caught it. Elated that Artemis had released the wind, he threw out his arms to feel it rush against his bare chest, and set his mind to war.

CHAPTER 22

Mount Olympus

Artemis flew through billowing clouds astride a swift Pegasus with Iphigenia clutched tightly in her arms. The winged steed landed lightly on a marble terrace framed by majestic solid golden columns. The goddess dismounted and set her charge down gently. She knelt in front of Iphigenia, and wiped away the girl's tears on the hem of her short tunic.

A leather cord kept Artemis's tight, black curls out of her eyes, and they bounced upon her shoulders as she spoke. "What a terrible fright you've had, but you're safe here with me."

Aphrodite approached with a hesitant step. "Have you begun hunting for mortals, Artemis?"

Iphigenia responded with a long, pitiful wail. She clutched Artemis's hand and gasped between broken-hearted sobs.

"This is truly a pathetic sight," Aphrodite mused as she circled them. "Perhaps you should send her back."

"Certainly not, fools wished to sacrifice her in my temple, but I've no thirst for an innocent's blood. She'll have a happy life here with the nymphs. Now please stop crying, dear child. Your day may have begun badly, but your life will be blissful ever after in this divine abode of the gods."

Iphigenia blinked away her tears and gazed up at Aphrodite. The beautiful goddess's long blonde curls were crowned with a wreath of roses and their heady perfume lightened her fears. "I have always loved you," Iphigenia whispered.

Aphrodite offered her hand to pull Iphigenia to her feet. "Of course you have, my child, and you must love Artemis even more. Now come with us, and we'll find the lovely nymphs and make a new home for you."

The goddesses had such a sweet smiles and light touches, Iphigenia danced away with them joyfully and never gave her Earthy home and family another thought.

Ares and Apollo blew away the clouds surrounding Mt. Olympus to observe the immense Greek fleet sail from Aulis on their voyage to Troy. "Have you ever seen so many ships united for a cause?" Apollo asked.

"Never, and it will make the coming war all the more exciting," Ares responded. He stood slightly taller than Apollo, with a lean, muscular build. His hair was a rich dark brown. He rubbed his hands together in glee, and his smoky gray eyes lit with a dangerous gleam. "I'll defend Troy so they won't be so painfully outnumbered. What's your choice?"

"I'm willing to take Troy's side as well," Apollo

agreed with a jovial shrug. "Aphrodite and Artemis should be with us."

Athena overheard them plotting and laughed as she approached them. "Hera and I will stand with the Greeks, as will Poseidon, so you'll never save Troy, my handsome ones."

"Would you care to place a bet," Apollo asked, a wicked grin gracing his full lips.

"You own nothing I'd care to win," Athena mocked. She knelt beside them to observe the fleet sailing northeast on the Aegean Sea. "With Agamemnon's wealth of powerful allies, Troy will quickly fall, whether you two like it or not."

It was now Ares turn to laugh. "No, my dark-haired beauty, mark my words, this war will last for many a year. When I get through with them, what's left of the Greek army will sail home on rafts made of rough wooden planks, all that will be left of their once mighty fleet."

Athena shook her head, tossing her helmet's plume in the air. "Months, years, what does it matter to us?" she scoffed, and she left to tell Hera how foolish Ares and Apollo had again proven themselves to be.

Paris and Helen rode toward his childhood home with the warriors Kastros and Orthis trailing at a respectful distance. Although Paris doubted any danger would befall them along the familiar route, a prince and his bride were always accompanied. "My first parents were very good to me. Please don't judge them by how little they own."

Helen swept a stray curl from her eyes. "Do you think so little of me? I can see what wonderful parents they are by how fine a young man you've become. I'll thank them for taking such good care of you. Or would it embarrass you?"

He nodded. "It will embarrass me terribly, but it will thrill them."

"Then I'll do so."

His mother heard them coming and peered out the door. Recognizing her son, she ran to greet him, but at the first sight of Helen, she halted and drew back. She brushed flour from her skirt and hid her work-worn hands behind her back.

Paris leaped from his horse and told the accompanying warriors to dismount and rest. He plucked his mother off her feet and gave her a lively turn before setting her down gently. "I've come home with my wife, Helen," he announced proudly. He handed his mother the basket they'd carried. "I've brought some treats from the city, superb wine, fine olive oil, and delicious little nut cakes."

Helen waited for him to grasp her waist and help her dismount. "I hope you like what we've brought, if there are other things you need, please tell us, and we'll bring them on our next visit."

Sotiria turned her attention to the contents of the basket rather than stare at her son's remarkably beautiful bride. "I didn't think you were ready to take a wife."

"Neither did I until I met Helen. Isn't she lovely?"

"Paris spoils me with compliments," Helen responded. "You've raised a wonderfully bright and thoughtful son."

His mother bobbed her head. "Your father is at the corral. Go and tell him you're here."

Paris circled the cottage at a swift jog, and Helen followed this second mother-in-law inside. She'd ridden by such small dwellings her whole life, but she'd never been invited inside one. The home was neatly kept. Windows let in the afternoon light and fresh air, but the aroma of garlic lingered. A table held jars of foodstuffs and utensils, a brazier was laid with wood for a fire, and sleeping pallets were rolled up against the far wall in readiness for the night. There were two crudely fashioned chairs, and when Paris's mother offered one, she sat down.

"Paris refers to you as Mother," Helen began. "I don't believe I've ever heard him say your name."

"It's Sotiria," she responded. She placed the basket on the table and unwrapped their gifts with a near reverent touch. "We've not seen Paris in many weeks."

"He's been traveling," Helen replied. When Paris returned with his father, she was relieved she'd not have to explain more, when their story was a scandal from beginning to end.

Agelaus crossed the threshold and upon seeing Helen, stopped as abruptly as Sotiria had. "We'd not heard of your betrothal, but good news is slow to reach us."

"We've brought wine to celebrate with you, and new cups."

"We have more than one clay kylix," Agelaus replied crossly.

That testy response surprised Paris, and he raised his hands in a helpless gesture. "I meant no insult. I was anxious for you to meet Helen. Should I have sent one of my warriors ahead to tell you that we were coming?"

Agelaus laughed at the thought, and Sotiria shot him a dark glance. "I'd rather not see the kings' warriors for any reason, so come and surprise us whenever you can."

Paris towered over Agelaus, and Helen wondered how he could have accepted the herder as his father. There was obvious love between them, but she couldn't imagine Paris being happy in such simple surroundings. They didn't remain long and had gotten away without being forced to relate how they'd met.

She raised her hand to her bare throat and missed the beautiful necklace Paris had made for her with the exquisite red stone she'd found. It was far too expensive a keepsake to wear while riding, or on a visit to a small village where no one would own such a treasure.

Even if news travelled slowly from the city to the countryside, by their next visit, Sotiria and Agelaus undoubtedly would have heard how she'd fled Sparta with their son. Clearly they would forgive Paris anything, and excuse him for being in love, but when she'd abandoned her family, would they be so generous with her? She sincerely doubted it.

Sotiria stood in the doorway and watched them ride away. She shivered and rubbed her arms. "What did you think of her?"

Agelaus stepped around her to return to the corral. "I fear I couldn't think at all. With such a lovely bride, we'll not see Paris often."

"Or maybe never again," she murmured under her breath. "It will break Oenone's heart when she learns Paris has wed another."

"He's now a prince. How could she have believed he'd come back for her?" Agelaus mused sadly. "She'll marry someone from the village and be happy enough."

"Maybe." She waited until the son she'd raised had vanished from sight, and unable to enter the cottage that now seemed much too small, she went out to her garden and yanked weeds from the ground with a fierce grasp.

Paris noted Helen's pensive frown and feared she'd not enjoyed their brief visit to his home. "They were surprised to see us. They'll be more hospitable the next time we're there."

"I thought they were lovely people," she countered. "It's simply difficult to imagine your growing up as a herdsman's son."

He took a moment to gather his thoughts. "I always felt, no knew, there had to be more, but I never expected how greatly my life would change. No man could have imagined someone as perfect as you."

She could think of many ways she might be described, but perfection wasn't among them. "I also sensed there was more to life than what I knew. Maybe we recognized that longing in each other."

He glanced over his shoulder and Kastros waved to him. "If we were alone, I'd take you under the trees beside the trail. You're a fire in my blood, Helen, and I'll never have enough of you."

"Nor I of you," she responded, but it seemed too simple a phrase. She'd always enjoyed poetry, and thought perhaps she'd compose some of her own.

When they reached the stable, there were no men waiting to see to their horses. "Where has everyone gone?" Helen asked.

Orthis dismounted to take her mare's reins. "We'll see to your horses, my lady."

"Thank you." She took Paris's hand as they made their way up the hillside to the palace. People were usually out conducting their daily business in the city, but that afternoon they were alone on the path. It wasn't until they had climbed high enough to see the sea that they found a crowd pushing and shoving for a better view of the shore.

Paris caught a glimpse of the dark warships on the horizon and took a firmer grip on Helen's hand. "Let's go on to the palace where everything will be easier to see." Fearing Menelaus must have gathered a vast army ready to fight, his heart thudded wildly in his chest. He didn't care what it cost him, but he would never let Helen go. He guided her up past saluting guards to the citadel, and found his whole family, along with their servants, standing against the crenellated wall watching the approaching fleet.

Helen raised her hand to shade her eyes, but until the leading ships were close enough to make out the markings on the sails, she merely dreaded, rather than knew they carried warriors from Sparta. Terrified, she grabbed Paris's arm and held on tightly. "I see my husband's ships, but there are so many others. Agamemnon must have brought all his Mycenaean allies, all the kings of Greece, but we couldn't have anticipated this, Paris. How could we have known?"

She'd just referred to her husband's ships, and he had to swallow hard rather than shake her to remind her that he was now her husband. He drew her into his arms. Hektor was standing nearby, regarding them with a hate-filled stare, and Paris knew a blistering condemnation was coming.

"Do you see what you've wrought?" Hektor shouted at them. "We'll fight the Greeks on the beach as soon as they land. Do you even own armor?"

"No, but I can use a sword," Paris called to him, feigning more confidence than he truly felt. He'd only practiced with Kastros and Orthis, but with ships stretching as far as the eye could see, there would be so many Greeks running ashore he'd be sure to hit a man with every hard swing of his blade.

Helen grabbed hold of his tunic. "You shouldn't be so eager to fight! The Greeks are battle-hardened warriors and should be feared."

He whispered in her ear, "I'm eager to protect you, beloved." Tears filled her eyes, and he took her hand to lead her into the palace. "You'll be safe here, everyone behind the divine walls will be. The Trojans also live for war. Hektor is our finest warrior, and he'll lead the fight. I'll follow his command, but stay well out of his way so he won't have a chance to strike me."

Helen wiped her eyes on the back of her hand. "He'd do it too, wouldn't he? I can't just sit here and hope you'll come back alive."

"Of course, you can, or stay with the other royal wives."

"What if they blame me?" she murmured under her breath. "Of course, they'll blame me."

"No, I'm the one Hektor condemns, and no one will dare harm you." He drew her close for a near-endless kiss. "Stay close to Priam. He's vowed to protect you. Menelaus should have believed him and remained in Sparta. He's the one who's brought war down on us, not you."

She shook her head. "No one believes that."

"I do," he insisted, and sprinted from her room.

Sickened by the coming tragedy, she lay down on her bed and broke into sobs. They'd hoped for a lifetime together, but they'd only been fools lost in sweet dreams. She cried herself to sleep, but a soft knock at her door awoke her. "Yes?" she called.

Andromache peered into her room. "Why are you weeping? The Trojans are very brave. They're magnificent warriors, who've made Troy proud, and after the Greeks suffer more deaths than they can count, they'll learn their folly and sail for home."

Helen pushed herself up, but felt dizzy, and lay down to rest her head on her outstretched arm. "The Greeks are skilled warriors as well. Too many will die today, and everyday until one side will admit defeat."

"They'll never drive us from Troy," Andromache exclaimed. She came close to sit down on the end of Helen's bed. "Our walls were built by gods, and they can't be breached. You must trust the gods to protect us."

Clearly, she shared Paris's confidence, but Helen knew the other side too well to believe the war wouldn't last until the last man fell dead from his wounds. "How can men play at war and give up their lives so easily?" she murmured.

"It's what they were born to do," Andromache responded. "Our son cried because he's too young to fight."

Helen thought of Hermione and was grateful to have given birth to a daughter. Her father had battled other kings for territory and whatever spoils of war he could bring home, among them women and slaves. She'd been too young to consider the cost in blood and pain, but none of those wars had involved the thousands of warriors she'd seen approaching today. They'd been mere skirmishes compared to what would surely befall Troy.

Agamemnon had seldom spoken to her, and he wouldn't have been moved to gather such an immense army merely to take her home. He had to want more. Perhaps he intended to rule Troy and the Troad, the land as far as the eye could see. Her brother-in-law was an ambitious man, and now that he'd reached the shores of Troy, she was stunned to think how far he might go.

Had she not fled Sparta with Paris, Agamemnon might never have turned his lust for power upon the people of Troy. She sat up slowly. "Is the city well-stocked with provisions?" she asked.

"Food is always plentiful here, and all our needs are met by the farmers and herdsmen in the surrounding villages. It isn't your place to worry over it anyway. While there is sure to be a dust cloud raised in all the confusion, don't you want to watch what's happening from the main tower?"

Helen closed her eyes and shuddered. "No, war isn't something I want to view, ever."

Andromache stood and smoothed out her tiered skirt. "Do as you please, but I want to watch my Hektor lead our warriors and send the greedy Greeks away in a sea of their own blood." She left as quietly as she had come and closed the door behind her.

Helen didn't respond to the young woman's vile comment, but the grisly scene was already painted in her mind, and she had no need to actually witness it. She'd played Hounds and Jackals with Andromache many afternoons, and they'd laughed and had such a pleasant time together. She doubted she'd ever again feel that carefree. She glanced toward the window where the shifting view of the sea had once fascinated her, but now the unfolding scene filled her with dread.

Achilles had sailed to Troy with fifty black ships manned by his famed Myrmidon warriors. A demi-god, he was the son of the sea nymph, Thetis, and Peleus, the great king of Thessaly. He'd tutored by the wise centaur Chiron on Mt. Pelion. Bright and eager to learn, he'd studied healing, music and mastered the skills of a fine hunter.

The fastest runner of his time, he'd earned the epithet: Swift-running Achilles. While he'd been too young to court Helen, he was old enough to join in this war. Golden haired and beyond handsome, as soon as his black ship had reached shore, he leaped to the sand, donned his armor, and ran to enter the fight.

The great red horsehair plume atop his four-horned bronze helmet swung with each blow of his sword. A fearless warrior, he delighted in every kill and eagerly sought the next Trojan foolish enough to face him. The battle lasted until sunset and men could no longer be recognized as being from one side or the other and they were forced to retire. He washed his sword in the sea, and found Agamemnon standing at a fire ring lit on the beach.

Agamemnon greeted him warmly. "Hail, Achilles, fortunately, the Trojans came out from behind their walls to fight us, and each day, fewer will live to return to the safety of their citadel. Troy will be ours before they realize it's lost."

Achilles glanced toward Menelaus, who appeared to be deep in thought. "Haven't we first come for Queen Helen?" he asked.

"Of course," Agamemnon agreed. "We've come for Helen, and everything else we can take."

Menelaus looked up with a rueful smile. "She is worth whatever it costs us, Achilles. You'll agree when you see her."

"I'll look forward to it," Achilles vowed, and strode back to his own men, the Myrmidons, who were as eager to fight as he for *kleos*, glory, everlasting fame.

Helen was still awake late that night when Paris entered her bedchamber. She sat up, and with only moonlight to illuminate her room, she could not see if he were well or if he had been injured. She slid off the bed to welcome him. "Are you all right?" she asked fretfully.

His wet hair dripped upon his shoulders. He picked her up and hugged her tight. "Fighting the Greeks was both horrible and exhilarating all at the same time. Orthis found armor for me that wasn't so heavy I couldn't move, and I waded into the fray with him by my side. When dusk came, none of the blood I washed off was mine, thank the gods. With the welcome we gave those Greeks today, many may seize the cover of darkness to sail away."

"If only they would all sail home," Helen cried and clung to him. "You were so certain Menelaus lacked the means or men to follow us, and we couldn't have been more wrong."

"Had I known, I would still have convinced you to come with me." He kissed her cheek and tasted salty tears.

She took a step back. "But had I anticipated this wretched warfare would be the cost, I never would have left Menelaus. Too many are dying on both sides because of us."

He drew in a deep breath and released it slowly before pulling her back into his arms. "I can't bear the sound of his name, and this is your home now. I'm speaking the truth, Helen. Don't doubt me. Once we'd met, I could never have left Sparta without you. What is done is done, so cease to worry over it. You're my wife, and that's all you need remember. The gods willed our union. Troy's walls are invincible, and we'll always be safe here."

Her anguish was too deep for his first tender kiss to touch her dark mood, but he kissed away her tears, and the soft curve of her breast, and his affectionate loving blurred her fears. He was a virile refuge, and for the night, she chose to glory only in being his wife.

Despite Helen's hopes, when the morning dawned, she saw the Greeks had failed to sail home during the night. Instead, they had set up a vast camp along the shore, fished, and began raiding inland for horses, cattle and any other food they could find to keep the thousands of warriors well fed. They spread over the Troad with relentless vigor, and each morning met the Trojans on the blood-soaked plain below their mighty walls.

"You must bring your parents from Mt. Ida into the city," Helen urged. "They have no way to defend themselves if Greek raiders want to take more than their cattle."

Paris paced her bedchamber. "I sent Kastros and a couple of other warriors to fetch them, but they were already gone. The cottage stood as we'd left it, and the village was deserted. Everyone must have fled inland rather than come to us. My father may have herded the cattle along with his neighbors', but I can only hope they've travelled well beyond the point the Greeks might follow."

"I doubt there is such a place." Helen seldom left her bedchamber, and she had no appetite for the meals Hecuba sent to her on trays, often decorated with a small vase of flowers. Paris would eat whatever he found when he came to her each night, without realizing she hadn't eaten her own meal earlier. She lived on watered wine and an occasional fig, and whiled away the time attempting to write poetry that unfortunately prompted near endless tears.

"We went on a hunt together, and you know I'm very good with a bow," she announced one morning. "I could stand in the tower with the archers and—"

Highly amused, he laughed at the thought. "The day Troy needs women to defend her will never come."

"There must be something I could do. Many men must be grievously wounded each day. Who tends them?"

He rested his hands on her shoulders. "There are healers adept with herbal remedies, but they are of little use to the dying. Don't concern yourself with them. Warriors expect to die each time they pick up their sword."

"Do you?" she asked, her eyes wide with fright.

"No, I expect to live forever with you." He kissed her with a tender passion and left her to face another troubled day alone.

Helen could take no more of her self-imposed isolation and tied her hair back with a golden cord. She donned her cloak and pulled the hood forward to shield her face. She'd learned her way around the palace and took care not to be seen as she made her way to the citadel wall where she'd have a clear view of the city below. She kept away from the others following the progress of the war. Noting tents on one of the first terraces behind the massive outer walls near the Scaean Gate, she thought it must be where the wounded had been taken.

The path was crowded with women and children, and with her head down, she slipped by unnoticed. She was nearly overcome by the smell of death before she reached the shelters. The men inside were dying, and she knew there had to be something she could do to alleviate their pain. A gray haired man in a bloodstained tunic appeared to be in charge, and she gathered her courage to approach him.

"What can I do to help?"

He cast her only a quick glance and failed to recognize her. "Bring water from the well if you wish. Many of these men will die of thirst before their wounds kill them. They will all bless you for your kindness, lady."

She'd never fetched water and swiftly found she couldn't lift a full amphora and had to bring water a half-jar at a time. Other women could carry an amphora on their heads with an ease that amazed her. They looked like slaves used to hard labor, but she had been raised to possess an entirely different set of skills, all useless here.

An older woman pushed her aside. "Take cups of water to men and stay out of our way."

Her hands shook as she filled the first cup, and the man at the end of the row closest to the opening of the shelter was so eager to drink he spilled more than he swallowed. "I'll bring more," she offered, and the next man and the next, begged for their share. Their wounds were bound with bloody bandages, and their faces were still smeared with the dirt where they'd fallen.

Once the men had slaked their thirst, she found a clean cloth to bathe their hands and faces. "Let me see your face," one painfully thin young man asked, his voice a husky whisper.

"I'd rather see yours," she countered and held his chin while she scrubbed away the last traces of bloody mud. "You must sleep to grow well."

He caught her hand. "Will you come back, fair lady?"

The scene was far worse than she'd imagined. She nodded, and he smiled as he closed his eyes. She went on to the next man, who proved to be little more than an overgrown boy. If these were Troy's finest warriors, then the city was sure to fall, and she'd be the first one thrown from the tower. With things so terrible here, the dire thought brought only a small spark of terror.

In the evening, Paris found Helen rinsing the hem of a skirt and scolded her for not calling a servant. "You needn't be doing a slave's work when there are so many eager to serve you, my love."

"I need something to do, and caring for my own clothing isn't a burden."

"Do you join the other royal wives during the day?" he asked.

She glanced over her shoulder. "I thought it best to avoid them."

"I didn't bring you here to live as a hermit. Now leave that and come out to the balcony with me. The stars are especially glorious tonight. It has to be a fine omen."

She dried her hands and went with him. He pointed out the constellation Orion, and three stars in the hunter's belt were unusually bright, but she'd seen too much misery that day to believe it might bode well. Sooner or later Paris would discover how she spent her days, but until he did, she'd not admit to tending the wounded. He would forbid it, of course, but she'd ignore him. She owed the wounded Trojan warriors all she could give and so much more. Her heart ached for them and for her young husband who saw only the glory of war rather than its tragic cost in lives.

CHAPTER 23

Achilles camp near Troy

Briseis was a princess of Lyrnessus, an ally of Troy, and when Achilles' warriors cut a deadly swath through the region, she became his prize of war. She was the only member of her family to survive the brutal attack, and after watching her husband die, she no longer cared where she was taken. She sat in Achilles' tent, head rested on her bent knees and wept until she could produce no more tears.

Achilles knelt beside her and stroked her tangled hair. It had once been styled in multiple braids, but now stuck out like handfuls of straw. "Look at me," he said in a soft invitation.

She turned her head, but her blue eyes were so swollen she could barely see. "Why did you let me live?" she asked.

"No warrior worthy of the name slays a beautiful woman," he answered with a sly smile. "Now drink this and rest until tomorrow." He held the kylix to her lips, but she took only a small sip of the watered wine. "Will you promise to remain here, or must I tie your hands?" he asked.

Too weary to run even if the tent burst into flame, she responded with a distracted nod.

He touched her tousled hair once more. "I'll leave the wine here where you can reach it easily. Rest, go to sleep if you can."

She heard him speaking outside the tent with a warrior who cast an enormous shadow, and hoped someone would soon kill them both. She rolled onto her side and closed her eyes. Although exhausted, the bloody visions of the day's horrors careened through her mind, and the screams of the dying echoed all around her.

Death had come upon them at a fierce gallop and ridden away drenched in blood. Her husband had fought bravely, but he and his warriors were no match for Achilles and his Myrmidons. Their beautiful palace had been overrun by the Greek savages, who had burned whatever they couldn't steal and carry away. She'd not even tried to hide, but she'd expected to die with the others, not survive as Achilles' whore.

She awoke late the next morning. A young man had brought her a freshly roasted fish, and the scent turned her stomach. "Take it away. I can't eat."

He sat down beside her. "I'll eat this one and bring you another later. I'm Patroclus, Achilles' comrade, and he asked me to look after you."

Her eyes were still so swollen she saw only a thin slice of him. She reached for the watered wine and took a sip. "Does he plan to share me?" she murmured.

"Of course not. Achilles is an honorable man, and he'll not mistreat you."

"He's a murdering thief," she countered, her voice hoarse with sorrow. "My presence here proves it."

Patroclus ignored the insult and continued eating his breakfast. "Young women always become spoils after a battle. That's the way of war, however distasteful it may seem to you today, you'll have a pleasant life with Achilles if you'll accept what your fate has become. You'll be honored too, for he is the greatest warrior in the world."

She turned away and closed her eyes. She heard him leave and was grateful to be left in miserable solitude. She hurt all over, and not merely from the rough way she'd been tossed upon a chariot and carried to Achilles' camp. Her sorrow ran so deep her spirit ached, and she thought she might die from grief alone.

Patroclus returned later in the day with an apple and cheese. He sliced the apple with his dagger and handed her a piece. "This is a remarkably delicious apple. You must give it a taste."

She took a bite, and as promised, it was moist and sweet. She licked the juice from her lips before it ran down her chin. Her mind a comforting blank, she couldn't recall the young man's name and didn't care. A piece of cheese tasted very good with the apple, and she chewed slowly.

"You appear to be feeling better," he said. "I'll have water brought to you so you can bathe, and it will improve your mood."

She looked down at her blood-smeared skirt. "My clothes are ruined, and I've nothing else to wear."

He rose and looked through the garments Achilles had brought to Troy. "This tunic will have to do, but I'll have the women, our slaves, find something suitable for you."

"Stolen from another woman widowed by your marauding?" She bit her lip before swearing she'd rather go nude, certain Achilles would quickly arrange it.

Patroclus went to fetch the promised water rather than argue, and she ate another piece of cheese. It brought the comforting taste of home, and knowing all she'd loved was lost, she wept again.

Achilles did not enter his tent for several days, and he found Briseis sitting right where he'd left her. "Briseis? Is that your name, girl?"

She nodded. Patroclus had loaned her his ivory comb, and she'd undone what was left of her braids and untangled the snarls. Her fair hair lacked any hint of curl and lay in a straight cape over her shoulders. Still clad in one of Achilles's tunics, she resembled an orphaned waif more than a grown woman.

"Have you been given enough to eat?" he asked.

She nodded and looked away.

"Patroclus enjoys your company, perhaps you'll soon be able to find a smile for me."

Appalled by the thought, she closed her eyes to shut out the sight of him. "You murdered my husband. How can you expect anything more than hatred?"

He dropped to his knees beside her and cupped her chin to force her to look at him. "Many men die in a war."

"The wrong ones," she hissed.

"Your husband fought well, but he was no match for me. You're fortunate I like a woman with spirit." He chuckled and released her. He stripped and bathed using water from a large clay basin and sorted through his clothing for a clean kilt.

Briseis looked away. He was a muscular, handsome man, with golden blond hair and blue-eyed, but evil from head to toe, and she had no use for him whatsoever. Outside the tent, she could hear men shouting to one another, laughing, as though needless death were a cause for celebration. When Achilles again knelt down beside her, she flinched at his touch. He leaned close to kiss her, but she felt nothing other than the unwanted pressure of his lips. He left without pressing for more, but she dreaded his return.

When it was Patroclus who next appeared carrying another roasted fish, she was so relieved she deigned to take a bite. It was a tasteless meal, but he ate the rest with undisguised gusto. A tall shadow crossed the front of the tent, the man who'd passed by before, and she feared a warrior of his size would take whatever he wanted without offering a single taste of apple or cheese.

Patroclus followed her gaze. "That's Ajax. After Achilles, he's our finest warrior. He's a head taller than the tallest of us, and carries a huge bronze shield none of us can even lift. You needn't be afraid of him. He knows that you belong to Achilles, and he'll not touch you."

"I belong to no one," she vowed darkly.

"Believe whatever you wish, it won't change the truth. A wise woman would seek the best future she could possibly create. If you treat Achilles well, he may take you home as his preferred concubine.

You'd be far happier than if he called you a slave and made you wash his laundry."

Too sad to care what became of her, Briseis looked down at her dusty sandals. She knew every fold in the tent, but wouldn't risk asking to go outside. Ajax might respect Achilles, but that didn't mean the camp wasn't full of men who'd expect him to generously share his prize of war until dawn.

"I hate you all," she murmured, her expression fierce.

"You'll grow to love us in time, everyone does," Patroclus predicted with a ready grin and left her to mull over what he considered to be excellent advice.

When Achilles returned, he took Briseis by the hand and lifted her to her feet. "Come look at the sea with me," he invited. When she proved to be unsteady on her feet, he slid his arm around her waist to guide her. He walked her through the camp to the shore. At his urging, she removed her sandals, and waded with him into the cool Aegean Sea. They stopped when it lapped at her knees.

He stepped behind her and wrapped his arms around her waist and hugged her. "The whole world lays beyond us. There's more than you can dream or imagine. We're on a mission of the gods, and you can share in our glory."

His voice was soft, but she wasn't fooled by the tenderness of his touch. He'd already taken everything she held dear, and if all he craved was the husk of a woman she'd become, then she would be his.

* * *

Agamemnon also took a female prize of war, Chryseis, a priestess of Apollo. She was a beauty with peach-toned skin, sparkling dark eyes, and hair as black as ebony. She refused to look at him or answer when he spoke to her. He had meant to be kind, but her indifference drove him past reason, and he raped her, repeatedly. She did not cry, moan, or beg him to stop, and disgusted he could not reach her, he picked up his sword and went to kill more Trojans with a particularly spiteful glee.

Sick with outrage and worry, Chryseis' father Chryses, a priest of Apollo, dared to venture into Agamemnon's vast seaside camp and beg for his daughter's return. He was ushered into Agamemnon's grand pavilion, but not allowed to see her, but the priest persevered. He was a tall man with long gray hair and a curly beard.

"You've come to pillage our land," Chryses began, leaning against his tall oak staff. "I will ease your task by paying a generous ransom for my daughter. She is a priestess of Apollo and was dragged from his temple. As a priestess, she should be respected as you would revere Apollo himself, and I beg for her honorable return."

Agamemnon took a deep drink of wine from his kantharos, but rudely did not offer Chryses any refreshment. "Chryseis is mine now rather than Apollo's maid, and I'll never set her free. Go home, old man, and forget you ever had a daughter."

Chryses tilted his head as he studied the Mycenaean king. "You're a brutal man, but I had hoped you'd possess some modicum of wisdom. I warn you each day Chryseis remains with you, Apollo's fury will burn brighter."

Unimpressed by his threat, Agamemnon turned his back on him. "Get out of my sight, old man, or I'll send you to Hades Halls with the sharp edge of my sword." Chryses's knees buckled at the thundered threat, but clinging to his staff, he left so silently Agamemnon had to glance over his shoulder to be certain he had gone. The high king laughed and his entourage joined in.

Chryses went to the seashore and with a heavy heart, raised his hands high and prayed for Apollo's intervention. "Chryseis has served you well, my lord. How much must I sacrifice to gain her freedom? Shoot your silver bow and punish these irreverent Greeks for this shameful blasphemy with your most dreadful plague." Tears rolled down his wrinkled cheeks. "Give me some sign that you hear my plea," he begged.

Apollo heard his faithful priest clearly. He had taken the Trojan's side in the war and had no affection for the Greeks. He swooped from Mt. Olympus like a shooting star and appeared in a blazing light. With a warm breath, whispered, "Trust me now, Chryses, and I will make everything right."

The god was gone in as blinding a flash as he'd arrived, only briefly blessing the nodding dolphins offshore with his presence. Chryses fell to his knees and praised him, and cried in his eagerness to see his daughter returned to the sacred temple site. Apollo rose to a thousand feet, drew his gleaming bow and shot glowing arrows downward from the ever-abundant supply of arrows in his golden quiver.

* * *

The following morning, twenty of Agamemnon's army could not rise from the ground where they'd slept. They burned with fevers and seizures shook them, countless other men stumbled and vomited, and before noon, hoards of them were dead. Some men lingered, coughing up blood and cursing their plight in hoarse rasps, but they were gone before dusk. Warriors lit funeral pyres to burn their bodies and the word *plague* was on every man's lips. Black smoke billowed over the Greek camp like a Titan's evil blanket.

During the night, a dozen more men began to choke and gag. Blood ran from their nostrils, fevers scorched their skin, and chills made their bones ache. They died struggling for breath, and their companions were so badly frightened, Agamemnon had to order men to add the bodies of the newly fallen to the still flaming pyres. Those chosen for the grisly task hurried about it and then ran into the sea to scrub away the foul stench of death.

All up and down the shore Greek warriors began to fall. Some were covered in huge weeping blisters, others vomited blood, and the deadly disease kept spreading while the symptoms became increasingly painful and bizarre. Men no longer lowered their voices to call the illness by its rightful name, and when Agamemnon's men were struck down more often than others, the troops began to blame him.

Unafraid to make the accusation out loud, Achilles gathered the Greek leaders and led them into Agamemnon's pavilion. The high king was seated on his camp throne, chewing a pork rib with obvious relish. Disgusted, Achilles drew himself up to his full height and spoke clearly, "The priestess you've taken for a mistress must be returned to Apollo, for surely his anger is causing this wretched plague. Send her away before we are all dead. Do it now."

Agamemnon met Achilles hostile gaze, and his expression contorted with a fierce fury. He glared at them all but found no sign of sympathy in any face. Squaring his shoulders, he shouted at Achilles, "If I must send her away, then you owe me another woman. Send Briseis to my tent, and Chryseis will be set free."

Infuriated by that insulting demand, Achilles reached for his sword, but the goddess Athena rushed to his side. She grabbed his long hair with a firm yank to stay his hand. Invisible to the others, she spoke convincingly, "You know who I am. Strike him now only with words, and a better chance for revenge will soon come. I promise, my dear Achilles."

No one moved while the goddess spoke, as though time had ceased to exist, and Achilles recognized the glory of the goddess and the wisdom of her words. He dropped his hand and everyone came back to life. "We have lost too many good men to this dreadful plague, and Apollo must be appeased to end it. I'll send Briseis to you only if nothing else will prompt you to do what's right, but first you must set Chryseis free. It will not be one without the other, but you've insulted my honor, Agamemnon, and I'll no longer follow you. You'll have to fight without me and my unmatched Myrmidon warriors. Believe me, you'll soon regret this day."

Before Agamemnon could respond, Achilles strode off toward his own camp, far from the deathly smell of the funeral pyres. Patroclus ran to catch up with him. "What are you going to tell her?" he asked.

Achilles responded with a filthy oath. "You expect me to give Briseis an excuse?"

His young friend shrugged. "I suppose it would be little comfort, but if it stops the plague, what does the fate of one woman matter?"

"Briseis matters to me," Achilles swore. "Go and make certain Agamemnon has freed Chryseis before you take her to his tent."

"You wish me to do it?" Patroclus's voice wavered.

"Yes, I'll not give Agamemnon the satisfaction of gloating over this vile bargain. Now go, and keep a watch on his pavilion before he dares to demand even more of us."

"As you wish." Patroclus waited as Achilles walked away, his head down, clearly so angry he could barely breathe. Agamemnon had to know he'd just made a worse enemy than the Trojan's Prince Hektor. Even if they ended the plague, Patroclus dared not think what calamity would next befall them.

He did as he'd been told, and waited in the shadows until he saw Odysseus escort Chryseis from Agamemnon's shelter on their way to Apollo's temple. He found Briseis alone in Achilles tent, and while he was uncertain what had occurred between them, she smiled as he entered, making his task all more difficult. "You must come with me," he stated firmly. "Gather whatever you have to bring with you."

She rose and searched his face for a meaning not in his words. "I have nothing. Where are we going?"

He'd grown fond of her, and had to cough to clear his throat. "Agamemnon has forced Achilles to give you up. It was not Achilles doing, so you mustn't blame him. Agamemnon is the commander-in-chief of our entire army. Achilles must comply with his commands."

Stunned, she gathered the sides of her tunic in her fists. "So he is sharing me after all."

"No," Patroclus exclaimed. "As I said, he was forced, but he'll no longer fight with Agamemnon. He's through with this evil war."

"Too late for my husband and our people," she remarked sadly. Achilles had been kind to her. She'd become less fearful around him, but her life had now taken another dreadful turn, and she braced herself for the worst. "I won't even ask what sort of man Agamemnon is, but thank you for the kindness you've shown me."

"You were never simply a conquest prize to me," he stressed. He raised the tent flap and she walked by him, her head held high, still a lovely princess even in a borrowed tunic.

The great Ajax strode through the Greek camp seeking Menelaus. He stood a head taller than all the other men and walked with a regal bearing. When he found Menelaus, he didn't hide his dismay. "Why didn't you try and reason with your brother? He's gained nothing by taking Briseis if we've lost Achilles, who not only fights well but also inspires all the troops. How can Agamemnon be such a fool?"

"He's never listened to me," Menelaus admitted with a hapless shrug. "I wanted only Helen, but he's after the riches of Troy. With that goal burning in his heart, nothing else has mattered. You should have argued with him."

Ajax swore a foul oath. "You know I vied for Helen, and I would have been a fine husband for her. I promised to come to your aid should anyone take her from you, and I'll fight by your side to win her back. But I've never liked your brother and he knows it. He wouldn't have listened to me. We should have anticipated how badly he'd react to Achilles' demand and been prepared for it. The fault is ours and doesn't rest on your shoulders alone. Still, you should have spoken the obvious: Achilles is worth more than a thousand pretty girls like Briseis."

"Yes, I should have," Menelaus reluctantly agreed. "The foul odor of the plague has made thinking too difficult." He sat in his tent looking out at the sea and longed for the days when Helen was by his side and life was filled with simple pleasures rather than the stench of this terrible war.

Once his temper cooled, Agamemnon realized what a grave error he'd made. He could not appear weak and approach Achilles, but he knew the young man was equally proud and would not return with his warriors without some consolations. But he was the high king, and he'd not grovel before anyone, let alone a man half his age. Achilles was an outstanding warrior, but he didn't know his place. There were others, mighty Ajax for one, who could battle with equal vigor.

When Patroclus brought Briseis to Agamemnon, he walked around the lovely girl, but felt not a flicker of lust. She was beautiful to be sure, but certainly was not worth his present trouble. When it occurred to him she might be useful in a later dealing with Achilles, he took her into a small shelter where he kept his personal supplies.

"Girl, you'll stay here and share my food, but do not cause me a bit of trouble because you'll find me a harsh man when I'm angry. Is that clear?" He turned to his guard. "Give her whatever she wants, but keep her here." The guard slammed his fist against his chest armor with a clang in salute and stiffened his stand.

Agamemnon's dark eyes held a threatening gleam, and his thick wavy beard only partly hid the downward curve of his mouth. "Be calm, young one, you're a prized piece in my grim game with Achilles and will come to no harm here if you behave." She nodded, and he left her to plan how he would attack Troy without the aid of Achilles and his men.

CHAPTER 24

Achilles shoved his own tent's guard out of the way and jogged down to the beach. Once on the shore, he shouted his mother's name to the sea. Thetis was a nymph, who dwelled in a splendid palace in the depths of the sea. She heard his first call, and swam to the surface attended by her sea servant girls, the Neriads. She waved her beautiful throng away, and emerged from the misty waves alone. She stepped lightly over the wet sand and came to stand beside him.

"I heard your cry, and it is always a joy to see you, my dear son. Do you have some need of me?"

He drew in a deep breath to steady himself, and related how greatly he'd been humiliated by Agamemnon and how fiercely he hated him. "He's the cause of the deadly plague decimating our numbers by taking a priestess of Apollo, and while he grudgingly agreed to return her, he demanded Briseis, my beautiful prize of war in her place to restore his lost status. I refuse to serve a tyrant, and

I won't fight beside him ever again in this wicked war."

She took his hand as they strolled along the shore and talked a long while. Rather than offer soothing advice, she took her son's side. "You should not have been treated so badly. Agamemnon is a fool, and he'll never conquer Troy without your help. You're the best of the Greek warriors, and you have no real rival in all the world. I'll go to Zeus and seek his intervention. He is very fond of you, and will be amenable to your cause, I'm sure."

Achilles kissed her cheek. Her skin was always warm, untouched by the chill of the sea. "I love you, Mother. You're the best of goddesses," he whispered.

She smiled and touched his fair hair. "I'm so proud of you, my great son. I'll speak with Zeus while you rest." She waited until he had returned to his tent to soar to Mt. Olympus. Zeus's palace circled the peak of the mountain, and she found him seated in the garden courtyard strumming a lyre. His nimbus, radiant beams of light, radiated from his glorious head.

"Thetis, how delightful to see you. Come and sit with me." He set the instrument aside to make room for her. "You appear troubled, my dear, has some misfortune befallen Achilles?"

"Indeed it has, my lord." She spoke quietly and blamed Agamemnon not only for violating a priestess who served Apollo, but also for retaliating against Achilles when he had urged him to do what was right. "He wants Briseis returned to him, of course, but more importantly, Agamemnon should show him the respect and honor he deserves as their finest warrior."

Zeus pulled his beard thoughtfully. "I'm growing weary of this war. Aphrodite and Apollo favor the men of Troy, while Hera and Athena are on the Greeks' side. I would prefer to remain neutral, although I've always loved the fair city of Troy, but I'm as angry as you are by the shameful way Achilles has been treated. Return home, and trust me to find a solution. Please don't wait until you have another perplexing problem to visit me, my lovely Thetis. I'll always be happy to see you here on Mount Olympus."

She kissed his cheek. "Thank you, Father Zeus. I knew you would help us." She dove through the clouds for the sea and entered the water in a clean slice without making a bit of a splash. Her Nerieds joined her, and they swam together to her palace in the ocean's depths.

Hera stepped out from the shadows, thoroughly displeased. "Thetis has come yet again asking for favors you're all too willing to grant. You always give in to a pretty face."

Zeus stood to pull his petulant wife into his arms. He smiled and said, "She is a pretty nymph, but you are a glorious beauty, my wife, and simply without peer."

Mollified for the moment, the goddess rested her head on his shoulder. "I overheard enough to learn Thetis expects you to help Achilles. I like the boy, he's both handsome and fearless."

"I like him too. Give me time to think, and I'll devise something clever."

She kissed his cheek before turning away. "You'll need to force Agamemnon to admit how much he needs Achilles and his warriors. It shouldn't be too difficult to prompt his thoughts in that direction."

"I hope not." Zeus returned to the marble bench and picked up his lyre. Perhaps he'd speak to Agamemnon in a dream. He turned the thought over in his mind, and considered it from every angle, until at last, it became perfection. If Agamemnon thought Troy would fall, he would send all his warriors into the battle, but at Zeus's bidding, the Trojan forces would overwhelm them. The costly battle would force Agamemnon to admit how greatly he needed Achilles, and Thetis and her son would be pleased. He laughed at his clever stratagem, and his exuberance resounded in violent thunder claps that made the Olympians shake.

Agamemnon awoke from a dream of battle so intense it had seemed real. He sat up and rubbed his eyes. Filled with an excited rush, he rose from his corded bed and had his heralds summon all the kings he had faced last night. They murmured their concern over the assembly, but Agamemnon quieted them with a broad sweeping gesture.

"I swear Zeus has spoken to me in a dream. He says we must attack today and Troy will surely fall. Go and make sacrifices to the gods, and we will surely triumph. Go, hurry! This is the day we will finally vanquish Troy!"

Ajax leaned down to whisper to Menelaus, "No more men have fallen ill in my camp. What about yours?"

"They are all well, as are all the other warriors assembled on the plain. Achilles was right to demand Agamemnon return Chryseis, but I did not hear Agamemnon praise his name."

"No, he appears to have forgotten the plague that cursed us with so many losses. We'll fight today, but Achilles will be sorely missed."

Menelaus nodded and went to gather his Spartan armor and weapons. He wanted the war over more than any other man present. Too anxious to eat, he tasted victory in every swallow of wine. His warriors felt his renewed sense of valor and vigor and followed him with glad shouts and up-thrusting spears.

As the Trojans prepared to battle, word spread that Achilles and his men had withdrawn from the Greek's forces and remained in their camp. They took heart, for without Achilles, the Greeks would be easily beaten, and sure of victory, Paris swung his sword in the air, eager to best them and send them home bloody with their losses. He swaggered into the battle ranks wearing his leopard skin cloak, and caught up in the thrill, he rushed ahead of the Trojan front line and shouted a challenge for a Greek champion to face him.

"All you Greeks, hear me. I'm Prince Paris of Troy. Send your bravest warrior, and we'll settle this war with a single combat. The winner shall have Helen and great treasures from the losing side."

Eager to accept, Menelaus leaped from his chariot and ran forward from the Greek ranks. "I'll fight you, Trojan," he yelled. "I'll cut down your shameless, thieving body and leave it for dogs to feast on! I swear it by Ares, the god of War."

Caught up in high spirits of the moment, Paris had offered his bold challenge without considering whom he might have to fight. Menelaus was clad in gleaming bronze armor, and his helmet was adorned with a white plume, but he was easily

recognizable by his red beard. Paris saw the fierce
hatred in the man's gaze as he rushed forward, as
eager as a lion on the hunt. Paris took a backwards
step and then another, his knees threatening to
buckle, but Hektor moved to block his way.

"You coward," Hektor whispered. "You had the
courage to steal his wife, but now you cringe and
can't face him man-to-man? Aphrodite may have
made you handsome, but of what use are fine looks
to you now? You must fight him or be the laughing
stock of all Troy."

His brother's bitter insults stung, and Paris
gripped the ivory handle of his bronze sword more
tightly. His first thought was of Helen and how
greatly he wished to make her proud of him. "I'm
grateful for whatever blessing Aphrodite my have
bestowed upon me, and I won't fault her for my
lack of courage. Have all the Trojan and Greek
warriors stand back and form an open circle for the
duel. Menelaus and I will fight for Helen and her
wealth. But first, we must all agree that whichever
man wins, it will be an end to this long war, and
there will be a sworn truce thereafter."

Hektor slapped his younger brother on the back.
"Muster whatever strength you possess and stand
tall. Troy's honor is at stake here." He stepped out
in the opening between the armies and waved his
spear with the royal pennant attached to catch the
Greek leader's attention.

Seeing Hektor striding toward him, Agamemnon
called to his archers to quiver their arrows. "Let the
man speak," he shouted.

Hektor possessed a booming voice that carried
well, "This challenge between Paris and Menelaus
should decide this war. Whoever wins the duel

takes Helen and will also take all her wealth. The rest of us will abide by a sworn pact of holy friendship and peace between our kingdoms."

Hektor's startling announcement was greeted with a hushed silence until Menelaus answered, his voice equally loud, "My quarrel with Paris has caused the deaths of too many brave men. I'll agree to fight him to the death, while the rest of us live in peace. Priam must seal this truce in blood. While we gather lambs to sacrifice, he must come down from his citadel to stand here on the plain with his son."

"We agree," Hektor shouted, and he sent two heralds to summon King Priam, and fetch the lambs. Agamemnon also sent a messenger to his ships for another lamb.

Eris, a goddess always eager to stir up strife, went to Helen disguised as one of Hektor's pretty sisters. "Come quickly, Helen, the war may soon be over, and you must see how it ends. Paris will duel Menelaus, and you'll be wife to whomever wins."

Badly frightened, Helen choked back tears. Her earliest memories were of Menelaus, for he'd courted her from the time she'd been a child. She had hurt him deeply by leaving Sparta for Troy, but her love for Paris had been all that had mattered to her then. The two men despised each other, and it was certain to be a furious and bloody fight, and the very last place she wished to be.

Aethra, Helen's long time companion, took her elbow. "You must go, child."

With the little woman leading the way, they soon reached the Scaean Gate. The white bearded venerated elders of Troy were seated high above them in the main tower. Their warrior years long over, they came each day to observe the battle playing out on the Scamander plain below. As Helen passed by, they were stunned by her beauty and sighed for their own lost youth.

"Is it any wonder the men of Troy and the Greeks have battled so long for such a woman?" one asked. "She resembles the radiant goddess Aphrodite."

Another leaned forward to whisper in awe, "Beauty, terrible beauty."

A more practical chief murmured, "She has caused far too much bloodshed and sorrow. Let her return to Sparta today."

Standing nearby, Priam called to her. "Come sit in front of me where you can see your kinsmen and your husband of long ago. I've never blamed you for this war, when surely it was the gods who brought this scourge to our shores."

Helen climbed to the tower and slipped into her place. "You have been so kind to me, my lord, but I regret the day I left Sparta with your son. The cost in blood has been far too high. It would have been far better for you all had I died."

"Hush, child, for the gods delight in playing with our fates, and we're only characters in their endless play." He surveyed the gathered armies. "I'm struck by the regal bearing of the man standing there. Is he a king?"

She followed his gaze. "Yes, that is Agamemnon, both a mighty king and adept with a spear. We were kinsmen once."

"Who is that man ramming his way through the ranks of warriors?"

"Odysseus from Ithaca. He's quick witted and not above treachery."

"Ah yes," Priam replied. "I remember him now. He came with Menelaus to ask for your return. I recall the depth of his voice. He was more eloquent than your Greek husband, but I would never have sent you back. Who is that tall man who towers over all the others?"

"Ajax. Menelaus often hosted him in his palace in Sparta. He has the size of a god and is a bulwark for the Greeks."

Heralds, breathless from running from the plain, reached Priam. "They are calling for you, sire, both your stallion breaking Trojans and the bronze-clad Greeks. They wish you to seal their oaths. Paris and Menelaus will fight with spears and Helen and her riches will go to the winner. The outcome of the duel will be an end to the war and bring a peaceful truce on both sides."

Priam leaned down to kiss Helen's cheek before summoning his chariot. She watched the dear man go and wondered if this would be the last day she would spend in his lovely realm. He had treated her so well, and she could not bear the thought he might lose his much beloved Paris. Tears rolled down her cheeks, for there would be unbearable sorrow no matter which man lost his life. There was the hope for peace, at long last, and the thought was all that kept her breathing.

When Priam's royal chariot reached the ground separating the two armies, Agamemnon greeted him with Odysseus by his side. The Greek high king acknowledged Priam with a nod, lifted his arms to pray to Zeus, god of glory, and to the sun, rivers and earth to bind their pact. They sacrificed the lambs, and drank from a great gold bowl filled with wine from both sides and poured it out on the ground in a solemn libation.

Unable to watch the deadly duel, when Priam knew Zeus had already chosen the winner, he returned to his chariot and rode swiftly back into Troy. Rather than return to the tower to watch what would surely be a ghastly spectacle, he went on to the calm of his palace. He would pace and worry alone there, but he gave no thought to the gods when his prayers were unlikely to sway them.

Hektor and Odysseus measured the ground for combat. The warriors on each side moved back to allow ample room for the fight. Two stones were used for lots, a light colored one for Paris and a dark hued one for Menelaus, and they were dropped into a gleaming bronze helmet. Hektor gave the helmet a hard shake, and Paris's lot leapt out. He would be the first to throw his spear.

With the first chance to wound his opponent, Paris's spirits soared, and he grinned at Hektor. He quickly checked his armor. The bronze greaves covering his shins had silver ankle straps. His breastplate fitted him well, and his plumed helmet protected his head and neck. He slung his silver handled sword over his shoulder, picked up his sturdy shield and finely sharpened spear. Battle ready, he stared at Menelaus, who was equally well armed. They began to circle each other round and round, their locked gazes deadly. Both Greek and Troy troops broke into war chants, and the low rumbling threats echoed all around them.

Seizing a chance to win by surprise, Paris hurled his spear with brutal force, but the spear bounced off the center of the Greek's round bronze shield. With the point bent, it fell useless on the ground.

Menelaus laughed and sent a prayer to Zeus for revenge against the man who had betrayed his kindness and defiled his wife. "Let me crush this bastard beneath my feet!" He took careful aim, and his spear pierced Paris's layered bull-hide shield, cut through his breastplate and even tore his war shirt. But Paris had swerved before he suffered a wound.

Menelaus charged him and could taste victory as he smashed his fine sharp sword down on Paris's helmet, but the bronze blade shattered into jagged pieces and flew from his hand. Without a weapon, he cried to Zeus and hurled himself on Paris to wrench him to the ground. Getting the better of the Trojan Prince, he grabbed the horsetail plume on his helmet and with furious strength, stood and with a great heave pulled Paris toward the Greek ranks. The raucous cheers from his warriors were deafening.

Stunned by the sword blow to his head, Paris fought to break free, but he choked on the helmet's braided chinstrap, and couldn't catch his breath. Aphrodite noted his dire straits and would not let her beautiful daring prince die. With power streaming from her outstretched hand, she snapped the chinstrap to free him and the helmet came away in Menelaus hand. The sly goddess then wrapped Paris in a whirling mist and sped him away to the safety of the palace.

Menelaus flung the empty helmet into the roaring crowd and grabbed his warrior's spear to continue the fight, but Paris had vanished. The Greek lashed his spear and turned around, seeking him out wherever he hid, but no one had seen him leave the battleground. Enraged with frustration, he shouted for Paris, but there was no answer.

Agamemnon rushed forward to seize the moment. "Hear me, Trojans! Menelaus has clearly won the duel, and Helen's fate has been decided. She must be surrendered to Menelaus before the day is through!"

Menelaus wiped away the sweat pouring into his eyes and gazed up at Troy's main tower. He wondered if she'd been watching from that height. He hoped she'd seen her lover turn coward and run. He raised his spear and shook it. "Helen!" he shouted. "You are mine!"

Once Aphrodite had Paris safely tucked in the palace, she hurried to the tower to summon Helen. "Come quickly, Paris awaits in your chamber."

Helen recognized the goddess by her rare beauty, but refused to heed her call. "Menelaus has defeated Paris, and rather than despise and punish me, he wishes to take me home. Go to Paris yourself. If you love him so, abandon the immortals on Mount Olympus and become his human wife."

Aphrodite's gaze filled with fury. "Do not provoke me, girl, or I'll have both the Greeks and Trojans curse your name for all eternity!"

Helen recoiled in fright, worn-out by too many sleepless nights and heartbreaking days tending the wounded. She closed her eyes and shook her head, but she couldn't shut out Aphrodite's hateful threats. She had simply suffered too much to withstand the furious goddess's abuse and reluctantly went with her into the palace. Paris had bathed and dressed in fine robes, and had he suffered even the smallest harm, it didn't show.

There were tears in Helen's eyes as she greeted him. "You've often boasted of how easily you'd beat Menelaus in a sword fight, but you fled the battlefield, and he won the day."

Paris rested his hands lightly on her shoulders. "The fault isn't mine. Athena helped him, but we have Aphrodite on our side. I'll fight Menelaus again tomorrow, but let's not waste anymore of today worrying about him. I've never wanted you more. You've enchanted me from the day we first met. Come to bed with me, and love me as you always have."

She did love him, or had loved him once, when time had stood still in the Egyptian desert. She followed him to their gilded inlaid bed, but she felt only sorrow at what their lives had become. Passion washed over him in a soothing balm, and he lost himself in her heat, but her troubled soul left her heart untouched.

The gods reveled on Mount Olympus. They gathered at the golden tables of Zeus's palace to drink nectar and feed each other luminous spoonfuls of ambrosia. The king of the gods was in an expansive mood. "Lady Hera and Athena may have allowed Aphrodite to spirit Paris away to Troy today, but clearly their favorite Menelaus has won the day. He'll return to Sparta with Helen, and Troy will continue to thrive under King Priam's rule."

Hera fumed and her robe swirled at her feet as she paced in front of her husband. "I say the war isn't over until the Greeks have vanquished that vile Troy."

"I hold Troy sacred, my darling wife, and what terrible wrong have the Trojans done to you that you would destroy their lovely town?"

She turned to face him. "I have defended the Greeks throughout this lengthy war and need not explain myself to you."

The Lord of Storms and Thunder stared at his belligerent wife with a narrowed gaze. "If I give you this to keep peace between us, then when I wish to tear apart a city beloved to you, you must give me my way."

Hera broke into a beaming smile. "So it shall be. Raze one of my favorite cities, Argos, Sparta or Mycenae, and I will offer no defense. For now, send Athena down to prompt the Trojans to break the truce."

"Fine," Zeus answered, for he had let Agamemnon believe he'd win the day, when he fully intended for Troy to triumph. "Fly at once, Athena, and see that the Trojans are the first to break the truce, and they'll overrun the Greeks." He may have given Hera her way, but the Greeks were still locked in a battle they couldn't win.

Athena donned her golden sandals and dived off the Olympus heights. She soared through the sky like a shooting star and plunged down among the warriors of both sides still milling about the plain and speaking of the truce. She quickly shape-shifted to become a Trojan warrior and sought out Pandarus, the finest archer of Troy. She greeted him warmly and easily tempted him into action. "Brave, Pandarus, shoot an arrow at Menelaus and kill him, and you'll win great fame. Prince Paris will praise your name and reward you handsomely. Swear to Apollo, the Wolf-god, and most glorious archer, that you'll give him many sacrifices when you return home."

Tantalized by her sweet promise of fame, Pandarus pulled a hawk-fletched arrow from his quiver and made that promise to Apollo as he drew back the string of his mighty back-bent bow. He held his breath as he took careful aim and sent the razor sharp bronze arrow flying. He saw Menelaus fall, and he leaped into the air rejoicing at his deadly accuracy.

Clever Athena had flicked the arrow so it only grazed Menelaus skin rather than do him any grave injury. The point pierced where his belt and breastplate overlapped and the guard shielding his loins. Blood ran down his thigh from the wound, but he was in no serious pain.

Horrified, Agamemnon dropped to his knees beside his fallen brother, and he took his hand. "The dishonorable men of Troy have broken the truce, now Priam must die and all who dwell with him!"

"No, don't alarm the men," Menelaus cautioned. "I've not suffered a mortal wound. My armor blunted the arrow's thrust."

"I pray you're right," Agamemnon responded, and he sent for the renown healer Machaon who came running to Menelaus's side.

Machaon deftly removed the arrow, and unbuckled Menelaus's war belt, breastplate and guard. He sucked the blood from the wound and applied the healing salves he carried. "It is a shallow cut, my lord, and will heal quickly, but what of the truce?" he asked.

Agamemnon grasped his brother's shoulder. "Rest in your shelter, Brother, I'll make the Trojans pay for betraying their sworn oath." With his sword in his hand, he rallied his warriors for if the Trojans wanted war, then he would give it to them, and he yelled a battle cry and charged with his incensed troops.

Hektor fought all afternoon, but even with the War god Ares taking their side for a while, he feared the Trojans might soon be overwhelmed. His brother Helenus came to his side with an urgent request. He spoke in a heated rush, "Go and have our mother make sacrifices of calves and a fine robe to Athena. We must turn the goddess's sympathy to Troy, or I fear we'll lose this war and all we hold dear."

Eager for all the help he could raise, Hektor hurried toward the city. He passed Zeus's holy oak tree and was quickly surrounded by Trojan wives eager for news of their husbands. They implored him with tragic, outstretched hands, and he quickly brushed their fingertips. He felt for them and his voice cracked as he spoke, "Pray to the gods," he told them and rushed on.

Queen Hecuba kissed his cheek as he entered her elegant chamber, her brow furrowed with worry. "My son, why have you left the battle?" she asked.

"I've come to ask you to make animal sacrifices to Athena to gain her favor. Gather a fine robe as well, Mother, and take them all to Athena's temple and pray for us to triumph over the Greeks."

"I will hurry to do what you ask, my dear, Hektor," she promised.

Hektor left her to seek out his wife, and a servant told him she could be found on the main wall near the Scaean Gate. He saw her as he approached and Andromache rushed into his arms and wept against his chest.

"I cannot bear this," she sobbed. "You possess a fiery courage, my husband, but if you are killed, your son and I will suffer terribly. The Greeks will make slaves of us and force us to do the most menial degrading labor. Your son was born to be Troy's king, not a slave to some hateful Greek warlord."

"Beloved," he murmured softly. "Send such awful thoughts from your mind. I'm alive and Troy hasn't fallen." He dried her tears on his fingertips and picked up his son to hug him close. "Zeus, I pray you let my son live to be known as a better man than his father, and may he forever be a joy to his mother and all of Troy."

He held them both, crushed them against his chest until he had to let them go. He picked up his shield and spear and turned to smile as he walked away through grateful Trojans who held out their hands to him and prayed he'd live to see his dear ones another day.

CHAPTER 25

The Trojans fought with great vigor, but the Greeks slowly gained ground. Apollo began to despair, and he confronted Athena by the great holy oak. "You are without mercy for my men of Troy, but both sides have lost too many lives. Let's end the fighting for today. I'll have Hektor challenge a Greek warrior to a duel, and the others on the battlefield will withdraw to watch."

Athena licked her lips slowly as she savored the idea. "I would enjoy seeing man-to-man combat among mortals. It can be particularly fierce and bloody."

"Yes, it can be," Apollo agreed. "I'll have Helenus move Hektor to make the challenge." He was delighted to have convinced Athena to bring the war to a halt, but he kept his smile from widening into a predatory grin.

Hektor doubted his troops could hold off the Greeks until nightfall, and when Helenus proposed he offer a challenge, he seized upon it as their best hope. He waited for a break in the fighting and then shouted at the Greeks, "I'll fight your chosen champion. Send someone to face me in single combat. If your man kills me, he may have my armor, but he must give my body to my people to carry home. If I slay him, I will take his war gear and hang it from Troy's walls as a trophy, but I will leave his body for you Greeks for his proper burial rites."

Agamemnon knew as well as the men whispering around him that only Achilles could best such a valiant warrior. Achilles had sworn he'd be needed one day, and surely that day had arrived. Menelaus waited for a man to take up the challenge, but only an uncomfortable silence surrounded him for no one wanted to face the killer of so many of their men. He called to his brother. "If no other man has the courage to face him, I'll fight him myself!"

"Are you mad?" Agamemnon scolded. "Your wound hasn't had time to heal."

"Then who will fight Hektor?" Menelaus replied. "Our honor is at stake!"

Lord Nestor was long past his days as a warrior, but he added his authoritative voice. "Is there not a man among us brave enough to take up Hektor's challenge?"

Spurred by that insulting taunt, several men stepped forward, Ajax and Odysseus among them. At Nestor's urging they each scratched their mark on a stone and dropped it into Agamemnon's helmet. Nestor shook it, and the one with Ajax's mark leaped out.

"Ajax!" the warriors all cried and Ajax shook his spear. "I can overpower Hektor, he's so small compared to me. He does not dazzle me." He raised his massive bronze shield and stepped forward to confront the Trojan prince. "Did you expect an easy victory, Trojan?" he shouted. "You've won the right to throw the first spear and begin the fight."

Hektor looked up at him. "Your great size does not mean you're a great warrior!" He hurled his spear and it slammed into but it failed to penetrate the thick layers of Ajax's shield. Ajax responded with a mighty throw that ripped through Hektor's great bull hide shield, but it also failed to harm him. Each man grabbed for his second spear and they continued to circle in a slow wary dance of death. Hektor gathered all his strength, but his spear again hit Ajax's shield, and swerved into the dirt with a bent tip.

On Ajax's next throw, his spear blade cut Hektor's neck, but undaunted, the Trojan fought on with blood dripping onto his breastplate. Hektor grabbed up a huge jagged rock and hurled it overhand. It struck Ajax's shield with a piercing metallic ring, and the Greek giant laughed. He quickly found his own boulder and threw it so hard it buckled Hektor's shield and knocked him flying into the dirt. Not willing to give in, Hektor quickly sprang to his feet and drew his sword ready to fight until the long shadows cast by the setting sun made it impossible to continue.

The match finally ended in a draw, and Ajax gave Hektor his purple war-belt. "It has been a good fight, Trojan. You're a worthy opponent," he blared out.

"It has been," Hektor agreed. "You deserve your fierce reputation." He handed Ajax his silver studded sword. More weary than he wished anyone to know, he made his way to the palace, but wisely had a healer treat the wound on his neck before he entered the royal chamber he shared with Andromache.

Her expression filled with terror as she saw his bandage, and she ran to him. He raised his hand. "It's a mere scratch, you needn't weep over me yet."

She threw herself into his arms and hugged him with all her strength. "I prayed to Zeus the whole day for your safety, and clearly he has heard my prayers."

Hektor drew her down beside him on their bed, but it was sleep he needed most that night rather than her tear-laced passion.

Paris heard about the duel from servants who had watched, and he returned to the room he shared with Helen elated with the news. "I wish I could have been there to see it, but from what I heard, Ajax gave Hektor only a slight wound. The Greeks have no man strong enough to beat my hero brother."

"Do I dare whisper Achilles' name?" she asked.

"For whatever reason, he's withdrawn with his men, so he poses no problem to us now."

She had a difficult time imaging Hektor getting the best of Ajax, but didn't want to hear any details of the battle. Paris strutted about their chamber, boasting about Hektor's prowess with a spear, and she saw him for what he really was: an excitable child. Menelaus would have killed him had Aphrodite not whisked him from the battleground, and yet he appeared to have forgotten how close he had come to leaving her a widow.

He was such a fine looking young man, so fit and full of vigor, but he lacked the depth of a rain puddle. She had allied herself with him so willingly, but surely Aphrodite had pushed her toward him, just as the goddess had softened his heart toward her.

Paris abruptly halted his pacing to face her. "I'll never give you up, but if I offer Menelaus a wealth of treasures, he may agree to end the war now and sail for home."

Helen drew in a deep breath and released it in a poignant sigh. "He was willing to fight you to the death. Do you really believe he'll accept gold in my place?"

"I'm uncertain what he might do, but it's worth a try, isn't it?"

"Go and speak with King Priam and ask for his wisdom on the matter."

He kissed her before he left to do so, but she doubted her former husband would accept anything less than her or her body to declare a permanent truce. She paced as she waited for her impetuous young husband and following his example, she cleared her mind of any thought.

At dawn, King Priam sent a herald to announce Paris's proposal. The Greeks stood around him listening intently as he spoke. He offered Menelaus riches to end the war and then added a suggestion from Priam that they suspend the war to burn the bodies of all the dead.

Agamemnon surveyed those standing nearby and saw not even a flicker of interest among the warriors for accepting Paris's offer. Menelaus came to stand beside him and shook his head. "Tell him no. It's Helen I want, my beloved wife, not the cold hardness of gold."

"The Trojans must have become desperate," Agamemnon whispered. "Victory will soon be ours." He stepped forward to address the herald and his troops. "Tell your king we refuse to exchange gold for Helen, but we will allow time for burial of the dead."

The herald saluted with a low bow and raced back to the citadel with his news, and the grim labor of building pyres and burning the dead began. Some soldiers gathered timber while others were ordered to collect the dead. Bodies had to be washed for many of the slain to be recognized, and men on both sides cried for their lost friends. It was a long and sad day.

The Greeks heaped earth upon the ashes of their fallen and continued the massive mound to create a rampart to protect their ships. The camp's new defense wall had gates and a wooden tower. A deep trench lined with sharp stakes in front added further protection. Satisfied they had enhanced their position, they fell weary onto their beds.

Zeus was not pleased his clever plan to aid the Trojans had not ended well, and he blamed the other gods for interfering in the war. "Leave the Greeks and Trojans alone, and don't think I won't expel you from Mount Olympus if you ignore my wishes."

Athena alone dared speak to the king of the gods, and she sidled up to him. "Couldn't we give them a little advice?" she asked, in a sweetly innocent voice.

Zeus stared at them all, his gaze as threatening as the thunderbolts he threw with such abandon. "Advice and nothing more. Is it understood?"

"Of course, husband," Hera responded, as though she was always an agreeable wife, and the other gods nodded their assent.

Thinking the matter done, Zeus hitched his marvelous flying horses to his golden chariot and flew to Mount Ida where he would have the best view of the day's battle. He had brought along his gigantic golden scales and dropped a sentence of death on each side pan. He held the scale lightly, bringing the two pans into perfect balance and the Greek's side dropped while the Trojan's side rose. Delighted the fates had blessed his dear city of Troy, he sent a blinding flash of lightning into the midst of the Greek forces. Terrified, the troops scattered and dashed for cover.

Overjoyed at their frantic dismay, Hektor called to his troops to charge and they pushed the Greek army back to their barricades. When darkness fell, Hektor rode in his chariot encouraging the Trojans to make camp on the plain where they would be ready to attack at dawn. "Warriors of Troy, have your food and wine, and tomorrow we'll drive the Greek devils into Poseidon's sea!" His men greeted him with loud cheers, and he thanked Zeus for his blessings.

As Agamemnon roamed through his camp, he saw only averted glances from his demoralized men. He blamed Zeus for the dire nature of their circumstances. "Zeus promised me in a dream that Troy would fall in flames. Clearly it was a false dream meant to cost us lives. If it is the will of the gods, then we must sail home while we still can."

A dispirited low murmuring greeted that sad pronouncement. Diomedes, a great warrior rose to object. "Go if you must, but I'll stay and fight with those who possess the courage to remain with me. We are Greeks, and we never retreat!"

Praise for Diomedes spread through the crowd, but Lord Nestor rose to speak of another path. "We must have our greatest warrior fighting with us again to turn the tide of the war. Make peace with Achilles, Agamemnon. He has been blessed by the gods with invincible powers, and we need him with us now for our cause to succeed."

Agamemnon hated to admit he had been wrong, and it cost him a huge slice of his pride to agree. "If I must, I'll make peace with Achilles. He'll need compensation, gold bars, splendid stallions, and I'll return his girl, Briseis, and provide other pretty slaves too. I'll even give him one of my daughters in marriage. Is that enough?"

Nestor rubbed his hands together. "He can't refuse such splendid gifts, Great King. Send his friends Ajax and Odysseus to offer them. Achilles will honor their presence."

The two mighty warriors sent up a prayer to Poseidon, lord of the sea, and made their way along the beach to Achilles' camp. They found him strumming his lyre, entertaining his friend Patroclus with songs of fabled heroes. The great centaur, Chiron, had tutored him well, and Achilles had a gift for music.

He welcomed his friends, offered them wine and a supper of venison and other meats roasted on skewers, and listened closely as they made what Agamemnon had considered a generous offer. He nodded thoughtfully and finished his wine before he answered. "I'm happy to see you both, dear friends, but I despise Agamemnon, and this awful war all for his profit. I have no quarrel with the Trojans and there is nothing Agamemnon could offer me that would move me to fight with him again.

"Mighty Zeus will protect Troy, for he loves the city. Go back and tell Agamemnon and all the Greeks to sail their black ships for home. They should save their own lives rather than help him lust after the glory of killing others."

Odysseus hung his head as they returned to their camp. "Achilles' anger runs deeper than any of us realized."

Ajax turned to look back over his shoulder. "Agamemnon should have known better than to humiliate our finest warrior in the first place. Don't blame Achilles for hating him."

"Blame profits no one," Odysseus stressed. "It's brave warriors we'll need tomorrow."

Agamemnon stared at the ground as Ajax and Odysseus reported their failure to win Achilles' promise to return to battle, but Diomedes was quick to offer advice.

"Be done with Achilles, and lead the troops yourself, Agamemnon. Show the Trojans how fierce a Greek war lord can be."

Surrounded now by cheering men, Agamemnon nodded, and vowed to fight for glory tomorrow.

The day broke with a forbidding red sky, and as they surged into battle, many Greeks thought it a bad omen. When Agamemnon was wounded and had to be carried from the field, Odysseus fought on. Diomedes stood with him and they waged their way into the Trojan ranks dealing death with every jab of their spears. When Hektor dared to come toward them, Diomedes swung for his helmet and the Trojan Prince fell, but he quickly recovered and withdrew.

Diomedes shouted in triumph, but suddenly an arrow pierced his foot, forcing him to retreat for the safety of his chariot. Never lacking for courage, Odysseus fought until he was wounded in the hip and blood gushed down his leg. He yelled for help and Menelaus half-carried him to his chariot while Ajax confronted the Trojans with his great swinging spear. Soon surrounded by the enemy, Ajax shifted his great tower shield to protect his back and retreated, but the Trojans kept coming.

With their situation dire, the Greeks were forced back within their crumbling barricades to their ships. Ajax fought with a fury and again faced Hektor who was equally brave and daring. They battled each other as the Trojans moved ever closer to overrunning the Greek's defenses to burn their ships and cut off any chance of retreat.

As he watched from Achilles' camp, Patroclus grew frantic and feared he would lose every friend he had ever had before the day was through. "Achilles, if you won't fight, let me go. I could wear your armor and lead the Myrmidons into the fray and give our friends a chance to regroup."

Achilles had seen enough bloodshed and reluctantly agreed. "You may wear my armor, but fight only to reach the ships. Go no farther, do not attempt to take Troy today."

Patroclus promised, eagerly donned Achilles' well-known armor and waving his sword, he led Achilles' famed warriors into the fight. Mistaking him for the mighty Achilles, the Trojans immediately fell back. Borne by the excitement of the moment, Patroclus left the cover of the ships and rushed after them. He pushed them back across the plain and ran even until he reached the great walls of Troy. Ignoring the danger, he tried to climb the high slanted stone wall.

Apollo saw him and knocked him down with a flick of his fingers, but Patroclus rose to try again, only to have the god shove him away. Not discouraged, and fearless in the heat of battle, Patroclus fought his way into the Trojan forces and this time Apollo struck him so hard in the back his helmet fell off and his armor ripped apart. Dazed by the blow, and left defenseless, he fell when stabbed in the back by a Trojan youth. Finally realizing it wasn't Achilles leading the attack, Hektor rushed forward and ran his spear through the badly wounded Patroclus. He tossed aside Achilles' armor clearly meaning to cut apart the fallen man's body.

Horrified by what had just happened, Ajax and Menelaus charged the scene and drove Hektor back meaning to rescue the body. Unwilling to lose the bloody trophy, the Trojans surged forward, but the Greek forces closed ranks, stood firm and dragged Patroclus' body away.

King Nestor's son carried the dreadful news to Achilles. "He fought so bravely, but Hektor struck him down."

Achilles fell to his knees and uttered a mournful cry that was heard all the way to the heavens. Patroclus had been his dearest friend, and he blamed himself for allowing the foolish young man to go into battle. He wept and could not be consoled. When Patroclus' body was carried to him, he rested the dear boy across his lap, kissed his forehead and wept anew.

Thetis heard Achilles' cries and swam from the ocean depths to the shore to reach him. "My darling son, favorite of Zeus, please cease your mourning."

He could not stay his tears, even for his mother. "Zeus may have blessed me, but I care little now that Patroclus is dead. I live now only to see Hektor die."

"Do not rush to vengeance," she warned. "Hektor has your armor and you will need another panoply. I'll go to Mount Olympus and ask god Hephaestus to create new armor for you in his workshop. His work is miraculously fine, your armor will be unlike any other in the world." She kissed her son and touched Patroclus cold cheek and hurried upon her way.

CHAPTER 26

Hephaestus's workshop was in his palace on Mount Olympus, and the talented god was delighted to see Thetis. He welcomed her with a sound kiss. "What can I make for you, dearest, gold jewelry, perhaps something combining pearls from the sea?"

"Your artwork is so lovely I wish beauty were my only concern, but sadly, my son Achilles is in desperate need of a new panoply of armor. The war is going poorly for the Greeks, and he must have your finest armor to lead their fight."

The god of smiths nodded thoughtfully. "I'll make him a set with both beauty and divine strength." He signaled to his golden automatons, and the mechanical maidens came to life and hastened to do his bidding. They brought bronze, tin and gold, readied the workplace, brought his hammer and tongs, and lined up around his flaming forge. He paused to give careful thought to the design and then furiously fashioned a shining shield thickly padded with ox hides. He began the decoration at the center with scenes of the sun, moon and stars.

Sparks flew around him as he pounded out the entire surface with a peaceful city with rejoicing people, and balanced it with a city besieged with war. He added vineyards filled with lush grapes and bulls prancing around a harpist playing for dancing boys and girls. A rolling ocean encircled the outermost edge. Greatly pleased, he grinned at Thetis. "This shield will never yield."

As Thetis stood back to observe the god's masterpiece in amazement, he next fashioned a bronze breastplate of equal beauty and a four-horned bronze helmet topped with a blood-red horsehair plume. He did not forget to make tin greaves to protect the warrior's shins from scrapes and wounds. He stood back to assess his work, grinned, and judged it among his finest.

Thetis was so thrilled she could barely find the words to thank him. "Among all the gods, you have always been my favorite. This wonderful armor will be the talk of Olympus forever."

Hephaestus blushed at her praise. "You are like no other, my lovely Thetis, and my favorite nymph."

Thetis parted with the marvelous set of armor and swooped down like a diving eagle to her mourning son's side. Finding Achilles still sitting with his dear friend's body, she laid the armor nearby. "We must see to Patroclus' burial, and I've brought new armor for you to wear when you avenge his death. Come look at it."

Achilles rose shakily to his feet, and had to wipe away his tears to see the glowing bronze armor. He picked up the heavy shield and traced the hammered design with his fingertips. "Hephaestus has created the whole world here."

"For you, my darling. It is all for you, the greatest warrior the Greeks will ever see. The Trojans will find you invincible and fear your name for all eternity."

"If any remain alive," he added darkly. Leaving the armor for battle, he kissed his mother and walked with her to the shore. She swam out with a graceful stroke, and greeted by her Nerieds, dove beneath the waves. He drew strength from her encouragement and turned his attention to the war. He sent a herald running to call for a new war assembly. Odysseus came running, and Diomedes as well. Agamemnon pushed to the front of the gathering troops to better hear Achilles speak.

The golden-haired warrior looked the high king in the eye. "Our feud is over and combat is all that should concern us now."

Lord Agamemnon took a cautious step toward him. "I still want you to have everything I've offered, gold and fine stallions and…"

"I have no need of them," Achilles responded with a firm shake of his head.

"I welcome your return, Great Achilles!" Odysseus shouted. "We need to give our brave army food and drink and a night's rest so that they may return to the battle with renewed vigor tomorrow."

"Agreed," Achilles responded. Men clustered around him eager to see him again in their midst, but he brushed them aside and returned to his camp, finally ready to put Patroclus to rest.

Odysseus urged Agamemnon to send Achilles the promised treasures despite his lack of interest in receiving them. The king did so, but only Briseis was welcomed.

"Patroclus was kind to me," she offered with her condolences. "I'll sit here with you to mourn him if I may."

Achilles took her hand and brought it to his lips, but he tasted only sorrow.

Paris brought Helen their finest wine from Thrace. "Drink with me. Tomorrow may never come, so let's glory in tonight."

She held the gold kylix in both hands to take a sip. The wine was almost as delicious as the gift of the grapes at home, almost. She closed her eyes to savor the flavor of the memory. "Thank you, this has an exquisite taste. Are the men not feasting together tonight?"

"I've had my fill of their tedious retelling of the day's battle. Had Ajax not defended the Greek's ships with such remarkable strength, we would have driven the Greek demons into the sea, and the war would have ended today."

A second sip of wine tasted even better than the first, and she smiled and licked her lips. "Perhaps the gods have no desire to ever see this war end. Ares and Athena may convince the other gods on Mount Olympus to indulge their insatiable thirst for mortals' blood."

He set her kylix aside, kissed her fingertips and drew her out on their balcony. Thousands of enemy campfires burned along the shore but darkness hid the men clustered around them. "The war will end soon. Hektor will attack at dawn, and if the gods are with us, we'll sweep our enemies into the sea and finally be rid of them."

Believing the gods were impervious to their pleas and sacrifices, she rested in his arms and thought only of him. He was so young, and she forgave him all his faults. "War or not, you have been the best of husbands, both kind and affectionate."

"Your favorite?" he teased.

"I'm with you, so there's no comparison."

He nuzzled her throat with light kisses. "The first time I saw you, I understood why I'd been born."

She recalled the curse surrounding his birth even if he had forgotten. She led him to their beautiful carved bed where they could pass the night lost in each other with wine flavored kisses. Even if it were only Aphrodite's spell, the lingering pleasure made her ache for more. There were times the gods could be useful after all.

Zeus stroked his auburn beard as he spoke to the gods gathered in his golden throne room. "You have all chosen sides. Hera, Athena and brother Poseidon, lord of the Sea, have encouraged the Greeks at every turn. While god of War Ares, and Artemis, Apollo and Aphrodite favor the Trojans. I will withdraw to observe today, but you must take care with your actions, for Achilles must not take Troy too soon."

Inspired, Poseidon rose to respond. "When I cause the mountains to shake, both sides will feel my power. Waves will crest over the Greek ships, and Troy's walls will tremble."

"Yes, do your worst," Zeus encouraged. "Create the ultimate battleground and let the warriors of both sides slip and slide upon the earth, let them roll and tumble, but live to strike again with their gleaming bronze swords and spears."

Poseidon laughed, eager to flip the earth like a carpet and send everyone flying.

The gods laughed with him, and Athena shrieked a war cry and led them into battle.

Hektor stood with his brothers Helenus and Deiphobus. "If the day does not go well and I fall, promise you'll take care of Andromache and my son."

Deeply concerned, Deiphobus touched his arm. "Have you had a premonition?"

Hektor laughed. "I've escaped the chill of death so often, it's already in my bones."

"We'll defeat the Greeks today, and you'll be with us tonight for the celebratory feasting," Helenus swore.

"Neither of you promised to look after my wife and son," Hektor responded, his expression dark.

"Of course, we'll care for them," Helenus vowed. "It would be an honor, but one I hope we need not fulfill."

Deiphobus nodded. "You have my word, brave brother. I'll see they live well."

Hektor drew in a deep breath and exhaled slowly. "I've grown weary of this war, let us end it today."

His brothers cheered, hastened on their helmets and beating their swords on their shields strode with him out onto the battlefield.

Achilles wore a grim grin as he donned the finest set of armor ever created and adjusted the fit of the breastplate. He clenched and unclenched his fists, eager for battle. He strapped on his sword and grabbed his two black spears. In his mind he could see

Hektor falling, and it sent a thrill clear through him.

Briseis walked around him. "You look as powerful as a god. Do you feel it?"

He donned his new helmet, fastened the chinstrap, and tossed the red horse-hair crest. His emotions were twisted with the anguish of losing his friend and entangled with a bitter hatred for Hektor. "I feel only a lust for revenge," he answered, and left her in a proud strut without kissing her good-bye.

Despite his vivid vision, Achilles caught only glimpses of Hektor in the melee, recognizing him by his bright shining bronze helmet. He hacked down many a Trojan warrior as he sought him out. Fleeing Achilles' bloody rout, what was left of the Trojan forces sped through the Scaean Gate for the safety of the citadel, but Hektor remained outside, finally ready to face Achilles.

King Priam pleaded to his favorite son from the high walls, "Come inside, Hektor! Live to defend our city and people another day."

Hektor stood firm. "I'll leave my fate to the gods." As Achilles ran toward him, he hurled his spear, but it bounced off the Greek's helmet, as a stone skips across the sea.

Apollo whispered in Hektor's ear, "When Achilles was born, his mother dipped him into Hades' River Styx. She held him by his heels, and the holy water washed over him to protect him forever against sword and spear."

Now understanding how the gods favored Achilles, Hektor gave up all hope of a fair fight and turned and ran. Relentless, Achilles was swift afoot and chased him, while King Priam and Hecuba watched the horrifying death race from Troy's tower. The runners circled the city three times.

When Zeus thought to save Hektor, Athena stayed his hand. "Leave him, he's a mortal, and his day has come," she argued.

Out of breath, Hektor stopped to face Achilles, but ably ducked when the Greek threw his black spear. He drew his sword. "If Zeus blesses me with a victory, I'll not harm your body, but return it to your people for proper burial. Will you give me the same honor?"

Achilles spit in the dirt. "No. You've caused me far too much pain and grief, and I intend to drag your body through the dirt until the last drop of your blood has been spilled." He gave a piercing war whoop and charged Hector, who fought bravely as the skilled warrior he was. Their swords clashed and clanged, and echoed against Troy's high walls, but Achilles at last swung a mighty blow that caught the Trojan in the neck and brought him down.

King Priam and his queen cried out in pain, for they'd now lost their dear son and Troy's chief defender. Helen stood nearby, but anticipating how the bloody battle would surely end, she couldn't bear to watch. Andromache, however, had seen it all, and now suddenly widowed, she collapsed in Helen's arms. While tending the wounded, Helen had found a strength she'd not known she possessed, and she called upon it now. A servant helped her carry Andromache to her room, and she called Aethra to stay with her.

That night, Paris described how Achilles had stripped away Hektor's armor and clothing and tied his nude body behind his chariot. He had then circled Troy on parade dragging his grisly trophy behind him in the dust. She clasped her hands over her ears unwilling to hear more. Now with Achilles fighting with the Greeks, Troy would surely fall. She clung to her husband, and feared for all those she'd come to love.

Achilles had his Myrmidons build such a high funeral pyre for Patroclus that it burned all night. At daylight, the last of the smoldering flames were doused with wine. The fallen man's bones were placed in a golden chest and buried beneath a high mound. Achilles also honored his lost friend with funeral games. There were contests of foot faces and with javelins, and the discus. The effort of sport swept grief from the warriors' minds temporarily, but like the rising sun, it was refreshed with each new day.

Apollo went to Zeus. "Hektor's body lays dishonored in the dust. He was always respectful of us all and made worthy sacrifices. He deserves a proper burial. What can we do?"

"It can be arranged," the god of Thunder replied. He contemplated the question at great length before deciding the best course. "I'll summon Thetis to convince Achilles to give Hektor's body to King Priam. Iris, our goddess of the Rainbow, will whisper in Priam's ear to send him to Achilles camp with a ransom to retrieve his fallen son."

Grateful, Apollo broke into a wide grin. "Thank you for your wisdom, as always."

"I was also fond of Hektor," Zeus reminded him. "Come, share some nectar with me before you go."

"I'm always proud to share a drink with you, Great One." Hektor completely forgotten, the gods spent an amiable afternoon.

* * *

King Priam interrupted his mourning to load a mule cart with gold and gifts to ransom his eldest son's body. Hecuba wrung her hands as she watched. "Have you lost your mind? How can you do this?" she begged. "Achilles will kill you too and then all will be lost for us."

An eagle flew overhead and Priam turned his wife so she'd be sure to see the magnificent bird. "Zeus's eagle is surely a good omen. The god will keep me safe. Rather than mourn for me while I'm alive, dear wife, prepare for Hektor's burial. I'll return with him soon. I feel the will of the gods."

Preparing for any eventuality, Zeus sent Hermes to guide Priam through the Greek lines, and past the sentries and guards. As they approached each sentry station, Hermes raised his magical golden snake entwined staff and rendered them invisible. Thus the Trojan king ventured unseen until he reached Achilles well-built shelter and entered. The great warrior sat with his Myrmidons circled around a central fire pit. All were shocked to see the Trojan king enter their midst.

"Do my eyes deceive me?" Achilles gasped. "Is Priam truly here?"

Priam met the young Greek's astonished gaze. He knelt before him and the Myrmidons were shocked when he kissed his hand. "Great Achilles, I do what no man has ever done. I've kissed the hand of the man who killed my son. I've come to ask you to remember your father's love. I beg you to honor him and allow me to bury my son. I've brought a ransom to pay for the privilege."

Achilles rose from his stool and raised the old white-haired man with him. He studied the sorrow in Priam's eyes and was deeply touched by his courage. He heard his mother's voice in his heart and understood what he should do. "You're an honorable king, Lord Priam, more honorable than the man who commands our army. You may take Hektor home with you."

The awestruck Myrmidons followed the conversation closely, shrugged and exchanged puzzled glances. They had the Trojan king within reach of their blades, and yet Achilles was giving Priam the gift of his son's body. They knew they must follow the lead of their warlord, and no one stirred or raised a hand against the elderly ruler.

Priam had brought a royal purple blanket to wrap his son's scarred and battered body so the sight would not mar his mother's dreams, but Apollo had protected the fallen warrior even in death, his body had not decayed. There was no terrible stench of death, and he was as handsome as he'd been in life. Priam wrapped him gently and leaving the gleaming treasure ransom, he mounted the mule cart, cracked the whip and started for home to bury the finest warrior Troy would ever see.

On Troy's high wall, Cassandra saw her father returning with her brother's body and began to cry to the gods with a pitiful wail. The sounds of her terrible grief spread over the city and brought others running. She called down to them, "Oh men and women of Troy, if ever you have welcomed our Hektor home from battle, come now and greet him one last time."

As the Scaean Gate opened, women rent their hair and clothes and men beat their shields with their swords or spears in a loud, grim rhythm. "Hektor, our beloved," they chanted.

When Andromache joined Cassandra none could bear to hear the new widow's lament when their own grief ran so deep. All of Troy wept with King Priam and Queen Hecuba and the royal family. The city had never seen such terrible grief.

Hector's body was tenderly washed, anointed with oil, and carefully wrapped in a fine linen shroud. Mourning for the fallen hero lasted nine days before his body was laid upon a high funeral pyre. Paris, Helenus and Deiphobus were among the brothers to collect Hektor's bones. The precious remnants of his life were placed in a golden chest embossed with rearing stallions, and it was buried beneath a great stone mound.

Hoping to escape notice, Helen stood back, but Deiphobus caught her eye. He was not as well-built as Hektor, but he was equally handsome as all of King Priam's sons were. He nodded, a brief sign of recognition she welcomed with a sad smile. The cost of the terrible war tore at her conscience both day and night, and his considerate greeting eased her sorrow only briefly. She returned to her bedchamber before anyone else noticed her in the crowd and waited for Paris to come to her as she knew he would.

It was late at night when he came stumbling into their chamber. He flung himself across the end of the bed, as he had so many times, and knowing his dreams would be dark and sad, Helen let him sleep.

Aethra sat with Andromache long into the night. "You mustn't kill Hektor in your heart," she advised softly. "Keep him with you always as strong and handsome as he was in life. Let him live again in your dreams."

Andromache listened to the elderly queen's comforting words, but they failed to ease her anguish. "My heartbreak will never end, and without Hektor, Troy is sliding toward ruin. Our men will still fight bravely, but without his fierce leadership they'll all fall away. It has all been for naught."

"You are very young," Aethra posed, "and life may give you many joys yet to come. Care for your son and be grateful every day for the love you shared with Hektor. Make it an endless blessing."

"Had I not cared so much, I wouldn't be in such excruciating pain now. I fear we'll all become slaves, and it won't be a life worth living."

Growing weary, Aethra rose and stretched. "You must make it so, child, as I have. It will all be up to you."

The next morning, the Trojans took up their shields and weapons, and the Greeks responded with a vicious attack. With Achilles to lead them, they fought with a new fury but the gods were still reluctant to let Troy fall. They played their perverse games from the heights of Mount Olympus, and argued as though the warriors on both sides were little toy figures carved of wood rather than men made of flesh and blood.

Helen returned to the tents were the wounded lay and sat with dying men. They were often so weak they mistook her for their mother or sweetheart, and she whispered the loving words they longed to hear. She closed their eyes when they drew their last breath, and choking back her own anguish, she moved on to the next man who called for someone dear. Her days passed quickly, and she kept no count of those lost for the number would have been too sad to contemplate.

In the days that followed, Achilles, Ajax and Odysseus fought together, each daring the other on. They battled with such wild fervor they routed the Trojans, forced them back against the Scaean Gate. Eager to follow them through, Odysseus pointed the way up the steep slope to Priam's palace at the top of the hill. Ajax shouted rumbling threats and brandished his long sword. Achilles looked up at the high citadel tower and saw Paris pulling back the string on a powerful recurve bow and raised his shield.

Apollo nudged the Trojan prince as he released the poison tipped arrow, and it found its mark in Achilles' heel, just as he had cut down two Trojan fighters. He grabbed at his heel, but the mighty warrior fell with a piercing scream and died before an incredulous Ajax and Odysseus had realized he'd been wounded. Ajax heaved his friend's body to his shoulder and recovered his amazing shield, while Odysseus fought with a wild jabbing spear to protect them all as they retreated to the safety of their own troops.

The Greek warriors formed a circle around Achilles' body, unable to believe their greatest warrior lay dead. Men fell to their knees crying, while others came running, certain the awful news spreading through the camp could not possibly be true. How could their mighty, beloved hero have been felled by a single arrow? Some crept close to touch his body with a gentle farewell caress, and they would carry that sacred moment with them for the rest of their lives.

A stolid Ajax carried Achilles' body through the astonished ranks to his shelter and laid him down to remove his armor. He set his four-horned helmet aside and unbuckled his breastplate. Odysseus came and stood with him. "I never thought I'd be the one to bury him," he said. "Nothing could be sadder, but his fame will live forever."

"We were as foolish as Patroclus and advanced too far," Ajax replied. "In the heat of battle, none of us thought of the risk, and Achilles has paid the price."

Funeral preparations began, with Achilles accorded the highest honors. His Myrmidons built the highest funeral pyre ever built and stood around it thrusting their spears up and down and chanting while the flames consumed the hero's body, "Achilles, Achilles!"

They collected his bones and buried them beside his dear friend Patroclus. Each thought the war had cost them far too much, but none was willing to go home without avenging their champion Achilles' death.

Ajax stepped forward to speak to the gathered assembly of grieving warriors. "I carried Achilles' body to safety to prevent it from being dishonored and desecrated by the vile Trojans. You know me to be a fierce warrior. I saved our ships from Hektor's attack, and therefore, Achilles' armor should be awarded to me. I'll always wear it into battle with pride."

Agamemnon glanced toward Odysseus, who rose to respond. "You are a great warrior it is true, Ajax. No one doubts your courage, or skill, but Achilles' armor should now belong to me." His deep voice rolled over the crowd in a convincing wave. He was more knowledgeable where strategy was concerned, a far finer orator, and used his talents well to compliment Ajax repeatedly, and yet emphasize why he was the man who should now wear the glorious set of armor the god Hephaestus had created for Achilles.

When the matter came to a vote, Odysseus was overwhelmingly chosen and awarded Achilles' armor. Ajax flew into a wild rage and cursed them all for relying on his strength, but denying him his just reward. His fury grew until he could no longer bear it, and he threw himself upon his own sword and died with a curse still on his lips.

The whole host of assembled Greeks stood in silent shock at the ghastly scene. Two of their finest warriors were now gone, and they feared the gods had cursed them all.

CHAPTER 27

Staggered by the painful loss of their finest warriors, Agamemnon welcomed the prophet Calchas to his shelter, hoping he could guide him in the best course of action. Slightly stooped with his clouded blue eyes focused above the high king's head, he spoke an intriguing premonition in a raspy low tone, "To defeat the Trojans, you must secure the bow and arrows of Hercules. The message of the gods is clear."

Agamemnon turned to the men seated nearby. "I would gladly send someone to fetch them. Philoctetes once owned the legendary bow. But where is he now?"

"He was bitten by a snake on the isle of Lemnos as we sailed for Troy and was too ill to continue the voyage with us," one man recalled. "We left him behind because his wound made him reek to high heaven," another offered.

"If he survived, he may be there still," Agamemnon surmised.

"I'll go for him," Diomedes immediately volunteered.

"You'll not go alone," Odysseus added. "I'll go with you." He turned to Agamemnon. "The men will fight bravely without us if they know we've embarked on such a vital mission to our cause."

"They will be so informed," Agamemnon promised. "Have you any more prophecies for us, Calchas?"

The white-haired man's laugh was a hoarse croak. "I will wait until you possess Hercules's bow before I offer any further revelations, Lord Agamemnon."

Eager to be on their way, Diomedes and Odysseus jogged down to the water. "We'll each take our own men," Odysseus began. "My ship is the swiftest."

"The war has lasted so long your men have undoubtedly forgotten how to sail."

"Then yours will suffer from the same failing."

Unable to decide which boat to choose, or who would be in command, they embarked in two ships and raced the wind toward the isle of Lemnos. Once the site of a rumbling, spewing volcano, the isle was now calm with a rocky terrain and gently curved beaches. The first to the shore, Diomedes queried the fisher folk who greeted them and soon found Philoctetes had indeed survived.

"He lives near Mount Hermaeus," a young man proclaimed and pointed the way.

Diomedes waited for Odysseus to reach the shore, and they made their way along a narrow inclined path to the stone hut Philoctetes had built for himself. He was thin, and gaunt, his hair and beard had grown too long, but they recognized him easily.

His eyes lit with surprise when he saw his old friends. He limped toward them. "You must have believed me dead, or you would have come looking for me long before this," he exclaimed.

"Alas," Diomedes replied. "The war with Troy has taxed both our minds and bodies all these years, but you appear to have survived and done well on your own."

Philoctetes shrugged. "The women are very pretty here, and the food plentiful, although unfortunately, the wine is merely passable. I lacked for the adventure of war it's true, but surely curiosity did not bring you two to the shores of lonely Lemnos. What are you truly seeking?"

Odysseus spoke softly, drawing Philoctetes near, "You once owned Hercules's bow and arrows. Do you have them still?"

"What made you think of those relics?" Philoctetes grew suspicious. "Have you run out of weapons to fight the men of Troy?"

"No, we've weapons aplenty, my friend. We've come to fulfill a prophecy of the priest Calchas," Diomedes confided. "Troy will fall if we have Hercules's bow and arrows."

Philoctetes sat upon a conveniently placed boulder. "You left me stranded here on this rock in the middle of the sea caring little whether I lived or died, and now you have need of my bow?"

There were sheep grazing nearby and a young girl stood shading her eyes as she watched them. "Your life appears to be a good one here," Odysseus surmised.

"It's not the one I intended," Philoctetes answered. "I'm grateful to be alive, of course."

"As are we all," Odysseus agreed. "Bring out the bow, so we may see it."

"You're known for your tricks, Odysseus," Diomedes countered, "but we'll not leave him stranded here again. Come with us to Troy, Philoctetes. Hercules's bow belongs in your hands. Warriors will follow your lead, and you'll be the one to turn the tide of the war."

The disheveled man looked toward the girl minding the sheep. "I can always return here," he murmured to himself. He rose and looked down at his tattered clothes. "Have you something proper for me to wear so the army does not mistake me for a beggar?"

"I'll be proud to share a fine kilt of mine," Diomedes promised. "I'll provide you with a handsome war-shirt," Odysseus added. "Gather whatever you wish to bring, and we'll be on our way."

Odysseus stood back as Diomedes followed Philoctetes into his hut. He grazed at the isle's uninspired landscape and had he been marooned there, he would have swum home.

Eager to present himself in the best possible light, Philoctetes bathed, trimmed his hair and beard and donned a new kilt and shirt before he accompanied Diomedes and Odysseus to see Agamemnon. He held Hercules's mighty bow made of a long-horned sheep's horn reinforced with wood, and he grasped the great leather quiver decorated with figures of Hercules's Twelve Labors, his legendary encounters with monsters and adversaries. "How may I serve you, my lord?"

Agamemnon broke into a wide welcoming grin. "How good it is to see you after all these years. You'll fulfill the prophecy when you enter the battle using Hercules's fine weapons, and all will regard you as a great hero."

"When I vied for Helen and swore my allegiance to Menelaus, I never expected to devote the remainder of my life to that effort," Philoctetes replied with surprising candor.

"None of us did," Diomedes muttered under his breath.

"We're fighting for more than a beautiful woman," Agamemnon countered. He argued for the increase in trade with the Black Sea cities that would make them all rich, and for the new lands that would be open to them all. "There is a great deal to gain," he emphasized. "Fight beside Odysseus and Diomedes today, and use Hercules's bow well."

"It will be my pleasure." Philoctetes regarded him with a knowing smile. "I have used the bow often to hunt the island's deer and wild boars and maintain my strength while on Lemnos. I won't fail you." He had fought the war often in his mind, but he had only imagined the magnificence of Troy, and the beautiful tiered city stunned him now. He followed Odysseus and Diomedes to the Scamander plain where the troops were preparing for the day's battle and held high Hercules's bow to whomever wished to see it.

Diomedes took him aside. "Wait for my order and aim with care. If Paris fights today, he'll be your main target. Do not waste an arrow on another."

Philoctetes understood, and he had always relished a hunt for men.

Helen knelt in the crowded, sweltering shelter caring for the injured when a helmeted Kastros carried the badly wounded Paris inside. She rushed to him and found a place where he could rest comfortably. An arrow had pierced his chest, and he was bleeding badly and breathed with great difficulty.

He gripped her hand and whispered, "Find Oenone. She can heal me."

Helen had never heard the name. "Who is she?" she asked Kastros, who was removing his helmet and trying hard not to weep over his prince he had guarded for so long.

"A maid from Mount Ida he knew in his youth," the warrior answered.

Helen believed Paris had suffered a mortal wound, but if there were any chance he could survive, she would gladly grab for it. "Hurry, you must leave at once to fetch her," she urged.

Kastros knelt beside Paris. "Oenone and her aunt, Chrisoula, have taken refuge in the city. I'll bring them here at once."

"Hurry. I'll have Paris carried into the palace, and you'll find us there," Helen responded. Warriors who had followed Kastros were eager to do her bidding, lifted the wounded man upon a long bull-hide shield, and carried him with slow, cautious steps to the palace. The women standing along the route covered their mouths and fought back tears at this latest tragedy for Troy. The king and queen rushed to their son's side, and wept as though he were already gone.

Helen gripped Paris's hand. She spoke of the love they'd shared, and prayed Aphrodite who loved him so would guard his life now. When Kastros returned alone, he pulled her aside so Paris would not overhear him.

"Oenone said Paris made his choice long ago, and she refused to come."

Helen knelt to kiss Paris's pale cheek and rose shakily to her feet. "I should have gone with you. Take me to her at once." She raised the hem of her blood-splattered skirt and ran beside the tall warrior. He led her through a maze of narrow streets to the home Chrisoula and Oenone shared with others. He knocked loudly at the door and called her name.

Oenone swung the door open. "I told you…" She stared at Helen, instantly fascinated by the lovely young woman.

"You must come with me to the palace," Helen stressed. "Paris believes you can save him, and you must try."

Chrisoula stepped behind her niece. "Helen," she remarked with hushed awe. "If Paris has fallen in battle, you're to blame."

She had accepted the blame for the war long ago and was untouched by the insult. "Please, he believes you can heal him, Oenone, and you must come with us now. He has very little time."

Oenone shook her head and sent her long dark hair flying. "Paris chose you. You heal him." She swung the door closed with a heavy thump.

Kastros took Helen's hand. "Oenone loved him, and she's never forgiven him for marrying you. Her heart has turned to stone, and she'll be the one to bear the blame if we lose him."

Helen squeezed his fingers. "Death has chased Paris from the day he was born," she murmured. "Let's hurry, we must be there with him even if there is nothing more we can do."

When they returned to the palace, Paris opened his eyes, and she took his hand. "Oenone?" he asked.

She shook her head. "We couldn't find her." She looked up at Kastros, and he understood the loving lie and nodded. She leaned close to whisper in her husband's ear, and her memories of their time together were all so dear to her now. "You are the great love of my life. I'll carry you in my heart forever. Do you remember the warm nights we spent in Egypt, where the sky was ablaze with shooting stars?"

He smiled at the memory and with his dying breath whispered her name, "Helen, my Helen…"

Hecuba collapsed in Priam's arms, and he offered what comfort he could find in his ravaged heart. He led her to a bench and sat holding her close as the terrible tragedy of death surged through them yet again.

A servant rushed in with Oenone running behind her. She looked back at the basket-carrying girl. "She says you've called for her."

Helen shook her head. "Oh, Oenone, whatever magic you possess is worthless now. He's gone."

"He's dead?" Oenone gasped. She fell to her knees beside her childhood love and heartbroken, burst into tears. She wept for the peaceful life they should have shared in the shadow of majestic Mount Ida, and cried Paris's name in mumbling sobs.

Kastros bent down meaning to haul the grief-stricken girl away, but Helen raised her hand. "Let her stay. She can do him no harm."

Hearing that Paris had been wounded, Helenus and Deiphobus rushed to the grim scene and drew to an abrupt halt when they found him dead. Helenus went to their parents, while Deiphobus knelt beside Helen and hugged her close. He whispered in her ear, "You'll be my wife now."

She still held Paris's hand fondly in her own to savor his warmth while it lasted, and could not believe he would call her his wife without allowing her even a day to grieve. She shuddered at his heartless demand. "This is no time to speak of marriage."

"There will be no argument," Deiphobus emphasized firmly.

Helenus frowned at his brother, perhaps he had overheard, and had she been forced to choose, Helenus would have become her husband. Sick of war, she would not set one brother on the other, however. With Hektor gone, Deiphobus was now the eldest of King Priam's sons, and he would have his way. She closed her eyes and remained with Paris until all too soon, Deiphobus lifted her to her feet and led her away. She looked back at Priam and Hecuba, but they were grieving too deeply to notice she was leaving with Deiphobus and Helenus refused to meet her gaze.

Aphrodite wept bitter tears for her beloved prince, and Apollo patted her back with a soothing rhythm as he offered his sympathy. "Mortals are such fragile creatures, and their lives so very brief. You loved Paris when he was at his best, when he was young, strong and almost as handsome as I am. Would you still grieve over him had he lived to be a frail old man?"

The distraught goddess wiped away her tears. "You offer very little comfort, Apollo. I loved Paris because he had such an innocent heart, and he chose me as the most beautiful goddess."

"As I recall, he chose you because you offered him the most beautiful woman in the world. Helen is the one he loved, not you."

"Liar! He showed his love with many offerings in my temple, and he loved me as I loved him."

"Go home and ask Hephaestus to make you something pretty to ease your sorrow. He loves to serve you in every possible way."

"Yes, he is a fine husband," Aphrodite agreed with a final choked sob, but she went instead to find Ares whose passions more closely matched her own.

Cassandra entered Helenus' room, but her twin turned away, unable to face her. "Alexandros should have died as a babe," she said. "He would never have met Helen, and we'd never have had to suffer through years of this catastrophic war."

"We did what we could when he was born," Helenus argued. "Father believed your prophecy and thought the boy dead. When he appeared fully grown, Father couldn't condemn him to death after the guilt he'd carried for so many years."

She circled him slowly. "While that may be true, there is an unusual darkness about you. What is it you intend to do?"

He drew in a deep breath and released it in an anguished sigh. "I can't bear to see Helen with Deiphobus, and I mean to go to Mount Ida to pray and think until my way becomes clear."

"Helen?" she mocked. "Your only concern is who lies with the bitch? If you want her for yourself, fight for her."

"I'd rather spare our parents the loss of another son."

"Are you afraid of Deiphobus? Is that what stays your hand?" she asked, a brow gently raised in question.

Insulted, he turned toward the window. "I've not wasted a thought on him. It's only Helen who matters to me."

Cassandra sat upon the end of his bed and smoothed her skirt. "She has bewitched you as she does all men."

"She may have, but have you never wanted a man so badly you could neither eat nor sleep for the painful longing for their love?"

Dismayed, she rose and went to the door. "When I look at a man, I see into his future, Helenus, and it never includes me. So I've not lain awake longing for a man to come to me who never will. Helen isn't meant to be yours. You may remain on Mount Ida until you're a withered old man, but it won't change what must be."

He responded with a sad, sweet smile. "You're forgetting that I also possess the gift of sight and know Helen will survive us all."

She shrugged. "It's true the capricious gods love her more than they love us. I'll miss you. Don't be away long."

Helenus bid her farewell and began to pack what little he cared to take with him for his journey.

Deiphobus led Helen to his own chambers. "As you can see, there is more space here, and the view is better too."

Not if it includes you, she wisely did not say aloud. "Will you not spare even a moment to mourn for your brother?"

"I'll grieve for Hektor until the day I die, but Alexandros, your pretty Paris, meant nothing to me. I've always wanted you, Helen. We all have."

He resembled Paris with his dark curls and brown eyes, but there was a lean meanness to him that warned her not to speak her mind. "It's a trick of the gods."

"Trick or not, you'll be my wife. Your things will be brought here where you now belong. Pass your days in whatever way you wish, but your nights will belong to me."

He inclined his head to kiss her, and while she didn't shy away, she didn't respond either. He'd come from the battlefield smeared in blood, and she focused on the floor rather than his mocking grin. "You smell like death," she said.

"So do you, beloved." He left her without seeking another kiss.

There was water in a small amphora. She poured it into a ceramic basin, and washed her hands and face to be clean of him. This chamber was larger than the one she'd shared with Paris, but it felt as empty as her heart. She sat down on the end of the bed and began with the first of her cherished memories of Paris. He'd brought light and laughter into a life she'd been merely walking through. He'd been a daring boy, and she'd loved him. Tears welled up in her eyes, and she sat alone, dreading the night.

When Deiphobus at last returned to his bedchamber, he was drunk and weaved as he crossed the floor. She hurried to his side and wrapped her arms around his waist to keep him from falling. She eased him down upon the bed, and he was asleep before she'd removed his sandals. Servants had brought her belongings from the chamber she'd shared with Paris, but unwilling to sleep beside the latest man to claim her as his wife, she returned to her former room and slept soundly.

She sat brushing her hair when Deiphobus woke, and if he had failed to discover he'd spent the night alone in his bed, she certainly wouldn't reveal it. "You appear to be overly fond of wine," she greeted him.

He leaned forward to rest his elbows on his knees. "Did I disappoint you?"

"Not as greatly as Paris's death, no."

"How long will it take for you to forget him?"

"The day after you forget Hektor," she countered, confident he felt too unwell to mistreat her. She'd shared her thoughts so easily with Paris, but his brother was a different kind of man.

He shoved off the bed, and caught himself before he stumbled and sat back down. "I'd no idea you possessed so sharp a tongue."

"Too many men are fooled by beauty," she cautioned. "It's another ploy of the gods."

"Help me dress. You can do that much for your husband, can't you?"

She laid aside her brush and rose. "Of course."

There was an icy stillness in her eyes that chilled him clear through. He'd longed for her from the day Alexandros had brought her to Troy. He'd dreamed of her, and no other woman had satisfied him. Like all of them, he'd been fooled by her beauty and now felt punished for it.

Helenus rode to Mount Ida alone. He'd brought a spear and bow and arrows to hunt deer and wild boar, but other than wine, he carried little in the way of provisions. He rode to the rocky crest of the mountain and camped there on the windswept summit.

The air was cool and crisp, but his thoughts remained a confusing muddle. He gathered branches from the fir trees to make a humble bed and went to sleep, but Helen, the lovely Spartan princess haunted his dreams, and he awoke the next morning far from refreshed.

Odysseus had led half a dozen warriors out to hunt, and when he saw a man had taken up residence on Mount Ida, his curiosity alone would not allow him to ride by without investigating. He approached the camp with a stealthy step, but found Helenus in a drunken stupor. He remembered the prince from his visit to speak to King Priam with Menelaus. Mount Ida was sacred to the gods, a favorite of Hera, and he wondered whether or not she might have deliberately provided him with a valuable hostage.

He kicked Helenus' foot, but had to bend down to shake his shoulder to wake him. When Helenus opened a blood-shot eye, Odysseus sat down beside him. "You are a long way from the battle, prince. Have you forsaken your Troy?"

Helenus recognized Odysseus, pulled himself up into a sitting position, shook his head, and instantly regretted it. He leaned over to cradle his aching head in his hands. "Never. I'm communing with the gods on sacred ground. Leave me be."

"A noble pursuit. Do you plan to remain here once Troy has fallen?"

Helenus responded with a hoarse snort. "Troy will never fall."

"I say it will."

"Troy is protected by the Palladium, a sacred statue of Athena, and the goddess guards the city well."

Odysseus had not heard of the Palladium, and he was immensely intrigued. "Who carved this sacred image of the goddess?"

With such a painful throbbing headache, Helenus could scarcely think. "No human. It fell from heaven, a gift from Athena, a promise of her devotion and protection of Troy."

"Is it made of stone or wood?"

"Olive wood, a tree sacred to Athena," Helenus mumbled.

"How have I never heard of this wonder?"

"The Greeks are known to be ignorant fools."

Odysseus laughed at the insult and jumped to his feet. He motioned for one of his warriors who came running, flashing spear in hand. "I'm taking Prince Helenus as a prisoner. He's very amusing, so you'll escort him to my lodge and see that he comes to no harm. Do you understand? He's not to suffer the slightest scratch or bruise while he's in your keeping."

"I'll treat him well," the man promised and saluted with his fist to his forehead.

Helenus squinted as he looked up at him. "We're on ground sacred to the gods. You dare not insult them by taking prisoners here. Go on your way and forget that we have met."

"You speak as though you were still a prince and expected to be obeyed," Odysseus replied. "That is no longer the case." He gestured for the warrior to pull Helenus to his feet and left them to continue his hunt.

Paris was mourned as a Trojan prince who had died in battle, and while the grief in Troy was not nearly so deep as it had been for Hektor, people wept for him too, and remembered their own loved ones lost in the long war. Deiphobus held Helen's hand tightly, as though he feared she might hurl herself upon the burning pyre, but the thought had not even occurred to her. She had cried for her lost love in private, and now stood dry-eyed beside her new husband surrounded by sobbing mourners.

In the coming days, she returned to the tents where the wounded lay. She remained late one afternoon with a young warrior with a bloody bandage over his eyes who kept calling for his mother. She had held his hand and whispered his name until he'd grown silent and slipped away. Now on her way to the palace, she heard a familiar voice and startled, turned back to gaze among those passing nearby.

A beggar in muddy rags and a stained pointed cap caught her attention, and when he spoke again, she recognized him by his deep voice. She hurried to his side and turned him away from the path. "Odysseus, if they catch you spying here, you'll not live to see another day."

He raised his hand to his lips and whispered, "Helen, you're as lovely as ever."

Exasperated, she shook her head. "Have you snuck into Troy merely to pay me compliments?"

He huddled down into his filthy garb and spoke in a conspiratorial whisper, "No, I've come to pray at Athena's temple. Will you show me the way?"

With her hood pulled low to shield her identity, she could move as easily about the city as he could in his disguise. She demanded the truth first and gripped his arm. "You're adept at the clever lie. Tell me why you're really here."

"You needn't know what's brought me here, just take me to the temple and leave," he answered gruffly. "If you were going to betray me, you already would have, don't deny it."

Had she not been so wretchedly unhappy, she might have summoned guards to kill him on the spot, but she already bore the responsibility for too many deaths. She paused to consider how best to proceed. "Have you come alone?"

He nodded. "Our fight is with Trojan warriors, not innocent citizens, women and children. You needn't fear I mean to attack within the city walls."

Wanting simply to be rid of him, she guided him to the blue columned temple and led him in. When he fell to pray at the feet of the Palladium, she realized why he'd come. "The image of the goddess will protect Troy for all time. You're known for your wily tricks, have you come to steal her?"

"I wished only to see it," he claimed. "There must be a secret passageway out of the city. Show me where it is, and I'll go and leave the Palladium untouched."

Had Paris still been alive, she would have left him to find his own way out of the city as he had found his way in. With a single chilling thought of Deiphobus, her decision was instantly made. She described where he'd find the hidden door cut low in the massive wall. Paris had bragged about it, or she'd not have known it was there.

"Stay here until dark and everyone will be inside having their evening meal."

"Are there many guards safeguarding the city?" he asked.

"I've no idea how many there may be. Be cautious and you'll not run afoul of them."

He caught her for a quick kiss and leaned back. "I've always wanted to kiss you."

Disgusted, she wiped her mouth with the back of her hand. "Now you can die happy," she replied and sped away.

Deiphobus usually ate with the men of the royal family in the megaron, while she ate with the women in the women's hall. When she entered their bedchamber to change her clothes for the evening, she was surprised to find him waiting for her. He looked displeased, as he often did.

"Why did you leave the palace?" he asked.

"I go each day to sit with the wounded, so they won't die alone. I've little to give Troy other than my company, and it's gladly given."

"You'll no longer leave the palace," he ordered. "Supervise the women who spin and weave, embroider your boleros and skirts, play games all afternoon. Do whatever you wish, but you'll no longer leave the palace unless I'm by your side."

"Am I a prisoner or your wife?" she responded too softly to give offense. She turned away, but he caught her elbow and forced her to face him.

"You're my wife, and you'll do as I say until the day I'm carried from the battlefield on my shield. Disrobe for me, I'll have you now before I dine with the men."

He'd bathed and his hair was still damp, so he smelled of soap rather than blood and sweat. Menelaus and Paris had been tender lovers who gave pleasure as well as enjoyed their own, but he took what he wanted seemingly unaware that she should also share in the bliss. It was always over quickly, for which she was deeply grateful. She tossed her skirt and bolero aside and went to the bed. She had cultured a lively imagination as a child, and it served her well now. Her thoughts were on the men who had truly loved her, and not the one grunting above her now.

Late that night, Odysseus led Diomedes around Troy's great sloping wall to the hidden entrance he'd used earlier in the evening to escape the citadel. "The door can't be seen for the acanthus bushes shielding it. We would never have found it on our own. The hinges are well-oiled and swing open without a sound. Let's wait for the guards to pass by before we enter."

"Why? If none are nearby we should go now," Diomedes argued.

Odysseus laid his hand on his friend's shoulder. "Hush, I hear someone coming."

Two heavily armed men strode by, their voices low as one recounted a day he'd fought beside Hektor, and the other offered his own memories of the fallen hero. Absorbed in their conversation, neither felt the presence of the Greek warriors hidden so close. They walked on, and would not have discovered the intruders unless they had tripped over them.

Odysseus moved forward slowly and Diomedes followed close behind him. The low door was so cleverly disguised it would have been impossible to find in the dark had Odysseus not left a cluster of stones nearby. Once inside the wall, they had to walk hunched over, brushing away cobwebs, and the cool narrow passage seemed to close in around them. With only daggers at their belts, they were relying on stealth rather than armor and weapons in this mission.

"Steady," Odysseus called. "I counted the steps, and the exit is just ahead."

Once they were into the city, they moved along close to the inner-wall with crab-like side steps. Oil lamps left burning in the temple of Athena drew them near, but they glanced in to make certain no one had come to pray before they entered. Diomedes hurried on to the Palladium and ran his hands over the highly polished wood. Light flickered on the face of the statue, making it resemble a living goddess.

"It's smaller than I thought it would be. Together, we can carry this out of the city."

"I thought so, but we must hurry." Odysseus grabbed for the head of the statue and lifted it from its stone base. He then removed his sea-blue cape and wrapped it. Diomedes took hold of the feet, and made clumsy by their sacred burden, they moved through the sleeping city with a slow shuffle to the opening in the wall. Traveling down the hidden passageway with the Palladium presented another challenge, and they struggled, but at last burst out onto the other side. They ran wide of the wall before returning to the beach where they could put down the stolen treasure and catch their breath.

"We should keep her hidden," Diomedes advised. "It will be enough that we have her, we mustn't incur the goddess's wrath by displaying the Palladium where it might be open to ridicule from our troops."

"I agree. We'll keep it wrapped and take it to Agamemnon's lodge, where no one will dare to search for it."

"Hurry, we must be done with this before dawn, for surely the Trojans will soon discover their precious Palladium is missing, and they'll all attack with renewed vigor."

"We'll be ready for them," Odysseus assured him.

Calchas licked his lips in delight. "We now have Hercules' bow and the Palladium, only one thing is missing."

"And what might that be?" Agamemnon asked. He glanced toward the Palladium that stood, tightly wrapped, in the corner of his lodge. He feared it would bring more bad luck than good if Troy did not swiftly fall.

"The gods command that you bring Achilles' son, Neoptolemus, to fight in the war," the seer proclaimed. "Then your army will be invincible and great Troy will be yours."

Odysseus rested his hands on his hips. "Is the boy even old enough to hold a sword, let alone fight with one?"

"He must be," Diomedes answered. "He lives on Skyros Island. I'll sail for him."

"No," Odysseus argued. "I'll be the one to go. You're needed here to inspire the troops."

"You also provide great leadership," Diomedes countered.

"Odysseus will go," Agamemnon decided. "It isn't a long voyage, but best it be begun quickly."

Odysseus put his fist to his forehead in salute, and left the royal lodge to ready his men and ship to sail.

Agamemnon noted Diomedes' frown. "I do not trust him either, but I need you here, and he can be counted on to bring the boy."

"Is this truly all that's needed?" Diomedes asked Calchas.

The seer bowed slightly. "Indeed it is, my lord."

CHAPTER 28

Word the Palladium, "The Spirit of Troy", had been stolen during the night passed quickly through Troy and its palace. The announcement was met with general horror, but only Helen knew who had taken the beloved sacred statue and how it had been done. She felt only a brief flash of guilt and promptly suppressed it. She observed Deiphobus with a wide, innocent gaze as he paced their chamber cursing the Greeks and damning the incompetent guards who were charged with keeping Troy's holy relic safe.

"How could the Greeks have scaled the wall and come and gone unnoticed?" he fumed.

Helen nodded sympathetically, as though she shared his dismay. When he turned away from her, he resembled Paris in physique and coloring, but there was no mistaking his identity when he wheeled around to face her. He had a multitude of expressions, ranging from his frequent anger to wild rage. His lip curled in a damning sneer.

"This is why you must not leave the palace," he ordered. "If Greek spies and thieves are moving among us, there's too great a danger they'll harm you. I'll not risk losing you, Helen, I won't. Do you understand me?"

She nodded, and didn't take a deep breath until he had left her for the day.

Thetis had foretold Achilles would die young fighting in a great war. In a vain attempt to spare her only son that fate, she had disguised him as a woman and hid him on the Isle of Skyros in the court of King Lycomedes. The handsome youth could not disguise his desires, however, and had sired Neoptolemus during an affair with Princess Deidamea. The handsome red-haired boy had been raised by his mother but took after his father and displayed both strength and remarkable speed as a runner.

When Odysseus arrived on Skyros's rocky shores with vivid tales of the Trojan War, Neoptolemus was eager to go with him. His mother wept at the tragic news of Achilles' death, and was reluctant to give her son permission to go.

"You must promise me you'll look after the boy," she insisted. "Swear it now."

"Our seer foretells a victory if Neoptolemus is with us. I'll guard him well, and he'll not come to any harm as we triumph over Troy."

Deidamea had early recognized a wildness in her son she doubted the small Isle of Skyros could safely contain. He was his father's son after all and born for heroic adventure. "You may go, my son, but when you're able, you must return to describe the Greek victory over Troy."

Neoptolemus kissed his mother's cheek. "I'll sing it in clever rhymes while I play father's lyre," he boasted. He quickly gathered his belongings in a leather bag and leapt aboard Odysseus's black ship his eyes aglow with excitement.

His mother waved from the stone dock until the ship with its distinctive wild bore sail emblem was no longer in view. Before returning to her father's palace, she strolled along the shore remembering Achilles, who would have been so proud of his handsome son. A shaggy Skyrian pony came over a rise and tossed his head in greeting. From the time he'd been small, Neoptolemus had loved riding the gentle ponies, and she was sorry she had no treat for this one.

Neoptolemus sat in the high prow of Odysseus's ship and laughed as the sea sprayed over him. "I want a ship of my own like yours!" he called to Odysseus.

"You shall have one," Odysseus promised. He'd found the boy to be bright and personable, but his close resemblance to Achilles was unnerving all the same. The lad was already tall and would undoubtedly grow up to be a well-built, muscular man. If he could keep him alive, and Odysseus had promised he would, but promises were not easily kept during war.

When they beached the ship near the Greek camp, he cautioned Neoptolemus sternly, "Agamemnon is the powerful King of Mycenae and the commander-in-chief here. You must show him the utmost respect."

"If he had need of me, he should respect me too," Neoptolemus replied with a cocky grin.

Odysseus laid his hands upon the boy's shoulders. "I intend to see you return to Skyros without so much as a scratch, but Agamemnon would have you whipped for insolence should you speak to him thus. Pretend he is Zeus if you must, but defer to him in all matters and smile only when he is smiling at you."

"Still, if I'm here to fulfill a prophecy...."

"Stop it!" Odysseus ordered crossly. "Our seer said only that you must be here, he did not foretell what might happen to you. Keep that in mind." He hurried the boy to Agamemnon's lodge. It stood out due to its size and royal emblem of Mycenae over its entrance: Two gold lions rearing against a sacred column. Odysseus stood close enough to cuff Neoptolemus if he failed to show the proper manners.

Agamemnon dismissed Neoptolemus with a hurried glance. "I can see Achilles in him. Find him a sword he can lift and teach him how to use it so he'll survive more than a single day on the battlefield."

"I already know how," Neoptolemus interjected, clearly insulted.

Odysseus slipped his arm around the boy's shoulders and wheeled him right out of Agamemnon's presence. "I'll see that he practices, my lord," he called over his shoulder. "Do you know what happens to lads who think they know more than their elders?"

Neoptolemus looked up at him. "Nothing good, I suppose."

"That's right. Now keep your mouth shut unless you're eating."

The boy laughed, but nodded as though he would.

* * *

Andromache could not be consoled. She had adored Hektor and sobbed for him from morning until night. Aethra came to Helen for help. "Please come and sit with her for I can not abide her endless grief. Young women are too often widowed, but she must find the strength to raise her son."

"Of course, I'll come." Helen took the petite woman's hand. "Deiphobus has forbidden me to leave the palace, so I need something worthwhile to do."

"I may have lived so long because that's always my quest, and I agree, it must be something valuable, not simply a mindless task to fill the day."

Helen hesitated at her sister-in-law's door. "Andromache has been pampered since she was a child, and it's possible there simply is no strength in her."

"Then you must instill some," Aethra demanded. She turned away and left Helen to deal with the tormented widow alone.

Helen entered Andromache's lovely chamber with its murals of blue flying fish, and found the young woman stretched out on her bed while a servant entertained her son. He was a handsome boy with thick dark curls and bright eyes. She went first to him and touched his hair. "What a handsome boy you are."

He was playing with carved wooden horses and plunking them down upon the floor as though they were running. "You're almost big enough to ride a pony," Helen observed.

Andromache pushed herself up on her elbow. "Oh no, he's much too small and would fall off and hurt himself badly."

"What he needs is a small gentle pony," Helen offered. "Shall we go to the royal stables and see if we can find one?"

"No, I'm too tired to leave my chamber today." She studied Helen with an accusing glance. "Didn't you love Alexandros? When you lost him, you took another husband within a day."

Helen sat down beside her on the bed. She carried her sorrow deep inside where it belonged only to her, and she never shared her heartbreak with others. "I loved Alexandros dearly and still shed tears for him in private. He'll always be a part of me. As for Deiphobus, he gave me no choice in becoming his wife. With a war surrounding us, I let him have his way rather than bring additional strife into our household. Do you feel well enough to visit Hecuba? Her sorrow must be twice as deep as ours."

Andromache swung her legs over the side of the bed. "How can I comfort her while I'm so sad?"

"If all you can do is hold her hand, come do it," Helen replied. "Your presence alone will be a comfort."

"What if we lose the war?" Andromache whispered, fear etched on her sweet features.

"That's not our concern today, is it?" Helen replied. She stood and offered her hand and Andromache came with her to visit their mother-in-law who could no longer remember how many of her children had died and who was still alive.

Neoptolemus watched Odysseus strap on his shining bronze armor and marveled at its beauty. He bent down to pick up the ornate shield and found it too heavy to lift. "Where did you find such a magnificent set of armor?" he asked.

Odysseus had been waiting for that question. Too many people knew the truth for him to lie. "The god of Fire and Smiths, Hephaestus, made it for your father. It was awarded to me after his death."

"I have nothing of his, and it should be mine," the boy challenged.

That he would claim armor he could not even lift amused Odysseus greatly. "It's meant for a man, not a boy."

Neoptolemus straightened up to his full height. He was growing so fast he thought he might soon be Odysseus's equal in stature. "Children aren't given swords and told to prepare for battle."

"True, but I expect you to remain in the rear of the ranks where no harm will come to you."

"An armorer should make a set of armor that fits me now. I'll grow into my father's in time."

"If you live that long, boy!" Odysseus blurted in frustration. "Now do as I say and stay well away from the fighting today. Must I have a warrior watch you, or will you be on your honor?"

Neoptolemus looked toward the shining Aegean Sea and thought of home. He didn't want to return to his mother with no thrilling stories to tell and sing. Perhaps they would come in time. "I'll go and watch from the beach. Will that be far enough away for you?"

"Yes, it will do." He waited to make certain the lad actually had gone that far before he joined his men. They had done all they could to ensure fate would be with them, and he strode into the fray with a new confidence and pride. When the fighting proven no easier than on previous days, but if anything more trying and vigorous, he wondered what prophecies the Trojans had heard.

When he sat with the other kings surrounding Agamemnon that night, he waited until every man there had complained of how stubborn an enemy the Trojans continually proved to be. When at last Agamemnon glanced his way, he cleared his throat before he spoke. "Lord Agamemnon, I'm often accused of having a cunning nature and relying on trickery, but perhaps that is exactly the course we should take."

"We all know you're clever, my dear Odysseus, what do you suggest?" Agamemnon asked, and all present leaned forward to hear.

Odysseus began devising a plan as he spoke. "If we convince the Trojans the war is over, they would lay down their arms and celebrate. If we staged a feigned retreat, but remained near enough to strike, we could catch them off-guard."

"No matter how drunk they got, they'd not leave the massive Scaean Gate to the city open," Diomedes scoffed.

"No," Odysseus agreed. "We do need a way through the gate, and I know how to do it." The men talked long into the night and by dawn, with Odysseus's leadership, they had worked out a plan so audacious, none regretted going without sleep.

Agamemnon chuckled to himself. "Epeius is good with wood. Summon him and we'll begin today."

Odysseus stretched the soreness from his muscles as he stood. "I'll send for him, but we must fight today with our usual spirit so the Trojans won't even suspect a ploy is afoot until after they've fallen for it. We'll need several days, but the war will soon be won, my friends."

"I won't mind killing more Trojans as we bide our time," Diomedes replied, and his companions joined in with raucous laughter.

Helen had slept poorly as she often did and was still in bed when Deiphobus burst into their chamber shouting, "The war is over! The Greeks have gone, vanished like cowards during the night, and they left behind a huge horse made of wood which must be meant as a tribute to Athena."

She sat up and pushed her hair out of her eyes. "How can this be after they've fought so hard?"

Deiphobus paced at the end of their bed. "They must have finally come to believe that Troy can't be defeated as long as the god of War, Ares, and Apollo guard our well-built walls, so they have withdrawn to their homelands. I care not at all why they have left. They are gone, and that's all that matters. Now dress quickly and come with me to view the giant horse. It's an astonishing sight, and we must decide what's to be done with this victory trophy."

When he was so happy and animated, he reminded her of an exuberant Paris, and she could barely stand to look at him. She had seen Odysseus in the city, and the Palladium had been stolen that very night. Clearly the Greeks were plotting something drastic but Deiphobus didn't appear to be in the least bit suspicious. She opened her mouth to warn him that something had to be amiss, but she'd be ridiculed if she offered to plot strategy for the Trojan army. Still, something was very wrong, and perhaps when she saw the horse, she could convince others of it.

She left her bed and dressed for the day, frightened by what it might bring.

* * *

Down on the beach, a growing animated crowd stood clustered around the mammoth horse but parted when Deiphobus and Helen approached. The smoking remains of the Greeks' camp were scattered along the beach, clear evidence in his view that they'd given up their quest to dominate Troy. Helen, however, was not fooled by the scattered litter, and her anxiety rose as she circled the massive statue. It was handsome in a stark, brutal way, made from fir trees felled in the nearby forest and fashioned into planks with the marks of axes and saws still showing. Its huge round eyes seemed to cast a disdainful glance on the little people below.

"What do you think of it?" Deiphobus asked.

"There's an ominous stillness about that it I don't like," Helen replied truthfully. She caught sight of Cassandra moving their way. "Let's hear Cassandra's opinion."

Cassandra shoved to the front of the awestruck spectators, clenched her fists and raised her arms in the air. She spoke loudly enough for everyone to hear, "This hideous horse is an evil trick and should be burned to the ground. Get rid of it now or we'll all come to grievous harm."

Laughter greeted her strong-worded prediction, and she scanned the crowd for support and found none. "Wait until my father comes," she called. "He may see this demonic beast for what it is."

Deiphobus shook his head and whispered to Helen, "She's still a beauty, but no one believes her mad ravings, nor should they. It's said she's cursed by Apollo, the god of Prophecy."

It was a warm sunny morning, but Helen felt the same eerie sensation of doom Cassandra had just described and shivered with a chill. The horse was solidly built with a broad belly that might hide many warriors within it ready to attack. Why did no one else see a danger that was so clear to Cassandra and her? As always, she kept quiet rather than draw attention to herself, but she felt badly torn. She'd found the joy of love as well as the anguishing sorrow of loss here in Troy, but the Greeks they had battled for so long were still men from her far away home.

Perhaps unwittingly, she'd chosen the Greeks' side when Odysseus had entered the city posing as a beggar. She'd been shocked by his daring, but not stopped him. Now the Palladium, the "Spirit of Troy" was gone, and this monstrous horse stood so ominously on the beach, silently daring her to speak out against it, but she couldn't find the words to damn her countrymen.

Priam and Hecuba rode down to the shore in the royal chariot pulled by a magnificent pair of white horses. He helped her to step down and stared up at the awesome horse with mouth agape. He'd been told it was large, but it was immense. He scanned the beach, but there were no warships pulled up on the sand, and no sound other than the brush of the wind.

Deiphobus greeted his father warmly, "Sire, a man who calls himself Sinon, hid rather than sail with the Greeks for fear of being sacrificed when they reached home. He told us the statute is meant as a tribute to the goddess Athena."

"Where is he?" Priam asked.

Sinon was pushed and prodded to the front. He'd been badly abused in a search for the truth and his clothes were rent and bloody. Priam viewed him with a suspicious gaze. "Speak up, man. Tell me the truth, and I'll spare your life."

"It is as he said, my king. I am a cousin of Odysseus, but he has grown to hate me, and I dared not return home with him. Now I mean to swear my allegiance to Troy and serve you all the rest of my days." He fell to his knees and bowed his head to the ground.

"Get up," Priam scolded. "Tell me what you know of this colossal horse."

Sinon lurched to his feet. "Calchas, the great Greek seer, advised the horse be built as a tribute to Athena and to atone for stealing her Palladium. The Greeks hoped to sooth the goddess's wrath and have a safe journey home."

Laocoön, the Trojan priest of Poseidon, joined them, and the crowd's attention shifted to him. After a swift march around the horse, he gave his own command, "I do not trust this huge horse. I fear the Greeks, even bearing gifts. Burn it now before its evil engulfs us all." He hurled his bi-pointed spear against the belly of the gigantic horse and all heard a strange rattling sound coming from within.

The crowd stirred, some taking up Laocoön's cry to set fire to the wooden beast, and others arguing to preserve it as a sacred gift. When Athena suddenly shook the earth beneath their feet, they bumped and grabbed for each other in a struggle to remain on their feet.

"You have offended the goddess!" a man cried.

"No, I speak the truth!" Laocoön shouted. "Burn the awful beast before it's too late!"

Athena blinded him with terrible pain, and still the priest damned the horse and ordered it to be burned. His two sons joined him and were frightened by the blood red glow of his eyes. He groaned, and they held his arms to keep him upright.

The horse had been built on massive wheels and men went running for ropes to pull it into the city, while others stared at Laocoön, frightened by his awful torment and certain they must avoid insulting Athena any further before they were all touched by her blistering rage.

Laocoön ignored the agony in his eyes to again demand the horse be set on fire. Furious now, Athena called forth two sea serpents from the ocean depths. They swam with lightning speed, breached the surface and set upon the priest and his sons. They were hideous creatures with long sharp teeth and their sinuous, scaly bodies sent up huge roiling waves as they slithered upon the shore. They ringed the priest and his sons, entwined them in their terrible grasp and squeezed with all their mighty strength.

Women screamed at the horrible sight, but no man ran to aid Laocoön and his sons who were dragged, hopelessly struggling and crying as the sea serpents constricted in brutal bands around them. The slithering beasts carried the nearly lifeless priest and his boys under the sea leaving behind only a single huge spray of glittering foam as they disappeared into the depths.

Deiphobus had pressed Helen's face to his chest to shield her from the gruesome sight, but he was as shaken as his father and mother. Priam held Hecuba, and they swayed together as she cried.

"We must take the horse into the city," Priam announced. "Clearly it's what Athena desires." He hurried his wife to his chariot and led the way.

A gray bearded elder shouted, "The goddess desires this wondrous trophy; do as our king commands. Take it into the city and let's rejoice in our long-fought victory!"

Helen and Deiphobus remained on the beach as scores of men worked to drag the wheeled horse with ropes and cables across the beach sand. He watched them sweat and toil at the task, while she gazed out at the sea. She had never seen a stranger morning, and still believed something even worse was bound to come to pass. She'd caught only a glimpse of the sea serpents as they'd first broken through the waves, but the frightful sight would remain with her for all time. Filled with dread, she shared none of the gaiety as women threw garlands of flowers over the wooden horse and welcomed it as it rolled into the city.

The war was finally over, and elated by their victory, the Trojans ecstatically danced around the horse, feasted and drank huge drafts of wine until they could no longer remember why they were celebrating. Music from lyres, flutes and high-ringing shaken sistrums added to the frenzied celebration, and it lasted long into the night. Too uneasy to take part, Helen remained in her chamber rather than dine with the other women that evening. When Cassandra came to her door, she welcomed her in.

"No one believes me," Cassandra cried, "but I saw something in your eyes. You're afraid too, aren't you?"

"I am," Helen readily confessed. "I fear the horse is Odysseus's doing, and that it will somehow bring us all great harm."

"I'll go and pray for our safety all night in Athena's temple. Perhaps she can be assuaged," Cassandra promised, and she slipped away.

Helen had never been fond of dancing and prayer, and after Theseus had abducted her from Artemis's temple, she found little value in temple rituals. Believing this could very well be the last night of her life, she combed her golden hair, put on her finest clothes with the beautiful gold necklace Paris had had made for her with the blood stone. She went to the window to keep watch and wait. The great dark horse rose up in the distance and looked even more evil in the flickering torchlight. When Deiphobus did not come to their bedchamber, she assumed he had fallen into a drunken sleep along with the other reveling men. She hoped he had his sword with him.

Menelaus arched his back and rolled his shoulders. They had climbed into the wooden horse before dawn and spent the day in its miserably hot and crowded confines. The air was rank and like the rest of them, he needed to relieve himself. They could still hear music growing faint from a long way off, but they waited, stiff and sore, for absolute silence.

Sinon had pretended to join in the Trojans' feast, but he drank very little of their potent wine. After the other men had either staggered off to their chambers, or fallen asleep where they sat, he made his way out of the palace courtyard at a light run. The wooden horse had been towed up to the citadel, as far as the temple to Athena, and he knocked against a foreleg.

"It's time," he whispered. "The Trojan fools are all in a drunken stupor."

Odysseus nudged Epeius. "Unfasten the latch. Be as quiet as you can be lowering the climbing ropes. We mustn't give ourselves away with victory so close at hand."

Menelaus had been one of the first men to climb into the horse, and he waited impatiently for his turn to get out. "I'm going after Helen," he cautioned his companions. "No one else is to touch her. Leave her to me."

Odysseus waited at the bottom to steady the ropes as his commandos slid down as agilely as snakes on a vine. "Walk around to shake out the cramps, and relieve yourselves off the road so we'll not slip in our own puddles as we make our way to the palace."

Once ready, the men followed Odysseus in a swift silent stream to the Scaean Gate, but no men had been left on watch. They raised the heavy bar to open it, and Sinon raced out to wave a torch to signal the Greek fleet waiting off the nearby island of Tenedos. Odysseus raised his sword and the killing began.

Helen smelled smoke before the flames became visible. The city was built in tiers with the palace at the crest, on the pergamon, the citadel, and as she watched, the fires leaped higher and higher licking their way up the hill. She heard men yelling to each other in the palace, frantically trying to mount a defense, but the Greeks were swarming inside the gates and no matter how valiant the Trojans proved to be, they'd awakened too late. At a severe disadvantage and with no time to don their armor, they were swiftly overwhelmed.

She sat on the end of the bed and put her hands over her ears to silence the cries and screams, but she couldn't smother her own thoughts. If the Greek fleet had returned, the palace would be overrun before dawn and far too many would die. Her fate, whatever it might be, would soon overtake her, but she drew in a deep breath and grew remarkably calm. She'd led an eventful life, been dearly loved, and loved in return. If she died tonight, she would not have missed any of life's joys, and she cherished her many blessings as she waited alone for whatever the fates would bring.

She heard a death scream from a guard in the hallway, her door flew open and crashed against the wall, and Menelaus appeared with a bloody sword in his hand. He tore off his distinctive helmet so he would be easily recognized, but she had expected him, after all. The war had changed him, but she recalled the day they'd met while she'd been playing with stick horses and soldiers in the dirt. Her brothers had been right, he had wanted her, even then.

"Have you come to kill me?" she asked, her expression warm, a reflection of their many shared memories.

He flung his gory sword aside, came toward her and knelt at her feet. He caught the end of a golden curl in his hand and brought it to his lips. "You are as beautiful as you were when I last saw you." Tears filled his eyes and ran down his cheeks.

When he had removed his fierce looking helmet, she saw his hair had become a silvery red and the lines at the corners of his eyes deep. He looked bone-weary, as though he had fought every day in the hated war. She loved him as she always had, but without the fiery passion Paris had kindled within her. She leaned close and kissed his cheek. "I've missed you."

He sat back on his heels. "You tore my heart from my chest when you left me."

She rested her fingertips on his lips. "It was so long ago."

"Yesterday to me."

They could hear screams, shrieks of agony echoing through the palace, and she winced at the sound. "I fear the innocent are dying, and I cannot bear their screams."

He stood, picked up his sword and helmet and offered his hand. "Come with me, my Helen. Fetch your belongings. Troy has fallen, and you'll not be back."

"I'll leave it all as plunder," she replied and went with him willingly. He led her through the palace the way he had come. She glanced neither left nor right, while terror swirled all around them. She clung to his hand, and they raced along the corridors out into the night. He gathered her into his arms and carried her away from the mayhem before setting her again on her feet.

He kissed her, long and hard, and she wrapped her arms around his waist. She relaxed against him, and their years apart fell away before the kiss ended. "I won't betray you again," he promised. "I'll be faithful until the day I die."

"You have much more to forgive," she whispered.

"No, if anything, I loved you too much, and cursed myself for it."

She thought him merely confused. "You are a good man, Menelaus, and the fault is entirely mine."

"Nonsense." He swept her up into his arms and carried her down to his flagship. "Stay here. We'll sail for Sparta at dawn."

She grabbed his sleeve. "Don't go back. Surely you've already killed your share of men tonight."

The reflection of the stars sparkled in her eyes, and he couldn't leave her, not ever again.

Zeus seethed as flames devoured his beloved Troy, and he grit his teeth rather than fling the lightning bolts tingling in his fingertips and add to the wanton destruction. Hera and Athena were singing and dancing around his golden palace, rejoicing in the ruin they'd brought to Troy, while Aphrodite and Apollo sat silently holding hands. Tears rolled down the Love goddess's cheeks and spilled into her lap.

"Are you happy now," Zeus asked his wife.

Hera ran her hand over his broad back as she danced by. "I'm thrilled clear to my toes," she proclaimed with a bubbling laugh.

The king of gods widened his stance and folded his arms over his chest. "Laugh if you will, my lovelies. You've won today, but our own battle is a long way from over."

Hera froze on tiptoe, and gazed over her shoulder at her mighty husband. "We're immortals, beloved, and the war between us will never end."

Believing Hera, Aphrodite wept all the harder.

Helen slept fitfully in her husband's arms and awakened to shouts as the Greeks swarmed the beach carrying and dragging their booty and moaning captives. A handsome red-haired young man came to their ship and stared up at her. He looked familiar, and she regarded Menelaus with a questioning glance.

"No, he's not mine. This is Neoptolemus, Achilles' son. Can you see the resemblance?"

"Yes, I remember him."

Awestruck, Neoptolemus continued to regard her far too closely. "So this is the famed Helen? You're as beautiful as I'd dreamed you'd be, but how can you still be so young?"

Menelaus laughed at the boy. "My wife is the daughter of Zeus, and she's blessed by the gods."

"Do you have a pretty daughter I might wed?" he asked, his hands rested on his hips.

Helen had thought so often of Hermione and hoped her childhood had been pleasant and sweet. "We have one you might wish to court when you're older."

"Is she as lovely as you?" Neoptolemus asked, his wide smile charming.

"Almost," Menelaus assured him. "If you have your father's speed and strength, you might win the games in her honor."

"I shall look forward to it," he replied.

Odysseus approached them, brushed Achilles' son aside, and the boy jogged away. "Without your silence, Helen, we could not have conquered Troy. Did they suspect they had a traitor in their midst?"

Menelaus bristled at that taunt and leaped down from the beaked prow of his ship. "You'll not speak to my queen in such insulting terms."

Odysseus shrugged off any shame. "I meant only to thank her," he exclaimed. "You can't deny that she played an essential part in both the beginning and end of this fateful war."

Helen knew she deserved whatever caustic blame others heaped upon her, but she refused to take any credit for last night's bloody victory. She looked beyond Odysseus and saw a little white-haired woman running their way followed by her maid.

"Aethra, you're safe. I feared you'd not survived the night." Menelaus gave Helen a hand, and she climbed down to the sand to hug the tiny queen.

"Don't crush me now!" Aethra sputtered as she broke free. "My grandson, Acamas, found me. He was a mere boy when I last saw him, but he's grown into a fine young man. Too many died last night," she mourned them only briefly with a sad shake of her head. Helen pulled her faithful maid up beside her.

"Emalia is coming home with me," Aetha exclaimed. "Agamemnon is taking Cassandra, and Andromache and Helenus were given to Achilles' son, Neoptolemus."

"Helenus survived?" Helen asked, astonished to hear it.

"He did," Aethra replied, "but not Hektor's baby son. Are you not curious about Deiphobus?"

"He's dead," Menelaus interjected, "with the rest of King Priam's wretched male spawn."

Sickened, Helen clung to his arm. "I can't bear the sadness here. How long must we wait to sail?"

"Everything will be sorted out soon," Odysseus assured them. "Summon your men and sail with the tide. I'll see you again when we reach our homelands."

Menelaus had lost no men during the night, and he was as eager to be free of the sight of Troy as Helen. "We'll leave shortly then. Have a safe journey home, my comrade-in-arms."

Odysseus laughed. "I have lived through too many years of war to want any excitement on the return voyage to my Ithaca. May you have a safe trip as well, my friend."

Helen kissed Aethra's cheek and bid farewell to the dear queen who had been her longtime companion. "I'll miss your wisdom," she told her.

"I've poured whatever I knew into you," Aethra scoffed. "Remember it all and you'll do well on your own." She took Emalia by the hand and hurried away to find her grandson and make plans for returning to Athens.

Menelaus helped Helen to again board his ship, and she sat facing the sea as she waited for him to summon his crewmen and prepare to sail. "What's become of my brothers?" she asked. "Is it a sad story?"

He kissed her before he replied, "It's a long and involved tale, and I'll tell you on the way home."

"Home," she whispered softly. She twisted her hands in her lap, and did not dare glance back until they were out to sea.

The once proud Troy lay in ruins still ringed with high-flaming fires. When Paris had brought her there, the once great city had shone upon the hill, like a sparkling gemstone, a glorious place filled with laughter and love. Tears blurred her vision, and she remembered the blissful days she and Paris had shared. They had been all too few.

"There was once a world, or was it all just a dream," she whispered, and as she turned away, her tears fell into the wine-dark sea.

*Turn the page for an
excerpt from*

SAVAGE
DESTINY

The Hearts of Liberty Series

Book One

Phoebe Conn

Accustomed to waking early, Alanna's late night vigil did not prevent her from following her usual routine and going out to the stable shortly after dawn. She swung open the door and nearly tripped over Hunter, who lay asleep in the straw piled just inside. She hesitated a moment, thinking the sudden burst of light would awaken him, but he continued to sleep undisturbed.

He had impressed her as being a proud man, and she wasn't surprised that he hadn't wanted to sleep in the house. Melissa had undoubtedly dismissed him with a remorseless vigor that had to have left him feeling both abused and bitter. His happiness wasn't her responsibility, anymore than Melissa's probable cruelty, but she could not help but feel sorry for him.

She knelt in the straw and reached out to touch his shoulder. "Hunter, it's morning, wake up," she urged.

Exhausted, Hunter came awake slowly, and because it suited his dreams, he mistook the blond woman silhouetted against the open doorway for

Melissa. He reached out to grab her arm, pulling her off balance and into the straw beside him. He closed his eyes as he kissed her and her initial reluctance to respond inspired rather than discouraged him. Peeling away her cap, he wound his fingers in her curls so she'd not escape his eager kisses, and he tried with a tenderness he'd not shown her at midnight to rekindle the passion they had shared all too briefly.

Taken completely by surprise, Alanna was so shocked by the Indian's sudden passion for her that she didn't have the presence of mind to struggle. Instead, she placed her hands on his chest and pushed against him with such a light touch it went unnoticed. Whenever Graham leaned down to kiss her, she turned her cheek, and therefore she was unprepared for a man who lacked such elegant manners, and instead took what he wanted. His insistent kisses weren't in the least bit unpleasant though, and her initial dismay gradually turned to a ready appreciation of what Melissa must have liked about him.

She savored the sweetness of his adoring kisses until she realized he had transferred his affections from Melissa to her with unseemly haste, and, unwilling to be a substitute for her cousin, she summoned the anger to shove him aside. "Yesterday it was Melissa you wanted, and now it's *me?* I had no idea men could be so fickle."

Finally realizing his mistake, Hunter let out an anguished moan. He sat up quickly and handed Alanna her cap. "You must forgive me," he begged. "I didn't see you clearly, and I thought you were Melissa."

For a few magical moments, Alanna had believed Hunter's enthusiastic affection was real. To learn that they were both victims of a silly mistake filled her with a sickening sense of disappointment. That the love which had flavored Hunter's kiss had been meant for her cousin, hurt far more than what she had interpreted as mere fickleness had.

"If I'm supposed to be flattered by that, I'm not," she blurted out as she struggled to stuff her hair under her cap.

Hunter watched her beautiful green eyes fill with tears and gestured helplessly. "What should I have said? Most people say my English is good, but there are times when I choose the wrong words."

"Or the wrong woman?"

"Please, don't laugh at me."

It was Hunter who now looked ready to cry, and Alanna feared she was treating him as badly as Melissa had. "I'm not laughing at you, certainly not. But even if I *had* been Melissa, you ought not to have grabbed me like that. What if she had come to tell you goodbye and brought Ian with her? At the very least he would have yanked out a handful of your hair, pulling you off her. I shudder to think what he would have done next. It's too dangerous for you here, Hunter. You've got to go."

They were both kneeling in the straw, but when she made no move to rise, neither did he. As before, her concern seemed real, and he longed to confide in her, to make her understand he had every right to be there, but he hadn't forgotten Melissa's threatened accusation of rape. He had not the slightest doubt that she would tell such a damaging lie either. It would not only be Ian he would have to fight then, but Byron and Elliott as well. If by some miracle he did survive the combined fury of their anger, he knew his claims that Melissa had willingly lain with him would never be believed in court. He did not know what the punishment for rape might be, but he was positive he didn't want to risk finding out.

"Melissa married the wrong man," he said instead.

"You were here only a few days in April. How could you have thought she might marry you?"

Again, Hunter dared not speak the truth, but despite the fact that neither he nor Melissa had made any promises, he had believed in the unspoken vows of her love. Now all Melissa displayed toward him was contempt, but in April, he would have sworn she loved him. He sighed unhappily. "I have money to pay for the *bateau*. Will you give it to your uncle?"

"No, you needn't pay for a boat. We have several, and one more or less won't be missed."

"I forgot how rich you are."

Alanna recoiled at the resentment in his tone. "My uncle has worked hard for everything he owns, and he's known for his generosity to others. Won't you need some food to take along? Come with me. Let's go to the kitchen and see what provisions we can find."

"You won't take my money?"

"No, of course not. You're Byron and Elliott's friend."

Hunter rose to his feet, and with a graceful tug pulled her up beside him. "Have I ruined things with you, so that we can't be friends?"

That his passionate kisses had been meant for Melissa no longer seemed important in light of his obvious pain, and she responded with a smile. "Yes, I'd be proud to be your friend. Elliott has nothing but praise for you, and I believe it's well deserved."

"Byron thinks I have a wild streak, and had he seen us a few minutes ago, he would know he was right."

He flashed a charming grin but there was definitely a wildness about Hunter that went far beyond his buckskins and long flowing hair.

SAVAGE DESTINY

available in print and ebook

Always a passionate lover of books, this New York Times bestselling author first answered a call to write in 1980 and swiftly embarked on her own mythic journey. Her first book, LOVE'S ELUSIVE FLAME, was a Zebra historical in 1983. Her forty-first book, a noir mystery, MURDER ME TWICE, is a December 2015 release. With more than seven million copies in print of her historical, contemporary and futuristic books written under her own name as well as her pseudonym, Cinnamon Burke, she is as enthusiastic as ever about writing.

A native Californian, Phoebe attended the University of Arizona and California State University at Los Angeles where she earned a BA in Art History and an MA in Education. Her books have won Romantic Times Reviewer's Choice Awards and a nomination for Storyteller of the Year. Her futuristic, STARFIRE RISING, won a RomCom award as best Futuristic Romance of the year. She is a member of Romance Writers of America, and Novelists Inc.

She is the proud mother of two grown sons and two adorable grandchildren, who love to have her read to them.

Dr. Gary Stickel received his Ph.D. degree from UCLA where he also taught classes in archaeology and theory. His major field expeditions and excavations have included Swiss underwater Neolithic sites, and excavation at the legendary "lost city of the Incas"—Machu Picchu in Peru. The Greek government gave him the honor to excavate at the legendary birthplace of Achilles, the great hero of the Trojan War—a site called Achilleion.

Because of his discovery of the oldest site in the greater Los Angeles area—Farpoint—dating back some 13,000 years, and his expert advice on the Lucasfilm "Indiana Jones" film series, the London Times called him the "Real-life Indiana Jones."

For the last few years Dr. Stickel has been searching for the lost Palace of Odysseus (from Homer's epic poem, The Odyssey.) And he may have found it already!